Perhaps no novel since *A Separate Peace* has so superbly captured the impact of a world at war upon a safe and sheltered environment as this richly haunting story.

We watch with enchantment as Suse evolves from a tomboy to a young person whose growth has been as remarkable as her blossoming into womanhood . . . "ELLA LEFFLAND WRITES FROM THE HEART, THE HEAD, THE GUT, AND MAKES HER READERS CARE. . . ."

—*PUBLISHERS WEEKLY*

"(MS. LEFFLAND) IS A NOVELIST OF REMARKABLE STRENGTH AND BREADTH. SHE HAS CHARACTER, STYLE, VIVIDNESS, SUBTLETY: MOREOVER, SHE HAS A FINE, HIGHLY PARTICULAR FEEL FOR PLACE AND A TACTFUL, DEEP AND INFORMED SENSE OF HOW HUMAN EMOTIONS OPERATE."

—*WASHINGTON POST*

"THE STUFF OF LIFE . . . STRENGTH AND HARD-TO-SHAKE PERSISTENCE. ELLA LEFFLAND IS A CONSIDERABLE WRITER."

—*KIRKUS REVIEWS*

RUMORS OF PEACE

Ella Leffland

FAWCETT POPULAR LIBRARY • NEW YORK

For my mother, and in memory of my father

RUMORS OF PEACE

This book contains the complete text of the original hardcover edition.

Published by Fawcett Popular Library, a unit of CBS Publications, the Consumer Publishing Division of CBS Inc., by arrangement with Harper & Row, Publishers, Inc.

ISBN: 0-445-04587-6

Printed in the United States of America

First Fawcett Popular Library printing: August 1980

10 9 8 7 6 5 4 3 2 1

Chapter 1

In later life, when I grew up and went out into the world, I was astonished to hear people speak of California as if it had no seasons.

Winter was long, it brought huge rains that swelled the creek to a brown torrent and made lakes of backyards, and it brought tule fog so thick that lights burned through the day, gleaming dim and haggard along the streets. Then suddenly one morning the trees stood sunlit, their bark still black and sodden, but tightly budded, and within a week, through banks of poppies, the creek flashed clear as quartz. Summer moved in fast and stayed long; the creek dried out to a powdery gulch, backyards cracked like clay, under a white boiling sky the town lay bleached and blistered in a drone of gnats; then abruptly the sky cooled, grew high and clear like blue glass, gutters of yellow leaves swirled, carried higher each day by winds that finally shook the windows, and once more the rain and fog engulfed us.

I liked the different kinds of weather, and though I myself was not methodical—my sister often informed me of this—I liked the weather in its ordained cycle. Whenever a gray day appeared in June, or a brilliant one in December, I felt uneasy, as if God had lost His bearings.

In the dark I plagued my sister with questions. She had metal curlers in her hair and lay with her back to me.

"Karla. Who's God?"

She would drag the pillow over her head.

I would stick my head under the pillow. "Tell me."

Silence.

Karla was a kind and generous sister, but at night she wished to sleep. And it was then that my questions came to me.

"Tell me."

Silence.

I would lie back again. I had no religious bent at all,

yet God had wormed His way into my thoughts. At Sunday school we learned about Christ, but He was only the son. I wished to get to the source. My parents said God was the spirit of kindness in each of us, but there must be more. Otherwise, why did the local nuns cause a fit of respect in even the worst Ferry Street drunk? Why did people say God damn, God knows, and God help us? But I was never able to put it all together.

One afternoon, walking by the construction site of our first skyscraper, a three-story union hall, I decided to climb up. At the structure's top, at the very edge, I looked out. Many-colored roofs and bright green trees stretched to the glassy bay. The big dry hills rolled golden into the distance. The sky was huge, blue, intoxicating.

After that I found I no longer asked about God, so I supposed that I must have caught sight of Him up there.

But for all the impact of that view, I never gave much thought to my surroundings. Thirty miles east of San Francisco, hemmed in by two high ranges of hills and the Suisun Bay, its population a fixed 5,000, Mendoza was as familiar and absolute as my face. We had an old yellow train depot, a long tarry wharf, and a large white ferry. We had a stone courthouse with a dome, an L-shaped Woolworth's with creaking floors, and a small dim library that smelled of flour paste. We had a tule marsh, eucalyptus groves, and tall scruffy palms, and we had steep dry hills that you could slide down on a piece of cardboard.

We also had Shell Oil refinery. It was our main feature, our reason for existence, but it was of no account to me. First, my dad did not work there, but at a body shop off Main Street. Second, the glaring storage tanks and belching smokestacks were not rewarding to look at, so why look at them?

That the whole area was industrial escaped me. Within a ten-mile radius stood Shell Oil, Standard Oil, Union Oil, the Hercules Powder Plant, the Benicia Arsenal, the Port Chicago Ammunition Dump, and Mare Island Navy Yard. When you took a Sunday drive, you could not help seeing these ugly, boring blots. But they quickly faded into the abundant countryside, and you forgot them.

6

My dad drove an old 1931 Model A Ford, black and shiny and high off the ground, so that you had a good view. When I was small, the whole family went on Sunday drives together, but by the time I was ten, in 1941, my sister was seventeen and my brother sixteen, and they had begun going their own ways. Karla wanted to be a painter and to study at the Hopkins Art Institute in San Francisco. Peter wanted to be a great drummer like Gene Krupa and tour the nation. Soon they would both go out into the world. But I felt that our way of life, like the seasons, should not alter.

I was happy, except for school, which sometimes caused me to run away. The varnished rows of desks, the cold, busy squeak of chalk on blackboard, George Washington's pale eyelids drooping at us from the wall—all this inspired me with a hopeless sense of wasted time, my object in life being to climb and swing from trees and other high things. I had thick yellow calluses on my palms that I sliced off with a razor blade. I planned to be a trapeze artist. With such an ambition, school could only be an intolerable bore, and so on occasion I ran away; but already at the outskirts of town the vast unknown wilted me, and I had to turn back.

I eked out passing marks, but I was late for class each morning, though our house stood directly opposite the grammar school. It was the bars and handwalkers I couldn't resist.

"You can play *after* school," my parents tried to drill into me.

I had no clue to their logic. What existed was the ever-fresh charm of the morning playground. This tardiness was the only sore spot between my parents and me, but though I regretted their unhappiness and disliked their scoldings, I never changed. And at least there were sometimes long periods during which the teacher seemed to grow numb to the sight of me sneaking breathlessly into my seat. No complaints were sent home then. I breathed easily, and life was as it should be.

Like all neighborhoods, ours had a gang held loosely together by grassfights, kickball, and faulty judgment. We built an airplane from old planks and tried to send it off a garage roof with struggling round-eyed Mario Pelegrino aboard (it was finally launched pilotless and nosedived to the ground). We traded comic books, slid down

7

the hills, and on Saturday afternoons hurried to the State Theater matinee, where we sent up wild cheers as the lights dimmed.

Of this gang, most of whom I have forgotten, excitable Ezio Pelegrino was my best friend. Mario was his brother, older than the rest of us, but with the mind and body of a small child. He had a coarse, squinty little face and was beloved by his mother. Now and again he took it into his mind to urinate in the street, and then a scandalized mother would appear at the Pelegrino door with the savage in tow, mouth cheerfully agape. A stout widow with black hair in a bun, Mrs. Pelegrino would shoot Mario a stern look while gathering him tenderly to her. "*Scusa, scusa,*" she always apologized, "he just a little bit cuckoo." We all liked Mario, even if we had tried to send him off in the airplane, and he followed us everywhere, except to the wharf. The waves scared him.

I always went with my dad when he fished for bass from the wharf. My dad was husky and warm to the touch. He was bald, with a fringe of sandy hair. He had a large nose like an Indian's, and sky blue eyes. When he fished, he was silent, like all the others who sat along the side with their poles. They never cared that the bass was so oily from Shell you couldn't eat it. They just liked to fish. Around the pier the water was brown and choppy, but farther out it was green and smooth. When I was very small, I thought the opposite shore was Denmark, the place my parents came from. Then I learned that it was only Benicia, a town like our own, and my brother showed me where Denmark was on his world map. I remembered it as a purple dot on the other side of an immense blue ocean.

When I was nine, I came home from school one spring afternoon and found Mama sitting at the kitchen table, her face in her hands. She was crying. She said Denmark had been invaded by the Germans. I understood that this must be a terrible thing, but the purple dot was so far away, the blue ocean so immense, that I could not feel the terribleness in my bones. I just felt sorry for Mama, whose face was so unhappy.

The next letter we received from Danish relatives was stamped on the envelope with the German word *Geöffnet* and an eagle standing on a swastika. The sheets inside were mutilated by scissors. I held the sheets up between my fingers and touched them with curiosity. And then suddenly wherever I turned I was confronted by this war across the ocean. Between Charlie McCarthy and Kate Smith the airwaves crackled with news of some desperate place called Dunkirk. At the matinee, *Pinocchio* was accompanied by a *Time Marches On* newsreel showing long gray columns of troops with cannons. In *Life* magazine there were pictures going back to the start of this war—apparently it had already been going on for many months—and I looked at rubble and smoke and the bodies of a potato-digging family lying dead and blood-spattered in a Polish field.

But when the magazine was closed, the radio turned off, the newsreel over, the vast barrier of the ocean returned. Mendoza was what existed. This which was real. This which you could hear and smell and touch. And gradually the war in Europe became just another part of the daily background, familiar but unpressing, one more thing belonging to the grown-ups with their eternal talk of politics and jobs and wages.

When I grew up, I realized that I and the Depression had been born almost together, but I was never aware of its existence. In our neighborhood everyone was the same, neither rich nor poor. We lived in small rented frame houses. There were always pennies for jawbreakers and a dime for the Saturday matinee. If I never knew a child with a radio of his own or a bicycle bought firsthand, I never knew one who went to bed hungry. When the Okies had rumbled through town in their dusty trucks, I had thought them glamorous, like Gypsies—the children sitting high and swaying on a heap of belongings. It never crossed my mind that they had troubles.

My own troubles loomed large at times. There was my constant tardiness. There was Ezio saying that Mario would probably die before eighteen. There were occasional shouting arguments between my parents, from which I fled. But then the domestic spat would pass, my teacher would sink into her numb phase, Mario was still far from eighteen, and life rolled on smoothly, as it was meant to.

On winter evenings, after slopping through my homework, I curled up with Andersen's fairy tales. A fire crackled in the wood stove, and there came a pleasant

9

muted din from the cellar, where Peter was relegated with his snare drum. Karla sat sketching at the dining-room table, and from the radio came the wise, confident voices of *Information, Please,* which my parents listened to over their evening coffee. When summer came, we moved out onto the front porch in the evenings. The crickets chirped from the dry grass. My dad's cigar glowed in the dark, an orange dot. From somewhere in the distance you could hear a game of kick-the-can. The night air was warm, the sky thick with stars.

Chapter 2

It was a warm, sunny out-of-place day in early winter. I was on my way home from Sunday school, loitering in the creek near the wooden footbridge. I had worked my way down to the edge of the torrent, which rushed through a fine dank smell of silt and decayed leaves. From the black branches above hung old birds' nests, soaked and raveled. The steep sodden banks glistened. I was throwing twigs into the torrent, where they bounced madly along like Ping-Pong balls.

Over the water's roar I heard something odd—shouting, but not the shouting of kids at play. It was a full-bodied adult voice, screaming out at a run. Swinging around, I stared up the bank at the trees. Whoever it was was running through the trees toward the footbridge, and suddenly, as my eyes widened, he burst into view and thundered onto the boards, a large man in full military uniform, swinging a rifle to his shoulder.

"Invasion!" he cried. "Seek shelter! Seek shelter!" And he fired into the air.

The report exploded through the gorge, jolting me from my feet. I felt a massive, icy engulfment, a deafening commotion, and when my head broke surface I was being shot downstream like one of my twigs. Thrashing, sinking, I was at once slammed into a knot of tree roots, where for a moment I hung on in total blankness. Then struggling out, my good Sunday dress glued to my body, I fled terrified up the bank on all fours.

As in a nightmare, I was the only person outside, running down streets abruptly deserted. Everyone had hidden behind locked doors. Gray armies in helmets were blocks away, they were rumbling their cannons through Main Street, loping alongside with fixed bayonets. Pounding down the sidewalks, I could not grasp why they had invaded us or how they had come so fast, in just the snap of a finger since I had left Sunday school. I only knew, with the horrifying certainty of the exploding gorge, that they were here.

Our front door was not locked. My family had not run for shelter in the closets. They sat innocently listening to radio music. Panting in the doorway, I knew I must grab their arms, pull them to safety—but this thought sent a heat of confusion through my terror. They were the older ones, the ones who knew. I could not grab their arms and force them into the closet, knowing less than they. Yet this time I knew more. I knew so much that I buckled under the weight of such knowledge and ran crying to my mother, who, with everyone else, was hurrying over to me.

I cried in a passion while they questioned and calmed me. No, we were not being invaded, something had happened somewhere else, a long distance off, and as they spoke, a voice broke into the radio music. "We interrupt this program for further news of the Japanese attack on Pearl Harbor—it has now been learned that casualties were extreme—an undetermined number of ships has been sunk and aircraft lost—we will keep you informed on any further—" Someone turned it down.

"How far away?" I asked shakily.

Thousands of miles, I was assured, in Hawaii. Who had told me differently? Who had frightened me? How had I gotten wet?

"A soldier. He shot a rifle. I fell in the creek."

Dad took my arm. "A soldier? He *shot* at you?"

"In the air. He was yelling and shooting."

"Where?"

"Down by the footbridge."

He went out the door. Mama, Karla, and Peter still stood around me. My hair was plastered to my skull; my muddy dress clung to me. The creek was a forbidden place, yet there was not a word of exasperation. It would have been more normal, more welcome. They were too gentle, and though behind their gentleness I now sensed something severe, it had nothing to do with my bemired dress, but with something much larger and more terrible.

"It's ruined," I wept, dishonestly, clutching my dress, narrowing all disaster down to this simple bedraggled garment.

Soaking in a hot bath, I pressed the washcloth to my swollen eyes. As a fearless tree climber, I was shamed by my terror, and by the fact that it persisted, in the form of a nervous intestinal knot. After I had dried my hair and changed into a clean dress, I put on a calm, interested expression as I returned to the front room.

Dad had come back with the news that my footbridge alarm spreader was old Hackman, a local alcoholic and World War veteran who had already been taken into custody by the sheriff. This soothed me for a moment, but the street outside was worrisome in a new way. No longer deserted, it now presented the unusual picture of all our neighbors wandering around in carpet slippers or aprons, gathering together in little knots, talking and looking around. Dad and Mama went out too. Through the lace curtain I saw them also talking and looking around. Inside, Karla was sitting in a temporary position on the arm of the sofa, leafing through the Sunday papers. Peter was stooped over the radio, turning the dial.

Suddenly there was a commotion from outside. A police car and a motorcycle policeman had screeched to the curb, motors running, radios blasting. The two men talked in shouts; then with a powerful kick of his boot the motorcycle policeman exploded the air and roared off, the car speeding urgently after.

With my calm and interested expression I turned to Peter. "Where did you say Hawaii was?"

He spread his world map on the floor and showed me. It was certainly very far from the streets of Mendoza, with the huge Pacific in between. But the knot in my stomach remained.

When Dad and Mama returned, they had no news. No one knew anything except what we had heard on the radio.

More bulletins flashed on. They were always the same.

Ships sunk, aircraft destroyed, casualties extreme. I did not know what casualties were, and did not ask.

Once, looking through the curtain, I saw a man go by carrying a pistol. I bit my lip and said nothing. Through the lace, the winter sun filtered bright as spring. A wrong, twisted day.

In the afternoon I went out on the front steps and sat down with Peter, who was waiting for a friend.

"They're talking about war in there," I said.

"That's right." His eyes were narrowed against the sun.

"Why? What do we care about Hawaii?"

"Christ, Suse, Pearl Harbor's a naval base. They bombed an American naval base."

"What does it matter if it's so far away?"

"Christ," he said again. He was not allowed to say Christ, but in his familiar gray cords and white shirt, with his blond hair hanging as always like a brush across his forehead, he seemed suddenly his own grown-up person, excited in a stern, preoccupied way.

"You don't make an unprovoked attack like that and get away with it," he said. "It means war."

I smoothed my dress tightly across my knees. "You mean war *there*, in Hawaii."

My words were drowned out by the honks of a jalopy pulling up, foxtail flying, sides scrawled with "What's cookin', good lookin'?" and "Hold your hat, here we go!" Peter's friend leaned out with a wry snort. "What a sitting duck, hey? Shell in our backyard? They'll wipe this poor old burg right off the map."

Peter frowned in my direction. His friend went silent. Then he smiled. "Just a lot of rumors, snooks. Nothing to it."

But I felt a bright, sickening hollowness, as if my bones had turned to air.

Karla had gone to the Sunday matinee with some friends. She came back within half an hour. The theater was closed. So was Dreamland roller skating rink. It grew clear to me that the town was readying itself. From the radio came an announcement that all schools in the county would be shut the next day. I swallowed and said, "Good, I can sleep late."

I was getting ready for bed. Mama had come in with me.

"I think it's been a bad day for you, Suse," she said, sitting down on the bed.

"No, it's been interesting."

"That man down in the creek wasn't right in his mind. I don't want you to go around brooding over what he said."

"I'm not," I assured her. "I know we're not going to be invaded." And I cast her a sidelong glance as I took up my pajamas. "I know we're not going to be bombed either."

My mother gave a nod, but it was indefinite. "Sit down here for a minute," she said, and she took my hands. "You know, Suse, even if nothing happens, people have to be prepared."

I nodded.

"A country has to take precautions, just in case."

I nodded.

"It's possible that we'll have air raid warnings, because that's part of being prepared. But it doesn't mean that anything will happen. I'm sure it will never come to that."

I nodded.

"So you're not to go around worrying."

"I'm not worrying."

"I hope not," she said.

My mother's face was smooth, with pink cheeks. She had warm gray eyes, and unlike the rest of the family's, her hair was dark, and was secured with large hairpins in a bun at the back. She always wore a hat when she shopped on Main Street. She always wore her best dress on Sundays, whether we went somewhere or not. It was a dark blue dress with a square-cut neck. As she went out of the room, I felt I was looking at the dress for the last time. We would never see next Sunday.

It was late when Karla came to bed, turning on the little lamp that stood on her dressing table. In the dim light, on my side of the room, my bureau top was crowded with worn-out rabbits' feet, acorns, marbles, and the skulls of small rodents. Karla's side was neat and cozy. She was always after me to put my relics away where she wouldn't have to look at them. "You want to

14

be a trapeze artist?" she would say. "Trapeze artists are very neat. They'd be shocked by this mess, Suse; they wouldn't let you into their union."

Now, suddenly, I felt I would do anything for Karla. I would sweep my possessions into the back of the closet, no, I'd throw them in the garbage can. I wanted to make her happy, because she was going to die. All of us were going to die.

She rolled her hair up in her metal curlers, got into her pajamas, and turned the lamp out. "I guess you'll have a million questions tonight," she said, climbing into bed.

I rolled over to her. "I'm going to clean my side of the room."

"I don't believe it."

"I will!"

After a long while, when I had not asked anything, she broke the silence. "Well, fire away."

"I don't have any questions."

The living-room clock chimed twice. I jerked awake. I had lain heavy-eyed, waiting for the sound of planes, until I could stay awake no longer. Now I woke to an ominous drone. After getting up, I went frozen-faced to the window and pulled the shade aside. It was a drone not of planes but of trucks, hundreds of trucks rumbling swiftly by, one after another, a few streets away.

"Karla!" I hissed, putting my ear to the pane. Army trucks, filled with defending troops. The invasion had begun.

"Karla!"

She sat up, rubbing her eyes.

"Listen!"

"What? I don't hear anything."

The sound was gone, as though it had never been. Shivering, I crossed the room and got back into bed. The clock chimed three times before I finally drifted off.

I woke to a gray, foggy morning. Karla was seated at her dressing table, putting on her lipstick before the mirror. She pressed her lips together, sucked them out of sight, nostrils enlarging. This usually interested me.

"There were army trucks last night."

"I didn't hear anything," she said, lips reappearing,

and patted her golden pompadour. "You dreamed it, honey." Going to the door, she leaned down. "Go back to sleep, no school today."

But I climbed from bed, sore with fatigue, and drew on my old pink chenille robe. Through the door came the sound of yet another radio broadcast.

I went tiredly into the living room and sat down with the others.

It was President Roosevelt speaking. His voice was slow, awesome.

". . . We will . . . make very certain that this form of treachery shall never endanger us again. . . . Our people, our territory and our interests are in grave danger."

My breathing came shallow. I crossed my arms over my chest, to hide its fluttering, and tried not to hear the voice.

Presently I was aware of silence. The president had stopped speaking. When he began again, it was with emphatic pauses, deep finality.

"I ask that the Congress declare that since this unprovoked and dastardly attack by Japan . . . a state of war has existed. . . ."

I looked slowly around the room at the others. It had begun.

Chapter 3

That night the town was blacked out. I watched Karla and Peter clothespin blankets along the curtain rods. A few blankets were all that hung between us and the bombs. But by now I was too exhausted to care, I only wanted to sleep, and as soon as my head touched the pillow, I was gone.

The next thing I knew Karla was shaking my shoulder. Wary and sober, with no heart for dawdling, I got up to prepare for school.

* * *

I saw with surprise that everyone was running and playing as usual. I had expected something military, I don't know what, each class standing in formation maybe. Puzzled, I advanced through the fog.

Red-nosed, bundled up, Ezio came dashing over.

"We're at war!"

"I know," I said, trying for enthusiasm.

He was husky, dark, with a home-knit cap pulled vigorously over his ears. He yanked it lower with both hands. "Lemme get at them Japs! Just give me a bunch of grenades and lemme go!"

"I guess they'll be coming to bomb us," I said casually.

"Let 'em try!" he yelled, rushing off.

I joined some girls from my class swinging on the bars.

"My cousin's in the Coast Guard—"

"So what, my brother's in the—"

"We had to eat in the dark—"

"We hung up this canvas stuff—"

"We hung blankets," I contributed, elbowing in and grasping the bars.

"Japs don't have eyelids, they can't close their eyes—"

"Who said so?"

"Japs are midgets—"

"So's Miss Bonder—"

A collective scream of laughter. Miss Bonder, our teacher, was so short that when she was on yard duty, you couldn't tell her from the rest of us except for her tall pompadour. Sometimes, when we were swinging from our knees, and our coats and dresses had fallen down around our waists, exposing our white cotton underpants, she would walk over and say, "Really, girls, have some modesty," and reprovingly point her pompadour at us. I saw her coming now, frowning at those who hung upside down, and it seemed to me that if we were going to be bombed, Miss Bonder would not be concerned with such a small thing as underpants.

Having had her say, and pausing to give my early arrival a grim smile of surprise, Miss Bonder strolled on. A little hope began burning in me.

When the first bell rang, everyone assembled before the flagpole as usual. If the enemy were on its way to destroy us, this would be the moment to announce it, now, as the flag went sliding up with a rattling sound.

But only the Pledge of Allegiance followed, after which the usual blithe disorder took over. For the first time in two days, I felt the knot in my stomach loosen. I felt my old warm craving to climb and stood eyeing the foggy handwalkers.

"Suse?" Miss Bonder said over her shoulder. My name, a variation of Susanna, was pronounced Seuseh by my family, and Sooza by everyone else, and now, for some reason, it had a beautifully familiar ring. Obedient, filled with the pleasure of temporary virtue, I followed Miss Bonder and the others into the building.

Class proceeded as always, pointless and boring. But I enjoyed my tedium, wallowing in Miss Bonder's monotonous voice as she went on about quotients and denominators.

But when she ended the lesson, she adjusted her rimless spectacles, which were attached to her blouse by two silver chains, and said, "I have an announcement to make. I want you all to pay very close attention."

I was not surprised. It was as though I had known all along that my relief was stupid, shabby, and worthless.

"As you know, our country is now at war with Japan. Although we're probably in no danger, it will be necessary to make some changes in our routine. In a few minutes we're going to have an air raid drill. This is nothing to get excited about; it's only a precaution. When the bell gives three short rings, I want you to get down under your desks—without a hullabaloo, thank you—and remain there until the bell rings again." She got up and went over to the windows. "No chatting, please. Let's just wait quietly."

A few moments later the bell split the air. I was under my desk before anyone else, pressed hard against the iron curlicues of its side. The rest of the class followed with a cheerful din, while Miss Bonder, hem flying, sent the Venetian blinds crashing down one after another.

Moments passed, filled with whispers and muffled giggles.

"No talking," warned Miss Bonder.

Silence descended. From behind the other curlicues, eyes brimmed with suppressed excitement. Down the aisle a hand stretched out, its fingers making elegantly grotesque movements.

When the bell released us, I climbed back into my

seat, covered with shame, hoping that no one had noticed my premature dive. My classmates seemed suddenly older than I, joined in some cheerful certainty that left me outside like a sniveling infant. Yet, without disturbing this humiliating feeling at all, I knew absolutely that I was the oldest one, alone in my understanding of what was going to happen.

At noon I went home for lunch. Drinking milk from my blue glass mug with Shirley Temple's picture on it, I commented lightly, "At recess the kids said there were Jap planes over San Francisco last night."

"I think it's all rumors," my mother said.

"I do too," I lied. I had never been a liar. Early in life I had found that lying was not for me; it was too bothersome, you had to stop and think all the time to keep stories straight, and they got mixed up anyway. It was much simpler to say everything just as it was; then, no matter what happened, you knew exactly where you stood with yourself and everybody else. But ever since Sunday I had been lying about this turmoil inside. Shirley Temple's dimpled grin seemed to come from another world, a vanished world.

"I guess Dad'll have to join the Army now?"

"At forty-nine?" My mother smiled.

"What about Peter?"

"Well," she said, pausing for a moment. "Let's hope by the time he's old enough the war will be over."

"How soon do you think it'll be over?"

"I don't know, Suse. Nobody knows."

Going back after lunch, I passed the superintendent of schools getting out of his car. Mr. Grandison was a stout silver-haired gentleman known for his fine tenor voice, with which, at every assembly, he regaled us with "On the Road to Mandalay." He was rosy-cheeked and smiling and always boomed a greeting when he saw you. Today he did not even nod but strode into the building with an ominous face. Maybe he was coming to tell the principal that all classes must be dismissed at once.

We were not dismissed, but we had another air raid drill right away. This time we were led in hurried lines down to the dim, cavernous basement. Afterward, back at my desk, I made a decision. I would run across the street to my house and be there with my mother when the bombs fell. If Miss Bonder tried to stop me, I would kill her. I liked her well enough, but if she tried to stop me, I would kill her.

During afternoon recess, new twists were added to the schoolyard talk. The bombers over San Francisco last night had been signaled by the Jap farmers in the valley, just outside town. They were spies and kept shortwave radios under their floorboards. Up in Seattle a Jap spy had already been beheaded, and the Jap spies in the valley would be beheaded, too. But they had already sent enough lowdown for the bombers to come back tonight and wipe out Shell. I plodded to the girls' lavatory with diarrhea.

When we got back to class, Miss Bonder rapped her desk sharply. "I have heard nothing but idiotic talk down in the yard. You've been spreading empty and very ugly rumors, and I want it to stop. I would have thought my class was above that. No more of it!" And she started us on our spelling.

They were only rumors.

I had to return a library book after school—*The Black Stallion*, which I had intended to renew but whose fascinating contents were suddenly of no interest to me. The lights of the little library gleamed through the afternoon fog. I went inside and handed the book to the librarian. Next to her elbow lay a folded newspaper with three red headlines showing.

Japan Planes
Near S.F. 4
Raid Alarms!

I brushed my hair weakly back. "Could I read this paper?" I whispered.

"Certainly," she whispered back.

It was our local paper, the Mendoza *Clarion*. I took it to a table and opened it to four smaller headlines, in black.

West Coast on Alert
All Bay Radios Are
Ordered Silent,
A Night of Blackouts

My eyes whipped down the columns of print.

Air raid alarms sounded on both coasts last night
. . . all army and naval stations were placed on the
alert . . . raid alarms on the Pacific coast started at
6:45 P.M., at which time there were official reports of
hostile aircraft . . . in San Francisco, police sirens
wailed through Market Street, and all lights went
out as searchlights swept the skies . . . the Golden
Gate City abruptly became reminiscent of London
and Rotterdam . . . in Seattle, more than 1,000
people roamed the streets, smashing windows of
stores burning lights . . . revealed at daybreak was
a gruesome reminder of the night's madness: a beheaded Chinaman, apparently mistaken for a
Jap. . . .

With trembling fingers I turned the page. There was a
new feature there, set off by two furled flags.

Contra Costa County in the War

We of Contra Costa County, especially those of us
living in Mendoza and other bay towns, are situated
in a prime target . . . antiaircraft units have been
installed on both sides of the bay, military guards
have been placed at refineries and plants, sandbags
have been banked around the sheriff's office . . .
highways have been cleared of all but necessary traffic . . . throughout the night of the seventh,
hundreds of army trucks passed through town en
route to various locations, carrying ammunition and
supplies. . . .

My army trucks. My dream, Karla had called them.
My teeth against my knuckles, I looked at another new
feature.

Sheriff O'Toole Reports:

Until an air raid siren has been installed, raids will be announced by an emergency warning of 11 fast beats of the fire bell. Turn off all lights. In the event of a raid it is advisable for citizens to retire to their basements. In the event of bombing, it is advisable to lie prone on the floor with the face down.

Keep cool. The enemy wants you to run into the streets, create a mob, start a panic. Don't get excited!

Old Hackman had gotten excited. But he knew. Seek shelter! Seek shelter! Tonight all of us would be lying facedown in our cellars.

I returned the newspaper to the librarian and went slowly outside. Across the street on the firehouse roof, men were hammering a stand together. People stood below, watching and talking. I went up and listened. The stand was for an air raid siren . . . Nagai's flower shop would close . . . the Philippines would fall . . . it would be a long war . . . it would be a short war . . . either way Mendoza was no place to be . . . men were on the courthouse roof with binoculars . . . crazy, what can they see in the fog? . . . Well the Japs can't see either. . . . Laughter. I walked on, down Main Street, and at Nagai's flower shop I looked through the plate glass window. Mr. Nagai was sitting behind the counter. He returned my look impassively, slowly crossing his arms. Going on, I tried to fit him in with the Jap bombers and the Jap spies in the valley, but he was Nagai's florist's between Buster Brown shoes and Sparacino's market, had always been, and could be nothing else. Anyway, my brain was tied in a knot like my stomach.

Someone ran directly into me from behind, knocking me off-balance. It was Mario, beaming from under a too-small aviator's cap with the flaps hanging down.

"Wanna go to Port Chicago?"

He always asked this, and if you said yes, and you always did, he was stunned with pleasure, tripping over his trouser cuffs and yelling, "I go get my car!"

But today the confident, feebleminded face angered me. "No, I don't want to go to Port Chicago," I snapped, and walked on. He tagged along. I suffered him silently for a few moments; then I said, "You're always talking about your car, but you don't have a car. You don't have a car, and you will never have a car. You'd better get it through your head."

But Mario enjoyed being addressed seriously, like a real person, and he walked along with a slack smile of enchantment. I turned to him. "Just because you're a moron, everybody's got to be nice to you."

Not my words, but my tone penetrated. His squinty eyes moved uncertainly to my face.

My own eyes dropped. I took hold of his warty hand and watched his face as it passed back to contentment.

It was going on four o'clock, already darkening. "I'm going home. You'd better go home, too."

We walked in silence, passing the three-story union hall, completed a year ago and already streaked with rust. "I climbed up there once," I told him, pointing.

He looked appreciatively.

We walked on. "I feel sick. Every minute I feel worse. You're lucky."

At his house I let go of his hand. With a wave, he went up the steps and opened the door.

"I hope we'll see each other again," I said as the door closed.

That night when Karla came in and turned on the lamp, I cautioned her.

"You shouldn't We don't have blankets up in here."

"Well, they can't expect us to go banging around in the dark. Anyway, it's a dim lamp."

I waited impatiently as she opened her jar of Sta-Bak and dipped her comb into the green goo. Combing a strand, she carefully rolled it up in a metal curler. She dipped the comb again. I began to seethe that she didn't go faster, yet at the same time I felt a pity well up for her, for her innocence. She knew nothing. Finally, the last curler was pinned in place. The lamp clicked off.

Under the door shone a crack of light from the dining room, where Peter slept on a couch. He was probably reading in bed. He was always poring over magazines for pictures of swing bands, which he cut out and saved. After a while the crack of light disappeared.

The house was silent. It was a small wooden house

23

painted mustard yellow like the train depot, with geranium bushes and pepper trees around it. I had always lived in this house and could have drawn a picture of everything in it, down to the smallest detail. The walls of the living room were peach, with a few comfortable spidery cracks. On the mantel-piece stood framed photographs, some old and brown. On the embroidered runner on a side table stood the radio, dark brown and shaped like a barn. The curtains were heavy lace, and the drapes were heavy, too, cranberry-colored. All the furniture was crowded, making it cozy. In the dining room, by Peter's couch, stood our round dining-room table. It was old, but a "good piece," as they said. When I dusted on Saturday mornings, I had to climb under it in order to get at the legs from all sides. They were heavy, ornate legs, and I knew their every curve by heart. Near it stood the wood stove. When a fire burned inside, the isinglass glowed amber. Tears were burning down my face into my ears.

I thought of the London children I had once seen a picture of in *Life* magazine, sitting in the subway singing and playing checkers while they waited for the bombs to fall. And the more I thought of their bravery, the more I gave way to my own wretchedness, until I was convulsed with suppressed sobs. And then, all at once, caving in totally, I saw our fate flash before me in full detail.

As though on a movie screen I watched us running into the cellar, knocking over Peter's drum in the dark, throwing ourselves onto the concrete floor. Our arms were tight around each other's backs. The drone of planes grew nearer and nearer until it was a deafening roar, and there came the whistling down of long, heavy bombs and the shock of a tremendous explosion that blew everything high in a splintering of wood and concrete and our own flesh and bones. And then, in the silence, the Japs with their bayonets came floating down in parachutes to creep through the rubble and stab and slice what was left of us. . . .

I lay knotted in a ball, so terrified I couldn't breathe. Then suddenly a powerful, boiling sensation flooded through me. I hated them. My eyes flared with a picture of Japs lying headless, burned, trampled down like beetles or lice or rotten vegetation. I hated them. Forever, with my whole being, I hated them.

I felt a long, quaking breath released and lay still. I was still frightened, but differently now. As though with control. And I no longer felt ashamed.

Chapter 4

The next day after school I got the paper from the porch and sat down with it on the front steps.

DEC. 10:   **War Raging in Philippines!**

The Philippines would fall. They said so downtown.

Contra Costa County in the War

All evening activities in local schools will be rescheduled for daytime . . . local chiefs of police have canceled all leaves . . . emergency Red Cross stations are being set up throughout county fire stations. . . .

I hadn't thought that far. Not everybody will be killed. Some would only be wounded. Maybe we would be among those.

Sheriff O'Toole Reports:

A pledge of wholehearted and undivided loyalty to the United States was given yesterday by the Contra Costa Japanese-American Association. We believe that most every Japanese here is a loyal American citizen, but those few who are not we have every facility to take care of in a lawful American way. . . .

Why didn't we line them up against a wall and shoot them? But I wouldn't mention this to my family, who kept saying it was a pity there were so many hysterical rumors about these people who had been farming here for generations.

I went over to the empty lot to play, and our games were wild and gory, filled with shooting and stabbing and the dying screams of Japs. I liked it very much, but after a while I felt something was wrong; my friends kept pulling back and looking at me the way they looked at Mario when he got carried away. So I went off alone.

DEC. 11:   Congress Votes War
                  On Germany, Italy

I had forgotten about Hitler and Mussolini. Almost everyone in Mendoza was Italian, but when I tried to think of Mrs. Pelegrino in her housedress being an enemy, I couldn't. Something here didn't fit. And there was Mr. Kroeger who delivered apple turnovers on Saturday mornings with a thick German accent. Dad and Mama hated the Germans, but they never slammed the door in his face. In fact they liked him. I liked him too. I felt there was beginning to be a place in my mind like a storeroom where I must shove things that didn't fit.

My face was the same, though. In the bathroom I would look at it in the mirror. My hair was the color of oatmeal, cut in a Dutch boy bob. My eyes were gray. I would look at myself until I felt embarrassed, but I kept looking. Then I would open my mouth and look down my throat. I couldn't see what was down there—heart, lungs, intestines—but it was me too. I liked it all, inside and out. It was all me, though I had never thought about it before, and I didn't really like to think about it now, because it saddened me to know that just when I began seeing myself so clearly I would be blown up.

DEC. 12:   Contra Costa County in the War

During air raid warnings, the sheriff's office on Station KPA will broadcast instructions. Citizens are advised to cut out the following list and keep it at all times by their radios.

WARNING SIGNALS
Yellow—Alert
Blue—Planes sighted, all lights out
Red—Bombing imminent, go to your cellars
White—All clear

Dad cut out the list and put it on the embroidered cloth in front of the radio. He had already signed up as a block warden, and he had a white metal hat and a flashlight that he kept on top of his bureau in the bedroom.

On the night of the twelfth, early in the evening, the fire bell dinned eleven times. By the time it was finished Dad had grabbed his metal hat and flashlight and an overcoat and was gone. Mama, Karla, Peter, and I sat down by the radio. Everything was very quiet. Only a small lamp was on.

"Yellow. Yellow," the radio voice said. "This is the yellow signal."

I sat quietly with my heart racing, my insides twisted up. I looked at the others. They were paying serious attention, but they did not look frightened. Peter even had a book in his hand, called *The Grapes of Wrath,* and after a while he put it under the lamp and kept reading. Every few minutes the voice said, "Yellow, yellow."

I sat looking at the floor, at Karla's extended foot, which wore a white Wedgie and striped ankle sock. I thought of Dad out on the street alone, and of the cellar. My bladder was building up such a pressure I thought I would die from holding it back. The clock on the mantel ticked.

Finally, after fifteen minutes, the voice said, "White. White. This is the white signal," and I got up in an ordinary way and went into the bathroom, and while I sat on the toilet, I rubbed and pulled my face and took one deep sigh after the other.

DEC. 13:   Sheriff O'Toole Reports:

A motor-driven air raid siren so loud that its wail can be heard for a radius of nine miles has been purchased by the city of Mendoza and will arrive within days, when it will be installed on the roof of the fire department. Manufactured by Belden Bros., Inc., at a cost of $627.82, the siren is powered by a Ford motor operated by remote control. . . .

I wanted it to come now. I lay awake every night because I feared the fire bell wouldn't be loud enough if you were asleep. If we got a real air raid siren, I could go to sleep at night. Ezio said the skin under my eyes looked dirty.

We went to the Saturday matinee. Ezio sat under the chandelier, but I wouldn't, in case there was a raid and it fell. It was *Small Town Deb* with Jane Withers, very good, but I couldn't concentrate. They say raids don't happen in the daytime, but if that was true, why did we have air raid drills at school, and why did men stand all day on the courthouse roof with binoculars?

DEC. 15:   **Sheriff O'Toole Reports:**

Keep your eyes and ears open at all times, especially around strategic spots! Be sure to take the license plate of any suspicious car. A little information tucked away by each citizen may be valuable to America. . . .

I went downtown after school with my Big Chief notebook. It was cold and drizzling, and the streets shone. On the hills to the right, Shell's big silver storage tanks were being painted black. I went to the post office first, and I saw people who looked as if they might be mailing a dangerous letter and followed them and wrote down their description, and if they got into a car, I wrote down the license number. Then I went down to the train depot, and I was surprised by all the soldiers and sailors suddenly filling the benches inside. There was nothing to write down here, so I went to Sheriff O'Toole's office, which was banked high on one side with sandbags, and watched for any spy in disguise who might shove a bomb in the shrubbery.

DEC. 16:   **Warning on Sabotage!**

The approaching holiday season is a period of increased danger from the fifth column. Sabotage activities, particularly on Christmas Eve, will require special vigilance from all citizens. Remember, surprise and treachery are Axis weapons!
    —Culbert Olson, Governor of California

*   *   *

28

That afternoon Ezio came with me. He said to Mario, "Go home, Suse and I have to go alone." Mario wandered away in the fog, looking back over his shoulder, his lip out. But Ezio was childish. He followed Mrs. Black, our third-grade teacher he had never liked, and took down her license number. When we passed the park, he crept around spying on old Hank the gardener, because Hank had chased him with a rake last spring for running through his flowers. And then on Main Street he saw Mr. Tatanian, the State Theater manager, and he followed him, too, because Mr. Tatanian had kicked Mario out awhile back for rolling down the aisle like a tin can.

But suddenly Ezio sharpened up and said he was going to look through Mr. Nagai's trash bin for coded messages. I didn't go with him; I waited at the corner. I tried never to think of Mr. Nagai. He had been shoved into my storeroom.

Ezio came running back through the fog with a little piece of paper with Japanese writing on it, and he shoved it under my eyes. "That rotten Jap! That spy!" he cried, and began running. We ran back to the empty lot where the kids were playing, and he handed the note all around. Everyone got excited and grabbed it from each other until it was so crushed and smudged you couldn't even see the pencil marks; then someone threw it in the air and they began killing each other in play, the scrap of paper completely forgotten. They were too harebrained to be patriots, they filled me with disgust. But I was glad they had forgotten about Mr. Nagai.

That night Mama said she was taking me to the doctor next week, because I was always tired.

Dec. 17: Germans Pushed Back from Moscow In Russ. Counterattack!

Moscow was so far away it didn't even count: but the Russians were our allies, and they were doing their best. Everything helped.

But here was a blow from Sheriff O'Toole.

Due to the immense demand for air raid warning devices, there will be a delay in the order of our powerful, remote-controlled siren. Until its arrival,

air raid warnings will continue to be signaled by the
fire bell.

Again, I lay awake into the small hours.

DEC. 18:   Frank Garibaldi
                            First Local
                            War Fatality

A cable has been received by Mr. and Mrs. Aldo
Garibaldi of 1402 Soledad Street that their son,
Frank, 21, was killed in the recent attack on Pearl
Harbor. Young Garibaldi enlisted in the navy in
1940, and was stationed aboard the *Arizona*. . . .

A long article, with his picture. I remembered him; he
used to deliver groceries. Red hair, green apron, he used
to whistle complicated things coming up the front walk.
I listened to my family talk about him.
I felt bad, too; but you understood that soldiers and
sailors would get killed in a war, that's what war was,
and if it just stuck to them, it would still be bad but not
so bad.

DEC. 19:   Hundreds of Oklahoma
                        Migrants Go Home

With the enormous increase of defense plants and
shipyards throughout the state, many of California's
"Okies" have at last found the profitable jobs they
left the drought for. But others, numbering in the
hundreds, have turned their dilapidated trucks
homeward. "Better to go back to the dust bowl,"
said Fred Simmons, 51, heading a line of trucks out
of Manteca this morning, "than stay here and be
bombed. . . ."

Why didn't we go to the dust bowl, too? Or at least we
could hike back into the hills and pitch a tent and live
there. But no one thought of doing this. They were like
the people in London and Rotterdam who stayed where
they were, I couldn't imagine why. I remembered that
potato-digging family in Poland or wherever it was that I

saw in *Life* magazine once, and I could have told them that they shouldn't have been digging potatoes in an open field. They should have run before the enemy came; then they wouldn't have been machine-gunned to death. But no one thought this way; no one seemed to understand.

DEC. 20:   **Sheriff O'Toole Reports:**

Our long-awaited remote-controlled air raid siren, so powerful that its wail can be heard for a radius of nine miles, will arrive Monday morning, December 22, by army truck in the city square. At 11 A.M., before its installation on the fire department roof, a demonstration will be performed by Sheriff O'Toole for interested citizens....

On Monday forenoon—it was Christmas vacation now—Mama took me down to the doctor's office. As we walked along the street I kept waiting for the siren's blast, and just as we were going up the steps there came a great hollow pop from the direction of the square. I wondered about this all through the examination, and as soon as we left the office we discovered what had happened, the whole town was talking about it. Right on the dot of eleven, Sheriff O'Toole had begun his demonstration, but before the siren gave out with more than its first breath, it blew up in a thousand pieces, wounding three citizens and a collie dog.

The doctor said my trouble was anemia and gave me iron pills.

DEC. 23:   **Sheriff O'Toole Reports:**

Due to yesterday's unfortunate incident, during which the city's newly purchased air raid siren exploded because of a mechanical fault, a new order for a siren will be made. Meanwhile, damages from Belden Bros. will be sought....

It was sabotage, but I couldn't even get excited about this; I could only think how long it would be now before we got another siren and I could go to sleep.

That night, past midnight, the fire bell dinned. I was

out of bed in a flash, pulling Karla. Then everybody was up, and Dad was running out, and the rest of us hurried to the radio. The voice said, "Yellow. Yellow."

Then it said, "Blue. Blue. This is the blue signal."

Peter turned off the small lamp. Mama, who was sitting next to me on the sofa, slipped her arm around me. I had a strange numb feeling, not what I expected. My eyes were frozen in the dark, and my brain was frozen too, so that all I knew was that the pepper tree was scraping against the house in the wind. It scraped for a long time.

"White. White," the voice said, "this is the all clear," and a moment later the fire bell dinned. Peter turned on the overhead light, and it came into my frozen eyes like a summer morning.

DEC. 24:   **Wake Island Falls!**

Christmas Eve was little. Even Dad's cigar smoke and the smell of roast pork were weak, as if a thinness had come into everything. The tree had only a few lights, to save on electricity, and that morning the blackout shades had arrived from Lasell's hardware, and we had them up, dark green, shiny, ugly. There were no Christmas packages from Denmark. We sang "Silent Night" around the piano, and Dad's and Mama's voices had a sound I couldn't place, as if they often wondered what was happening in their home country, and tonight they were wondering most. Opening the presents was nice, though not exciting the way it used to be. But I was happy just that we were still alive.

Christmas morning was crisp and icy, with frozen puddles in the driveway and white frost on the grass. In the cold, clear sky you could see barrage balloons hanging over the bay.

Chapter 5

Under cover of darkness, people had been throwing rocks through the windows of the Jap houses in the valley. The Japs had their own school out there that flew the flag of the rising sun (of course it had been taken down right away), and all the schoolhouse windows had been broken, too. But now in early January something happened closer to town and closer to my heart. In the outskirts of town lived a white chicken farmer and his Japanese wife. One day in broad daylight, while these two were away somewhere, vandals broke in and slashed the furniture and turned on all the faucets so that the place was flooded when the couple returned.

These vandals understood, but who backed them up with a firing squad? Even important people understood, because I now read the San Francisco papers when I was at the library and ran my finger under statements by governors, generals, and famous columnists:

> Why treat the Japs well here? They take the parking positions. They get ahead of you at the stamp line at the post office. Let 'em be pinched, hurt, hungry, and dead up against it. Personally, I hate the Japanese, and that goes for all of them.

and

> Japs live like rats, breed like rats, and act like rats.

and

> A Jap's a Jap! It makes no difference if he's an American or not.

These people understood, but no one listened. The Japs were given all the freedom they wanted to pull their net more tightly around us. Ignorance and blindness were all around me, even in my parents. When they exclaimed over the flooded house, I kept silent. And it seemed wrong that it should be this way, that I, a sixth grader, should be the one to understand. It turned things around, pulled the pattern of life out of kilter: my parents blind, and I miserably wise.

I pondered the facts I had gathered since Pearl Harbor. I knew now that our enemy had been scheming against us for years. Everyone, even my parents, talked about the Jap officers of the oil tankers who used to walk around town with cameras slung over their shoulders like tourists, taking snapshots of Shell, which were now in the hands of their Air Force. I remembered very clearly a little round-faced officer in black tunic and black cap who took a picture of me one summer when I was small, sitting in the schoolyard swing. I had smiled because he was so nice, bowing and beaming and wriggling his fingers. Now I and everyone else realized what these officers had been up to, with grins on their faces and death in their hearts. Only no one would shoot the Japs in the valley, who were just as murderous, with their wireless sets and rocket flares under their floorboards.

In this dark new year of 1942 Dad quit the job he had had as long as I remembered and went to work at Moore's Shipyard in Oakland, twenty miles away. He drove off in the old Ford before anyone else was awake, and returned after dark.

Mama joined a group of Red Cross women who met three afternoons a week to roll bandages for wounded soldiers.

Ezio threw away his knitted hat and replaced it with an army overseas cap he found on the street.

Downtown was a crowded place now, filled with soldiers wandering around between trains, with sailors from Mare Island and Port Chicago, with construction workers who were building a garrison by the creek. A lot of servicemen took a special liking to Ferry Street with its fourteen saloons crowded into three blocks, and sometimes you saw them staggering out in the rain and throwing up in the gutter. But most just bought picture postcards at Reed's stationery to send home or walked around looking at girls. They made wolf calls at Karla.

One tossed me a dime and said to call him up in ten years. I pondered his idea that he would be alive in ten years. He was probably whistling in the dark; if I were a soldier, I would throw dimes everywhere if it made me feel better. Soldiers got killed. You saw them in *Life* magazine with their arms sticking up from the snow like iron or lying half covered by sand on littered beaches. That was what it meant to be a soldier.

I continued lying awake far into the night. My grades had slumped disastrously, and now Miss Bonder had a talk with my mother, who sat me down that evening with her and Dad, not for the first time. What was really wrong? they wanted to know. And it was proof of my long careful deception that they did not point a questioning finger at the war. After the understandable hysteria of my creek plunge, I had shown no more and no less concern with the war than anyone else my age. I collected tinfoil. I said optimistic things. And now I was even smart enough to bring a comic book to read under the lamp during air raid alerts. But I could not sleep at night, and my grades were failing.

My parents were unhappy, and I was unhappy for them. I promised myself that as soon as the siren was installed and I could sleep again, I would make it up to them by becoming a top student.

The great day arrived the end of January, with a sound the enormousness of which no one had ever imagined—a madly amplified cow's moo blasted first in the middle register, then in the bass, this pattern repeated nonstop for five minutes. With each alert, satisfied reports came pouring in from Pacheco, Port Chicago, and Port Costa—all six or seven miles away—that the blast could be heard as though from next door. But here in Mendoza people leaped from their chairs, dogs raced under tables, babies screamed themselves into convulsions. Sheriff O'Toole was finally approached to lower the intensity, which he did with reluctance. Even so, the alarm remained a heart-jolting bellow which no one could possibly snore through to his death, and I was finally able to fall asleep after only an hour or so of ingrained vigilance.

At school, in spite of my vow, I merely plodded back to my former mediocrity. Nor had my other vow been kept: my side of the bedroom remained as cluttered as ever. It seemed that the only real changes in life came from outside and were forced on you. Like the war itself, or my classmates' sudden chatter about next fall and junior high school—a glamorous Spanish-style building I had no desire for, with its lawns that no one played on and its trees that no one climbed.

Feb. 15:   Singapore Gives Up!

That same day I came across a picture in *Life* that I wanted badly. It was a picture from a Malayan town called Kuala Lumpur, and it showed a Jap soldier who had tried to crawl out of his tank and been burned to a crisp. His head stuck out of the turret, skull-like, and as though covered with tar or black molasses, a few wisps of singed hair hanging over the empty eye sockets. By expressing interest in a neighboring feature on palomino horses, I was able to have this issue for myself without raising suspicion. I kept it on a shelf with Andersen's fairy tales and my comic books, and each night before going to bed, I indulged myself in a long, fulfilling scrutiny of the incinerated skull.

Feb. 24:   Santa Barbara Shelled!

It sent me to the bathroom with acute diarrhea. Afterward, as we sat listening to the radio news broadcast, I drew swift, detailed pictures of beheaded, limbless Japs bleeding from every pore, then quickly scribbled them out, in case anyone should look over my shoulder. The announcer's final words, making me sit back and swallow, were these: "The purpose of war is still to kill people, and it can still happen here just as it happened at Pearl Harbor."

It came the next night. At one o'clock in the morning, to the shattering blasts of the alarm, we hurried into the living room, pulling our bathrobes around us. No sooner had we turned on the radio and sat down to wait than the voice said, "Red. Red. This is the red signal. Go to your cellars. We repeat, this is the red signal. Go to your cellars immediately—"

"Well," said Mama, standing up.

Peter clicked on his flashlight. As in a dream, we walked quietly through the dark house and out the back

36

door. It was a cold, moonlit night. The wind whipped our bathrobes as we went along the back of the house to the cellar door. We waited while Peter groped with the latch. He seemed to take forever, but I felt no urgency, only a huge exhaustion, a sense of unreality. He swung the door open for us, and single file we descended the steep concrete steps as he stepped inside and closed the door above us. In the blackness someone bumped into the drum and sent it over with a crash.

Joining us with the flashlight, Peter beamed it on the old steel cot awaiting us. On its rusty springs lay a pile of emergency blankets covered with oilcloth. Below it stood an emergency chamber pot. The springs creaked as we sat down in a row. We spread the blankets across our laps. The beam of light went off.

I felt the wire springs pressing sharply into my buttocks. In my nostrils was a close, dank underground smell.

"It's like sitting on razor blades," Karla whispered.

"It's just for a while," Mama said, also in a whisper.

And Peter whispered, "It's just another drill."

But I was sitting next to him and I could feel a muscle working in his thigh, as if his heel were moving nervously up and down.

We waited in silence. In my plaid slippers, my feet were already numbed by the chill of the concrete. I sat exhausted under Mama's arm, looking into the blackness before me.

At length we heard brief, official voices outside. Block wardens, talking on the corner.

"I wish Dad weren't out there," Karla whispered.

And Peter whispered, "Come on, you know O'Toole's been dying to test the red alert." But the muscle in his thigh was still working.

Time must have passed, but there was no sense of its passing. It was part of the heavy stillness of this dark cave in the earth. Now and then someone moved a little with a creaking of springs, or there came a sudden chattering of teeth. But above all were the enormous black silence and the abiding quality of ears listening, and the sense of unreality.

When the drone of planes was heard, there was a collective turning of heads, like a delicate current in the darkness. Mama's arm gathered me slowly into her. The unreality faded. I felt drool fill my mouth, sliding out the corner. As the drone grew louder, it began reverberating under the soles of my slippers, in the wire springs of the cot, in the porcelain of my teeth, until it became a maddening roar directly overhead, and then the bombs were released, plummeting, and with an abrupt crushing up of my body I heard them whistling down, and everything ended in a shattering blast of white.

I was breathing, but with difficulty, crushed deep into something rough. Gradually it came to be the familiar roughness of Mama's terry-cloth robe. Her arm was like iron around me. It slowly relaxed as silence ebbed back. Everyone whispered at once.

"Were they our own?"

"They came so low!"

"I thought—"

The walls resounded with the blasts of the all clear, and numbly finding my face, I wiped the drool from my chin. Peter jumped up with a clang of released springs and pulled the string of the overhead bulb, illuminating the fallen drum, the damp cellar floor. These sights seemed, beyond all understanding, of great beauty and perfection. I watched Peter's blond hair fall brightly forward as he reached down to the drum. I looked at Mama, whose face was brilliantly clear and focused, as if under a magnifying glass.

"You were very good, Suse," she said, still in a whisper, smoothing my hair back with a hand that trembled slightly.

A reply was in order. I must form words and speak them. It was a moment before they came. "I was cold, though."

"Frozen stiff, you mean!" exclaimed Karla, shivering with pleasure.

Because now even the cold was beautiful. Outside, the wind felt clean and sweet; the pale moonlit yard gleamed. When we sat down to hot Ovaltine in the kitchen, the night had turned cozy and festive. And when Dad safely rejoined us, saying that it had been an unfounded alert off the Golden Gate, I felt the good heavy hand of sleep on my lids.

But I jolted awake in the dark. The illumined drum

was gone, the clean wind and cozy Ovaltine. All that remained was the whistling down of the bombs and the white shattering blast.

Chapter 6

In March the FBI broke into the Santa Cruz home of a Nisei couple and discovered sixty-nine crates of colored flares and signal rockets.

That night I gave a prayer. I had never prayed before and was not sure how to phrase the words of a prayer. I wanted to ask that the Japs in the valley be gotten rid of before they brought the bombers in. It must be clear, direct.

"Sheriff O'Toole," I whispered, "shoot them in the morning."

One cold, blustery afternoon I saw something in the post office that kindled my hopes. Alongside the "Be Prepared" and "Back the Attack" posters was a new one, "The Mask Is Off." It showed a slimy-faced Jap with buckteeth removing a smiling mask with one hand, while clutching a dripping dagger in the other. Now even the solemn post office was in on it. Now something would happen.

On the morning of March 27 all Japanese Californians were given forty-eight hours in which to dispose of their homes and businesses. When they had done this, they were loaded onto trucks, buses, and trains and taken to detention camps.

I was outraged. They had stuffed their wireless sets in the false bottoms of suitcases and baby buggies. They would escape from the camps and spread into the countryside to work from there. It was a measly, pointless move. Those who tried to kill you should be killed.

I heard my parents talking in the living room.

"The shop went for almost nothing," my Dad said.

"It's hard to believe," Mama said, knitting on a khaki muffler. "It's disgusting."

They were referring to Mr. Nagai. I didn't want to think about Mr. Nagai. I pushed him deeper into my storeroom and went into my bedroom, where I took my *Life* from its shelf and studied the burned head with an enravished loathing. I had never shared my burned head with anyone, but tomorrow, even if he was too scatterbrained to appreciate it on the right level, I would show the picture to Ezio. I felt a great need, tonight, to share. I felt at sea, all alone now, with the empty, silent valley.

The next morning I brought the magazine to school, but it quickly vanished from my thoughts. Ezio was yelling to a group by the swings.

"Those bastards, I'll kill 'em!"

"Who?" I asked, squeezing up to him.

"We've got to get out of any military zones! And what's military here! That bunch of crummy barracks? I'm impressed! I'm impressed!"

"Get out?"

"Get out! Any Italians that don't have citizen papers, like my mother! We've got to go ten miles outside city limits! We've got to go to my uncle's in San Ramon—"

I stared at him. "How long?"

"For the whole war," answered another Italian pupil, of whom several stood listening. They only seemed bewildered. None carried on like Ezio, who struck his thigh with his fist and yanked his overseas cap down.

"What do they think, we're a bunch of Japs? I *hate* Tojo! I hate Hitler! I hate Musso—"

Miss Bonder's tall pompadour passed through the crowd. "Ezio, please don't shout. It just makes things worse."

"It doesn't either!" he yelled in her face.

"That's enough. Lower your voice." And she turned to us, thinking for a moment before she spoke. "I know it's hard to understand, but in wartime things sometimes have to be done that seem unfair. All we can do is cooperate and do our best to end this war as soon as possible."

They were a teacher's dry, empty words. It was Ezio who was real, furiously smoothing the sides of his overseas cap, standing on trembling legs as if he had just run ten miles and was ready to collapse.

It was, as Ezio said many times during the next

month, the most stupid idea the government had ever had. Some of the Italians leaving town had sons in the armed services. Not only that, but those who worked in town, even at Shell, could get passes to go to their jobs. What sense did that make if the government was afraid they were going to plant a bomb by an oil tank? It was rottenness and stupidity, the whole country wasn't worth a nickle, let it rot. When Bataan fell, Ezio spoke of it with a contemptuous sneer, as if had he been consulted he might have spared us such a defeat, but at this point would have had to be begged to do so.

The day before his departure I told him I would come to his house in the morning to say good-bye.

"The hell you will. I don't want a bunch of jerks hanging around."

He must have seen the hurt look in my eyes. He said sullenly, "You can say it now."

I stood looking at him, not knowing how to phrase a farewell.

"Well. Good-bye."

"Good-bye." He crossed the street, not looking back.

But I spied on him the next morning, from the big date palm down the street from his house. In blue jeans, sport jacket, and no overseas cap, his face set in an expression of aloof efficiency, he was helping his uncle load the car. Suitcases were strapped to the roof; the back seat was piled high. Mrs. Pelegrino, a brown coat over her print dress, a kerchief around her head, was trying to keep Mario by her side.

"Mario go to Port Chicago!" he yelled, twisting and pulling. "Mario go to Port Chicago!"

"Shut up, sweetheart!" she cried. "You make Mama crazy!"

"*Andiamo*," the uncle called, getting in behind the wheel. With a last glance over her shoulder, Mrs. Pelegrino climbed in and settled Mario on her lap. Ezio got in after her and slammed the door. Framed by the window, his flinty, lifted profile moved down the street, and he was gone.

Two days later the house was up for rent.

Chapter 7

Behind Sheriff O'Toole's office a model air raid shelter had been completed. I went down inside and looked. It was snug and clean, but somehow seemed a worse place to die in than a cellar. By the train depot there now stood a hastily constructed USO canteen. The Native Daughters of the Golden West passed out sandwiches and coffee, and from the windows you could hear "Don't Get Around Much Anymore" and "That Old Black Magic" blaring from the jukebox. Mr. Nagai's flower shop, painted and redecorated, had reopened under a new sign: "Modern Miss Apparel." On May 6, Corregidor fell.

But the fullness of spring gathered as always. For weeks the sky had been a hard blue, and the breeze was cool. Now the sky softened, the wind vanished, the air hung hot and fragrant. Trees rustled green and heavy. Above the calm, glassy bay the hills loomed emerald green.

At school sweaters were pulled off and tied around waists. Then they were gone for good, along with pounds of hair, for everyone seemed to have had his or her hair cut, the girls' shorn straight and clean high across the neck, and the boys' clipped so close their ears stood out. Bare-necked, bare-armed, I felt a rippling freshness on my exposed skin. In the backyard, I helped Peter and Karla plant a victory garden.

All at once the Saturday matinees showed nothing but war films, ranging from *The Commandos Strike at Dawn* to *Abbott and Costello Join the Navy*. Clark Gable and Victor Mature were in uniform. Even Elsie the cow's husband Elmer wore an overseas cap. Classmates' older brothers and cousins disappeared from soda fountains and jalopies, leaving behind blue stars in windows. Windows were filled with all sorts of information: "Block Warden" and "We Buy War Bonds!" and "Quiet, Please, War Worker Sleeping." In car windows there were

42

pasted gas-rationing coupons and stickers saying "Give 'em a Lift!" and "Dim Lights After Dark!" At school we wrote essays on What America Means to Me. We bought defense stamps. We turned in big balls of collected tinfoil. In music class we kept to the patriotic strains of "America the Beautiful" and "My Country 'Tis of Thee," adding more raucously at recess "I'm Gonna Slap a Dirty Little Jap." Housing tracts mushroomed through the country. The stores downtown were crowded, though there was a shortage of zippers, alarm clocks, soap, fountain pens, boxed candy, even of matchbooks. Everywhere you saw people use wooden kitchen matches to light their Fleetwoods, a new and apparently dissatisfying brand that had sprung up in the absence of Camels and Chesterfields. Everyone had money to burn; but sugar, coffee, and butter were a luxury, and you stood in line at the market with your little green ration book and carried your groceries home in the same paper bag until it fell apart. Dresses were suddenly short and skimpy, with no pockets or ruffles, to conserve cloth. In place of nylon stockings, women covered their legs with tan makeup and drew on black seams with eyebrow pencil. But more often they wore pants called slacks. They worked in shipyards and defense plants. Some of them lived alone, their husbands having been drafted, and with greasy wrenches they repaired their own cars, and with hoes and mowers they cut down the lush spring grass in their backyards and planted victory gardens.

We planted beans, potatoes, and spinach. I liked working with the black pungent clods, pressing the seeds down. I envisioned the first frail shoots and then the sudden springing forth of foliage, surely a miracle. And I wondered if it was just spring that made everything seem better or if it was the fact that despite our disastrous chain of military defeats we had not yet been bombed.

It would not do to feel too sure. What the enemy banked on was our becoming relaxed, careless, as we had been before Pearl Harbor.

One day I looked at Peter and felt a shock. All at once he was tall, and he had taken to combing his hair back from his forehead with brilliantine. His nose and cheekbones had sprung into prominence; his jawline was sharper; he had a gaunt, chiseled, mysterious look.

43

"You don't practice anymore," I told him.

"Practice what?"

"Your *drum*."

"Oh, that." All he talked about now was becoming an architect. He got a job on Saturdays selling shoes at Buster Brown's, and he put on a tweed suit and a yellow knit tie and sauntered off, pausing at the corner to light a Fleetwood. It was only too easy to picture him in uniform now; he could be one of those tall, gangling soldiers downtown on a last leave from Camp Stoneman, which was a few miles up the bay. It was where the troops were loaded onto gray carriers that plowed through the Golden Gate toward the screams and crossfire and jungle quicksand of the islands.

But Peter wouldn't be eighteen for another year, and the war might end by then. Sometimes I felt my mind leaping recklessly past the war, to all the years beyond, life streaming on and on, in sunlight, like a river. But I always pulled back. To want that, to pinpoint it, was to hang it with a bull's-eye for demolition. You had to use camouflage, even in the privacy of your own mind.

I was studying my mason jar, which was filled with mildewed oranges from which I hoped to grow penicillin.

"I really wish you'd put that out of sight," Karla murmured, doing her homework.

"I have to check it. Anyway, what about your jar?"

She had her nylons stuffed in a jar.

"That's to *keep* them from rotting."

"Well, these oranges have to rot."

"Oh well," she shrugged, and gave me a smile. "It doesn't matter." She didn't care about my side of the room anymore because she would be leaving soon. She would be graduating from high school in June and had won a scholarship to the Art Institute in San Francisco. In the fall she would move there.

I received a postcard from Ezio, in his huge scrawling handwriting that had to bunch up at the edge. He rode his uncle's plow horse, Mario had a big boil on his seat, so long for now. If only I could take Ezio with me into junior high school, that red-tiled palace where the girls shrieked and the boys slouched and, in spite of this mutual unattractiveness, walked with their arms around

44

each other. My hated but familiar grammar school life was rapidly drawing to an end.

There was something I should do before leaving. During air raid drills Miss Bonder no longer pulled down the Venetian blinds against the possibility of flying glass. When I pointed this out to her, she had replied, "Thank you, Suse, but I think I know what's necessary and what's not." I felt it my duty to report her to Sheriff O'Toole, but it seemed underhanded. Anyway, the rules all seemed to be letting up. The school drills were not as frequent as they had been, and the nighttime alarms came only every ten days or so. I was beginning to feel the passing of a crisis, as if I had suffered a violent cold that had passed from its sneeze-exploding crest to a dry, chronic chest pain, a kind of natural condition, manageable.

On the last day of school the sixth-grade classes had an orangeade party in the town park. When it was over, everyone in our class crowded around Miss Bonder to say good-bye. Even the rowdies crowded up to her side with rough good nature, and some of the girls hugged her tearfully and stood back, wiping their noses in the excitement, which was such that I too cried, "Miss Bonder, good-bye! Good-bye!" and felt we were taking leave of a saint, a supernatural being suffused with great light. But as the clamor died down and we dispersed along the streets, I felt this shining figure sink back into a tall pompadour, a sour smile, and a dangerous attitude toward Venetian blinds. Even if things were letting up, I should report her as a threat to our safety. Then suddenly it struck me that we would never be coming back to her classroom, and my concern with the Venetian blinds blew away like smoke. It would not be me the flying glass hit.

I walked along thinking how glad I was that George Washington's drooping eyelids were gone for good. How he must have bored everyone with those eyelids. Even without him, American history was boring. What was America? Beyond California there was a haze, with the Rockies sticking out there, Chicago farther on, and New York at the end. That was more or less what I had put down in the What America Means to Me essay. Miss Bonder had written across it: "The subject is not meant to be a joke. What do you pledge allegiance to? What do you collect scrap metal for? Please rewrite." And so I had thought more deeply and written, "I collect scrap metal to defend my family, and my house, and my backyard, the crickets in the grass, and the sow bugs under the back stairs." This time she scrawled, "Bugs do not enter in. You do not grasp the idea." I didn't really know why I had put down the sow bugs, except that they were under my back stairs and they belonged in my reason. And if I didn't grasp the idea, I didn't care either.

At which point I reached home, handed Mama my squalid report card, and summer officially began.

Chapter 8

At noon Mama would roll down the shades and sit fanning herself with a newspaper. The hills glared bone white. The sidewalks hurt your eyes. You could smell the rank mud and crusted salt from the tule marsh and tomato aroma drifting in hot waves from the cannery. These smells were as fine as the smells of spring, and finest was the prickling scorch of the creek, where every summer Ezio, Mario, and I went searching for deep, clear pools. This year I climbed alone through the dry grass, narrowing my eyes for a jade green glint. Though I knew there was nothing here but a few stagnant crannies, I kept looking anyway, certain that the clear green pool lay around the next bend. But without Ezio and Mario, I wandered out early.

I would climb up in the hills, or go down to the wharf, or walk around town, looking at things. When I passed Dad's old body shop, I thought of how he used to walk to work and how he had time to eat breakfast with us in the morning and always got home from work while it was still light. The shop was an interesting place, dim and smelling of paint thinner, and Dad was always there when you dropped in. He would look up from what he was doing and smile hello and put his arm around you, and he would show you around the sanding and noisy banging, and sometimes someone would be welding, sending up a magnificent shower of sparks. If you came by around noontime, he would wash the grease from his hands and face, and you would walk home together for lunch.

I would wander on, drift into the library, look for something to fascinate me. One day the librarian suggested *The Three Musketeers*. When I returned this two days later and asked for more like it, she gave me *The Count of Monte Cristo*. After that I downed *Les Misérables* and *Notre Dame de Paris*, enthralled by this place, France, with its furious swordfights, its mysterious sewers, its hunchback swinging on cathedral bells. Then, in our own bookcase at home, I came across a book called *Madame Bovary*, and though it had neither swordfights nor sewers, I liked it best of all. It had a special realness that made it possible to taste the food the people ate, to feel with their fingers the wallpaper and the bark of trees, and to smell with their nostrils the morning steam rising from rivers. In spite of Emma Bovary's incomprehensible mania for clothes and sweethearts, in spite of her terrible death, the book possessed something which only in later life did I crystallize as beauty. When I finished the last page, I started all over again.

Then something entirely unexpected happened. A six-week Red Cross swimming program for children began.

Three times a week we piled into a yellow school bus, whizzing past the ex-Jap walnut and pear orchards, past dry fields and big oaks, into dusty foothills, and then we were bouncing along a dirt road with the dust rising behind us, and Mitchell Canyon pool burst into sight, green and sparkling. The bus windows were open, and we could already smell the chlorine, and we were pushing to the door with our rolled-up towels before the bus had stopped.

For three hours we were immersed. Only occasionally did I slosh onto the wet burning cement to catch my breath as feet pounded by and screams and splashes filled the air; then I would scramble to my feet and dive back in with a whoosh of engulfing deafness, my eyes drawn to slits by the water's rush. Smooth and soundless as a fish, I swam deep inside the green-blue world, and if I looked up, I saw among the blurred bodies, the sun's blaze of silver across the surface, with pale coins of light dappling down.

Blue-lipped, fingers like white raisins, we bought licorice sticks afterward at the refreshment stand and piled back into the stifling bus, where through the dust and jolting we sang:

> There's a place in France
> Where the naked women dance,
> And the men go around
> With their trousers hanging down

which ended in bursts of knowing laughter and an unfavorable look from the driver, a tough-faced lady with gray curls under a battered sun visor.

When we passed the San Ramon cutoff, I felt a wave of melancholy, remembering Ezio and Mario. And when we reached the outskirts of Mendoza, I gave thanks that it had not been bombed in our absence. Yet, with a sunburned elbow out the window and licorice sweet in my teeth, I could not find it in my happiness to linger over these things.

By the time the program was over my hair was chlorinated a rich green hue. "Sort of off-viridian," mused Karla, who knew colors. I didn't mind. It was my badge and my memory. Plug-earred and sodden, I was content to return to my books. I remained happy.

One afternoon this happiness overcame me. I was in the backyard, doing nothing. All at once I felt my heart expand, and I swung my eyes blissfully through the yard, and I knew—not with crossed fingers, but with a clap of certainty—that nine long months had passed and we would never be bombed. I flopped down on the ground with a stunned smile and sat there with no thoughts at all, except that later on, when the shade from the house had crept across the yard, Mama and Karla would come out with a pitcher of lemonade, and we would sit at the old card table, whose top would still be brick warm from the sun.

And then a strange picture came to me. That potato-digging family lying dead in a Polish field, they must have lived in a house and sat in their yard at an old table drinking lemonade or whatever you would drink in

48

'oland. The children must have spread their hands on the warm tabletop, and it must have felt real to them; they must have felt real to themselves, as I felt real to myself. A wave of astonishment passed through me, a wave of disturbance; I didn't want to know this surpassingly strange thing, but the picture was growing, for the parents must have felt real too, and the people in the bombed cellars of London and Rotterdam, the soldiers lying dead in the snow with their arms sticking up like iron, and in the jungles, rotting. They had all been real inside, important. Frank Garibaldi in his green apron, coming up the steps whistling his complicated tunes, he must have been important to himself, the shining center of everything. He must have hated to die. He must have cried out and covered his eyes.

They all must have, and it was too much to know, too painful, too pitiful, too huge and boundless, and why should I have to see such a thing now, just when I knew we were safe, and I had found happiness again? I pressed my hands to my ears, as if that would squeeze me back into my happiness, but I felt like a pond when a stone has been dropped, and ripples spread out as though set in motion forever. For these terrible ripples would go on forever, would be with me forever, even if my own yard were never bombed, even if only good things happened to me for the rest of my life.

Chapter 9

Good things were not to happen, in any case. Soon after, we had our first blue alert in months. A rash of torpedoings broke out in coastal waters. Rumors began spreading that Jap balloon bombs were floating inland. Sheriff O'Toole reported in his column that those who had been lulled into a false sense of security should take heed.

Chastened, I took a long step back into the shadows.

When Karla moved to San Francisco, we drove her there and saw her settled into a rooming house. She was

49

excited and happy, but when she kissed us good-bye, sh
didn't seem quite as excited and happy, and I wondered
if she would feel as lost in a room of her own as I would
now feel. I tried to console myself with the fact that she
was far better off here in San Francisco. People often
said San Francisco was a safer place to be in than Mendoza.

On the way home, sitting with me in the back seat, Peter began talking to Dad and Mama about his own plans
after graduation next year. He was hoping he might
squeeze a couple of months of college into the summer.

"What about afterwards?" I asked, with my calm, interested expression.

"Basic training, kiddo."

I was silent for a moment. "If you practiced your
drum, maybe they'd put you in the band and you could
just go around in parades."

"Not a chance. That would be too logical. They don't
put musicians in the band, they put cooks in the band.
Musicians they put in the kitchen. Swimming instructors
they put in, let's see—desert training." He laughed.

But I saw nothing funny about the Army.

Over the back of a chair hung a new plaid skirt and
yellow sweater. A pair of saddle shoes, my first, stood
underneath. I sat at Karla's dressing table, carefully slic-
ing the calluses from my palms with a razor blade. Then,
after sweeping the pieces of hard skin into the wastepaper basket, I climbed into bed, where my feet encoun-
tered a cool vastness on Karla's side.

The next morning, in my new clothes, my hair brushed
to a green gloss, I set off for the unknown. It was a
hazed, sultry morning, and I walked past the creek and
gravely alongside the garrison storm fence, behind which
stood a stark scene of army trucks, artillery, brown rows
of barracks. A troop of soldiers was drilling with rifles.
The barked commands echoed all the way to the entrance of the junior high.

I pulled the door open on a sea of unfamiliar faces, the
girls with high pompadours like Miss Bonder's, the boys
with pointed Adam's apples and deep voices, everyone
yelling, waving, shoving, sweeping me along in a mad
tide to the auditorium.

There, as soon as the hubbub died down, Mr. Gran-

...dison welcomed us with "On the Road to Mandalay," and I felt more at home. Twisting around in my seat, I was pick'... out the scattered faces from my class when a large ... ...cher in a gray suit shot his arm out and poin... ...ı me to turn around. Humiliated before the entire student body, I slid down on my spine, not even hearing the speeches and instructions that followed. Then we were surging back into the corridor, where the big teacher in gray stood planted, answering inquiries with "Down the hall! Up the stairs!" like one of the Gestapo men in the movies who would as soon beat you to a pulp as look at you.

But my homeroom teacher seemed nice, and I breathed more easily. Only for a moment—a dark fact was spreading through me; of my old classmates here, each was a "poor worker" like myself, or worse, and the rest were from other sixth-grade classes, among them loud messy Eudene who had a screw loose, and Dumb Donny Woodall. I had been demoted. These were the fools rounded up from each class and shut away together like cats with the mange. I took my seat with a hot, shaky feeling, knowing I must not look at my new clothes and remember how pleased Mama had looked as I set off, or my throat would tighten and I would not be able to say, "Here."

For having introduced herself as Mrs. Miller, the teacher was calling roll. I found no comfort now in her pleasant, friendly voice. It was an indulgent voice, reserved for peabrains. I sat with rapidly blinking eyes fastened on my desk, which, I noted with another wrench, was not a desk at all, but an ordinary chair with a traylike arm to write on—a useless piece of furniture to dive beneath in an air raid.

The name Suzy Hansen was repeated several times before I realized it referred to me. I said with my tight throat, "It's not Suzy, Mrs. Miller. Sooza."

"Sooza!" Eudene yelled at her.

"Please, dear, we don't yell. Sooza, then. Peggy Hatton?"

A girl I had never seen before, apparently new, looked up from the doodle marks she had been making on her binder. Her hair was red and frizzy and stuck out in two chunky pigtails. The rest of her was also chunky, filling to tautness a plain white middy blouse and black skirt.

She had a quiet, modest air and luminous green eyes that blinked earnestly as she spoke. "Excuse me, please, but that name's wrong. It's Rochelle Hatton."

Mrs. Miller looked again at the sheet she held. "It says Peggy here."

"No, excuse me, Mrs. Miller, but it's Rochelle."

"I'm sorry, dear, I think we must go by what it says on the list. That way there's no confusion. Angelo Iaconi?"

The girl gave a solemn blink and resumed her doodling. I saw that she was drawing squares within squares, appropriate, whether she knew it or not, to the tedious years that lay before us.

After roll call came the choosing of locker mates. I stared frigidly ahead, wishing no mate, no locker, no junior high school, and was irrationally stung when I remained unchosen. The new girl also having been passed over, Mrs. Miller paired us off, and the class proceeded into the hall to the lockers. I set my lunch pail inside with a mournful bang. The Hatton girl gave a cold click of the lock. We did not speak and exchanged only the brief, cool look of people who have been brought together on the basis of an inadequacy.

The morning passed with increasing confusion. Where was Miss Bonder, deficient, but at least not fragmented into seven different faces? Why, when Dumb Donny Woodall raised his hand to go to the bathroom, did the teacher say to attend to those things earlier? Why, at noontime, did the eighth and ninth graders carry brown paper bags instead of lunch pails? And why did they have each other's names inked all over their saddle shoes? Because they were all friends, like my old class, which was eating lunch together on the lawn. I decided to take my lunch down to the creek. Maneuvering around the Gestapo teacher, who was patrolling the grounds, I jumped behind a tree and climbed down to privacy. Opening my blue lunch pail, I listened gloomily to the sound of garrison trucks mixed with the strains of dance music from the gym.

But in homemaking class that afternoon there were two refreshing moments. The first came when Eudene dropped her shoulder bag and some cigarettes rolled out. She was ordered to the principal's office, and she left us with a loud laugh, swinging her hips. Eudene had broad

52

hips to swing, a big bosom to point with, a strong smell of sweat, and a coarse, sallow face under tangled sauerkraut hair. She had been kept back for so many grades that she was now fifteen years old. But this did not bother her, and in fact nothing bothered her. She seldom knew what was going on, but she always enjoyed herself, yelling and smashing your ribs with her elbow. These junior high school teachers didn't know what to make of her, and despite my resentment at having been demoted to Eudene's level, I admired the way she had gone to her destiny, laughing and swinging her hips, leaving the teacher with lips parted.

Then, shortly after, the teacher spoke admonishingly to the quiet Hatton girl. I saw that she had slid down in her seat and sprawled her legs out.

"Sit up properly, please, and pay attention. What was I just saying?"

"You were saying sit up properly, please, and pay attention."

The teacher frowned down the roll sheet and, finding the name with her finger, looked up. "We have no room for smart-alecs here, Peggy."

"I didn't understand what you meant," said the girl, her green eyes widening. "I really didn't." She had sat up, aligned her feet, and neatly folded her hands in her lap. "And excuse me, please, but it's not Peggy. That name is wrong. It's Rochelle."

"I'm afraid that's between you and the registrar's office," said the teacher, and at that moment the air raid bell sounded and we were led into the corridor like a herd of cattle for the roof to crash down on. All today's anger and disappointment burned into the ceiling as I stared up at it, and I vowed to send off a scathing report as soon as I got home.

Dear Sheriff O'Toole,
    This is to tell you that in junior high school they make you stand in the hall during the air raid alarm where the ceiling could crush you. You can not use the desks to get underneath and they do not take you down to the basement either. I am a student there. Thank you.
    P.S. Miss Bonder at the grammar school does not pull the venetian blinds down so that the flying

glass would not cut the children. I am not there but they are. Thank you.

With a dictionary at my side I got the spelling of each word right. It took a long time, but it was worth it. I mailed the letter on the way to school the next morning and felt better. But as I passed the garrison, my thoughts sank down under war everlasting. Nor had I done my homework. Nor did I know anyone. A lump of melancholy grew in my chest.

But at lunchtime everything changed.

Maybe on the grounds that we were, irreversibly, locker mates, Peggy Hatton invited me to eat lunch with her.

With eyes lowered to hide my relief, I accepted. "But you don't have any lunch," I added, seeing her empty hands.

"I go home to eat."

I hesitated. I was not supposed to go to strange houses.

"Come on, kid," she urged.

"All right."

We walked down the street, leaving the school behind. The day spread out in a hot blue blaze, filled with salt tang and sudden promise.

Chapter 10

I hate this school," she said.

"So do I."

"The teachers won't even call me Rochelle. It's my *name.*"

"How come it's Peggy on the roll call sheet?"

"How do I know?"

"You mean Peggy's some completely wrong name?"

"That's right."

"That's funny. I wonder why."

But I could see that my companion was not one to pursue a subject relentlessly. She seemed already to have dropped this one. Her round stomach was comfortably thrust before her, and she walked with a pleasant, solid roll.

"Are you new?" I asked.

She nodded.

"Where did you go before?"

"Clara Bebb's, in the valley. It's a boarding school."

I gave her a closer look. I had seen boarding schools in movies, and the girls were snobbish and beautiful. They rode horses with English saddles and swam in pools surrounded by urns of wisteria. None of them looked like Rochelle. But for all I knew, they left these stumpy ones out of the movies.

"Did you have a swimming pool?"

She gave a nostalgic nod.

"Why do you want to go *here* for?"

"I don't." She turned a slow, heavy-lidded look at me. "They kicked me out."

"They did?"

"After the sixth grade they make a decision, on if you're too untamed. They like the bookworm type. I was too untamed."

"You were?"

"I don't care. Only I liked it there, I had a lot of friends. This is our uniform."

"I had a friend. His name was Ezio."

"We didn't have any boys, just brothers if they came on visiting days."

"I've got a brother. And a sister."

Her round face took on a sudden hardness. "I've got a sister. But they never brought her along to visit."

"Why not?"

"Because. She's insane."

"Really? Ezio's brother was insane. He used to go to the bathroom in the street."

"She doesn't do that."

"What does she do?"

"I don't want to discuss her. I detest her."

We turned onto a broad, curving street lined with weeping willows. "Do you like Mendoza?" I asked.

"Are you kidding? Run-down old refinery town?"

"What do you know about it! You just moved here!"

"No I didn't. We've always lived here."

That was strange. I had never laid eyes on her, never

heard of a Hatton family. There was a lady foot doctor on Estudillo Street named Hatton, a woman with cropped hair like a man's and a cigarette always dangling from her mouth, but as far as I knew she wasn't even married.

"How come I've never seen you around?" I asked.

"Because I'd be in school all year, and in the summer I'd go to camp at Tahoe. Only I can't anymore unless I improve."

We had come to a broad, velvety lawn where a gardener in a sun helmet was moving a sprinkler.

"Is he a Jap?" I whispered.

"Filipino. How do you pronounce your name again? I want to get it right in case they're home."

"Who?" I asked uneasily, looking at the house. It was large, imposing, made of gray stone, inset with long, cathedrallike windows. "Sooza," I said in a hushed tone as she pulled open the door, a great rough-hewn affair with an iron knocker.

"Anybody here?" she yelled, and taking my hand, she led me down the hall to the kitchen.

There, amazingly, sat the lady foot doctor from Estudillo Street. She was smoking and reading a newspaper over the remains of lunch. Next to her sat a man, also smoking and reading a newspaper. Across from them sat a girl of about fourteen or fifteen, spooning up a bowl of soup. She had piercing green eyes that never left my face as we approached the table.

"This is my friend Sooza," Rochelle announced, "and this is my mother and father."

The lady doctor glanced up pleasantly from her paper.

"And this is Rudy!" cried Rochelle, stooping down as a brown dachshund barreled into her arms, barking wildly. After setting him down with smacking kisses between his eyes, she went to a cupboard and took out two plates. But I could see that the table was meant for only two people, not three or four, let alone five. Yet it was a big kitchen and could have held a banquet table. Rochelle was trying to cram the plates in.

Dr. Hatton looked up again. "Dear," she asked me, "would you mind eating at the drainboard? Peggy, make your friend a nice sandwich."

"Rochelle. And she brought her own lunch."

"Fine," murmured the doctor, pushing up a pair of

imless spectacles that had slipped down her nose and returning to her paper.

"Is that okay, Suse?" my new friend asked, flopping down very hard next to her sister.

I nodded and went to the drainboard. I sat down on a high stool and opened my lunch pail. I felt very nervous because I could feel the insane girl's eyes boring through me.

Suddenly, sharply, she spoke. "Why is your hair green?"

"It's—it's from swimming. The chlorine—"

She stood up. She was slim and wore a beautiful wine-colored dress of the sort you would expect to see on a grown-up person and black open-toed pumps. Across her shoulder was draped a silk shawl with a fringe. Quickly, intently, she crossed the room to my side.

"Is it a permanent condition?" she asked. She had a strong British accent.

"No. It—it'll fade—"

She stood studying my head. I squinted sideways at hers. The eyes were the same green as Rochelle's, but brilliant rather than luminous. The features were finely chiseled, framed by loose auburn curls. It was a deadly serious face.

"What are you staring at?" she asked.

"Well, you—you're staring at me—"

"That is an entirely different matter. Your hair is green. An attractive enough shade, but patently abnormal."

"Why don't you shut your trap?" Rochelle yelled. "She can have any color hair she wants, it's a free country, we're all born equal!"

"Oh God!" cried the girl. "This is the stale commentary we have to live with! What a threadbare repertoire! What a—"

"Well, you—" Rochelle began.

"Don't speak to me!" she snapped, returning to her seat.

After a moment Rochelle turned to her with a smile. "You've got mayonnaise on your sleeve."

The girl recoiled, clutching her arm. "Estelle, she's gotten mayonnaise on everything!"

"Well, wipe it off, dear," her mother murmured.

"She is a complete and utter swine!"

Mr. Hatton lowered his newspaper. "I would like som peace and quiet," he said in a low voice, and the kitchen fell silent. The sister wiped her sleeve with angry swipes of a napkin. Rochelle was busy eating. She was eating a great deal, including large spoonfuls of mayonnaise, which she downed with a sharp eye on her parents, who were not looking in any case. They both wore tan windbreakers, his with trousers, hers with a straight skirt. Their hair was similar, hers coppery and his carroty, and the same length, since hers was shingled. After a while, putting out their cigarettes, they got up and left the room, discussing Stalingrad.

The older girl rose too, abruptly. "Rudolph will now give his celebrated imitation of a frankfurter." She clapped her hands smartly, and the dog fell over. "Bravo, Rudolph!" she cried, and glanced at her watch. "I must dash or I'll miss my train." And with her hurried, intent walk, she left us.

I hardly knew what to say. "Why does she talk like an English movie?"

"She thinks she sounds better that way. She's insane. Listen."

I listened but heard nothing.

"Wait a minute."

Presently, from another part of the house, there came a terrific yelling. Rochelle led me down the hall to peer around the arched entryway to the living room. There the girl stood with clenched fists, crying, "I will not! I will not!" while Rudolph, who had raced ahead of us, danced around, leaping and barking. Mr. Hatton observed the scene from a chesterfield, while his wife stood before the girl with a coat in her hand.

"It might turn cold later on," Dr. Hatton said patiently.

"It will not turn cold!"

"Take it along, Helen Maria."

"I will not! I want to wear my shawl!"

"Wear it over your shawl, dear."

"It will look repulsive! I will not!"

Dr. Hatton gave a sigh. "Go on then. Catch pneumonia."

Sweeping up an armful of books, the girl strode from the room, throwing a furious look at our two prying faces.

"That's not nice," Dr. Hatton remarked to her younger daughter. "Helen Maria is not a sideshow."

My companion nodded agreeably, and we started back to school. Up the street we could see Helen Maria walking along very fast. She turned and looked at us. Then, tossing her head, she hurried on.

"Why was she so mad about the coat?"

"She's always having fits over something."

"Where's she going on the train?"

"Berkeley. UC. She's in her senior year."

"Of *college?* How old is she?"

"I don't know. Fifteen."

"She must be a genius."

"*She* thinks so."

"What does she study"

"I don't know. Greek and junk like that." There was a bitter, suffering tone to her voice, yet also a grudging boastfulness. "Estelle and Jack said she was reading at eighteen months. What a freak!"

"You call them Estelle and Jack? How come?"

"I don't know. That's who they are."

"You've got a really odd family," I complimented her.

Chapter 11

The next day I again accompanied my new friend home. This time only Rudy was in. Rochelle took me into the living room, where she flopped down on the chesterfield, which stood at an angle, as if someone had once searched for something behind it and never bothered to push it back. "Horrible room, isn't it"

The walls were burnt orange, the carved furniture massive, the lampshades of brown parchment stitched with leather thongs. There were a lot of podiatric supplies standing around and a lot of clay pots holding withered cactus plants. Above the mantelpiece, on which rested a dusty Spanish galleon and a burned-out light bulb, scowled a life-size matador in somber oils.

"We call it Dorothy's Dungeon. It's my Aun Dorothy's brainchild. We hate it."

"Why don't you change it?"

"I don't know. We never get around to it."

Her own room was magnificent. My room was small and cozy. The plaster walls were light blue and now, since Karla's departure, Scotchtaped with pictures of horses and boats and mountain ranges torn out from old *Lifes*. The linoleum was maroon with a blue pattern, and the drapes, setting off white curtains, were also blue. This carrying out of blue throughout the room was Karla's doing, and it provided a pleasant background of grace and symmetry for my clutter. It was a perfect room, and I would not have had another; but I stood awed by Rochelle's.

It was very big, almost too big, and covered with a very thick dusky rose rug. All the furniture was white, splashed here and there with bright throw pillows. The walls were papered in a pink and white flower pattern, and it was a room drenched and glittering with sun pouring through French windows that stood open to the back garden. Everything in it was extremely neat. Rochelle explained that she had been promised a phonograph if she kept it clean for a month.

"You want to see hers?" she asked, and took me back down the hall, where she cautiously opened a door. "Ixnay, don't go in. Nobody can go in."

It was a room like her own, very large and sunny, but on the floor were small Persian rugs, and there was a fireplace, and the walls were lined with books. Here and there on the shelves stood small white statues of naked people or people in robes, all missing an arm or two.

"How come the statues are broken?"

"That's how they are. That's how your Greek statues come."

Through the French windows I caught sight of the gardener raking.

"I'm sorry, he looks like a Jap to me."

"Well, he's not. His name is Annuncio, and he's a Filipino. The Japs are all gone." She sounded impatient. She wanted me to look at the room.

"Is that Greek?" I asked, pointing to a picture of some ruins.

"Yes. Your Greeks are a very ancient race. They left many ruins. Those are peacock feathers."

A brass vase holding three peacock feathers stood by the bed, which strangely enough was just a mattress on the floor, covered with a heavy spread that looked like a Persian rug. On the spread lay some books and a pack of Fleetwoods.

"She smokes?"

"With a holder. She thinks it makes her interesting. Over there's where she studies." She pointed to a desk piled with binders and untidy stacks of paper. Nearby, against a portable phonograph, leaned a long row of record albums bearing such unfamiliar names as Shostakovich and Vivaldi.

"Those are your classical composers. All she does is study and listen to music." And giving a loud, repulsive blurt, she shut the door and took me to the kitchen. "Next time I'll show you Jack's workshop downstairs. He's a marine architect at Mare Island."

"Mare Island could be bombed."

"Oh well," she said, throwing open the door of the large white refrigerator. Most people I knew kept their food in iceboxes and coolers. Nor did anyone I know have a telephone in the kitchen and another in the hallway. Many people, including my own family, had no need for a phone at all. There were floor gratings for the heat to come through. They didn't look very inviting. A wood stove crackled nicely, and on winter mornings it was exhilarating to race from your icy bedroom and warm your clothes on the stove top until they were roasting hot to climb into.

"He does inventing down there," she said, filling up the table with bowls and jars. "His father was an inventor too. He got rich off a thing to bottle soda pop with. That's all you need, just one idea. I'm going to be an inventor too." She fell abruptly silent, spreading white oleomargarine on a piece of bread and layering it with cheese, deviled egg, and sardines.

"I may be a trapeze artist."

"I've got this aunt," she said, cramming a corner of the sandwich into her mouth. "You can't guess what she is. A mortician. My aunt Margaret." And she sat back with a food-muffled chortle. "I'm named after an undertaker."

I glanced over at her. "I knew your name wasn't Rochelle."

She lowered her sandwich.

"It doesn't matter to me," I said, opening my lunch pail. "I'll call you Rochelle if you want me to."

"Because I am a Rochelle. I am not a Peggy."

I nodded, though I did not follow this.

Swallowing, she smiled. "At Clara Bebb's we had contests. Listen." And she delivered herself of a rich, protracted belch.

"I didn't know you could do that at a private school."

"You can do it anywhere. Try it."

I shook my head. You could not belch at the table. At meals you behaved with decent manners. It was a special place, the table—and suddenly I saw the Polish family simultaneously seated at theirs in the backyard and lying machine-gunned in the open field. Everything in the kitchen, all sounds, smells, colors, seeped away into a stillness.

"Are you mad about something?" I heard Rochelle say.

I looked up. "No. Why?"

"You've just been sitting there, not saying anything."

I kept sitting there, not saying anything, but looking at her now. "Do you ever—" I hesitated.

"Ever what"

"Think about the people who get killed in the war?"

She gave a reflective nod. "I think it's terrible. I think everyone should live in peace and brotherhood and have enough to eat."

It was so exactly right, so beautifully expressed. Looking at the round face across from me, I began to feel a shimmering realization of our friendship, as if this were the moment of its baptism. There was a fluttering in my chest as I sat forward. "I feel exactly the same way, Rochelle. And then you look at the pictures in *Life*, like there's one of a Polish family machine-gunned in a field, and you know that they eat and drink—I mean they did—just like we're doing, you and me right now, and they were as real as us—and now they're dead and finished."

"I know," she said with a sad nod.

But I didn't want a sad nod. I wanted her own dead Poles, her dark cellar, her burned Jap heads.

"But how do you really feel, I mean——"

She sat thinking. "Well, I feel bad. Killing's a terrible thing to do."

She spoke sincerely, but it was not enough. "Do you hate the Japs?" I asked with sinking hope.

"Sure," she said, reaching for the pickles. "Don't you?"

I only nodded, the kind of a nod you give in place of an answer too big to articulate. And dropping the subject with disappointment, I felt a strong need to hurt her.

"If your father's an inventor, why doesn't he invent a bigger table? This is a cruddy table."

She looked down with mild surprise. "It's sort of small, I guess. They bought it when they got married, and I guess they just never thought of getting a bigger one later. Anyway, we practically never eat together."

"Yeah, well that's a cruddy way to live."

"Really?" she asked, not offended, only curious.

My nastiness faded. She looked so accepting and content sitting at the little table behind her jars and bowls. If she had no Poles or burned Jap heads, maybe it was just as well. Because I realized that what I liked about her was that she made me feel cheerful, as if nothing were very important.

Chapter 12

The internal organs of the female, our gym instructor warmly informed us, were like a little sack. A little basketball, if you will, suspended from a thread. When you were small, you could jump around to your heart's content, but as you grew older, the little basketball grew heavier and the fragile thread came under greater strain, which was why you didn't see lady bronchobusters and prizefighters. Did we all understand so far? And she gave a reassuring smile behind an uplifted forefinger.

Silence. Nods.

Well, then. Exercise was fine, exercise was necessary, but within limits. Now that we stood on the threshold of womanhood, these limits were about to be put into effect. Which brought her to the point she wished to make. When we crossed this threshold, we would not be asked to take part in games, for it was during our monthlies that the suspended basketball was at its most vulnerable and must be treated with special care. We would say, "Excused," and sit quietly in the locker room, chatting or doing homework.

A ripple of titters.

"It's nothing to giggle about, girls," she said benignly. "You'll see that it's a very natural thing, a very marvelous thing. It's Mother Nature," she concluded with a cheerful toot of her whistle, dismissing us.

I touched my stomach uncertainly, with some anger. "Mother Nature," I whispered contemptuously to Rochelle, "a little basketball!"

"Mother Basketball," Rochelle threw scornfully over her shoulder at the instructor's back.

But within days Rochelle was pretending to have crossed the debilitating threshold in order to sit back from toe touching and basketball and munch U-No bars in the locker room. Whereas I pushed myself to the limits of these activities, to prove that my insides did not and never would hang from any flimsy thread. Mother Basketball was much taken by my zeal and flashed me smiles of commendation, but I could not forgive her for the picture she had painted of my insides, and I refused to smile back.

Rochelle could not understand this. "She's really nice," she would insist.

"I know she's nice. I like her."

My friend gave me a look of puzzlement.

I had the same puzzled response to her when she spoke the degrading word, "Excused," when she grew wide-eyed and sweetly courteous before my parents and store clerks, and when one day she announced, "Forget Rochelle. From now on it's Sandra," and a week later ousted Sandra for Adrienne.

"It's too confusing," I said. "I'm calling you Peggy." She sulked, but only for a while; then she was Peggy without complaint. Nothing left a dent; she always popped out again as if made of rubber. It was bewildering, but it was the quality in her I liked; as if her rubberiness made it less worrisome that even when I laughed the hardest or ran the fastest, the great joy no longer came.

I liked doing things with her too. We chewed gum surreptitiously in class and developed a sinister background for the Gestapo teacher, Mr. Lewis. We studied as little as possible, united by the philosophy that being at the bottom of the heap was good enough reason not to try. I showed her my favorite books, Andersen's fairy tales and *Madame Bovary*, and my mildewed oranges, and introduced her to my spying trips, and dragged her down to the creek, where she puffed along good-naturedly, never minding if she tore her clothes or stepped in a dog pile. We spent a lot of time at each other's houses. She liked Mama and Dad very much and said Peter was really keen, and when she met Karla one weekend, she thought her very glamorous. She said I was lucky to have a sister and brother like that.

I felt a passionate loyalty to her and accepted all that she said about the intolerable Helen Maria. But the outrageous creature, with her brittle English accent and strange clothes and fits of anger, was seldom in evidence, nor were her parents. The family rarely collided for lunch and was never home in the afternoons when I went there from school with Peggy. Or if Helen Maria was, she kept severely to her room.

But one afternoon she walked directly into the kitchen, where Peggy was having a snack, and seated herself at the table with us. She wore a sea-green dressing gown. A pencil was stuck behind her ear. "My sister informs me that you read. What, precisely?" And she added crisply, "My sister herself is an *aficionada* of dreadful little mysteries featuring girl detectives. Well, speak up."

"I like to read H. C. Andersen," I said nervously.

"I have never heard of him."

"He just writes fairy tales."

"Do you mean Hans Christian Andersen? Why didn't you say so? Who else?"

"Flaubert." Flawburt, I pronounced it.

"Who?"

"Flawburt. He wrote *Madame Bovary*."

Peggy leaned forward. "Madame Ovary."

"Go on. Ignore her."

"Well," I said, with an apologetic look at Peggy, "also Alexandre Dumas and Victor Hugo."

Helen Maria gave a minor nod of approval. Then, withdrawing her pack of Fleetwoods and a long amber cigarette holder from the pocket of her dressing gown, she lit up with a large flourish.

"That doesn't make you look any better," Peggy said, imitating her with her hands.

Her sister gazed at her coolly, then turned to me. "Peggy is actually a highly intelligent person. At least one assumes so, considering the genes."

Peggy's lips parted. Her whole body seemed to expand.

"There are problems, however. At Clara Bebb's she fiddled her time away."

"Oh?" I said as Peggy's eyes jumped back and forth between our two faces like those of a tennis spectator.

"I should probably have kept an eye on her, but we led separate lives there."

"Were you at Clara Bebb's too?"

"Yes, it was from there that I matriculated."

It sounded improper to mention, vaguely shocking, like "menstruated," but I nodded.

"She matriculated with honors," said Peggy.

I nodded again, blushing.

"You don't matriculate with honors," Helen Maria told her. "You graduate with honors." She turned back to me. "Since then I've commuted to college in Berkeley. I would prefer to live there, but my age is against me. Peggy and I have always found Mendoza lacking."

Peggy's eyes lit up like lamps at this bracketing, but I was offended. "Mendoza is the best place," I said. "Haven't you ever been in the creek? Haven't you climbed around the hills?"

"I have not."

"You should."

"I'm not a pantheist. That's not my particular cup of tea. But your ardor is laudable."

I wished she would not use unfamiliar words. Only because these were accompanied by a brief smile did I know she was saying something favorable.

"In June when I graduate—"

"She's doing four years in three," said Peggy.

"—I shall leave Mendoza. Forever, I hope."

"She's getting a scholarship to Oxford, in England."

"England?" I said. "What about the war?"

"Yes," said Helen Maria reflectively, "I have certain pregnant feelings about the war," and I gave a start as the cigarette butt suddenly shot from the holder into the ashtray.

"There's a button on the side," Peggy explained.

"It was given me by our aunt Dorothy, who ruined our living room," said Helen Maria. "She is a gifted but tragic woman."

"A wino." Peggy nodded at me.

There was a silence.

"What do *you* read?" I asked boldly.

"Apart from my curriculum? At the moment, *Lord Jim*." She stood up and gave a dry, artful pause. "But I differ with Joseph Conradically."

With that she swept from the room.

Chapter 13

Peggy said she had never seen Helen Maria so chatty and decent. She didn't like people and people didn't like her; she scared them. She had no friends. It was amazing that she had come out of her room of her own free will and talked and been decent.

I wanted to know more about her war feelings. What did she mean by pregnant? Well, said Peggy, she didn't mean pregnant, that was for sure, she hated boys. Did she hate the war? Well, said Peggy, she said it damn well better not keep her from going to Oxford, and she hated the way her train was so crowded with soldiers and duffel bags that she had to sit in the ladies' lavatory.

But I was sure a genius would have more than that to say about the war, and I planned to find out.

"Do you suppose a genius knows everything?" I asked at the dinner table.

"I doubt if there's anybody who knows *everything*," Dad said with a smile, and Mama agreed: it wasn't possible.

"Well—but maybe that's not true," I said.

"Why?" asked Peter. "You thinking of becoming a genius?"

"No. I just wondered. Peggy's sister's a genius."

"That oddball you've talked about?"

"Don't call people oddballs, Peter," Mama said.

"Well, she sounds like one."

"She's a genius," I said, returning to my food. And geniuses knew everything.

OCT. 20:   Showdown in
                      Solomons Near!

The blinding jungle sun, the thunk of bullets piercing bone, the smell of rotting corpses. Peggy pulled me on from the newsstand. She had been awarded her phonograph (secondhand, because there were no new ones to be bought), and we were on our way to the Melody House to buy her first records.

There were large colored pictures of Gene Autry, Carmen Miranda, and Deanna Durbin on the wall. Peggy said to the clerk, "I don't want that kind. Have you got anything classical?"

The clerk took us to a section marked "Serious." "Strictly classical," she said with a beaming look at Peggy. "And I'll tell you something, it's nice to find a youngster who likes good music, and not all this boogie-woogie they go in for now."

Peggy went round-eyed and demure with pleasure, and we each gathered an armful of albums and went into the glass booth to play them. She chose *The Sorcerer's Apprentice*, *Scheherazade*, and *Malagueña*.

As soon as we were back in her room, which already bore signs of creeping disorder, she put *Malagueña* on the turntable and set the needle down.

The first majestic chords rolled out, and thrilled, we stepped back with our arms crossed. Peggy glanced at the door, which she had left open.

Presently Helen Maria appeared in her sea-green gown and leaned against the jamb.

"Is that what you bought?"

"*Malagueña*. Played by José Iturbi."

"I could have predicted it," she sighed.

The younger girl looked at her uncertainly.

"Good God, where is your taste?"

Peggy was silent a moment. "You can't come in here. You can't come in my room."

"I am not in your room. I have no desire to be in your room."

"You filthy barn owl! You rotten dodo!"

"Oh God, if you could ever say anything worth listening to."

"You freak!"

The older girl's lips tightened just perceptibly; then her eyes flashed. "I suggest that when this record is finished, you sit on it!" The eyes flashed to me. "Last year she sat on Estelle's glasses. They were instantly pulverized. At Clara Bebb's she was famous for sitting on things with her highly capable, big lardy behind. It was her only distinction!" She turned and left.

Peggy tore off the record and shattered it against the wall. Rudy got up and waddled over to sniff the pieces. "Come on," she said gloomily, sitting down on the dusky rose rug with her Marcia the Navy Nurse paper doll set. I poked through the paper wardrobe for Marcia's helmet and battle fatigues. But Peggy was brooding.

"She made me sick from the day I was born. At Clara Bebb's they made her the queen of the place. She never even had to go to class, the teachers went to *her* room. How would you like to be somebody like that's sister?"

"Well, you didn't have to pay any attention to her."

"Oh, *God!*" she exclaimed, just like Helen Maria.

"Come on, I'm playing."

"Well, at least I'm not a freak." She gave a sharp little smile. "That's what we called her. She pretended she never heard, but finally she had a big screaming fit, and she screamed that I was persecuting her and she'd never come near me again. Well good! That's how I liked it!"

"It's funny, she was so nice the other day. Look how she said you were highly intelligent."

"I know," Peggy sniffed. "It's my turn."

I handed Marcia over. "She's the last nurse on Corregidor. She's barely alive."

Peggy pulled off Marcia's fatigues and slapped on an evening gown. "She escaped. She's at the Top of the Mark."

"She's still got her bandages on."

"No she doesn't. She looks terrific. They ask her to be a Hollywood star."

69

"She's famous overnight."

"She marries Victor Mature." Suddenly she stood up. "I can play anything I want." Banging *Scheherazade* on the turntable, she sat down again.

"She's back in the cave," I said. "The Japs keep throwing grenades in, but she keeps throwing them out—"

"The clerk said they were classical. She ought to know, she works there. I don't give a damn anyway." But she glanced up as Helen Maria's figure passed swiftly down the hall.

"They explode in the Japs' faces," I said, "but more Japs keep coming—"

Helen Maria swiftly retraced her steps back along the hall.

"An improvement of sorts!" she called out, flashing by.

"You want to hear?" Peggy yelled.

The doorway remained empty for a moment; then Helen Maria reappeared, tentative, arms crossed.

The music wove softly through the room, which was coppery with the setting sun. Peggy sat very still, her stout pigtails lined with fire. Helen Maria was also still, listening, eyes lowered. I felt something unusual was happening, something was beginning. Helen Maria stepped into the room. "I must leave momentarily," she whispered, arranging herself in a white wicker chair.

When the last beautiful note faded away, Peggy said quickly, as if afraid her visitor might vanish if silence fell, "I love music. I'm going to be a composer."

Helen Maria made no objection. And she showed no signs of leaving. She even drew her feet up under her. "You'll ruin your needle," she said. "You'd better turn it off."

Peggy did so.

"I've got needles," Helen Maria said, "in case you ever need more."

She was so pleasant, so quiet, sitting there in the coppery light. It was my moment.

"Helen Maria, would you tell me what you think of the war?"

She answered without hesitation. "War is the natural result of Du Pont's and Krupp's devotion to luxury."

I didn't understand that. I would have to put that aside.

"How long do you think it will last?"

"It's already lasted too long."

"Do you think we'll win?"

"Who knows at this point?"

"Do you think the Japs will bomb Shell?"

"Since it would reduce Mendoza to a little black smudge, I certainly cherish the hope."

"You'd be a little black smudge too," I said resentfully.

"Only if you take me literally." She turned to Peggy. "Is your friend always preoccupied with things military?"

Peggy nodded. "She's always killing off Marcia with hand grenades."

"She doesn't get killed," I protested. "She hasn't gotten killed yet!"

"And who is this unfortunate Marcia?"

"A paper doll," I said.

"Oh God," sighed the genius, and seemed prepared to leave. But she paused on the edge of her chair. "You might try to do something interesting. You might try to read a play."

"A play?" Peggy asked quickly. "What play?"

"It would have to be simple, of course. You could give *Lady Windermere* a go." And she went to get the book.

"She's never come in here before," Peggy whispered. "Never!"

The play was not a success insofar as Peggy and I stumbled over large words and forgot the multiple roles assigned us, but Helen Maria was swept away. She took Lady Windermere's part, singing out her lines in a high dramatic voice, shaking with laughter, and sometimes even grabbing the sleeve of Peggy's middy blouse to keep from collapsing.

I was sorry to leave in the middle of all this, but it was getting late. As I walked home, I reflected that though the music had been pretty and the play fun, I wanted my questions answered.

Chapter 14

My questions were forced to wait. Helen Maria resumed her solitude, no doubt embarrassed after so much shaking and collapsing.

It was appropriate that my questions must wait. War itself was a matter of waiting. The barrage balloons hanging; the military guards at Shell, marching back and forth; the rusty cot in the cellar, also waiting. It was the waiting that made you nervous, the not knowing, the not being able to get your hands on anything. At the front I would know what to do; I understood that perfectly, in my bones. Give me a solid Jap lunging, and there would be no hesitation. Cut his throat.

Nov. 21:   **Russ. Counterattack**
                  At Stalingrad!

It was going all right over there, but the war in Europe had never been more than a back room of the real war, and that was going badly. Once things had looked up, with the Battle of Midway. But that was a long time back now, and there had been no more victorious headlines.

When my birthday came, I didn't want a party. I didn't see how there was anyone to invite, outside Peggy, since I had been separated from my regular old classmates. But Mama said I must certainly invite some of my new classmates, they must be just as nice as my old ones. And so I asked those who were always enthusiastic about everything and would be sure to accept, such as Eudene and Dumb Donny Woodall and a few others, and of course, Peggy. It was a good party.

Before going to bed that night, I looked at myself in the mirror. I was twelve. But I still looked the same. I was still short, still thin. My calluses weren't as thick, but I could still feel their hardness. My face was the same. I was still here.

When Karla came home on visits, it was almost like old times. In bed, I plied her with questions about San Francisco. Did she swim in the ocean? Did she ride the cable cars? Did her art professors wear berets?

And what about me, she wanted to know, how was junior high?

Not so hot. Too big and mixed up. The teachers weren't so hot either. Did she know Mr. Lewis, the ninth-grade algebra teacher? We called him the Gestapo agent. He patrolled the grounds at noon. Peter said he used to kick the wastepaper basket across the room.

Yes, Karla had had him too, and he kicked the wastepaper basket once, but he was all right.

What about the gym instructor? Mother Basketball, we called her. Had she told Karla's class about a stupid basketball and little thread?

Oh Lord yes, was she still talking about that? She had some weird ideas, but she was a nice old thing.

But hadn't Karla been mad?

No, why should she be mad? She had come home and asked Mama about the subject, and that's what I should do. Unless I'd like to talk about it now, with her, Karla.

No, it wasn't important, and besides, I was sleepy.

The real reason was that I no longer asked Mama or any of the family about the things that worried me. These things were black question lumps, some bigger than others, some enormous. Would we be bombed? Would they feel sick if they saw me breathing over the burned Jap head? Why it had happened, that day in the backyard, that I should know what it was inside the flesh of strangers, like the Polish family, and that it should bring such a piercing sadness even in the cheery crowd at the Saturday matinee.

Sometimes I was on the verge of asking them, but a feeling would cover over me, which was a good feeling and which kept me from asking. Because if I didn't draw them into my black question lumps, if they remained apart from that dark confusion, remained just as they were, it seemed that somehow, when the barracks were torn up and the barrage balloons taken down, they would be the same as they had been the day before Pearl Har-

73

bor, and we could all go back to that day and start again fresh from there.

To ask my questions of Helen Maria was a different matter. She was not family, friend, or anything. She was a genius. Geniuses belonged nowhere, they weren't even exactly human, and not just because they acted strangely, which Helen Maria certainly did. Genius was more than that. The word was pale, lofty, like the sky in early morning when you had a feeling of the world's lid being lifted away. I had seen that in Helen Maria's eyes, when she wasn't saying anything, when she was quiet.

But I would have to wait for her to emerge from her room.

She did, one day. If she was still embarrassed about the play, she didn't show it. She was very clipped and British as usual, but quite decent. She presented no quiet moment, though, for me to ask my questions.

Peggy went downtown early to shop for Christmas cards. They were hard to come by this year because of the paper shortage, but store clerks liked her round face and fat pigtails, and she returned with seven cards heavy with glitter. They were for her teachers.

"Why?" I said. "We don't like them."

"It's the Christmas spirit, for heaven's sake. Love thy neighbor."

I felt the Christmas spirit too, if not to the extent of including teachers. Last year we had been stunned by Pearl Harbor, but this year the holidays seemed more normal. Peter took me with him downtown to shop for Dad's and Mama's gifts. He wore a fedora, and though it made him look too old, he looked good, and I was proud of him. Karla came home for a week. The three of us decorated the tree, again with only a few lights, to save on electricity, but they looked better this year. The blackout shades were drawn, but Dad's cigar smoke smelled strong and full, and by saving up rationing stamps, Mama served roast pork as always. When we sang around the piano, Dad's arm around me, and mine around his warm and solid waist, it came to me that maybe in this new year of 1943 he would stop working at the shipyard and be home again, maybe 1943 would be the year the war would end.

74

* * *

Over at Peggy's house, Helen Maria wanted to know how foreigners celebrated.

"Foreigners?"

"Yes. You Scandinavians."

I told her.

I learned that other people opened their gifts not on Christmas Eve but Christmas morning. I learned that others ate not roast pork but turkey, and that they were not served rice pudding with a hidden almond that brought a prize. Maybe I had known these things, but I had not thought about them. I thought about them now. But just because we ate roast pork, how did it make us foreigners? Helen Maria must be using the term very loosely.

"Customs are fascinating," she went on. "Unfortunately, we ourselves are rather hit-or-miss."

That was true. The large handsome tree stood nicely decorated; but its raw wooden base was exposed, and none of the podiatric cartons had been cleared away for the festive season.

"What is picturesque about our Christmas is the relatives. You should meet them someday."

"Aunt Dorothy, you mean."

"No," said Peggy from her pile of gifts. "She lives in Mexico City. She's a wino."

"Must you keep using that term?" asked her sister, but Peggy was busy leafing through her girl detective books and rattling her games. Now she held up a powder blue coat with a dark velvet collar.

"I'm wearing this when we go back."

"Good," I said. She would welcome 1943 in this fine new coat.

But when we returned to school, there was nothing better about the Pacific war. Not only was nothing better, but Mrs. Miller's eighteen-year-old grandson had been killed in New Guinea, and she was not at her desk. It was Peggy who took up a collection among us to buy her a sympathy present.

"Under the circumstances," said Helen Maria, as Peggy wrapped the gift in her room, "I consider a cocktail shaker highly inappropriate. Also, it's cheap-looking."

"I don't think it's cheap-looking. Is it, Suse? Anyway, what else can you get for a dollar fifty except handkerchiefs or something? This is like something special."

"I shall agree with that," said Helen Maria.

On the morning of Mrs. Miller's return, Peggy brought the gift up to her desk. Mrs. Miller had been elderly when we last saw her; now she was shriveled, like a shoe left overnight in the rain. I had an abrupt sense of doing something wrong by looking at her; but, gravely, Peggy was setting down the box, and now she stood back with eyes respectfully lowered. Mrs. Miller silently read the attached card, then began unwrapping the box.

I realized, too late, that Helen Maria had been right. A cocktail shaker was inappropriate because it was for good times, and I cringed as I saw, very clearly, merged as one, the soldier's white dead face and this good-time thing sparkling from between his grandmother's hands. How could Peggy stand there so serene as she looked down on her horrible error?

But Mrs. Miller said, after a pause, "This was very thoughtful of you, class. I'm very touched . . . thank you." And she smiled a faint but extraordinarily intimate smile. There was tenderness in it, which we had never suspected, and also a wry twist of amusement, and through these things, the deep, implacable sadness of the grown-up, which you were almost never allowed to see.

She patted Peggy's arm. Peggy tiptoed back to her desk.

After that we all had a special stake in Mrs. Miller's welfare, made less noise, were more cooperative. And she for her part seemed to have a soft spot for us, and maybe especially for Peggy, who had after all thought of the gift.

Mother Basketball, too, had grown fond of Peggy. Peggy loved cookies, and one day she dug into the family's sugar ration and made herself a batch of brownies that came out black and evil-tasting. Instead of throwing them away, she put them in a colorful little tin which she presented shyly to Mother Basketball. It was strange, but whatever unwanted thing Peggy gave, it was always accepted with gratitude. Soon after she was appointed Towel Supervisor. This office allowed its holder to leave the gym floor early and retire to the towel counter, where, if you were Peggy, you didn't stack the towels in readiness, but sat reading comic books inside your binder until the rest of the class came pounding in, sticky and out of breath, for their showers. The boldness of the overseer went with this office, and Peggy bloomed with authority, with a kind of casual omnipotence that took her through the intimate, steaming locker room like a floorwalker. This was a habit of hers that was to bring us both to grief.

Dad and Peter bailed out the cellar in hipboots. Inside my galoshes the cheap wartime soles of my saddle shoes were beginning to rot. Behind the garrison storm fence the soldiers wore black shiny capes and slogged around in a field of mud. For blocks you could hear the roar of the creek.

I took Peggy down there one day after school, to show her the torrent close up. She thought it very powerful and impressive, but as she turned with this compliment, she gave a wild stumble and plunged over the side. Horrified, I looked down, but she had not rolled into the water, only into a tree stump, and was crawling back up the bank on her belly. "Christ," she groaned, standing up in the rain and peering down the front of her powder blue coat. Black muck was ground into the entire length of the fabric. "Why do we have to come to this stupid place anyway?" she demanded as I silently handed her her muddy books.

The whole world was made of mud. She lumped along the street on two clods. The gutters rushed with muddy water. Behind the storm fence the soldiers in their shiny capes squelched in mud to their ankles. When they were sent to the front, they would die in the mud. There would be the thunk of a bullet, and they would fall in the mud, and it would fill their mouths.

Silently, I followed Peggy into her house. There we were met by the unforeseen. Dr. Hatton was rarely home in the afternoons, but today she was just hanging her windbreaker up in the hall as we came in.

"Good heavens," she said, touching her spectacles. "Is that mud?"

Peggy looked around the hall.

"On your coat. Peggy, is that your new coat?"

Peggy looked down at it, surprised.

"Do you wear that lovely coat in the rain? Good heavens, Peggy, do you play in the mud with it?"

Peggy looked at her solemnly.

I wondered if Dr. Hatton would say good heavens again. She looked bewildered. She looked bewildered for several moments. Then she sighed and shook her head. "It seems to me you could stop and think sometimes." And she began looking through the mail on the table.

"Your mother's a real sport," I said as we tracked our mud through the Dungeon to Peggy's room. We were just taking off our coats when Helen Maria put her head through the door.

"I have an announcement," she said crisply. "You're invited to my room." Then she sped off.

Peggy looked at me. "Her room."

It was the inner sanctum, the secret temple. After pulling off our galoshes, we hurried after her down the hall.

Chapter 15

We stood close together, like visitors in a cathedral. There was a cheerful fire in the fireplace. A sweet-smelling plume of incense issued from a copper ashtray. From the phonograph came a light, gay piece of music.

"Do sit down," said Helen Maria.

We seated ourselves tailor fashion on the floor, where she had placed two throw pillows. On an electric ring a pan was heating. Next to it stood a plate covered with a napkin. "Please let me know if there's anything special you wish to hear after the Mozart," said Helen Maria, standing over us like a grand hostess in her sea-green robe, hands graciously folded. "And I hope you like spiced wine," she said, going over to the pan and breathing deeply of its aroma. After pouring the contents into three cups, she handed us ours; then she whipped the napkin from the plate, revealing a half dozen French pastries, which she set before us. "Please help yourselves. There are two for each."

Arranging herself on the Persian spread, she sipped

from her cup. We followed suit. It was a strong, fuming concoction, rather pleasant. We sat drinking and chewing, waiting for our hostess to speak. Behind her the rain streamed down the French windows, making a gray blur of the garden.

She dusted her fingers off. Gracefully she inserted a cigarette into her amber holder. She seemed quiet, serene.

"Helen Maria, what do you think of the war?"

"Are you back on that again?"

"No, but—"

"War is stupid. Man is stupid." She lit the cigarette with her fine, sweeping flourish. "That is all ye know on earth and all ye need to know."

I thought for a moment. "Everybody?"

"Of course not. There's always been a tiny minority of thinkers. But they've never made any difference. Take your other pastry."

I had a vast, sinking feeling. On the turntable the Mozart record came to an end and spun hissing.

"I hope you'll appreciate Mahler, whom I'll now play," said Helen Maria, getting up and crossing the room. A few moments later a soft, desperately forlorn melody filled the air. My eyelids felt heavy from the wine; my eyes grew filmed with sadness.

"What about the people who get killed?" I said as she sat down again. "All the refugees, and the soldiers and army horses. . . ."

"Can she include horses with people?" Peggy asked through a mouthful.

"Why not?" I said. "They hurt like us."

"Not quite," corrected Helen Maria. "They can't reason. They lack a concept of extinction. Their pain is a simple physical one."

"Well, they hurt!"

"Of course. I'm simply pointing out the difference between man, who is highly developed, and the lower order of animals, which is not."

"You said man was stupid!"

"I should say. The lower orders aren't stupid at all. They don't go in for bombast and bamboozlement."

"I don't understand that!"

"What are you so angry about?"

"Because it's not what I mean—not what I'm talking about!"

"Yes, what exactly are you talking about?"

"I don't know. Just that the war's happening . . . while we're sitting here, it's happening somewhere else, and it doesn't matter if you can't see it, because you know it. . . ."

"Ah," she said, nodding thoughtfully. "Imagination is all very well and good, but you mustn't overdo it. You can't dwell on misery and death. That way lies madness."

Worriedly I lifted my eyes.

"At best you'll wind up in the Salvation Army. You'll wear a black bonnet and sing 'Rock of Ages' on street corners."

Peggy gave an amused snort.

"Please don't snort, Peggy. And you've had three pastries. One of those was Suse's."

I didn't care about pastries. I wanted to go home. But my body was heavy; my eyes seemed to drift.

"Are you enjoying the Mahler?" asked our hostess.

I shook my head. "He makes me too sad."

"Oh, buck up, for God's sake. Don't take everything so personally. Are you enjoying the wine?"

"I'm drunk," Peggy smiled.

"Don't be. I hate a drunk."

We both sat straighter and tried to look alert.

"Now. Let's talk about something worthwhile. What have you been reading lately, Suse?"

"*Madame Bovary.*"

"Again?"

"I've read it four times. I like it."

"Certainly one likes it. I myself like it. I understand what Emma was up against. Those shopkeepers and notaries and priests. What a dreary lot."

"I think they're interesting," I said, rubbing my eyes. "How they lived and everything. I like how they're different from how it is now. I mean they didn't have airplanes or refineries. . . ."

"My dear friend, just because they used tallow candles and blotted their letters with sand doesn't mean they weren't dreary. Flaubert despised them. For that matter he wasn't too keen on Emma because she was a sloppy

80

thinker. All romantics are sloppy thinkers. And that's what you are, a romantic."

"Me? I'm not romantic. You mean like kissing?" Peggy gave an interested grunt and sat forward.

"I mean you've taken literature's crowning glory of realism and varnished it over with romanticism. Do you realize you've read this book four times and never understood it?"

I looked down again, invaded by a cold doubt.

"You'd have been very unhappy a hundred years ago," she said, getting up and turning the phonograph off. "You'd have worn a tight corset and never been able to go hiking. You'd have been married off at sixteen to an old man. And then you'd have died of a mere flu. But these things you blithely ignore. You're no better than those housewives who read silly historical novels and recline there in the past. But the past is no better than the present, and was usually worse. It's no place to recline in."

So then, the cobbled streets and moonlit duels were not what they seemed. Hunchbacks did not swing forever on cathedral bells, or Emma gallop eternally through green forests, but all was thin and false, and I could not recline there. But I had a thought.

"You study ancient Greece. You must recline there."

"I do not recline. I stride about, exercising my mind. Besides, that was a glorious age."

"The age of Plato," Peggy told me sleepily.

"Pericles," corrected Helen Maria, shooting her cigarette butt into the ashtray. "Of course, to the world, ancient Greece is *parti avec le vent*—gone with the wind. I have no delusions. When I become an archaeologist and unearth an ancient city, it will make no difference to the swarming masses."

"Who?" I saw gnats, hornets.

"The masses. Man. Man is not impressed by knowledge. He just goes on making a mess of things."

Again I had the vast, sinking feeling.

"But what the masses do is their business, and what I do is mine. As a student of history, specifically of Greece, my business is the clarification of a man's experience."

"But you said man is stupid—why would you want to know about them? I mean if they're stupid and they

81

don't pay any attention to you and you don't pay any attention to them, I mean if you and them aren't even connected—"

"If you say 'I mean' once more, I shall vomit! And, Peggy, it's rude to fall asleep!"

Our hostess's speech was growing more and more clipped, while mine was becoming more slurred and difficult, but I said again. "But why do you want to study man then?"

"Because! If one is interested in history, one studies man! One would hardly study reptiles or rock formations, would one?"

"No," I said, but I was lost. My eyes were drifting in circles. I tried to stifle a yawn, but it broke through loudly, just as Peggy's head sank down on her chest.

"What a choice crew," the genius whispered slowly, as though to herself. Then suddenly she clenched her fists. Her face turned bright red. "Get out!" she cried, leaping to her feet.

We staggered up as she hurried over to us, grabbing us by the arms and dragging us to the door. "Get out! Get out!" she cried again, flinging us from the room.

Maybe it was just as well if the genius was through with us, I thought later. Because I had had enough of her answers, which just made everything darker and worse.

Chapter 16

The next day in gym, as I was stepping into my cubicle to undress and shower, Peggy the Towel Supervisor strode to my side with an official order: "Come with me."

I followed her down the row of cubicles until she stopped before one and opened the curtain. From behind the second curtain inside I could hear Eudene singing "Besame Mucho" in the shower.

Peggy pointed to a brassiere lying on the floor. It

looked huge and hugely interesting. Peggy lifted it up between thumb and forefinger. It was a terrible-looking thing, gray and sweat-stained, its straps held together by rusty safety pins. It hung enormous and shapeless, and shameful too—even if it had been clean—like one of those medical trusses you saw in store windows.

"Poor Eudene," I whispered.

Poor Eudene's big wet face emerged from behind the curtain. "What're you guys doing!" she yelled over the noise of the shower.

"I can't hear you," Peggy said pleasantly. She was always good in an emergency—clear-eyed, innocent. Calmly she deposited the garment on the wooden bench as Eudene turned the shower off. When the face reappeared, Peggy said, "I may need one of these, so I thought I'd have a look at yours."

Eudene gave her a careless squint! "You're fat, kid, but not where it counts."

"Who's fat?"

Eudene threw her head back and let out one of her big donkey brays. She was not cast down by the brassiere, whose every stain and rusty pin she knew we had inspected.

But Peggy cut into the laughter. She had her authority. "This is temporary fat. By the time I'm your age I'll have a terrific figure."

I had not known she planned along these lines and frowned at her. But maybe she only meant to point out Eudene's great age and embarrass her for being fifteen years old in the seventh grade.

"How old do you take me for?" asked Eudene, her gray eyes growing smoky, almost exotic. "I bet you think I'm right up there. A guy the other night he took me for twenty-one."

"You like that?" I asked.

"Sure. I like to be right up there." Then with a robust shiver, she yelled, "Clear out, you guys, I'm freezing my ass off!" and came barging out rump first, reaching for her towel on the peg, a glimpsed enormousness of pale quivering flesh, a sudden matted brown armpit. She was like a piercing sense of upturned earth, something secret and unexpected that spread waves of nameless alarm as we whirled around and flapped through the curtain.

"You wanna meet me after," she yelled, "I'll tell you about that guy!"

"If she takes showers, how come she's always dirty!" Peggy demanded angrily, hurrying along.

"I know!" I agreed, but I was not thinking of Eudene's grooming habits, and I sensed Peggy was not either. What I was thinking about, stamping into my cubicle, was what lived beneath that ordinary skirt and sweater Eudene was pulling on this minute, that white, quivering nakedness, that swampy armpit breathing in secret under her sleeve. It was all wrong, and it made me angry. It was wrong that such strangeness should suddenly be there—that nude, billowy whiteness, somehow grave, as though heavy with fate, perhaps known already to a man's hand, a hairy, sinewed, sliding hand. . . .

"You don't want to meet her, do you?" Peggy asked through the curtain.

"No, do you?" I said, coming out.

"No, do you?"

We hung around, unable to make up our minds, until we noticed that Eudene had gone in any case.

"I'm extending another invitation," said Helen Maria as we came down the hall to Peggy's room. She was unsmiling, cool. But she had forgiven us. Relieved, nudging each other, we followed her to her room. This time there was no hot wine or French pastries, but the fire crackled as it had the day before, and the sweet smell of incense once more filled our nostrils. With the Eudene experience fresh in my mind, I hoped the genius would discourse on flesh. But she was aimed in the opposite direction. "Do you believe in God?" she asked us, stretching out on the Persian spread.

"No," answered Peggy. "I'm an iconoclast."

"What is an inconoclast, please?"

"It's when you don't believe in God. Isn't it?"

"No. It is not. I disapprove of the way you pick up my words and use them inaccurately. You shouldn't be content with the approximate. Why don't you look in the dictionary? Why don't you seek?"

"I do seek."

"You do not. You're a born disciple. That's your problem."

"I'm not a disciple. I break rules!"

"You break rules because you're lazy or you wish to draw attention to yourself."

"I do not!"

"You do," said her sister, not unkindly. "And you must change. You must become an independent thinker. But go on."

"I don't want to," said Peggy sullenly.

Helen Maria turned to me. "And what about you?"

"I don't believe in God," I said. I had not formed this thought before, but as I sat there, I knew it was true. After God came to me on the union hall roof, I had never thought about Him again. I just knew He was around. Now I knew He wasn't. He hadn't been for a long time. "I used to," I said. "But I don't anymore."

"Were you required to attend church? Our family, I rejoice to say, has never been sucked into the tentacles of organized religion."

"Well, I had to go to Sunday School, but He didn't have anything to do with that. He just came along on His own."

"An independent experience. Good for you."

Peggy threw me a sour look.

"There is no authority for God," Helen Maria went on. "The Greeks understood this. You were right to turn your back on the rotting superstitions of the cloister. Go on. What was your experience?"

"I don't know, I never even thought about Him. He was just around, in the hills and the sky."

"Ah, yes, you're the pantheist. But tell me, how does a pantheist lose faith?"

"I don't know, He just disappeared. . . . I think it was when the war started."

"The war again."

"And she'll join the Salvation Army," Peggy said sharply. "That's what you said. And that's not turning her back on anything, that's not being an independent thinker. Is it!"

"*Brava*, Peggy," said her sister. "Now you show the spirit of inquiry."

Peggy shrugged, but her cheeks pinkened.

"And I did say that. I don't say she *will*, but she *could*, if she doesn't rid herself of this preoccupation, which is both lopsided and useless."

She got up and stood before us, very tall from our

vantage point on the floor, the firelight flickering on her sea-green robe. "There is nothing worse than a disunited soul."

A hush spread through me. She had put her finger on it. "How do I get rid of it?" I asked carefully.

The green eyes flashed down. "Do you know what the Greek concept of God was?"

"No."

"Excellence. Striving for the highest. For clarity, vision, and balance."

"How did they get it? What did they do?"

"They examined their lives."

I sank back on my pillow. It was a disappointment. It sounded like tests and homework and drudgery.

"That doesn't sound like God to me," said Peggy, made bold by her triumph. "God should make you good and kind."

"You're quite right, Peggy," said her sister, sitting down again. "But it is thinking that makes you good and kind."

"Can it make you bad?" I asked quickly.

"Of course. Wrong thinking. But right thinking brings virtue and freedom."

"How do you know if you're doing it right or wrong?"

"That," said the genius, reaching for her cigarettes and holder, "that," she said, lighting up and blowing out a stream of smoke, "is the question."

Again I sank back with dashed hopes, but Peggy was in strong spirits, once more the Towel Supervisor. Briskly, officially, she spoke. "We know a girl at school who can't think at all. She's been kept back three grades. She's a mess."

"What type of mess, precisely?" inquired Helen Maria.

"Well, she's sloppy, and she's really big, she's got this big rear end and everything. She doesn't know what's going on half the time, and she's always laughing and punching you with her elbow."

"But she's nice," I said. "But she wears this big dirty brassiere, it's like a harness."

"Does she speak in complete sentences?" Helen Maria asked.

"I never noticed. I think so."

Peggy crossed her hands, interlacing the fingers. "We

think," she said quietly, "that she goes all the way with men."

"Ah," mused the genius, taking a puff. "*La Grande Horizontale*."

"I mean, we think she goes all the way with men," Peggy said again.

"Why not?" asked her sister. "Why not?"

Peggy and I exchanged a look. We had not expected such simplicity; we did not want it. We gathered our mystery back into our laps and said no more about Eudene.

Chapter 17

We stood outside the gym entrance, waiting. At last Eudene came blustering out, her fingers scratching in her hair, which was always greasy at the roots. She might not be Rita Hayworth, but we stepped up to her.

"Hi, you guys!" she yelled, which she always yelled, even if she had seen you twenty minutes before.

"We want to know about that guy," Peggy stated with her authority. "The one who thought you were twenty-one years old."

"Sure!" And she began searching for something in her big squalid shoulder bag.

I glanced around, concerned that Mr. Lewis might stride around the corner with his vicious eye and see that Eudene was telling us of flesh. "Should we go somewhere?" I whispered to her.

"Sure, let's go."

Gym was our last class; everyone was hurrying off. It was a dark, windy, showery day. Peggy was in her powder blue coat, somewhat wilted since its trip to the cleaner's, I in my yellow slicker, and we both wore bandannas that flapped in the wind. Eudene, by contrast, was coatless, bareheaded, her sweater sleeves rolled to her elbows—too dumb even to notice the weather, but unquestionably the leader as we walked off together, a superior being taking us on a forbidden and mysterious journey.

She was still looking through her bag, making a terrific racket in its bowels as we crossed the lawn. We turned onto Las Juntas Street, at whose end you could see a chunk of leaden bay and a warship. I wondered if this man of Eudene's was a sailor. Or a soldier. Was she searching for his photograph? A love letter? Or something more unusual—

Eudene kept searching, lifting her head only to yell a greeting at passing classmates, until the students had thinned and we were walking alone.

"Remember that guy, Eudene?" Peggy asked. "You were going to tell us about?"

At that moment Eudene found what she was looking for, but all she fished out was a stick of unwrapped gum embedded with lint and tobacco, which she shoved into her mouth with her palm.

"Well he was this guy," she said, chewing juicily, "and he sees me and he says hi babe you got a nice little town here and would I want to show him around, like where could he get something to eat? So we go down to Meloni's and we have a spaghetti dinner, and he says I figure you're about twenty-one years old."

We waited for the rest, but unbelievably, she was done. She just sauntered along, chewing, her profile framed against the ugly black storage tanks on Shell hill.

"Didn't he say anything else?" Peggy asked. "Didn't he flirt?"

There was a bellow of delight, and Eudene's left elbow rammed the powder blue coat.

"Was he a soldier?" I asked, and suffered the other elbow.

"Didn't he *do* anything?" Peggy asked. "I mean afterwards—you know what I mean."

Eudene threw her head back, still bellowing, and rolled her eyes heavenward. "Do I know what you mean, kid!"

"Well, tell us! What he did!"

But our guide looked suddenly stupid beyond belief, as if she had come to a blockade in her mind and was trying to squeeze around it or push through it. "We had a spaghetti dinner." She wasn't sauntering now. We hurried alongside, shifting our books in our arms.

"*After* the spaghetti, Eudene!"

"You said you'd tell us!"

"Get outta here," she said in a low voice.

Peggy grabbed her sweater sleeve. "He told you to take your clothes off, didn't he?"

Eudene began to run, her sauerkraut hair streaming, her big bosom bouncing in her sweater.

"Didn't he!" Peggy cried, still hanging onto the sleeve as we ran alongside her. "He took you some place and took your *clothes* off!"

A cheap hotel room whirled through my mind—Eudene's clothes dropping to the floor, the white flesh exposed, the soldier's hands quivering, pouncing. My mouth went cold as I pounded along at her side.

"Didn't he!" Peggy demanded, stretching the sleeve as the three of us thundered along. Eudene was pincered between us, so close that she smelled like the tule marsh, her secret armpits steaming, her face deep-pored and oily. I hated her for doing this disgusting thing in the hotel room, and I hated her for not telling. I wanted to give her a kick, but we were going too fast. I delivered something just as good.

"If he bought you dinner, he must've known you'd do it! Why else would be bother with somebody like you?"

"Right!" cried Peggy.

Eudene's face swung around, the lips laid back like those of a mauled animal. My steps faltered; the two of us fell back. Her sleeve pulled out of shape, Eudene kept running, and now she gained the corner and disappeared around it.

We walked on in silence. A thin rain swerved down. There was an iron weight in my chest.

"I don't know why we did that," Peggy said at last, in a timid voice.

My voice was timid too. "Where do you think she went?"

"Home, maybe?"

"I know where she lives."

Once more we began running, using all the shortcuts I knew.

Eudene lived on the road leading along the bay front to Port Chicago. The houses there were big and had once been very fine, but now they were ramshackle and divided into apartments. In the front yard of Eudene's building stood a rusty car on blocks. We went behind it and waited.

89

The rain was heavy now, carried by strong gusts of wind that splattered loudly against the car. At intervals Peggy gave a profound sigh. Her eyes were anxious, unhappy. I tried to take my mind off Eudene by thinking of her surroundings. It was a dangerous place to live, with Shell right across the street, the hills dark and cindery in the rain, the black tanks stretching into the distance. But behind the houses lay the railroad tracks, and the marshes and the bay, and it must be nice to live where you could hear the ferry bell clanging across the tule. The houses were nice too, in their run-down way, with huge windows filled with tiny panes, like houses from ancient Paris. At night, sleeping under those windows, you would have all the stars spread out above. But it did no good to think about these things.

Peggy was looking with mournful surprise at her legs. "I'm wetting my pants."

Our eyes met. The Towel Supervisor out of control, and I with my chest of cast iron. What if Eudene had run away and never came back, and we had to go through the rest of our lives like this, sick with remorse, hating ourselves?

At that moment we saw her coming up the street. We hurried from around the car. Eudene planted her feet apart on the wet sidewalk. She wrapped the strap of her bag around her hand. The gray eyes were flat, stony.

"We apologize! We were only joking!"

"We want to be friends again—"

Eudene remained as she was, the bag held ready.

"Hit us," I told her. "Hit us!"

Her stony look turned to one of cold suspicion, but she raised the heavy bag by its strap, whipped it around and around in a vigorous warm-up, and unleashed it with a brutal smash against my neck. It felt wonderful, it took care of all my guilt, and with my whole soul I loved Eudene. I wanted to see her happy, celebrated, laden with medals. I groped for some dazzling compliment.

Peggy found one, rubbing her smacked neck. "I love the color of your hair, Eudene. It's practically blond."

Still hard-faced, Eudene pulled a damp strand to her eye and looked at it.

"It's naturally wavy, isn't it?" I asked.

She gave a cool nod. "I never need a perm."

"Lucky you, mine's straight as a stick!" Grabbing a

hank from under my bandanna, I tugged at it disgustedly as Eudene's lips finally, slowly, turned up in a small, superior smile. It was as good as a medal on her chest. I hoped it would bring her strength and happiness forever.

"We've got to go, so long, Eudene."

"You'd better dry off good and not catch cold," Peggy told her with concern.

"Yeah." She walked off across the muddy yard.

"So long, Eudene."

"So long."

Peggy leaned down and scratched her ankles, where the urine had run into the tops of her socks. "I don't know why I did that. I never wet my pants for years."

I didn't know why she had done it either. I could no longer grasp the reason. My chest was light.

But that night in bed it all came back. I thought of Eudene lying under her Parisian window. Probably she never washed her hands or brushed her teeth before climbing under the blankets—just a big satisfied mess chewing her worn-out gum and enjoying the stars without a worry. And what I felt now was that she would never enjoy the stars again. There would always be a black spot inside her that we had put there, a black wound that would make the sky seem too cold and dark, so that she couldn't sleep. But I wouldn't mention these sad thoughts to Peggy, because of the Salvation Army.

The next morning at school, a pale gray bruise on my neck, I worriedly observed Eudene for signs of a haggard night. But she didn't look haggard, and she didn't look hateful either, though she wasn't as friendly as she usually was. It was a couple of days before she was back to normal; but then she waved us behind a tree for a comradely puff on her cigarette, and I knew that her blurred, skiddy mind had triumphed. Probably the only thing she had kept from that horribly disputed spaghetti evening was the voice of the soldier, releasing those magic words, "I figure you're about twenty-one years old," and putting her right up there.

But I wasn't wrong about the black spot. Except that it was in me, not Eudene. Every time I remembered that I had said, "Why else would he bother with somebody like you?" I felt an unbearable shame. It was flesh that had unhinged me, flesh and slithering hands. I pushed them deep in the storeroom of my mind.

Chapter 18

FEB. 2:   Stalingrad
                Recaptured by Russ!

FEB. 7:   Guadalcanal Victory!

"It could be over by the time you graduate," I told Peter.

"Are you kidding?" He was busy polishing his shoes on the back porch.

"No, it could."

He squinted, holding up a loafer. "It's just getting started. Look at those hundreds of islands in the Pacific. Look at—"

"I don't want to talk about it. It's boring."

"Ah, to be twelve again," he murmured, smiling and attacking the shoe again with his cloth.

"Your shoes look terrific," I said sadly, thinking of those hundreds of islands. "They really shine."

And I saw that Peter himself looked terrific and really shone—with his blue eyes clear and bright, and his chiseled features glowing, as if the skin gave off a radiance—and though he was much older than I, it seemed that I was glimpsing all youngness and brightness and freshness as he stood there on the rainy back porch, working over his brown loafers.

Sometimes when we all sat together at night, Dad reading the paper and Mama knitting a khaki muffler or sock, and maybe Peter playing a game of Chinese checkers with me, I would wonder if Peter would look like Dad when he was Dad's age, stocky, bald, and if I would look like Mama with my hair in a bun, and I wondered how Dad and Mama would look then, in thirty years, ancient, bent; but it was impossible to visualize, to go that far into the future—if in fact there would be such a future—and I would quickly burrow back into the warm familiarity of the present, wondering something else—what did people do who didn't have cozy evenings together at the end of the day? I should think that without them the outside world would be too hard, too confusing, too much.

Yet the Hattons never got together. It was Dorothy's Dungeon that was the problem. It was too gloomy to sit in, so they kept to their rooms. Helen Maria's, of course, was her temple. And the parents' room had sofas, desks, everything they needed. As for Peggy, she loved her room, which had collapsed into an unspeakable mess, much worse than mine. Her two remaining records had long since paled on her; but she listened to *The Shadow* and *Fibber McGee and Mollie* on the radio, and she had a big enough allowance to keep her curled up with comic books and candy bars, and she had Rudy curled up at her feet.

Everyone seemed happy with this way of life, meeting as they came and went. Sometimes they converged for dinner. Sometimes they entertained guests in the dungeon. The guests were usually Aunt Margaret, the undertaker, and Grandmother. The lady mortician, who cracked morbid jokes which Helen Maria found "appalling but witty," looked like a gray-haired version of Dr. Hatton, except that she wore pin-striped slacks and argyle socks with sandals. She lugged her accordion along and, in a rousing voice, sometimes joined by Peggy's off-key soprano, regaled the others with "Santa Lucia" and "I'm in Love with the Man in the Moon," which Helen Maria found merely appalling. She approved more of her grandmother.

This was a large wobbly woman with a swept-up bun of fine white hair, and a hearing aid which was on the fritz and for which she could not get parts, because of the war. Throughout dinner—at a perfectly ample table in the dining room—she would bark, "What? What are you saying?" giving the instrument in her ear frequent angry twists. She was extremely fond of Peggy, who ran and fetched things for her, shouting, "Here you are, Granny!" and "You're welcome, Granny!" with her wide-eyed, angelic look.

Helen Maria's attitude toward her grandmother was detached but admiring. "She has a remarkable constitution; for instance, she gave birth to Estelle at the advanced age of forty-eight, soon after which she accompanied our grandfather over the Dolomites with an alpenstock. She's ninety-three now, with her own teeth and unimpaired mental faculties, continuing to read French fluently. She has willed her body to science."

I was impressed. But it was the other side of the family that interested Peggy: the grandfather of the soda-pop invention, who had awakened rich one morning, and Aunt Dorothy, whooping it up down south of the border.

"You may have Aunt Dorothy and her whoopee," said Helen Maria. "She's a sodden bore."

"She's had four husbands," Peggy told me, undaunted.

"Every time she gets a divorce she comes and cries on Jack's shoulder," said Helen Maria. "Then she tries to do something nice in return, like ruining our living room. She was once a brilliant, talented woman who has let her life slip through her fingers."

When we were alone, Peggy said, "Well, I'd rather have four husbands than one. You get more variety."

"I suppose." But who cared about husbands, one, four, or four hundred? Peggy was hard to follow at times, yet in a way I wished I were her. Such as when we came across a drunk one day lying in the park with his claw of a hand around a bottle. While I entertained a few useless thoughts (poor old man on the ground all alone), Peggy was stuffing into his frayed coat pocket all the money she had on her. She was always giving things away. Outgrown toys to church bazaars, an overlarge sweater to Eudene, once-read comics to Annuncio's children. She never stumbled around, brooding; she did good things and moved on, and if she changed horses in midstream she didn't care. And she had no real viciousness in her, not even for the three people she said should be shot: Hitler, Tojo, and Mr. Lewis. Even her bitter attacks on Helen Maria were *parti avec le vent*, as the genius would have put it—gone with the wind. Swept out with a clean broom. You only had to look at Peggy to know she was a happy person, a "growing person," as Mrs. Miller said each one of us should be.

*　*　*

One day, when we were going through the park, I recognized a figure sitting on a bench. He was dressed in gray work pants and a red lumber jacket, but I knew him by the way he sat: leaning forward, fidgety, on the alert. I saw the big cleated boots that had pounded over the bridge. I saw how his knees were spread apart with his hands lying on them palms up, as if cradling a rifle, and I saw how calloused and ugly the palms were, like yellow horn.

"What's wrong?" Peggy whispered. "What're you stopping for?"

I was on the brink of hurrying on, yet I couldn't help staring at this man who had smashed my world to bits in the space of a minute. The face was tight-skinned, flushed in patches. It should have been shot between the eyes, with his own rifle. More than I wanted to get away from him, I wanted him to know this, and I narrowed my eyes with all the smoldering grievance of fifteen long months.

"What's wrong?" Peggy whispered again. "Listen, I'm going."

Old Hackman met my stare from under loose, wrinkled eyelids. It was a gummy, jittery look, yet strangely sure in some way, full of dark knowledge. And to my horror, cutting through all my hatred, I felt a kinship with him, like a bond of blood. He knew. And I knew.

I turned and ran, plowing into Peggy.

"What did he do? Did he say something dirty?"

I hurried on, feeling my palms.

"Was he crazy?" she asked.

The calluses had gone down so much that I no longer sliced them off with a razor blade. But underneath the outer skin I felt the hardness, a definite horny hardness.

"Do you think my eyes look all right?" I asked, stopping.

"What d'you mean?"

"Do you think they ever looked—not right or something?"

"What d'you mean, like cross-eyed?"

"No. I don't know."

"Tell me what he *said*."

"He didn't say anything."

The sky turned clear and warm in April. Downtown, after two winters of rain, the sandbags around Sheriff

O'Toole's office were a hard, cohesive brown mass. On buildings and fences war posters hung faded in the brilliant spring light. No one glanced at them. The war was old, old, yet it would not end.

I enjoyed Helen Maria's salon, which had become a regular part of my life, yet I never heard what I wanted to hear: something strong and bright which could be stood upon like a rock. In fact, even comfortable old ideas I had never thought to question were put to the test time after time; far from having my storeroom illuminated, I found my entire mind becoming a hodgepodge of uncertainties. Nor could I withdraw from the salon. Helen Maria was almost a friend, and a friend was a precious thing. Also, if I left now, with my bunged-up brain, I might remain this way for life. I could only stay, hoping that the genius might yet reach out with the golden word.

One night, when I was staying over with Peggy, Helen Maria came into the room. She wore a coat over her pajamas.

"Would you care to invoke the gods?"

"Sure," said Peggy, already out of bed.

"Put your coats on. Follow me."

She led us out of the darkened house to the street. It was past midnight. We walked along in slippered feet.

"Where are we going?" Peggy asked.

"Mount Olympus."

We passed the silent junior high school and the silent garrison. We passed the creek flowing eerily in the dark, and we passed my house lying moonlit and sleeping—a strange, set-apart feeling to see it so. Finally, we passed the community hospital, behind which rose a hill crowned with eucalyptus trees. We climbed this hill, and inside the circle of trees we sat down and rested.

Then Helen Maria got to her feet, lifted her arms, and spoke into the mild night.

"O Artemis, come thou now to these eyes. O Zeus, show thyself in thy glory. Achilles, I wait for thee!"

She paused. "No, I'd better do it in their own language." And she spoke again, in Greek, her face serene and happy in the moonlight. When she was done, she bowed, spreading her arms in a gesture of gracious welcome.

I looked up at the trees, soaring into the starry night. The air carried a sweet smell of dewed grass. We waited.

After a while Peggy said, "Have they come yet?"

"Yes." Helen Maria sank down beside us with a smile. "They came. And now they've gone."

"How did they look?" I asked.

"Magnificent. They were just above the trees, with the moon behind them, and they were colossal. Then they soared away."

"Did they say anything?"

"They didn't have to."

"What did they wear?"

"Really, this is not something that can be gone over, like a railway shedjule."

"Shedjule?"

"Schedule, if you must."

"Why did you say shedjule?"

"Because I prefer the phonetics of our English cousins."

"I didn't know you had English cousins. Have they been bombed?"

"Oh God, let's leave before the spell is destroyed entirely."

Our journey back seemed longer and colder; but Helen Maria was buoyed by her experience, and she walked briskly along, now and then exclaiming on the beauty of the night.

The house was as we had left it, dark, slumbering, ignorant of moonlit gods. We filed silently through the Dungeon and down the hall, past the parental bedroom from behind whose door surged Mr. Hatton's manly snores. "Our parents are still deeply in love," Helen Maria informed me. "And now, good night."

I followed Peggy back to bed, where Rudy still lay asleep, unaware of our absence. There was something wonderful about our secrecy, our mysteriousness, and I only wished that I too had seen something—the hint, at least, of a colossal arm or foot.

"Did you see anything?" I asked.

"No," Peggy yawned. "And she didn't either."

"She must have, to make her that happy. Don't worry, she saw them."

But now that I thought about it, it was wrong for someone who hated religion and superstition and any-

thing that you couldn't weigh and balance and discuss—
it was wrong for someone like that to glow with mystery,
the way the saints glowed in the stained glass windows
of the Catholic church. The way superstitious people
glowed when they wished on the first star or found a
lucky penny on the street. I felt a flash of indignation.
How could I find the one solid truth through her if she
herself didn't know?

Chapter 19

Very shortly, even before his eighteenth birthday in
June, Peter would have to report to Oakland for his
physical. I wished him failing eyesight, punctured
eardrums, flat feet, and even—it was terrible—a very
small but real heart murmur, like the one Dumb Donny
Woodall said his 4-F cousin had.

At dinner I would urge these many infirmities upon
my own brother, staring across my plate at his unsuspect-
ing face, until at last I was so consumed by guilt I had
to give it up. By the time he left for Oakland, driving off
with Dad one cold predawn morning, I had pinned everything on a happy error. The overworked army doctors
would swing around from their probing and tapping, and
in their haste, on Peter's report sheet, a check mark
would accidentally by dashed off by 4-F instead of 1-A.

Since the notification would not come for several
weeks, there was a good while yet to brood hopefully on
the Army's capacities for mistakes.

Peggy no longer wore her cherished Clara Bebb uniform but, like everyone else, went in for sloppy Joe
sweaters and jangling charm bracelets. She also wanted
to wear her hair free, but when it was unplaited, she
looked as if she had been plugged into an electric socket.
She also wanted to be slender, but she liked to eat. She
said these things would change by themselves when she
turned thirteen; she said you got smoothed out when you
entered your teens, it was the way things went. She put

such stock in her approaching birthday, June 3, and mentioned the date so often that it began to take root in my mind as something of international importance. It was in fact a date that would precede many significant events: Peter's own birthday, his high school graduation, Helen Maria's university graduation, and, possibly, Peggy's and my promotion into eighth grade.

The more Peggy talked about the miraculous gateway of June 3, the more my thoughts centered on it, and fortified by the recent Allied victory in North Africa, I decided that on that day all across the globe, the white flags of the enemy would appear. They would appear for Peter, and for the soldiers and the Polish families and the army horses, and for myself, and even for Helen Maria, who wanted only to sail for England. A world of people sailing, like white swans let out after winter.

The morning of June 3 unfolded without news of a cease-fire. It was a Saturday; the house was quiet. Dad was working at Moore's overtime. Peter had gone to his job at Buster Brown's. Mama was ironing my good dress for the party. The war would end later, I decided. Around dusk, when the first pale stars came out.

The party took place in Peggy's back garden. Her braids were pinned up, and she wore an expression of beaming, adult charm. The whole class came. Even Peggy's parents put in an appearance, Mr. Hatton bringing out some folding chairs with the defensive glare of someone stepping into a lunatic asylum, and his wife, with genial squints through her cigarette smoke, hurriedly pouring the orangeade. Helen Maria did not attend.

It was a very loud, fine party. Peggy's charm disappeared at once; she talked with her mouth full; she opened her gifts with shrill cries, waving around a comic book or hair ribbon, and got up a game of tag that went strong all afternoon. But toward the end she did something odd, suddenly announcing that she must thank Dumb Donny with a kiss for his penholder. Perspiring with heat and jubilation, she chased him up against a plum tree and pressed her puckered lips against his mouth. That she would want to kiss anyone, I didn't approve of. But that she would want to kiss Dumb Donny Woodall—who slid from her grasp with a frightened snort—that was truly insane, unless it was that he was small and weak and could be experimented on.

But it didn't ruin the party. There was more tag, more cake and orangeade, and I went home at dusk as the stars came out.

At midnight, the war still in progress, I closed my eyes with bitter, yet somehow not unexpected disappointment. Now but for the grace of a careless check mark, the mailbox would yield up the long stone gray envelope of a draft notice.

The week progressed to its cold conclusions. Helen Maria graduated *summa cum laude*, with no Oxford to go to. Peggy and I barely scraped into the next grade. And Peter, even before receiving his diploma or celebrating his birthday, took from the mailbox not a long gray envelope, as I had envisioned it, but a short white one.

Greetings, it said.

After days of brooding over the situation, of fidgeting and pacing, the genius joined Peggy and me for a walk downtown. People looked at her. She dressed in a grown-up, citified way, with an artistic dash, and though she didn't have on her fringed shawl, she wore a dramatic scarf pinned with a scarab. They were probably also looking at the way she walked, for she went rapidly along with her head in the air. Soldiers jumped aside with exaggerated courtesy, and one even bowed deeply, after which whistles and laughter went up behind her. She never broke her stride. Her eyes were hard.

"What is there to see on this street!"

"We could go down to the wharf," I suggested.

"What will I do on a wharf!"

Eager for her to meet Peter, I tricked her into Buster Brown's by not mentioning that my brother worked there. Though Peter was surprised to see me bring her in, he was friendly; but Helen Maria suffered the introduction with such staggering hauteur that I didn't know which shocked me more, her face or Peter's, which lit up with amusement.

She flung out the door, Peggy and I hurrying behind.

"Don't take me to meet people! I don't want to meet people!"

On the leafy residential sidewalks she calmed down, but she was distracted, brooding. Of course, she would start graduate work at Cal right away, she said, but there was so little in her field offered in summer. Nothing to sink her teeth into. Why couldn't she be at Oxford!

That night I asked Peter what he had thought of her.

"Quite a dish."

"A dish?" I had never thought of Helen Maria as a dish.

"Looks like Gene Tierney. Too bad she's such a character."

"She's not a character, she's a genius."

"So you keep telling me. So what's she hanging around with a couple of twelve-year-olds for?"

"Peggy's not twelve. She's thirteen."

In the restless days before her summer courses began, Helen Maria came out with us often. She discovered places she was interested in, like Al's secondhand store filled with old books, and the Catholic church, through whose dim interior she would lead us, condemning superstitions and describing carnal priests often ringingly enough to lift and turn a devout head, and the courthouse with its Corinthian columns, the only building in town she sanctioned.

One day she even ventured to the Saturday matinee with us. She had a book under her arm—*Faust*, it was called, written in German—because she meant to go to the ladies' room and read if she didn't like the picture, which was *The Leopard Man*. She stood in the tumultuous line with a revolted expression on her face, but once inside, she loosened up, whereas I immediately tightened, for though I had sat through countless matinees without being bombed, I still crowded down the aisle with dark fatalism. About five minutes into *The Leopard Man*, Helen Maria retreated to the ladies' room. She told us afterward that the picture was jejune and to look the word up in the dictionary. But she came with us the next Saturday, and the next.

I realized why when I happened to glance at her as she handed her ticket to Mr. Tatanian, the manager. When he returned the stub to her palm, her face reddened, and with lowered eyes she darted him a smile, swinging around and bumping headlong into me.

"What's wrong?" I asked.

"Your face is all red," said Peggy.

"Whose face!" she snapped, and plunged into the crowd.

I thought about Mr. Tatanian during the movie. He had a strange color, as though he had been steeped in root beer, and sad, sour, heavy-lidded eyes, and bushy hair streaked with gray. He was silent and lumbering, and he was considered a cheapskate because he collected the tickets himself. It had also been said (by Ezio) that he did things with the usherettes in his office, but I never saw him look at them with lust, though they were glamorous in their flaring trousers and short red jackets covered with gold braid. Except that Mr. Tatanian kicked you out once in a while, he was no one at all to give any thought to.

In his army notification, Peter had not been told what date he would be inducted. It was more waiting in the dark, but he didn't seem to mind. He had decided it would be pointless to start a summer course at college and have to leave midterm, so he was working full time at Buster Brown's, and on Saturday nights he went off with friends to the bowling alley or took a date to the State Theater. He said if it weren't for gas rationing, they could all pile into somebody's jalopy and zip down to Oakland or even to San Francisco; but they were stuck, and I knew that like Helen Maria, he found Mendoza lacking. But he took it with better grace. Maybe it was because he had more than two friends.

It seemed stupid that I had once thought the war was old and wornout just because of some faded posters. More soldiers than ever clogged the streets, Dad's shipyard was going full blast, *Life*'s pages still choked on smoke and corpses, and in Helen Maria's salon one day I had listened with dismay as she mentioned a Seven Years' War, a Thirty Years' War, a Hundred Years' War.

One morning another short white envelope arrived. Peter was to be inducted for active service on August 14.

With Peggy beside me, I looked out the bus window on our way to the first day of the Red Cross swimming program. The outskirts of town had grown from a couple of gasoline stations and roadside taverns to a sprawl of trailers and grocery stores. The town of Concord had tripled in size, its surrounding orchards replaced by row after row of heat-blistered wartime housing. Quonset hut schools had sprung up, even a Quonset hut movie theater. The whole place was like a military post that went on for miles, swallowing up the countryside. But gradually the cool green walnut and pear orchards resumed, and the big dry hills with their dottings of scrub oak, and finally we were jolting through the dust of the dirt road, and the sparkling pool burst into sight.

How long a separation it had been, how like paradise to smell the perfume of the chlorine and to sprint madly from the dressing room in a running dive over the side. The cold, engulfing roar and the clear green depths with sunlight dappling down like coins sinking and turning. When I had no more breath left, I shot up into the joyous confusion and looked for Peggy, who had been smitten by an Esther Williams movie and meant to perfect her style and become an aqua star. I expected much from this graduate of Clara Bebb's turquoise pool, who in addition had spent all her summers at Lake Tahoe, but she was an earnest, splashy swimmer who progressed toward me in a maelstrom, head up and eyes tightly closed.

"How do you like it!" I cried.

"Terrific!" she cried back, continuing on her stormy way.

Panting and goose-pimpled, she paid eager attention to our instructor—an athletic young woman in a black swimsuit and black bathing cap, a whistle clenched between strong, bared teeth—and at the end of the day she flopped down in the bus, damp, candy-laden, in the same soaring spirits as I.

If it weren't for August 14, this day would have had to be counted as one of life's perfect gifts.

JULY 11:   Sicily Invaded!

Far from winding things up over there, they were starting a new front. Having filched Peter's world map, which he never looked at anymore, I unfolded it on my bed and studied it. What were they doing in Sicily? Why did they keep fighting in places so far from Germany? North Africa, Russia, now Sicily. If they couldn't load the troops onto planes and drop them on Berlin, which would seem the sensible thing, why at least didn't they aim for some invasion spot where they wouldn't have so far to march to Berlin? Up there, by the town of Genoa.

103

Or better yet, Holland. That would make more sense than Sicily.

Even after Helen Maria had started her summer courses, she kept coming to the Saturday matinees with us. She began bringing Mr. Tatanian's name up in an off-hand way, the way she might have made some casual remark on the ticket seller or the usherettes, except it was never them, just Mr. Tatanian.

She wrote a poem entitled "To the Nation of Armenia" and read it aloud to us. It was about ancient battles and kings, but I knew it had to do with Mr. Tatanian because one of her casual comments was that his name was Armenian. She probably thought we weren't smart enough to put two and two together. But it wasn't hard, and it bothered me that a genius was in love with somebody who had been collecting tickets in the State Theater doorway for as long as I could remember. After the reading of the poem Peggy left the room to make a sandwich, and I took my courage in my hands.

"Do you like Mr. Tatanian?"

Helen Maria looked neither surprised nor displeased by the question. She merely said, "Chemistry is a strange thing."

"Chemistry?"

"Body chemistry. Your feelings simply cry out to a stranger. There's no accounting for it. You're completely and utterly at its mercy."

A picture of an epileptic flashed through my mind. You walked by some man, maybe a toothless wino, and suddenly your body cried out to him and you went into a fit even as you stared at him in horror. You might even wind up marrying him.

"Would you marry him?"

"Certainly not. I don't intend to marry."

"But if your body chemistry cried out, if you couldn't live without him—"

"My dear friend, haven't you heard of free love?"

"No. What is it?"

"It is this. If you can't live without a man, you live with him, but you don't ask permission from church and state. You are above that. That is free love."

It didn't sound free. Having to live with someone like Mr. Tatanian because your body cried out to him. All

104

that blushing and bumping into people. It was anything but free.

"You mean you want to live with Mr. Tatanian?"

"Oh, really," she said, and there came the awful blush. "I haven't planned anything, you're always so literal."

I thought she was annoyed, but she showed no desire to drop the subject. Glancing at the door, as though hoping Peggy would not return yet, she smoothed the skirt of her dress. "I've learned his first name. It's in the phone book. George . . ." she said, looking up.

As if the name were miraculous.

"That's interesting," I said. I felt I had to say something.

She nodded. Her blush deepened. "He's different—don't you feel that? He's like an exotic plant in a desert."

"I guess so," I replied uneasily. "But I mean I've known him all my life."

And I sensed that in her eyes I too was miraculous, for having been part of Mr. Tatanian's existence for so long. Her behavior was abnormal, murky. Peggy's footsteps could be heard coming back along the hall.

"Can't you get out of it?" I whispered.

"Of what?"

"Body chemistry."

The green eyes flashed. "I wouldn't wish to!" And as Peggy entered with her enormous sandwich, her sister cried, "Welcome, stout sibling!" The conversation had put her in a wonderful mood.

But it had done nothing for me, except to strengthen my opinion that the wisest course was never to ask anything.

Chapter 20

The following day the swimming instructor likened Peggy to a windmill, and she quit the program. Swimming was bad for your hair anyway, she said on the bus home.

"You could wear a cap."

Caps were ugly. Look at the instructor's. And she was ugly enough without it, with her big horse teeth and muscles. And when she took your arm to guide your stroke, she crushed all your bones. Peggy could live without that.

"And do what?"

She would find something, don't worry. There was more in life than swimming.

But she found nothing. The next time I came to her room she was lying on her back on the unmade bed, wearing her big gym shorts and a red halter, her hands clasped behind her head. Her sweaty legs were stuck to a litter of comic books and movie magazines. Rudy turned in circles for a cool position, his mouth drawn back in a panting grin.

"Let's go down to the wharf," I said. "It's cool there."

"I don't feel like it." She yawned and sat up and began cutting pictures from a movie magazine with a pair of blunt-nosed children's scissors.

"We could play blackjack," I said.

"It's too hot."

Maybe she was feeling low because being thirteen hadn't smoothed everything out. Her hair was fuzzy, and her body was still fat. I was glad, but I didn't say so. After a while, because she didn't want to do anything, I wandered out.

JULY 25: Mussolini Imprisoned!

By August 14 the war might be well on its way to ending. With its dictator locked up by its own government, everything was over for the long purple leg on the map. As soon as the island at its toe collapsed, our troops would jump across to the purple mainland and swarm northward, up through yellow Switzerland and pink Austria, into the black heart of the Reich. Then, as soon as Berlin was kaput, the troops would be loaded onto ships and planes and rushed around the globe to the hundreds of stubborn, bloody islands in the Pacific, which would at once surrender to our superior numbers.

I spoke to only one person about this theory. "Wait a

while," I breathed down at the black eye sockets. "Wait till after Sicily, all you Japs will be a bunch of skulls."

Everything in Peggy's room had changed. On the wall was a sign:

> *I, Margaret Louisa Hatton, am on a diet.*
> *I will not bring food into this room.*

Bread crusts and candy wrappers had vanished. On the dresser stood a framed movie magazine picture of Errol Flynn in a turban, and next to it gleamed a giant-size jar of Sta-Bak. Peggy's hair was unbraided and swamped flat with the pale green goo, which dripped down her freckled, slightly less plump shoulders.

"I've lost five pounds," she said.

I became aware of a smooth lamentation in the background. "What's that?"

"A record. 'In My Arms.' That's him singing, Frank Sinatra."

"So that's him." I stood listening. "He's not much."

An exasperated tongue click, then briefly: "Do me a favor. I bought this, but it won't go around my back." She was holding up a fancy pink brassiere, all lace and satin. After slipping it on over her red halter, she tugged behind her back at the two ends, trying to make them meet.

"No good," I agreed with satisfaction, glancing at the price tag. "Two fifty out the window."

"I want you to tie the ends together. Here." She handed me some string.

Grudgingly, I did as she asked and watched her turn this way and that before the mirror. The cups were empty and crumpled, but she didn't seem to mind. "It's gorgeous, isn't it?"

"Better than Eudene's anyway."

She looked suddenly annoyed. "Suse, I want to tell you something. You're going to have to do something about your appearance."

"Why?"

"Because. You don't look human."

A knife stab, deep to the heart. "I don't?"

"I mean maybe I'm overweight, I admit that, but you're a complete skeleton. You need a gaining diet. And bleach that chlorine out of your hair. Get rid of it. You can't go around that way."

"I think I look all right," I murmured, fighting down an urge to turn to her mirror.

"Well, I'm sorry, you don't. I'm not criticizing, I'm just trying to help."

I looked at the wrinkled shelf of her brassiere, at the mired hair which was drying and sticking out in clumps.

"*You* need help."

"Oh, I'm just experimenting," she smiled. "Wait till you see me when I'm done."

I went down the hall to Helen Maria's.

"She is wrapped up in her cocoon," said the genius, standing before an electric fan that blew tepid air across the room. "Soon she will emerge and offer herself. She'll go simpering about like a sugar plum, begging to be nibbled."

"How do you mean?" I asked, running a finger over the bony knob of my wrist.

"I mean she's found her métier. And what a waste, because Peggy has intelligence. But what has her goal turned out to be? To have her sojourn on earth justified by the opposite sex."

"How do you mean?"

"I mean she wishes to be admired by men."

"Well . . . what about you and Mr. Tatanian?"

"You jest, I hope, in drawing a parallel. I like *him,* not the entire sex indiscriminately. And I don't look to him to authenticate my existence. It's ignoble. It's pathetic. She's going to turn into my aunt."

"The one in Mexico City?"

"Yes, Aunt Dorothy. Who, incidentally, plans to descend on us this fall with her latest attachment. One has a headache already."

We were into August now, but Sicily did not fall. And an unbelievable thing was happening here: Japs were being released from the detention camps, filtering back.

"Can you beat that?" I told Peggy. "They're letting them out!"

She didn't answer. She had taken up exercises, vigorous knee bends accompanied by loud grunts of *one,* two, three, and *four,* five, six, until she had done twenty and staggered back to mop her face with a gray sock, fingernails flashing red, hair in a scarf wound punishingly tight. Then she would put on a new record, of which she had many more now: Ginny Simms, Dick Haymes, more Sinatra. She had new pictures around Errol Flynn: Tyrone Power, Victor Mature, Sinatra again. She was always looking in the mirror, sometimes sucking in her cheeks and raising an eyebrow, smolderingly, like Marlene Dietrich. She wanted to discuss movie stars and singers and was not happy with my poor reception, preoccupied as I was with the Japs. The irritated tongue click. Her back suddenly facing me as she touched up her toenails.

Into the oven stillness of my backyard I would take *War and Peace*, a book Helen Maria had recommended. The ground lay cracked and purplish in the white glare. Under the walnut tree the air was clammy with pinpricks of oil dropping from the leaves. The shade lay pale and hot on the dry grass. I would sit down and try to concentrate. But who were they, all these people with their unpronounceable names, who never stopped talking about dispatches, coronations, executions, fetes? In all their pages of conversation, only one remark leaped out clear and sensible: "Tell me what this wretched war is for?" I kept coming back to that, but the speaker didn't pause for an answer, which was not offered in any case. And as I sat there, I would see the print blur in the heat waves, as if it were under smoked glass, and I would plod back into the house and lie on the dining-room couch, the book heavy and shut on my stomach.

This was how I spent my days when I wasn't swimming. Sometimes I would rouse myself to do errands for Mama or go marketing with her downtown, and in the late afternoon we would work together in the cooling green of the vegetable patch. Sometimes, when she had friends in, I would join them for cake and iced tea, being of an age now to be invited as long as I changed from my shorts into a dress and used good manners.

They talked about food prices and rationing, about the heat, and about the heat of Sicily, where one had a son fighting; they talked about young so-and-so, who brawled with the soldiers, and pretty such-and-such, who had eloped with a sailor, and they talked about Sheriff O'Toole's high blood pressure and his unsightly sandbags, and sometimes they leaned across the table to whisper, laughing in warm, ladylike gusts, pressing a nearby arm or hand in their pleasure. They were nice to me, asked about my swimming lessons, and said I was growing tall, which I wasn't, and when I finished the cake and iced tea, I took my leave feeling good because Mama had friends she could talk with and wasn't lonely.

One afternoon, sitting under the walnut tree with my book, I saw the back porch door open, and Peggy came out.

"Want to take a walk?" she asked, crossing the glare of the yard.

I dropped the book and scrambled to my feet. "Maybe. I don't care."

"How do you think I look? Your mother said I looked terrific."

"My mother doesn't say terrific."

"Well, she said *nice.*"

She did look nice. She must have lost another five or six pounds by now, and though she wasn't slim, she wasn't a big fat girl anymore. She wore a crisp chalky blue full skirt and a crisp white peasant blouse and spotless white Wedgies matched by a dainty white purse. The most outstanding thing was her hair, which hung to her shoulders all of a piece like a big catcher's mitt, a dense complex of fiery glints and gleams.

She touched it. "Rosemary oil, I just discovered it. It works wonders."

"Where do you want to go?"

"Oh, just around." She started down the driveway with small, new, dainty steps. "I really like your mother, I always have. She's so nice. And she's so attractive. And she has such a cute accent."

"She doesn't have an accent."

"Of course she does. They both do. It's so cute."

"Cute? They're not cute."

"I didn't say *they* were cute, their *accent's* cute."

"But they don't have one."

"You just don't notice it, you're always around them. When's Karla coming home?"

"I don't know." How could they have an accent? I would have heard it. You couldn't live with somebody for twelve years and not notice something like that.

What was all this small talk about family anyway, as if she had suddenly become one of the iced-tea ladies? That tiny purse. That mincing walk.

Except that she was going faster now, and from the tiny purse she grabbed a stick of gum, unwrapped it, and slapped it into her mouth. All at once she was her old corky self, chewing openmouthed as we hastened along, scratching an itch on her behind, even banging out a belch from times gone by.

But it was all nerves, I realized later, for on Main Street the gum flew to the pavement and she pushed open the door to Buster Brown's, saying over her shoulder, "Don't you want to say hello to Peter?"

He was trying shoes on a customer. We waited at the counter. I saw that Peggy's face had become a mask of apprehension, as if earwigs were crawling up her leg. When Peter came behind the counter to make out the sales slip, she kept shifting from foot to foot and staring over his head at different places on the wall. The cash register rang. The shoes were wrapped. She began clearing her throat in a low, testing way; beads of sweat stood out on her upper lip. The customer departed. Peter stuck his pencil behind his ear.

"Say, who's this? Don't tell me it's Peggy?"

"Hello, Peter," she said in soft, sliding tones, breathlessly, and took hold of my hand. "We were just going by and we thought, why not drop in for a minute? So here we are . . . it's certainly a hot day, isn't it? And how's the shoe business these days?"

She was twisting my hand painfully as she got through all this, but above the tortured activity her face wore the calm, round-eyed expression she used on parents and teachers, only the smallest blush hinting at her inner turmoil. Finally I yanked my fingers free and held them up, blowing on them, but this had no effect on Peggy. Her eyes were filled with Peter.

He was saying business wasn't bad, and it was hot all right, 104 degrees, and as he spoke, I saw with horror that she was very slowly sucking in her cheeks and that the left eyebrow was rising high, high, in Dietrich's sultry arch.

Coupled with the still-round eyes, this expression gave her an effect of weird astonishment. Peter glanced away, rearranging some pads and pencils, and I saw a hint of a

111

smile on his lowered face. But when he looked up, he was serious.

"Well, I'm glad you dropped by. You look very nice today, Peggy. Nice hairdo."

She had to release her cheeks to reply. "Thank you, Peter," she drawled in a low, husky voice, "I'm so glad you think so." Then, as the eyebrow came slowly down, she turned gracefully away, saying that we had to be going, and gave him a last look over her shoulder, drawling once more in the low, husky voice, " 'Bye, Peter . . . see you later."

Outside, she walked to the next building and leaned against it, heaving a deep sigh.

"You acted like a nut. Peter thought you were a nut."

"He did not."

"You were making insane faces."

"I was not."

Just then our ears were assailed by a piercing whistle as a soldier passed by. Looking back over his shoulder, he winked hard at Peggy, screwing up his face in a virile knot.

"He winked!" she whispered, clutching my arm.

"So what, they'll wink at anything."

But she was already walking on, her eyes bright and darting, the world her oyster.

Chapter 21

The fighting in Sicily had not ended when August 14 arrived. I woke very early and lay quietly until I heard the house stir. Karla, home for the weekend, was still asleep. I raised the shade, put on my shorts and shirt, and woke her. "It's getting late."

Breakfast was leisurely, jolly, almost like a Christmas morning breakfast. But the moment came. Chairs scraped back. Dad went out to the garage to get the car. The rest of us walked into the living room, where Peter's suitcase stood with his tweed jacket folded over it. He picked up the jacket and threw it over his shoulder and lifted the suitcase. Mama's eyes had reddened. He hugged her, kissed her cheek, then did the same to Karla. I went out and got in the back seat of the car, and Peter got in the front with Dad. As we drove off, Dad beeped the horn, and Peter leaned out, waving to Mama and Karla on the porch.

The draftees were gathered at the American Legion Hall, which was not a hall but a tiny brick building standing on a dry little lawn with a cannon on it, also little, painted gray. Dad parked behind a Silver Trailways bus. The draftees, twenty or thirty of them, were standing around or sitting on their suitcases on the lawn. A sergeant in summer khaki, sweating darkly under the arms, stood writing on a clipboard.

I reminded myself that the bus was only going to Camp Beale, near Sacramento. It was a sorting-out place before they were sent to basic training, and basic training itself would take six weeks. Much could happen in that time, and I concentrated hard on my Sicilian theory; but it had no effect today. I watched Dad take his hands from the wheel and turn and shake hands with Peter and embrace him. Then Peter got out with his suitcase. I got out too, and he gave me a hard little hug—I saw the rim of his ear, the comb tracks in his hair. I got into the front seat with Dad, and we sat for a minute while Peter walked over to the others, turned, waved. Then Dad started the motor and drove around the bus, a rectangular blur of silver.

In white shorts, a paisley blouse knotted above her midriff, Karla sat out in the sun that afternoon. Her face was tilted back, her eyes under dark glasses. I sat next to her, at the old card table, shading *War and Peace* with my hand.

"You're turning into an intellectual," Karla said.

I shook my head. "I'm stuck in Book One, and there are fourteen more of them and two epilogues." But at least, having consulted the dictionary, I could say the word *epilogue* with confidence. Peggy, for instance, would not know what an epilogue was.

Peggy, at that moment, came around the corner of the house, wearing her blue skirt and crisp white blouse. "Hello, Karla." Breathless, seating herself quickly, ignoring me. Karla, like Peter, expressed amazement at the change in her appearance, and Peggy sat there smiling and wide-eyed, smoothing a big lump above her forehead, supposedly a pompadour. She asked Karla all sorts of silly questions, about hairdos, and if sunbathing was good for you, and who was her favorite singer. I kept reading.

"Peter left today, didn't he?" she asked.

I closed my book. "This morning."

"It's too bad. He was so nice."

"What do you mean 'was'? He still is. Nothing's happened to him!"

She traced her finger slowly on the tabletop. "I'll miss him."

"What do you know about it? You're not even related."

"Karla," she asked, "do you have a boyfriend in the war?"

"Not exactly. Not a steady, just dates."

"Karla, when they leave, do you miss them?"

"What do you keep saying her name for?" I said. "She knows what her name is."

"Don't be so nasty," Karla told me, getting up from her chair. "We'll all miss Peter, Peggy included."

"You're not going in, are you?" Peggy asked, eyes filling with disappointment.

"I've got to, I'm red as a lobster. Good luck with the diet, Peggy. When you get to Hollywood, you'll be the new Rita Hayworth."

Peggy smiled through her disappointment as the screen door closed. Why did they all encourage her when she was already so filled with herself? But I was luckier than she. I could write letters to Peter, and I could go inside to Karla, which I did. But even with Karla home, the house was like a shell today. Mama's eyes still looked red. Dad, who never talked a lot, was quieter than usual. The four of us sat on the front porch that night, as the stars came out one by one, and I kept seeing Peter standing on the dry little lawn with the cannon on it, his tweed jacket over his shoulder.

In the days that followed, I stayed close to Mama, to make her less lonely. But the one thing that might have brought her comfort I could not articulate. For as soon as I thought of putting my Sicilian theory into words, it lost all substance. I tried to make her happy in a different way. I said I would get straight A's when I went back to school. But if this made Mama happy, I don't know; she said it was good news, but it was clear that it was too much for her to absorb. It was certainly too much for me to absorb, and I was thankful for the weeks that still hung between me and my return to school.

Aug. 18:   **Sicily Falls!**

I waited. Nothing happened. The days went on, yellow and fierce already in early morning, bleached by noon to a colorless haze, and finally deepening to the plum blue stillness of evening, and nothing happened.

When *Life* came the next week, it summed up the Sicilian battle with photographs of dry hills like our own, ruined villages, dead bodies, and close-ups of dusty captured Germans under the caption of "Hitler's Best." Hitler's best had gone down in defeat, but the title of the article was "What Happens After the Sicilian Victory?" Nor were the newspapers or radio more enlightening. Nothing was happening.

Peter was sent to Camp Crowder, Missouri. He wrote that it was interesting. Some of the men were straight from the hills, and the first morning at breakfast one had stabbed another's hand to the table with a fork because he reached too close to his plate. He said his hair was shaved off, and it felt good because it was even hotter there than here. He was fine, and he hoped we were too, and he was looking forward to seeing us at the end of his training.

I wrote him back. I wrote about the swimming lessons ending, and about the vegetable garden, and how I meant to get good grades when I went back to school, and told him how much we were looking forward to his furlough.

Just before school started, Peggy had a relapse. I discovered her in Helen Maria's room with her hair tied back in a clump and a licorice stick hanging from her mouth. The genius was observing her sister's return with mixed pleasure and severity. "It's about time you came back down to earth. But it isn't necessary to revert totally. Don't go back to your overeating."

"Don't worry," said Peggy, chewing loudly. "You don't have anything to worry about."

"I'm not worrying, Peggy. I have more important things to worry about than your diet."

She lay down on her Persian spread and put a cigarette into her amber holder. But she didn't light it. It was too hot to smoke, almost too hot to talk. Through the glare of the French doors I saw Annuncio in his white sun helmet taking his tools from the shed.

"I've noticed that you have an unusual interest in our gardener. Have you read *Lady Chatterley's Lover*? I've read the unexpurgated edition, printed in Florence, 1928."

"I see," I answered, having picked up this phrase from Helen Maria herself, who used it when she was not interested. I was not interested in Lady Whoever's lover, since he was probably not a Japanese passing for a Filipino. Anyway, Helen Maria was too hot to go on.

"I don't know why I'm not in England," she muttered, fanning herself with an issue of the *American Linguist*.

We sat in silence. A fly buzzed madly against the glass, trying to get out.

"May I let that fly out?" I asked my hostess.

"Certainly."

I opened the French doors, feeling an oven blast in my face as the fly sped off. Annuncio smiled up from his raking. Hypocritically I waved and flopped down again.

"Suse is using her summer constructively, reading Leo Tolstoy," Helen Maria was telling Peggy. "She will return to school enriched. One also hopes her general comprehension will benefit."

"My grades, too," I said.

"I'm getting good grades when I go back," Peggy stated. "I mean it."

"Good news from both of you. It's been a wonder to me that the two people I consort with most should be academic failures. It's an irony, if you know what I mean."

We nodded. If we had not, she would have sent us to look up the word in her dictionary, and it was too hot for that. There was another sluggish silence. Peggy and I wandered out.

"Are you really going for good grades next year?" I asked.

"I don't want to stay in dumbbell class. Nobody in dumbbell class is popular."

"Eudene is. Everybody likes her."

"Eudene. Eudene's a *joke*. I'm talking about something else. You've got to have good grades or else you're just nothing. It's just lumped together that way—the kids who know how to act, the ones who count, they get good grades. I don't mean fantastic, that's just as bad as lousy, I mean just good. You've got to make College Prep. Then you're set."

I had a feeling that the messy hair, the licorice stick—they weren't a real relapse. She spoke too seriously. She meant to be one who counted.

Chapter 22

On September 6, when school began, there was still silence from Italy.

Waiting for Peggy on the entrance steps, my lunch in a paper bag, my binder carelessly held, I watched the bewildered seventh graders with a feeling of greatness. Yet it was warming to see these little old schoolyard playfellows of the past, and for a moment I wanted to run over and be one of them. But Peggy had arrived. "How do I look?" she asked. Her lips were bright orange, and so were her fingernails and toenails. She wore a bright orange dress and her white Wedgies and carried her dainty white purse, and she had gotten her hair shaped into a long, smooth curve topped by a superabundant pompadour. She hurried inside.

But there was too much confusion at the assembly for anyone to take notice of her, and afterward, with "On the Road to Mandalay" echoing in our ears, she was further disappointed to find that Mrs. Miller was teaching some eighth-grade subjects this year and would be our homeroom teacher again. Peggy felt it made our new status less exciting, but I was happy to see Mrs. Miller again and to see her put a deserved damper on my friend, whose spirits were zooming as the girls crowded around her with compliments on her fantastic change.

"Peggy," she asked, "have your parents said you could wear lipstick?"

"Oh yes, Mrs. Miller." The great round-eyes look. "I can even bring a note."

Forged, of course. But Mrs. Miller believed her. "Well, I'm sure they don't mean for you to wear it so thick. Please wipe some of it off."

Peggy did so, but when we went on to our next class, she said, "I like Mrs. Miller, but she's really behind the times." And taking out her tube of Tangee and a little mirror, she reapplied it thick and bright.

At noon she led me out to the lawn.

"Aren't we eating at your house?" I asked.

"I don't eat lunch anymore." Carefully she spread out the skirt of her dress and sat down. "Besides, I'm going to the noon dance."

"You don't know how to dance."

"I taught myself, with a booklet."

"That won't be any good."

But she wasn't listening. As I took my sandwich and apple from my bag, she leaned back on her elbows and gracefully threw her head back so that her profile was presented for everyone to admire. It was an admirable profile, I had to admit, almost as perfect as Helen Maria's, but with everything more upturned; by now she had lost pounds and pounds, and her neck was slender, and so were her arms, and her legs, too, crossed before her. But she had chosen a ninth grader haunt to sit in, and they all were too busy among themselves to notice her.

Suddenly her eyes narrowed. "I'll make him smile!" she exclaimed, catching her lower lip between her teeth. The Gestapo agent was coming along the walk.

"Are you crazy?"

She was already on her feet.

"What will you say?"

"Wait and see." And round-eyed, demure, she walked over to him. "Oh, Mr. Lewis?"

His grim, sour face looked down.

"I have a message for you, Mr. Lewis. From Peter Hansen. You had him a few years ago in algebra?"

My eyes bulged.

"Well, he's a friend of mine, and he wants to study ar-

118

chitecture when he gets out of the service. And he said he learned more in your class than anywhere else, and that you changed the course of his life."

"Hansen?" said Mr. Lewis, in his grim, sour voice.

"Peter Hansen."

"Don't remember him." He started past her but turned. There was the faintest touch of a smile on his hard lips. "But tell him fine. Good."

"I will, Mr. Lewis," said Peggy shyly, smiling back. She returned leisurely to my side. "Well?"

"Peter never said that. You lied."

"So what, it made him feel good."

"I don't count it."

She didn't care. She was looking boldly in the direction of the gym. "Okay everybody, here I come!"

These weekly dances were apparently popular. The gym was already crowded, mostly with girls in a huge bunched-together group which Peggy pushed and elbowed her way through, dragging me behind. I saw there was another, smaller bunch against the wall, all boys. Then there was another bunch, very small, standing around the phonograph with Mother Basketball. These were The Ones Who Counted, to use Peggy's phrase, and the student body president himself was putting the first record on. "Paper Doll" began blaring from the loudspeaker, bouncing hollowly off the bare walls. The student body president strolled onto the dance floor with a neat button-nosed girl, and Others Who Counted followed, and then some of the boys against the wall began wandering over to us bunched-up girls. I felt Peggy's hand grab mine and crush it painfully, as it had at Buster Brown's. Her eyes were so excited she made me think of a horse filled with locoweed, wild to leap over the corral fence.

But when she was asked to dance, she exclaimed uh-uh! and jumped back and even crossed her arms in front of her. The boy was moonfaced, slow-moving, with a line of dark fuzz on his upper lip. He looked down at her crossed arms, blushed to the roots of his hair, and moved off.

"I hope they don't think I'd even consider him," Peggy murmured, looking around worriedly.

"You hurt his feelings."

"I did?" Surprise, remorse; she craned her neck to spot him, then swung back to the music. "Well, I can't just say yes to every single boy who comes along."

But no one else asked her during the whole thirty-five minutes we stood there. It was I who danced.

Running around popping his gum, Dumb Donny grabbed me. Neither of us knew how to dance, but tangled up and scuffling, we progressed around the crowded floor, and it was exhilarating, like the days we all played together in the schoolyard, yet I also felt spasms of pride to be part of the noon dance, not that my partner was much: short, bony, with blond hair tarnished green from summer pools. In fact he looked just like me. But we were having a good time, and when the record ended I hurried back to the brilliant orange splotch of Peggy's dress.

"Did you see me dance?"

She didn't hear me. Her face was taut. Both hands held the strap of her white purse, as if for support. The walls began to reverberate with the last number. And suddenly she was gone from my side. I pushed through the crowd and caught up with her outside, hiding behind a pepper tree. She was crying bitterly, her face pressed against the rough bark. "What was wrong with them?" she sobbed. "I'm pretty, aren't I . . .?"

But I didn't know anymore. Maybe she was too orange. Her pompadour too overwhelming. Her eyes too wild. Maybe she had scared them off.

"They're just stupid," I said. "They wouldn't know how to act with somebody special."

"You think so?" she asked, her eyes still streaming.

"Of course I do."

We could hear Mother Basketball's whistle ending the dance. Now everyone would come pouring out the door toward us. Bent over, shielding her face with her hand, Peggy allowed me to lead her away, into the main building to the lavatory.

There she submerged her face in a basin of cold water. It seemed to calm her. She blotted the skin dry. She repainted her lips and combed her hair. She looked at herself in the mirror, serious, cold.

"Fuck them."

"What?" The word had an ugly, deep-cutting sound.

"You heard me. Fuck them." This time she blushed as

she said it and dropped her eyes, but whatever the word meant it seemed to do her good. She threw her things back into her purse and snapped it fiercely shut. "Bunch of jerks—wait till next time!"

She flung open the door and walked out.

SEPT. 9:
Italian Surrender
Unconditional!
Allies Pouring In!

The long silence finished at last! The whole country ours! And as I threw the newspaper down, my theory was jubilantly vivid, like a newsreel in Technicolor. A week's march up purple Italy, another week to black Berlin, and then the yellow-infested islands of the Pacific.

"It was too big," Peggy said the next day, patting a diminished pompadour. "I think it looks better this way."

"It looks terrific!"

SEPT. 10:
Allies Prepare
For Italy Battle!

Unwillingly I read further. General Eisenhower was appealing to the Italian people to drive the Germans from their soil; but the German army in Italy was powerful, and he realized there was no hope that the country would fall like a plum to the Allies.

"Maybe Mrs. Miller wasn't completely wrong. Maybe it was too gooey-looking. It's better just one layer like this."

"I suppose so."

SEPT. 11:
Fierce Salerno Battle!

Salerno, way down there at the bottom, hundreds of miles from the northern border.

"Nobody wears Wedgies. Nobody who counts, anyway. You know what they wear? Loafers. With a penny stuck in front."

I gave a shrug.

"Aren't you coming? What's wrong with you anyway?"

"I don't know."

"Well, I'm going now. I want to get there early."

She went off across the lawn. Her pompadour was down to a modest mound. She wore a pale blue dress; her lipstick was light, her nail polish gone. On her feet were well-polished brown loafers with a bright penny stuck in the front of each.

I kept sitting after I finished my lunch. I didn't feel like doing anything, but after a while curiosity sent me slowly over to the gym. I squeezed through the big bunch of girls like refugees huddled together for safety, but Peggy wasn't among them, and it was awhile before I even thought of glancing toward The Ones Who Counted—Towks, I was beginning to call them in my mind. There she was. Holding a record, smiling, talking.

I stared, trying to understand how she had managed it. Then, glancing at Mother Basketball, I saw how. Certainly, Peggy, you may help bring the records from my office. Just put them there by the phonograph. Oh, so-and-so, Peggy's giving us a hand. You know Peggy, don't you? And that was that. They probably didn't even connect her with pigtailed fatso from last year. She was a fresh new person. And now, as I watched, this fresh new person was led out on the dance floor by a tall Towk. I knew she must be bursting and fainting inside, but on her face was only a neat little sociable smile. What iron effort, what control; and I remembered that look she had given herself in the mirror, that deadly, cold look. And I remembered her bitter tears that day and Moonface's bitter blush, and I looked around at these chatting girls huddled for courage, and it seemed that there was no pleasure here at all, but that it was a battlefield of fear and pain and desperate measures. I turned and pushed my way back outside.

Four days later, when Salerno fell, it was clear that all progress north was to be made inch by bloody inch.

Chapter 23

In spite of everything, there was Peter's furlough to look forward to. He would be coming home the first week in October, only for two or three days because it would take him two days to get there by train and the same back. But even to see him for two or three hours would be something.

The late summer heat was intense. At night, when Dad came home from work, the house was as stifling as it was in the daytime. But he said it was cool compared to the hulls of ships when you were working inside them, and everything was relative. This was something Helen Maria often said—everything was relative. But it seemed to me that either a thing was or it wasn't, and it shouldn't make any difference how it compared to something else. Yet here was Dad saying how cool the house was, while Mama and I roasted. It was something to think about. As for Peggy, the heat made her irritable, and she complained constantly about her triumph, which had been great but inconclusive. The Towks now said hi to her in the hall, but no one asked her to eat lunch, or to join a committee, or to go to a party. It was because she was in a dumbbell class. She set about to change that.

In study hall, while I sketched exploding Zeros with pieces of Jap flying through the air, Peggy bent over her homework. Nothing could break her concentration, not whispers or offers of gum or covertly produced comic books, though I tried them all. After school she went home loaded down with books.

She bored me. I bored her. Yet I cherished the hope that she would somehow change back to what she had been and like me for what I was, green hair and all. Looking at the slim cheek bent over a text, I felt pangs of nostalgia for my old, fat, ignorant Peggy.

Others didn't. Mrs. Miller praised her. Her parents praised her. Helen Maria praised her.

"I'm very impressed," the genius told me, while Peggy smiled at the floor with ill-concealed satisfaction. "It's a remarkable breakthrough. But I always knew she had it in her; it was just a matter of application. And what, if I may ask, has become of your own academic resolution?"

I had planned to improve, but somehow, improvement had lost importance. I stood thinking of a newspaper item I had read earlier that day.

War on Japs Just Begun

Don't start selling your war bonds. The war in the South Pacific is only a prelude to the fight that is to come. We will lose thousands of men, scores of ships, hundreds of planes, and tons of supplies before we even make a dent. . . .

It made it seem useless to pore over the irrelevancies of schoolbooks. I shrugged my shoulders at Helen Maria's question.

"You didn't even finish *War and Peace,* did you?"

"No. It was too hard."

She gave me a cool look and turned her attention back to Peggy.

A messenger boy from Western Union handed me a telegram through the screen door. My heart lunged. Telegrams brought catastrophic news, and I saw through the cellophane slot of this one that it was from Missouri. I ran through the house into the backyard, where Mama was talking with a neighbor over the fence. Biting my lip, I held out the yellow envelope.

She took it, saying to the neighbor, "It's from Peter, when he'll be coming in."

She read it, and a look of disappointment came over her face. "No, he can't come," she said slowly. "He's got the flu."

We went back into the house together.

"Could he come after?" I asked.

"I don't think they can do that," she said, sitting down at the kitchen table. "He'll be going overseas."

"We won't get to see him at all before he goes?"

124

"I don't think so, Suse." She sat with her chin in her hand, looking down at the green oilcloth.

A letter came a few days later. He was in the infirmary and mad as hell to spend his furlough there. It wasn't even bad flu, but they kept him in bed with a thermometer in his mouth. The only time the Army showed concern about you was when you didn't want them to. And he had wanted so much to get out here and see us all before shipping out. They had gotten their orders. They were going to England.

England. Not the bloody, steaming jungles of the Pacific. And not Italy either. But England, which hadn't even been bombed in more than a year. Thank God. Thank God for England.

"And what will they do in England?" asked Helen Maria. You could tell she was jealous, she didn't want anyone else to get there.

"Guard it maybe," I smiled. "Save Oxford for you."

But she had no sense of humor when it came to Oxford.

I began wondering myself what they were going to do there. And gradually I came to understand that they were going to prepare for an invasion of Europe. It was what Dad thought. It was what the newspapers thought. Far from being a safe harbor, England was to be the launching place.

With Peggy locked away studying every day after school, I got back into the habit of going down to the library, where there was a variety of newspapers and magazines to read. I was looking specifically for news about the invasion, but I read everything that pertained to the war.

One unbearably hot afternoon I sat back, socked in the face by a brief article in *Time*. It explained that dragged-out silence in Italy this summer. It said that the Italian surrender had been preceded by a long conference in Lisbon between Italian emissaries and the Allies.

My concept of surrender was vastly different. The head of the collapsing army shoved a scrawled note of defeat into the hand of a messenger to take to the enemy encampment. There, waving his white flag at a blood-spattered, hate-filled sentry, the messenger begged to be

125

taken to the commanding general. Through smoke and corpses he was led, and in a bullet-torn tent, with bloodshot eyes and bags beneath them, the general read the note with such violent scorn and joy that the messenger before him shook with terror.

These enemies had sat around a polished conference table. They had shuffled papers, sipped glasses of water, calmly gone over points. How could they hold themselves back, they whose armies had been at each other's throats since North Africa? How could they keep from flinging themselves across the table and smashing each other's faces? Why had the Polish family been killed if these leaders didn't even let go with a clenched fist? In such restraint, in such cordiality, there was something more horrifying than death itself. I scraped my chair back and left.

The buildings glared bone white, their shadows long, black, sharp-edged. Oil-blackened Shell workers were walking home, swinging their empty lunch pails. Cannery women in tomato-stained slacks, their hair bound up in kerchiefs, made for the Ferry Street bars. Shopgirls in thin flowered summer dresses strolled arm in arm, their pompadours wilted. Soldiers squinted, smiled, whistled, their summer khakis darkened with sweat under the arms and down the spine. They squinted at me too; they always did, because of my hair. I returned their looks today, shading my eyes with my hand, thinking, "Go home. Get on the train. Why should you fight if they sit around a table like that?"

Then I was certain I had lost my mind. God help us if our army got on a train and went home! Had I forgotten the bombers? And the Jap spies filtering back this minute from detention camps? But something was frighteningly wrong, out of kilter, and I kept walking, head down, passing from glaring pavement to black shadow, trying to grab hold of what it was.

There at the end of Ferry Street stood the four-thirty train from Berkeley. The old signal man in baggy trousers waved his red flag in slow arcs as the warning bell went *dingdingdingding* and soldiers with duffel bags ran down the USO steps to the surging khaki crowd by the train; the depot doors kept flinging open, their windows flashing like diamonds; from the open windows of the USO Glenn Miller's band music floated through the

126

scorching air. The crowd pushed noisily in the heat and dust, yelling at each other, clattering up the steel steps into the train, hanging out the open windows. Then there was an explosive hiss, steam rose up around the engine, and the conductor cried, "All aboard! All aboard!"

From this hectic scene Helen Maria was rapidly emerging, her books against her chest. I watched her. In an ordinary summer dress and no shawl she looked like anybody else, except for her walk, very fast, and with her head high. Soldiers smiled and whistled, and one kept blocking her as she tried to pass. Eyes fixed haughtily above him, she stepped off the curb and continued along the gutter at an unbroken pace, returning to the pavement when she had left him behind. She took notice of nothing. Not the clacking billiard rooms, or the barbershop with its many moose heads inside, or the mysterious bail bond offices, or the sleazy hotels, or the noisy bars one after another. On she came, oblivious. I tapped her shoulder as she passed.

"You know the conference in Lisbon?"

"I do not," she said, as I fell in alongside her. That was a nice thing about Helen Maria, you didn't have to waste time with greetings and small talk.

"After the fall of Sicily. A meeting between Italian emissaries and the Allies."

She was usually bored by my concern with things military, but it may have been the urgency in my voice that caused her to raise a responsive brow.

"They discussed the terms of Italy's surrender," I said. "They *discussed*. They were *enemies*, and they sat there politely discussing!"

The brow dropped. "What do you want them to do? Shoot one another?"

"Yes! Or why should the soldiers? If those big ones don't hate each other, why should the soldiers?"

"I believe I once explained to you that war is an economics-based phenomenon. Those in charge have nothing against each other on an emotional level."

"That doesn't make any sense."

"What's more, soldiers don't hate each other either."

I looked at the brilliant green eyes, astonished to hear a genius say anything so hopelessly, so embarrassingly incorrect.

"Let's take Verdun," she continued, shifting the

127

sweaty books in her arms. "On Christmas Day the Allied soldiers climbed out of their trenches, and the Germans out of theirs, and throwing their rifles to the mud, they proceeded to have a jolly game of soccer."

"You don't expect me to believe that."

"Don't you know about the friendships that were struck up in bomb craters? Yank and Kraut sharing rations, exchanging family snapshots?"

"I'm trying to be serious!"

"God, it's like talking to a wall. Go to your history books if you don't think I'm serious. Read about war, if you're so interested in it. Read about Verdun."

"Verdun wasn't an important war," I said defensively.

"Verdun was not a war! My God, don't you know anything? Verdun was the longest, bloodiest battle of World War One. A field where they lived like rats. Not important, indeed! They'd be so charmed to hear it, the million or more who died there."

My face burned, but I kept to my course. "Don't tell me they didn't hate each other. Don't tell me they would have stayed there if they didn't hate each other."

"That's exactly what I am telling you."

I could have struck her. How was I to talk with someone who would not use reason? "Then why *did* they stay there?" I snapped, to force her into a corner.

"Because they were told to."

I did strike her then, except that it was my own thigh, meant as the back of her calm, smug head.

"Let's cut through the park," she suggested, turning. I could not speak for anger, and all at once the heat was choking, intolerable. Then the scorching air, colorless and glaring as gravel, went out like a light bulb as we were enveloped by cool, lofty greenness. Except that it was not really cool, just not boiling, as if you were walking through tepid water. Old men in rolled sleeves sat on benches. Young mothers in shorts rolled flushed babies along in buggies. Soldiers lay asleep on the lawns, children playing among them. I still clutched my anger, not knowing what to do with it, and was further angered to see that Helen Maria was enjoying the shade without a care in the world. Sinking down on the grass, she put her books aside and pushed her damp hair from her forehead.

128

"Well, what are you standing for? Are you still annoyed because they played soccer at Verdun?"

I sat down sullenly.

"Why do you insist that everyone burst with hatred?" she asked, lying back on an elbow. "Isn't it more practical not to hate, since the enemy will more than likely become the ally afterwards, and vice versa?"

Again I was electrified by the urge to strike her. I yanked up a handful of the short grass. When I spoke, my voice came out oddly pinched. "You make it sound like a game."

"Because that's what it is."

"It is not!"

I sat mangling the grass in my palm, trying to get my voice under control. I said quietly, "They hate us, and we hate them. We hate them, and we'll always hate them."

"Ah," she said reflectively. "Hatred as something to hold it all together. To give it point. Since nothing else does."

"It's not to give it anything. It's how it is."

"Fascinating," she nodded slowly. "Yes, I quite understand."

I nodded too, feeling calmer, as if I had narrowly escaped obliteration. Now the soccer game faded, and the shared snapshots, and the prescribed, ratlike dying. All sank back under the strong, comprehensible tide of vengeance and bloodlust.

"Tell me something," Helen Maria said suddenly. "Why are you so interested in our gardener?" But she didn't wait for an answer. "Sometimes he has trouble, people take him for a Japanese. Once a woman visiting across the street came over and made a very unpleasant scene with Jack. Well, to me Annuncio looks like a Filipino, but I don't know. Sometimes I wonder. Do you, too? Is that why you look at him?"

I nodded, surprised and pleased by her admission.

"I really think he should be sent to a detention camp," she said.

"Except the camps are no good, they're all coming back. They ought to—" But something in her face cut me off. She was listening too closely, her eyes slightly narrowed.

129

"They ought to be done away with," she prompted. "Isn't that right?"

And then I realized she was still arguing, but slyly, leading me on.

"Answer quickly," she urged. "Don't hedge."

I remained silent, not daring to say yes, unable to bring myself to say no. And in her eyes, for the first time since I had known her, there grew a look of contempt.

"Were you among the brilliant minds that flooded the house of that mixed couple?"

"No."

"But you approved?"

I said nothing, growing very still inside, wary.

She sat up slowly. "So this is what your fine hatred is all about. You realize, of course, that what you feel isn't even hatred, only a scabby hysteria that attacks inferior souls. Cretins. Lynch mobs. Medieval witchhunters. Nonthinkers, the lot. That's the company you're in."

A powerful self-protective instinct was layering me, as if with coats of hard, deflective pearl. Remote, encapsulated, shrewd, I lifted my eyes. "That's the company *you're* in. I didn't say anything."

"That was the Socratic method of question and answer I was using, for your information."

"I don't know, but you said Annuncio should be sent to a camp, and that they should all be done away with. A... you're always right. So I didn't say anything."

"Just a moment, please. You said the camps weren't enough."

"I know. The bad Japs can come back with the good ones, but why should the good ones be there in the first place? There ought to be some way that's fairer. That's what I was saying, but you didn't let me finish. You said they should all be killed. But even if you think Annuncio's a Jap, you shouldn't want him killed."

"I do not want Annuncio killed! That's just the point I'm making! Where is your brain? I'm speaking *against* prejudice and terrorism. I'm taking you to task for your trashy mob mentality."

"But I don't know what you're talking about. I don't hate them." The lie came out surprisingly easy, and I even looked at her searchingly as I said it.

"Then what is all this hatred you've been rhapsodizing
130

over since Main Street? What are you talking about? If you even know?"

"Well, I know." Carefully looking down at the grass, carefully choosing my words. "I know I hate cruelty and evil, and Japan is cruel and evil, and so is Germany. But I don't hate Annuncio. I look at him because if he's pretending to be a Filipino, I wonder how long he can get away with it and stay safe. I don't hate the California Japs."

"I wonder. How do you see the color of their skin?"

"I don't know. Brass."

"Does it occur to you that we look like peeled bananas to them? It behooves a racist to think about that. I assume you're in league against Mexicans and Negroes as well?"

"No."

"Why not?"

Mexicans, Negroes, they didn't belong to an enemy nation. She was accusing me of something I couldn't even begin to follow, and I felt the honest resentment of someone unjustly attacked. "You're trying to twist me into something I'm not," I protested. "Just to be right."

"Not at all. I'm merely using the Socratic method. And I'm relieved if I'm wrong. But let's return to your statement about Japan and Germany. You say they're evil and cruel. Granted, one knows about Japanese atrocities, and one is well aware of the persecutions in Germany before the war, but the horrible fact is that at one time or another, all nations have ..."

She talked on. I nodded now and then, but I was not listening. From deep within my pearl, I was savoring my safety. She had dislodged nothing. Now and then a phrase floated through, as if from a great distance: "Man is stupid because he allows evil, but he's not evil in himself ... you can't hate nations, they're only people, you might as well hate everyone in this park ... you're expressing patriotism in its most primitive form, it must be nipped in the bud. ..." Slow nods of my head, as if mulling her wisdom, but I was thinking that there was great advantage in talking with someone who thought you were dumber than they; they never saw very far inside you because they didn't think there was very far to see. Still, I had come dangerously close to some sort of demolishment. I would never again throw out my deepest

131

questions. It was better to remain locked up in the dark with them. This I knew absolutely, once and for all.

She had come to an end. "I must be getting on home," she said, gathering up her books. "I'm glad we talked. I think you may have learned something."

"Yes," I agreed. "I have."

Chapter 24

Peggy was so impressed with herself as a scholar that she was hard to bear, but in a way she was easier to be around, more zestful and communicative, like her old self.

"It all fits together," she said. "It's sort of exciting, even."

"Really," I said.

"I wish you'd let Peggy inspire you," said Helen Maria. "You should listen. Do you realize that every night she drills herself in grammar and spelling? Do you realize that she enhances her lessons with supplementary reading of the *Encyclopaedia Britannica*? My set is gone, you'll notice. It's on temporary loan to my sister, at her own request."

It was too much. I couldn't picture anyone laboring over pages not even assigned. We were in Helen Maria's room; it was late in the afternoon, hot but not broiling. Peggy had changed into her old baggy shorts to be comfortable, and that was heartening, if only she would stop talking about her studies. But she was walking back and forth with bright eyes.

"What I mean, it really fits together. It's amazing. Like yesterday in Science, remember we were studying rocks? Okay, now listen. Last night when I was doing homework on General Lafayette I looked him up in the encyclopedia, and there were a lot of references to the French Revolution, so I looked up the French Revolution because I didn't know there was one. Well, first thing I came to was the word *feudal,* so I looked that up in the dictionary, and the definition mentioned the word *vassal,*
132

so I looked that up, and it came from the word *upo*, so I looked that up, and it was from the Greek word *hypo*, which means 'under'—and that came right back to the science lesson! *Hypothermal.* 'Under' plus 'heat.' Molten rock under the surface!"

Helen Maria stood gazing at her sister. Her eyes were shining.

"I guess that's interesting," I said. "You mean it makes sense."

"Absolutely," said Peggy,

"You mean it really does. It's all connected up."

"Of course," said Helen Maria. "That's what learning is all about. I have been trying to tell you that for ages. From ignorance and confusion, learning leads *out*."

"Out where?" I asked. A sudden glimpse of the black, starless sky.

"To more learning, greater understanding. One fact unfolds another. Liken it to a great flower opening."

"One big flower?" I asked carefully.

"The flower of knowledge."

I could see it. A big golden rose, with the petals fitting smoothly together and opening one by one to release its light, until the whole flower blazed like the sun. I nodded thoughtfully.

"Yoo-hoo!" someone called from the front door. "Anybody home?"

"What's that?" asked Helen Maria, turning her head.

A clatter of high heels across the Dungeon.

"It must be Aunt Dorothy!" cried Peggy.

"Oh God, what is wrong with the woman! She's not supposed to arrive till the weekend!"

The heels clattered down the hall. Peggy flung the door open.

"Peggy, darling!"

She didn't look like a wino. She was tall and redhaired, with a small white hat perched on the side of her head. She wore a navy blue suit with white ruffles sticking out in front, and she had very white teeth, very pink cheeks, and very red lips. There were a lot of rings on her fingers, and she carried a pair of white gloves in her hand. She stood in the doorway, hugging Peggy, then beamed at the genius.

"Helen Maria!"

Helen Maria extended her hand.

"How grown-up you've got, both of you! And Peggy, so slender! Estelle mentioned it in her letter, but I never *dreamed*—Roger! Roger! Come meet these two beautiful children! And who is this?" she asked warmly, smiling at me.

"It's my friend Suse," said Peggy. "And this is my Aunt Dorothy from Mexico City!" I said hello over the threshold. Aunt Dorothy did not attempt to step inside the sacred chamber, no doubt having learned from previous visits. Gesturing eagerly, she brought a tall gentleman into view and clasped him around the waist. He was interesting-looking, with sunken cheeks and haggard eyes and rather long pale hair like an Englishman. He wore a dark blue jacket with gold buttons—a blazer, Helen Maria told me later, possibly the first blazer ever to be seen in Mendoza.

He shook hands with all of us, smiling tiredly, then smiled tiredly at Aunt Dorothy.

"We've been on that miserable train for days," she told us. "The coaches are just swarming and choking with soldiers, poor things, how can they sleep, but they do! We didn't catch a wink, ourselves, we are *staggering* with fatigue, we must absolutely have some sleep or we'll die on the spot!"

"Of course," said Helen Maria in her finest, most British tones. "The guest room has been prepared."

"Oh, but Roger insists on being stuffy." Aunt Dorothy shook a coy finger at him. "He thinks he should stay at a hotel."

"If there is one," he said.

He must be joking. "Of course we've got hotels," I told him. "The Travellers' is the best. It's on the corner of Main and Alhambra."

"Yes," said Helen Maria. "It's charming. It will remind you of a pesthouse in Whitechapel." Her accent was more pronounced than I had ever heard it, as if each word were chipped from a block of ice. But there was nothing icy about her smile.

"Well, I'll just have a try," he said with his weary smile, and started off. Aunt Dorothy went down the hall with him, Peggy tagging along.

"She must lead him a dog's life," said Helen Maria. "He looks exhausted."

"Well, he's old."

"Nonsense. He's about the same age as George."

Exactly. Mr. Tatanian was old too. Odd how she liked them so creased and frazzled.

"Aunt Dorothy's gone to lay down," Peggy informed us breathlessly, slipping back inside.

"Lie, and what's there to be so breathless about? They're not royalty."

Peggy ignored this. "Isn't she fabulous?" she asked me.

"She doesn't look like a wino. I thought she would look like a wino."

"She's taken the cure," said Helen Maria. "Which accounts for the strained look."

"She doesn't look strained," Peggy objected. "I think she looks very gorgeous, in this very grown-up sort of way."

"I should hope she looks grown-up, at the age of fifty-five."

"I don't care. She's fabulous. And you ought to see their luggage, it's fabulous. His is maroon and hers is cream and they've got stickers from everywhere. He just took his overnight case because the cab already left. I told him Jack would drive his suitcase down later."

"I can't feature him in that fleabag," said Helen Maria.

I gave her a cool look. The Travellers' Hotel was Mendoza's finest; hardly a fleabag. And even if it had been, Roger looked too worn-out to be disappointed in anything. I wondered if his constitution had been shattered in the London blitz.

But Peggy felt he was continental. "Bulgarian, maybe."

"Bulgaria is Axis," I told her contemptuously.

"He's English," Helen Maria broke in. "It's there in the vowels. He's one of your roaming British expatriates."

Peggy hitched up her big shorts and said she'd better get into something decent for dinner.

"He is to dine with us tonight?" asked Helen Maria.

"That's what they said."

"What a bother." But she walked immediately to her closet. I left her pulling out a dark red velvet dress which looked both too hot and too fancy to wear till Christmas.

"You know where Roger was born?" Peggy hailed me the next morning. "Bend, Oregon."

"Bend, Oregon?"

"The accent goes away when he's drunk. Take my word, kid, he's never even *been* to England. He doesn't even have any money. He said he used to, but twenty-nine did him in, it's a roulette number I figure. And Aunt Dorothy sat there looking just miserable because he showed up drunk and kept talking and talking and finally fell asleep at the table with pudding on his chin. He was really disgusting. I felt sorry for her."

"Helen Maria must have been furious. She liked him."

"I know, she got all dressed up and everything. She was really mad. Afterwards she said something about him to Aunt Dorothy, I don't know what, and Aunt Dorothy said don't be so hard on people and started crying. This morning she didn't smile or anything. I hate to say it, but she was more fun before she went on the wagon."

A few days later the visit was declared a failure. Roger stayed in his hotel room, pestering Aunt Dorothy with phone calls, which she answered in angry whispers, hanging up with an anxious hand. She wandered around the house, drinking ginger ale until it came out of her ears, and she didn't want to visit Estelle's relatives or take a walk or go to the movies, and when they had a barbecue in the garden, that didn't cheer her up either. All she did was talk.

"All she talks about is when she was young," said Peggy. "Or how she hates ginger ale. She's really boring. And there's this creepy feeling I get, like she wants to eat me up. I never go near her."

Peggy pleaded homework. Helen Maria kept to her chamber. Mr. Hatton disappeared into his workshop. It was poor Dr. Hatton who was maneuvered into the Dungeon and placed in a chair before the fireplace, to sit listening as their unhappy guest talked on and on, breaking off only to feed the roar of the flames. She had used up almost all their wood. The weather was warm, but she claimed she was frozen to the bone.

Chapter 25

When I went over the following Saturday, the fireplace was black, the whole room smelled of burned wood. Sitting by the cold grate, Aunt Dorothy was still talking. Her face with its bright mouth was startlingly pale in the room's dimness. In emerald green lounging pajamas, her red curls piled high, she was puffing on a cigarette with quick stabs that made her long diamond earrings shake. Quietly smoking and listening, Dr. Hatton with her short hair and plain skirt seemed blotted out. I took my time going by. Aunt Dorothy's voice was lowered, but hard and intense. On her lap she held her ginger ale glass in a clenched grip, as if she didn't mind if it broke her hand. There seemed something fabulous about her, after all, something larger than life, sitting there so white-faced with the portrait of the matador scowling down at her, and her own eyes shooting fiercely through the curling smoke, not even noticing as I passed.

I found Peggy in Helen Maria's room. She was brushing Rudy on the step of the French windows, which stood open to the warm early afternoon. Helen Maria was working at her desk. Her green eyes looked up.

"Is she still talking?"

I nodded. "And she sounds mad."

"That's the strain of not drinking. We'll all rejoice when she leaves tomorrow."

"I feel sorry for her," Peggy said, tenderly brushing one of Rudy's long ears. "She didn't have a good time."

"And why not? Because she makes one wish to escape her. That's why you're here in my room."

"I know. She was more fun when she drank."

Helen Maria turned around in her swivel chair. "She was never fun, Peggy. She was slaphappy, which you may have found appealing. I did not. I could only think that this nitwit might have been a front-rank painter." She pointed her pencil at me as I sat down on the step. "She was outstanding. An outstanding student at Pratt

137

Institute. I once had a drawing of hers, just a quick sketch of a boy's head, but masterful—"

"You've still got it," said Peggy. "I saw it on your desk."

"That's a lie! I threw it out long ago!"

Peggy was silent.

"Her future was vast. She betrayed it. She collected husbands and lovers and face creams and silly hats and became a drunken bore. Now she's sober and a worse bore. Estelle's about to collapse. Even Rudolph is half demented."

"She keeps calling him Doris," Peggy explained.

"Doris." Helen Maria sighed. "A dog from her golden youth. Everything is from her youth." She turned back to her work. "*Cependant,* why talk about her, she talks enough about herself."

"But you've got to give her credit," Peggy said. "It's hard to stop drinking. That's what Estelle says. She says Aunt Dorothy's a trooper."

Helen Maria turned a page. "I don't consider her a trooper. I consider her posthumous."

"Well, she tries to be nice. Like the living room. She didn't *try* to ruin it."

Helen Maria looked around from her book. "One doesn't need to try, Peggy, when one has degenerated to a tenth-rate talent. I'd like to turn that unspeakable bullfighter to the wall."

"Did she paint that?" I asked. "That's good!"

"Good! Have you studied the perspective? Have you drunk in the garish flesh tones? Have you seen how she's hidden the hands? Do you know why she's hidden the hands? Because she can no longer *manage* hands! That's how bad she is." Compressing her lips, she turned back to her work.

Dr. Hatton could be heard going along the hall to her room, released at last. Peggy took a pack of cards from the pocket of her shorts. We began playing a whispered game of blackjack.

The afternoon unfolded to a great hush, as if the smallest carrying sound might undo Aunt Dorothy's plans to leave. From Mr. Hatton's workshop below came an infrequent dim clunk. Now and then Helen Maria turned a page. Rudy lay like a dropped shoe. Slowly the sunlight deepened, throwing a gold wash across the cards.

I heard Helen Maria's chair squeak suddenly around. The door had opened to a crack. Aunt Dorothy's face peered in. "Hello, hello," she sang out, twisting through with her glass, not looking at all fierce now, but warmly sociable, completely at ease. Ice cubes clinked as she crossed the room. She held her glass cozily, rocking it gently, and plumped herself down in a chair as streaks of spilled liquid soaked into her emerald green bosom. Smiling all around, she clamped the glass between her knees and reached over to help herself to a pack of Fleetwoods on the desk. Helen Maria had risen. She stood stiffly by her chair, watching nervously as her aunt began a long, fumbling process of lighting up, twisting her face into a hard-breathing knot of absorption.

"You know, sweeties," she said, loud and slurred, finally getting the match blown out, "your mother's an angel. And I mean that. Your mother's an angel, putting up with all my *miserere*, and I've given out no little *miserere*, you don't have to tell me—don't even tell me. Here's a big fat apology for boring everybody to death." She lifted the glass with a slosh and drank. Peggy and I moved slowly inside and stood together near the wall.

"I was doing fine till Roger cracked," she said, lowering the glass. "I was doing great. We both were. What you wouldn't know, it's a lot easier if your sweetie's off it too." She took a deep drag on her cigarette, letting the smoke roll thickly out her nostrils. "But I should've known he'd crack. All right, so what? Estelle says Dorothy, you can do it on your own, yes Dorothy, you can! you just keep looking at those five solid months behind you!" She slid a forefinger slowly around the rim of her glass. "Your mother's an angel, the only thing is, she doesn't know anything." She gave her head a sudden shake. "But I don't want to talk about me, I want *you* to talk—"

"I think we should get Estelle," Helen Maria said in a small voice.

"Nonsense, let her nap. I wore her out. Wore everybody out. Jack's hiding, you don't have to tell me. All right, who cares? I mean that, it's all right, sit down and be comfy. Don't look so sepulchral. Don't take it so bloody serious." She finished her drink and set the glass unsteadily on the floor.

Helen Maria seated herself on the edge of her swivel

chair. She looked nervous, disapproving, yet her voice had a strange catch in it. "Aunt Dorothy, if that's your first drink, it's not fatal. One slip doesn't—"

"My fourth, sweetie. And don't lecture. I feel good, what's wrong with that? Sit down, you two!" She scribbled her cigarette at Peggy and me. We sat quickly on the floor.

"Now I want to hear everything, I mean that. God, just look at you, Helen Maria, so pretty and grown-up. And Peggy! So slim and darling. You're Hatton girls all right, I mean that for a fact, heartbreakers, it's in the genes. Who's your little friend with the hair?" She looked at me with warm, benevolent eyes. "What is it, sweetie, green? My God, it really is. Green hair . . . or is it just me?" And she gave a deep, rich laugh.

"No," I answered shyly. "That's what the Ferry Street drunks think too, but it's really green."

As soon as I spoke, I was stricken. Peggy looked horrified. Helen Maria took over swiftly.

"This is our friend, Suse, whom I believe you met the day of your arrival. The green you refer to is the result of swimming-pool chlorination."

Aunt Dorothy was still laughing, but silently, her fingers slowly rubbing her eyelids. Then she looked down at her lap with a sigh.

She looked old in the afternoon light. I could see that her red hair was tinted, dry and brittle-looking. Under the eyes hung soft, puffy bags. Around the mouth were lines that branched down to the jaw in spidery cracks. A white flake of cigarette paper was stuck to her lower lip. The earrings sent a soft spray of pink and blue specks across her powdered cheek, just where the mouth turned up faintly, ruefully, with its little tatter of paper stuck to the lip.

The earrings flashed. "You know what you've got, sweetie?" she said to Helen Maria. "Flair. That lilac dress is perfection, most redheads wouldn't dare, but you would, and I would. That's flair. You got that from me, not them, God knows. Oh they're darlings, but windbreakers, *wind*breakers!"

"Our parents are of a practical turn," said Helen Maria coldly.

"Oh I know, God love them," she smiled, mashing out her cigarette in the ashtray on her lap and with fumbling concentration lighting another. "You'll be one of the great beauties of your generation, sweetie, and Peggy too, it's all in the genes, you're lucky or you're not. Hatton women are lucky. Marvelous genes. *Thank* your genes. Thank you, thank you, I thank thee, God, for all shimmering things, for skies of firecolor coal . . . firecoaler color . . . oh hell, Hopkins anyway, who's talking about poetry, we're talking about you and Peggy, and I want to hear everything, everything. Peggy, tell me everything. . . ."

"Well. I'm in the eighth grade now. I'm getting good grades. And I'm Towel Supervisor in gym class."

"That's wonderful, Peggy. And you went on a diet, was it hard?"

"Not too. I wanted to look good."

"I was a little plump at your age, then the pounds just fell away like magic. I just kept getting prettier and prettier. A painter stopped me on the street once—"

"I know," Peggy murmured.

"I must have been, oh, fifteen, sixteen—"

"Sixteen."

"There were tears in his eyes. A face—"

"In a thousand."

"A face in a thousand. That's what he said." There was a faraway look in her eyes, which were a golden color. "You'll get used to it, people stopping you. Oh God, and in this town, crawling with soldiers—" A flush broke beneath the powder; the gold eyes burned. "Don't ever expect a minute to yourselves, can't even walk down the street—that's the price we pay!" She laughed, moving the ashtray around in her lap; then her eye caught the amber holder on the desk. "Ah, the old holder." She beamed.

"I use it on occasion," said Helen Maria.

"You shouldn't at all, sweetie, not yet. You're too young."

"I am a graduate student at the university."

Her aunt nodded, smiling at the amber gleam. "You know, I used that crazy thing in my heyday, you can't imagine how *outré* I felt, running around with my sophisticated holder . . . ah, God, those days were wonderful, and you've got it all before you . . . ."

"I don't intend to have a heyday."

"Good gracious, sweetie, I should hope you will—with

those looks? You're on top of the world, and I mean that, oh Christ do I mean that, this crud, you call it skin? I don't know what the hell it is!" Her fingers were digging deep into the folds of her face, to the bone. Then the hands returned with a plop to her lap. From between the ring-laden fingers rose a thick plume of smoke which made her eyes water. "I should've stayed in Mexico. All those damn trains, all those damn duffel bags, couldn't even move. Poor old broken-down Roger. Get old, you get old men. Can't keep up, nothing left, not a spark in bed. . . ."

My face broke into flame. I had never heard anyone speak this way, actually admitting they had experienced sex, inviting you to envision them in its dark clutch. Helen Maria's eyes dropped. Peggy's head was lowered.

But Aunt Dorothy was continuing along some more innocent track now. ". . . Evenings we used to take canoes out on the lake, a whole group of us . . . boys and girls . . . girls wore long dresses then, not like now . . . long, white, pretty dresses . . . I never wore a stitch underneath, my body was smooth as glass . . . I always slept naked. . . ."

Just cooling, my face began to burn again. Peggy glanced worriedly at her aunt.

"I used to lie there, and I'd cry . . . I don't know why, for the pleasure of it . . . I was all smooth and fresh, like a rose. . . ." She sat gazing at Helen Maria, her golden eyes soft. Slowly, awkwardly setting her ashtray aside, she got to her feet and wobbled over to her. Gently she tried to lift her niece's rigid chin.

"Exquisite," she murmured. "Exquisite. . . ."

And turning carefully, as if afraid of falling, but with intent, luminous eyes, she crossed over to us.

"And Peggy, a more flamboyant type . . . nobody has eyes like that. Ocean pools . . . men will drown in them. . . ."

I saw Peggy's face twitch with embarrassment. But her eyes were wide as she waited for more.

Aunt Dorothy tried to touch the nose with her finger, but couldn't get it in focus. "A retroussé nose is a charming, charming feature. Thank your genes, Peggy, thank your genes. . . ."

Finally, she turned to me. "You may do someday. . . ." She came wobbling closer. I could smell sweet, pungent perfume in waves. "Get rid of the hair . . . but first-rate bone structure . . . bone structure is very important . . . yes, this is first-rate bone structure. . . ."

I felt like a horse at auction, yet there was nothing cold in the way she spoke. In fact she seemed to be speaking to each of us from some passionate depth, some fierce burning center, and I knew now what Peggy had meant when she said her aunt seemed to "eat her up." The eyes were eating the flesh from my bones.

"You don't know what it's like yet," she said, turning, swaying a little. "None of you, you don't know what it's like, men wanting you . . . oh, God, they want you, they want you, your breasts, your—"

"I must protest, Aunt Dorothy!" said Helen Maria, standing up.

"Oh, shut up, sweetie, relax . . . that's your problem." She took a few uneven steps. "Enjoy your youth, for God's sake, it won't last . . . I mean that, here's somebody who knows. . . . All right, all right, what am I crabbing about? I've had a good long haul, haven't I?"

And all at once, noiselessly, she began to cry.

Rudy came waddling in from the garden, but she didn't call him Doris, she didn't call him anything. With her face squeezed into a thousand lines, she looked older than ever, but the horrible thing was that she seemed like a child. Helpless and asking and needing, with her hands hanging open at her sides and the tears pouring down her face. It was that terrible turnabout again, the grown ones suddenly powerless and needing, making your heart pound with the wrongness of it. It made me hate her, and I fought down the pity that banged along with my heartbeats. How long was she going to stand there anyway, blubbering because she was old?

Helen Maria went over to her. "It's all right, Aunt Dorothy," she said with that odd catch once again in her voice. And she smiled, the only truly kind and gentle smile I had ever seen on her face. Putting her arm around the older woman's shoulder, she helped her from the room.

Chapter 26

Aunt Dorothy was sent to a clinic in San Francisco. Every day in study hall Peggy dashed off a cheery little note ending with a line of Xs and several plump hearts. Sometimes she would ask me to add a few words, but I would only scrawl, "Hello, from Suse." I wanted to forget Aunt Dorothy.

So, apparently, did Helen Maria. She never spoke of that awful day in her room, never mentioned her aunt's name. Then one day I saw that she had pinned above her desk a small and very delicate sketch of a young boy. I glanced over at her but saw from her severe expression that I was to make no comment, so I didn't.

Whatever became of haggard, roulette-playing Roger in his beautiful blue blazer, no one knew. After Aunt Dorothy was sent away, he borrowed money from the Hattons to pay his hotel bill. Then, leaving town, the bill unpaid, he was heard of no more.

Mama and Dad and I waited for Peter's first overseas letter. When it came, Mama read it aloud to me after school. Then I read it myself. Then, when Dad came home, Mama read it aloud again, even before he changed his clothes. Then he read it himself. Then I read it again. It said October 23, Somewhere in England. A couple of words in the letter had been censored, not scissored out, like the Germans did, but laid over with a square of black. It was cold and rainy, he said, but the countryside was beautiful, very green with rolling hills and big hedges along the roads. There were about censored men in the camp, it was a good size. He was training as a machine gunner. They hadn't gotten a pass yet, so he hadn't met any English people, it was still like being in Camp Crowder. He was looking forward to getting out and seeing London, it was censored miles away. It was a long letter and said a lot more, including that he missed us and thought of us often.

144

The heat loosened, blew away, leaving the sky glassy and high. The wind crowded the yellow leaves in bursts along the gutters and twanged eerily in the garrison storm fence. Behind the fence the soldiers were in warm jackets now. For months they'd gone around with their sleeves rolled up; sometimes you even saw them in undershirts, dog tags glistening in their chest hair. Peggy said chest hair was all right if there wasn't too much. But too much was better than too little. It was repulsive if there was none. Still, it shouldn't be a mat. Now she wouldn't have to worry about all this, with everyone covered up.

She could concentrate on other important things. She was jitterbugging at the noon dances now, and she got up the nerve to ask home a girl Towk to help polish up her steps. She seemed to like this Towk, whose name was Bev—a girl as neat and pleasant and dull as Peggy herself was becoming—and often, instead of hurrying home to study after school, she went off together with Bev. But she kept her grades up; she seemed to have energy for everything. In study hall—where she no longer dashed off her daily greeting to Aunt Dorothy, who had gone back to Mexico City—she was a demon of application, reading with knit brows, scribbling down notes, chewing her pencil. I no longer whispered or offered gum. I sat sketching my exploding Zeros, and sometimes it was Bev who was blown in small bits from the cockpit.

The end of November I had my thirteenth birthday party. Peggy showed no interest in grabbing Dumb Donny, she received Eudene's elbow smash with a grim sigh, and when I blew out my candles with a silent wish (every Jap dead and the war over), all my guests clapped exuberantly except Peggy. She ate no cake and left before the festivities were over, pleading tons of homework.

After that it was all downhill. She won an interclass essay contest on the meaning of patriotism, she was invited to Bev's Christmas party, and when school resumed after the holidays, she had been elevated to another class. She was gone, bodily, unbelievably.

Nineteen forty-four. I walked around downtown in the heavy fog. It seemed that the whole war, even with an in-

145

vasion in the works, even with Berlin bombed daily, was a dead end. It would go on forever, getting nowhere. Already it was as if it had been with us always. Streets had never known lights at night. Barrage balloons had always hung over the bay. The most ancient, permanent-looking structure in town was Sheriff O'Toole's stained and hardened wall of sandbags.

In the hall I would catch a glimpse of Peggy walking along talking and laughing with her new friends. She looked completely relaxed, all her furious work behind her, and in passing she would send a warm but distracted smile in my direction. I didn't smile back. We still had gym together, and there she even came over a few times and tried to be nice, but I rebuffed her. This pleasant, groomed thing had never inspired any interest in me except for the old Peggy who still breathed inside it, and now old Peggy had breathed her last. I saw my beloved friend drowned, lying fat and forgotten on the ocean floor.

With an elective to choose, I had taken up the snare drum. I found myself soothed and comforted in music class, which was hardly a class at all, just a few students scattered through the dim wings of the auditorium stage, practicing in solitude. As I sat at the mottled drumhead and lost myself in a long, steady tattoo, I felt strangely content. Under dim pools of light the floor shone scuffed. Music stands glinted, their ink-spattered scores the color of honey. Against the wall a long row of folded chairs disappeared into the darkness, where a jumble of dusty props could be made out. The drum roll mixed with the strange twilight seclusion, as if time had stopped, leaving me free of all worldly cares.

I resented the music teacher's intrusion. From his tiny office he would emerge, reluctantly, to hear our lessons. When he sat down, pulling up a chair with an old flattened cushion on it, you had the feeling you were about to cause him pain. Inclining his face against two fingers—it was a heavy-boned face, lined and sallow—he would sigh, "No, straighten your wrists," and sit back with an impatient nod. His eyes were small, pale blue, distracted. But his nostrils were great, cavernous, tragic. He wore a wine-colored velvet jacket over a soft shirt, and foreign-looking shoes, woven, with open toes, very old and scuffed. He had spent a year in Europe before the war, and it was rumored that he was composing a symphony entitled *Europana*. It was no wonder, with such a background, that his hands went to his ears as he approached a beginner scraping on a violin or that he was not amused when a boy got his thumb hopelessly stuck in the intricacies of a French horn. Yet in a way Mr. Kerr seemed a kind person. He smiled when he saw you in the hall, and he was a surprisingly mild grader, maybe to make up for his deep sighs and curt nods.

After school, a black beret on his head, he paced outside, waiting for his wife and a large sheepdog to fetch him in an old wood-paneled station wagon. Before the car even stopped, he leaped inside and, in a tumult of barks and grinding gears, was borne swiftly away. I never glimpsed the wife—she drove too fast—but it was rumored that she sang *Lieder*, whatever that was, and wore purple eye shadow.

In the dim light Mr. Kerr's scalp shone through thin strands of brown hair, but at the sides the hair was thick and uncut, mixed with gray, curling over his ears. His hands were very big, with freckles and reddish hair on their backs. It was said he could span an octave and a half. He told me I had a feeling for the drums and began spending more time with me. No longer could I indulge myself in my tattoo, protracted to the point of trance. I had to learn notes, beats, measures. Mr. Kerr's foot thumped as he marked my timing; often his voice broke in angrily. I listened and learned, afraid to do otherwise. When my tormentor honored me with a smile, I expressed my resentment by not smiling back. He never seemed to notice. There was much he didn't notice. One day he remarked, "Girls don't usually take up drums," as if he had only that moment noticed I wore a skirt. Boys, girls, to him they were all the same: short people affixed to musical instruments.

When I went to the Hatton house now, it was to visit Helen Maria. She was deeply disappointed in Peggy, whose burst of academic passion had fizzled out to an unremarkable B average and who now spent most of her time entertaining friends, trying out dance steps, and fussing over her wardrobe. The genius's efforts to prod me into accomplishment were now resumed. When I told

147

her I was taking the drums, she said there was no future in it.

"I don't care about the future. You ought to see where we practice, it's backstage. It's an interesting place, it's got a dramatic feeling. And our music teacher is living in sin."

"Free love isn't sinful. You should purge yourself of these narrow attitudes. How do you know?"

"Well. He's supposed to be married, but he doesn't wear a wedding ring."

"That means nothing. Neither does Jack."

"Maybe not, but I know Mr. Kerr's living in sin—I mean free love."

"How do you know?" she asked again.

But I could come up with nothing. In fact, until my remark popped out, I had never thought of Mr. Kerr's love life, and I was surprised that I held an opinion on it. It gave me an uneasy feeling, to be carrying an idea around without even knowing it.

"You shouldn't spread rumors about people. It's immoral."

"Why? If there's nothing wrong with free love?"

"Any untrue statement is immoral, it doesn't matter what it is. Only the truth is moral. Even a child knows that."

She was irritated because she was so interested in free love and would have loved to hear about someone who was actually doing it. But I was glad to leave the subject.

Chapter 27

Having nothing better to do one rainy noon in February, Eudene and I wandered into the auditorium where the orchestra was rehearsing. Jacket off and shirt sleeves rolled up, Mr. Kerr was working very hard conducting "Song of India." Hunched over, arms outspread, he waved his baton in one hand while with the other he made deep, scooping motions, as if to drag the musicians bodily from their chairs.

After a while Eudene yawned and scratched her sauerkraut hair. "Who wants to listen to that?"

"It's not bad," I objected, watching.

She smashed me with her elbow. "Let's go."

But my eyes were fastened, as if mesmerized, to Mr. Kerr's arms. They were hard-looking, hairy arms, and as they raised higher, the shirt stretched taut across a broad, muscular back.

"I'm going," said Eudene.

I beat her to it, getting up and walking hastily out the door.

"Have you got a cigarette?" I asked.

"Sure."

"Could we have a puff somewhere?"

"Sure."

I felt uneasy, not myself. In movies a smoke always helped.

The next day after my lesson, the sheet music happened to slip off my stand as Mr. Kerr departed. It fluttered down next to the chair he had used, and to reach it more easily, I slid over onto his cushion. As my thighs sank into the unexpected den of body heat, a keen sensation shop up my spine, an exciting, tingling rush of heat that seemed to envelop and melt my heart. I sat immobile, staring straight ahead. It was an intensely pleasurable feeling, but its very intensity was alien, shocking.

It lasted only a moment. I scrambled back into my own chair, feeling frightened and looking nervously around. In the shadowy distance, Mr. Kerr was instructing the boy with the French horn. I looked at him a long time, as he stood there sallow-faced and irritable in the dim light. Then my foot shot out, kicking his chair away from me.

All through the day I worried. It had happened. My body had cried out to someone I didn't even like. Who next? What next? What if I carried inside me a dark, secret weakness for any warm chair a man had sat in?

By the time the last class was dismissed I had decided to try something. Setting my jaw, I slid into the still-warm seat of the boy opposite me. Nothing. I tested the next one. Nothing. I stood up, relieved.

But they were only schoolboys. Mr. Kerr was a grown

149

male, and that must be the difference. What if I was powerless against the body heat of all grown males—half the chairs of the world?

Throwing on my slicker, I hurried out into the rain and walked directly to the Hatton house. I knew that Helen Maria wasn't home today and that I had no excuse to go inside, but I opened the door and stepped into the hall. The hush of the rooms was so great that I went into the Dungeon tiptoeing. There I took off my slicker and sat down on the chesterfield, which still stood at its careless angle from the wall. I gripped my hands in my lap. The rain blew and spattered against the long dim windows.

After a while the front door opened. I stiffened at the sound of Peggy's voice. Helen Maria said Peggy never came home from school early anymore—why of all days did she have to today? A sense of criminal guilt gripped me, a housebreaker, and I fought down the urge to jump up and hide behind the chesterfield.

She came through the archway with Bev and another girl and stopped. I looked at the three faces, each with a little bud of lipstick at its center.

"Hi," Peggy said, in a neutral tone, and I knew she thought I had come to break into her charmed circle.

"I'm waiting for Helen Maria," I said stiffly.

"She won't be home till about nine tonight."

"I know. I'll wait."

She looked surprised. It was a ridiculous thing to say, but I couldn't think of anything else.

"Sure, if you want to," she said, and paused uncertainly, as if she felt she must ask me to come along with the others to her room.

"I'll wait here," I said more stiffly. "I want to read." I took a magazine from the side table.

"Okay," Peggy nodded, and they moved off. The two other girls smiled at me, nicely enough.

Watching them go out, I felt a sudden certainty that for all their grown-up ways they were more innocent than I, that they would be horrified to know the real purpose of my visit, that their lives were smooth, clear, and virtuous, deeply to be envied.

The magazine was a podiatrics journal. I put it back and resumed my wait, listening to Sinatra crooning through Peggy's closed door.

It was at least another hour and a half before the front door opened again. Mr. Hatton came into the Dungeon, the newspaper under his arm.

I cleared my throat. "Hello, Mr. Hatton."

He glanced over at me. "Hello, Suse," he murmured, opening the paper as he continued toward his room.

I watched him passing. One more step and it would be too late. I sat forward, squeezing my knees. "Could I talk with you?"

"Hm?" His eyes were on the paper.

I had planned what I would say. I spoke quickly. "I'd like to talk about your profession."

"Hm?"

"Would you—sit down for a minute?"

I could hardly get the words out; they seemed on top of everything else so rude and demanding. But with only a slight frown he came over, sitting down at my side. I had never seen him so close. He had many freckles. Even the bags under his eyes were freckled.

"I want to be a marine architect."

"Good. Fine. You'll like it."

He seemed already on the verge of rising.

"But I'm not strong in math."

"Got to be strong in math. Work on it."

"What about—what about English?"

"Got to know what you're reading, of course."

I ransacked my brain. "I like to read. I read a lot, because I like to read."

"Good. Always a good thing."

His eyes had strayed back to the newspaper in his hands.

"It sounds like a good profession," I said. "I know I'll like it."

"Got to like what you do."

"I think I'll be good at it."

But he was no longer responding. I feared an immediate departure. My eyes dropped to the headline. *Cassino Battle Rages!*

"They should have invaded in the north," I said.

"Too easy," he muttered, as if to himself. "This way they'll divert the whole German force for months." He slapped the headline. "Is it worth it, though? Look at the losses already. This monastery is something awful. A fortress."

"I know. It's held out for a month already."

151

"God-awful."

"I hope they shoot Mussolini."

He nodded, reading on. I hoped he would read for a long time. But after a few minutes he began rising.

"They should have gone in at Genoa. Don't you think so?"

He nodded again, but I could keep him no longer. Still reading, he shambled off. It had been long enough, though. I touched the cushion; it was sufficiently warmed. Holding my breath, I slid over and sank into its sultry depths. Nothing, nothing, and more nothing.

I sat quietly for a while, at peace. I didn't have to worry about every male in the world. Just Mr. Kerr, which narrowed it down to something manageable.

Chapter 28

The next day when Mr. Kerr sat down by me at practice, I averted my eyes. When I had to answer something he said, I addressed the drum. This was how I would manage it. He would not exist.

But by the end of the week I was curious to know if his spell was still in force, and when he left me, I moved over to the cushion on his chair. As fearsomely as the first time, the strange feeling thrilled up my spine, spread piercingly into my chest, melted my heart.

He stood regarding the finger work of a bassoonist.

He was like a bomber that blew everything up and flew off high and safe. I stood up in the gloom and for the second time gave his chair a hard kick. A chair was no longer a chair; a teacher wasn't a teacher; your own insides were no longer your own insides. I had an odd thought then, not odd in itself, but out of place. If I had gone along to that Jap house in the outskirts, there wouldn't have been any slashed furniture or running faucets, no such puniness. I would have drenched the rooms with gasoline, locked the couple inside, and burned the place to the ground. The black, sticky skull sticking out of the tank. It made me feel better, thinking of this.

"What's that geranium doing sticking out of the mailbox?" Dad asked one night at bedtime as he was putting the hook on the screen door.

"A geranium?" Mama asked.

"How funny," I said, blushing. "I wonder who could have put it there."

"Probably some neighborhood kid," Dad said, and went out and removed it. But it was I myself who had stuck it there, on a sudden impulse, for the mailman. It was he who brought us news of Karla and Peter, and it seemed so decent of him; he was so dependable, like the Pony Express. He deserved at least a geranium.

The news he brought from Karla was that an agent from the Disney studios in Hollywood had been up to the institute, and she was thinking that she might go down there. Not if she had to sit at a factory belt drawing the same rabbit's tail over and over, but if she could do some original work. She would have to look into it.

Peter had been promoted from buck private to PFC, and he had been to London twice now. He had been to a music hall review, a Shakespearian play, and Westminster Abbey. He wrote about the red double-decker buses and how people called you "chappie" and "luv." He said the city was leveled in places, big sections of rubble, and how there were props all over the place holding up sides of buildings. He wrote how Big Ben sounded and how it was to hear it as you walked along the Thames at night, in the fog.

I told Helen Maria about the Thames; it was so poetic, she would like it. But she seemed sad. And I realized, looking at her face, that missing out on Oxford was not just an ordinary big disappointment, it was the greatest disappointment of her life.

I hesitated, embarrassed to offer comfort. "You'll get there afterwards, Helen Maria. After the war."

"Oh yes, I suppose so."

I didn't add: if ever it ends.

Mr. Kerr's power began spreading from his chair. The current flashed through me when he took my wrist or if his shoulder happened to graze mine. It left me red-faced, staring at the floor. Often he did not take my wrist or graze my shoulder, and then I had to brush against him, to know if things continued as fearfully as before, which they did.

One night in bed, as I was drifting off, I had a kind of dream. I was walking along a road. It was a warm summer night. I came to a large Parisian mansion and knocked on the door. Mr. Kerr opened it. His jacket was off, and his shirt sleeves were rolled up. A full moon hung overhead. Faint music drifted through the door.

"What beautiful music," I said. "Who is playing?"

"Not my wife, it is a phonograph. I am alone now; she has gone away."

"That is too bad."

"Not at all."

And now the blue eyes looked deep into mine as he slowly extended his hand and said in soft, low tones, "Come in, Suse."

It was sublime; it was terrifying. I burned the whole thing up in a flaming vision of the Jap house.

From then on, every night, I had this fantasy. It never progressed beyond the soft, low invitation to come in, but it was enough, it was far too much, and I always ended it with the roaring destruction of the Jap house.

Outside the French windows the rain poured down. A cozy blaze crackled in the fireplace. Helen Maria had made hot wine, and as she poured it, I thought she looked unusually happy, almost to the point of bursting. But I had something important to ask, and I got it in before she could speak.

"How's Mr. Tatanian?"

"Who? Don't even remind me. It must have been the heat."

She was free! Released! It was what I had hoped she would say, yet now that she had said it I was disappointed.

"Love should be eternal," I said.

"That is boring."

"But you can't forget him, just like that."

"Why not? He's in the dreary past." She handed me my wine and sat down on the Persian spread with hers. "Waste no regrets on Mr. Tatanian. He's quite content collecting his little tickets."

Little tickets—he who had inspired a poem to the nation of Armenia. It was not as it should be.

"Now, listen, do you want to hear something smashing?" she set her cup aside and crossed her legs tailor fashion, putting her hands on her hips.

"All right," I said.

"I'm moving to Berkeley."

I looked, shocked, at the radiant face.

"In April, when I turn seventeen. Jack and Estelle have agreed. Just a boardinghouse, it won't be the same as having my own apartment, but I'll be independent." She screwed a cigarette into her amber holder, lit it—but without the flourish; she no longer made those grandiose sweeps—and blew the smoke out through a smile. "I'll do exactly as I please. I absolutely can't wait to leave."

I looked over at the fireplace.

She was silent for a moment. "Listen, Suse . . . I want to tell you something. You've been my only friend . . . we're true friends. I'll miss you."

I looked away from the fireplace, at her face, which was embarrassed and severe. I couldn't speak; I had nothing at my command except an overflowing heart and a tight throat.

She took a brisk sip of her wine. "When I'm settled in, you must come down and visit. You can take the train, and I'll meet you at the depot. I'll show you the campus, and we'll eat out at a restaurant. Maybe you can even stay overnight."

"That will be nice," I said, clearing my throat.

"Yes, we must look forward to that."

When would the invasion begin? Dad didn't know. The newspapers didn't know. No one knew. That was the whole point, it had to be kept a secret. Waiting, waiting, always the waiting. And Peter a machine gunner. If only he would get the flu again, so he would be flat on his back when the others left. Except they were brothers of someone too, thousands and thousands of them. Impossible to hope for thousands of cases of flu. And if it did miraculously happen, there would be no invasion, no end of the war. However you looked at it, there was no way out.

"No way out," I said, looking into the rain.

"What are you, talking to yourself?"

155

"I guess." I took the butt Eudene held out. We were standing under a pepper tree at noon, having a puff.

"When you talk to yourself," she said, "it means you've lost your marbles."

"I lost them a long time ago, Eudene."

She began singing, "I lost my marbles at the stage door canteen. . . ."

At least I had Eudene. In a way she was like old fat Peggy. She made life seem less serious.

But overnight Eudene changed. She sat at her desk in silence. At lunchtime she didn't eat. She didn't roll her eyes and smash you in the ribs. She didn't want to talk. After a few days I wrote a note and put it before her on her desk. "What is the matter?" She glanced at it, chin in hand, and continued brooding.

One day she didn't come to class. The next morning she wasn't there either. By noontime I had decided to go to her house after school. Getting my lunch from my locker, I turned to find Peggy beside me. I felt a shock of joy, for this was old drowned Peggy raised from the depths, standing gracelessly on heavily planted feet, hair carelessly combed, mouth untouched by lipstick. She had come back.

"This awful thing happened, Suse . . . I think you'd like to know. Aunt Dorothy died."

So that was the reason for her appearance. It wasn't that old Peggy had come back.

"We just heard this morning. . . ." The eyes suddenly squeezed into slits, shone with water. "She committed suicide."

I looked at the tight mouth, the chin trembling. Why did she come to me? She never bothered with me otherwise. "What'd she do, hang herself?"

Peggy looked down at the floor, trying to speak. "Pills," she said in a little gasp, and kept looking at the floor. "I don't really remember, but when she was here, I don't think I was really mean or anything?" The wet eyes looked up.

"No, I suppose not. You just ignored her. You wouldn't talk to her. I suppose it wasn't really mean, except she must have thought it was."

The eyes looked down again.

"You treated her like a bore. I'm only telling you what you told me."

She didn't look up again. Turning, she walked slowly away. I felt a blow of remorse but stood firm as she made her way to the girls' lavatory, no doubt to lock herself in a stall and cry. I had only spoken the truth. The truth was moral; the truth was just. And Peggy, the door swinging shut behind her, would have to live with it.

I rang the bell and waited. I waited a long time. Shell Hill towered behind my back, dark and cindery in the rain, its black storage tanks glistening. Poor Eudene, one direct hit and there wouldn't be a piece left of her on the face of the earth.

But solid and real, she opened the door, standing in a threadbare bathrobe, looking sick and tired out and not happy to see me. But she let me in and walked heavily down the hall to where she lived.

It was just one room, huge, cold, and gray as an aerodrome. But there were the Parisian windows, and I went over to them. The bay was silt yellow, broken everywhere by whitecaps. Overhead the dark clouds merged and shifted, all at once exposing a cauldron so glaring that all the raindrops were lit and broke against the glass like diamonds.

Eudene took no notice of the splendor. Crawling under the blankets of a ratty chesterfield, she looked at me uneasily, her face chalk white, darkly discolored under the eyes. She said she had the flu.

It was an odd visit. She kept saying she didn't feel like talking and I couldn't stay, yet she talked more than I had ever heard her, mostly about her grandmother, how religious she was, how she kept screaming about hell and damnation. I didn't even know she lived with her grandmother. I thought she lived with parents like everyone else.

Abruptly she said she wasn't coming back to school. She was moving away.

"Why?"

She only glared at me. She was terribly nervous and irritable, and the whole time I was there she kept asking if I believed in hell and damnation. I kept saying no, and she kept saying, "What do you know about it?" It was useless to open my mouth. I looked around the room, so

157

big and bare, with its gray floor like an ice rink. Poor people were supposed to live in tiny cramped rooms. It was a fact of life, and a logical one, because they kept warmer that way. I looked at a framed picture of Jesus on the wall.

"Where is she anyway, your grandmother?"

"The arsenal. She works there."

I couldn't imagine a grandmother working anywhere; they were too old. But this one was apparently different. She thought she looked like Sonja Henie, Eudene said—and here came the old bellow of laughter, but black with scorn—and she was getting remarried next month. "She said I could keep living with her when she got married, and I never even *wanted* to! But now I want to, but she says no because she's so godalmighty religious and pissed off."

"About what?"

"Nothing!"

I was getting tired of the visit, but I stayed because Eudene looked so sick and unhappy. I sat listening to the rain battering the windows, and to a dreary ping-ping from the icebox.

"What'd you come here for?" she asked. "Just to spy?"

"Spy? What d'you mean? I just came to see how you were—"

"Well, this is how I am!" she cried, sitting upright and grabbing herself all over, as if plucking a chicken. "Go on, tell them all you seen me and what I look like, I don't give a shit!"

"What d'you mean?"

"You're so stupid!"

"*You're* the stupid one! I can't even figure out what you're talking about, that's how much sense you don't make!"

"Maybe I don't want to make sense!"

She was absolutely a lost cause. I sighed and shook my head.

Eudene had a trembling look around her mouth, as if she were going to vomit. A chair stood next to her with a chipped enamel basin on it, and she pulled it closer. She leaned over the basin, holding her greasy sauerkraut hair back with both hands.

I stood up quickly. "Get better soon!" I called, hurrying to the door. Closing it behind me, I had a sense of having done something wrong, or at least of not having done something right.

In the hall I saw a woman coming through the front door, closing a dripping umbrella. She wore overalls and a lumber jacket and had a lunch pail under her arm. As we passed, she threw me a brief glance. Her face was like a walnut, topped by dark-streaked yellow bangs. She didn't look religious, she didn't look like Sonja Henie, and she didn't look like anybody's grandmother, but she turned in at Eudene's door.

That night in bed it all came to me. But how could a member of the eighth grade be pregnant, even sweaty, big-bosomed Eudene? It was one thing to suspect her of doing fleshly things with men. That at least was alive in a dark mysterious way. But being pregnant was like being dead. You saw them all over town, war wives, very young, with protruding bellies and a toddler already whining and dragging at their skirts. Their faces were deaf-looking, like cows' faces; all they did was shop, cook, change diapers, and drink coffee in a pablum-smeared kitchen with some other young mommy just as deadly washed-up as themselves. They were so dreary that when you saw them on the street, you made a detour around them, thankful that you were a free, high-stepping schoolgirl.

Eudene's grandmother was right to scream damnation at her. Eudene had let down the eighth grade, she had let down youth and freedom everywhere. And if she had to sit for nine long months in an unwed mothers' home, with an ugly uniform over her big filthy brassiere and ballooning belly, eating thin soup and fearing the devil's pitchfork, it was only just.

But I thought of something Aunt Dorothy had said to Helen Maria. Don't be so hard on people. I was hard on people too. Eudene. Peggy. Aunt Dorothy herself. I had pushed Aunt Dorothy so completely out of my mind that I hadn't even felt bad about her death. But think of her doing that, cramming those pills down her throat, and now she was lying cold under a mortician's sheet in Mexico City. Or maybe she was already buried, in the dry Mexican ground. Inside her coffin it was black, not one gleam left of a white dress or silver lake at twilight.

159

I saw her standing in Helen Maria's doorway in her navy blue suit and small white hat. I wanted to see her loud and horrible, sloshing her whiskey glass around. It hurt me to think of her laughing and hugging Peggy in the doorway. I wondered if she was buried in those clothes; would she turn to dust in her navy blue suit? But she was already dust when she came; she swallowed all those pills because she'd been for a long time broken and burned-out inside, a heap of rubble. And a terrible thought suddenly came to me—it was like that day in the backyard, a frightening, hurtful rippling out, some kind of knowledge that would never end, now that it had begun. For what if war wasn't only bombs exploding, and blood and screams, but someone smiling in a doorway?

Chapter 29

I primed myself to apologize to Peggy the next day, but she looked recovered. She must have found something to ease her pain, probably those little get-well notes, which had required neither time nor thought nor even the neat, clear hand she used for her lessons.

As for Helen Maria, when I said I was sorry about Aunt Dorothy, she gave a curt nod. I only stayed a minute.

Now it was early April, and Helen Maria was moving. Inside the sacred chamber stood a black battered trunk that must have belonged to the grandmother in the days when she had hiked across the Dolomites with an alpenstock. On brittle stickers, faded to the palest honey color, you could read the names of foreign cities. Paris, Rome, Berlin, London. How small and quiet they seemed on these stickers, cities that screamed at you now in black headlines.

Helen Maria was looking everywhere for her toothbrush. "I've packed it—all right, it stays there! I'm not unpacking a thing!"

She was all set to go, although she wasn't leaving till

the next morning. Her coat and purse lay ready on a chair. Book-filled boxes covered the floor. The walls were bare; the desk was cleared. She walked among the boxes, taking out a book, putting it back, lighting a cigarette, restlessly smoothing her hair.

I sat down on a box.

She talked a great deal. She talked about her boardinghouse. It was three blocks from campus. Her room was right under the eaves, marvelous. The house-mother was a retired art instructor with a braid, a woman of the world, marvelous. Finally, all her fellow roomers were marvelous. Independent spirits like herself, and some were even foreign, refugees from Central Europe who had gotten out before the war, women with burning eyes and hair drawn back in a bun like Rosa Luxemburg. . . .

They couldn't have been through much if they had gotten out before the war. In fact, how could you have refugees without a war? And who was Rosa Luxemburg? But I no longer asked questions, so I said nothing.

And there was a lovely large living room where one could entertain male callers, and she had seen some interesting callers the day she was there. "One in particular, with jet black hair and blue eyes."

"Four-F, or he'd be in the Army."

"It's no concern of mine if he has kidney stones or a deviated septum; that's not what I'm interested in." She paced, smoking. On her face was a look of daring that I had never seen before. Again she swept her hair back. "I think in the evenings it must be quite nice entertaining there. It may be rather pleasant."

It probably would be.

"Of course I'll miss Jack and Estelle."

"You will?" I was surprised.

"Of course. Peggy I shall not miss."

We listened for a moment to Frank Sinatra's croons seeping down the hall. Helen Maria resumed her pacing. I envied her her restlessness, her coat thrown over a chair. A new and perfect life, starting tomorrow morning.

She began rearranging her books in the boxes. It was clear that she didn't want a long visit. I got up, and suddenly I was overcome by an old, dog-eared, stupid hope that I hadn't had for a long time. Now that we were parting, she would at last hold out the golden word.

"I'll write when I'm settled in," she said, coming with me to the door, "and we can arrange for your visit. A Saturday morning, maybe, and you can stay the weekend. I'll put up a cot in my room. You'll love the place."

No, I wouldn't. I didn't like anything about it. But looking at the animated green eyes, I said, "I'm glad you're so happy."

"I could be happier." She blew smoke sharply through her nostrils. "Things happen. That you don't expect. Like someone dying. Oh, I don't know, it makes you think. Just that you can't go back and do things over. That's all." She shrugged, then smiled and shook my hand. "Take good care of yourself, Suse."

Still waiting, I stood looking at her.

"*Lebe wohl*," she said softly, closing the door.

The German dictionary at the library yielded up *lebe wohl* after some searching. But it wasn't the golden word. It meant farewell.

"Come in."

"Come in, Suse."

"Come in, Suse, my great love."

"You are here at last, my beloved Suse!"

"Suse, you are here! Come in, come in, my heart is bursting. Your hair, your eyes, your passionate soul. I must have you! The storm of a kiss!"

Here, in this moment, the rest of the world is gone. All that exist are Mr. Kerr's blue eyes and low, throbbing voice. There is no end of variation on his welcoming speech. I add a word, take it out, put in others. The speech grows longer each night, richer, more passionate. Where have these glorious words hidden in me, to suddenly pour forth like this now? I stand breathless, I dissolve in his moonlit eyes, and then I destroy everything in flames because it is too much.

The days are warm now, with high fluffy clouds. On Sunday afternoons Dad and I putter around the victory garden, where we've planted new seeds. The creek is clear and gurgling, its banks green and glossy, alive with white butterflies. Behind the garrison storm fence the soldiers are always stopping and stretching, lifting their faces to the sun, as if they had come out of a cave. Downtown, Sheriff O'Toole's sandbags have dried out from the rain, servicemen disgorge from winter bars and pool halls, shopgirls again walk arm in arm in thin flowered dresses. The streets are crowded and lively. Cassino has fallen; the Russians have broken through to Rumania. Spring will bring victory, maybe even without an invasion.

One day, in the course of my lesson, Mr. Kerr touches my wrist and I feel nothing. Afterward I plump down on his cushion. Nothing. I look across the room at him, stunned by this loss. He stands listening to someone scraping on a violin, having done all this to me and now pulling it all away. I feel a fury mounting, yet I am somehow thinking of his nostrils, which are not only too big but hairy. The fury sinks; I feel oddly quiet and a little embarrassed. And gradually, as I continue my practicing, I feel relief and joy. I am free.

A few days later, going through the gym entrance, I collide with the boys' coach. I've never given him a second glance, a boring-looking man with slicked-back brown hair, but in one second I am again lost, the old thrill zinging through my body. Doomed, I stare at his back as he passes on.

Chapter 30

It was Coach Thaxter who now opened the moonlit door. His brown eyes burned into mine.

Then one day Mr. Villendo, the science teacher, happened to touch my hand in returning a paper and electrified me. Mr. Villendo had black double-sized eyes behind thick glasses, and now it was his black double-sized eyes that burned from the door.

Soon after, Mr. Lewis brushed past me with his heavy Gestapo tread, and I felt a world-weary acceptance along with the piercing thrill and the evaporation of Mr. Villendo.

How unclear Mr. Lewis had been until this moment, just a gray suit and a nasty expression. But now I beheld his thick smooth brown hair and dark gray eyes and wide firm mouth. When he opened the moonlit door that night, he spoke in a tragic way:

"Ever since I first saw you, you have sank deeper and deeper into me. You may think I am a harsh person, but I am not; I am misinterpreted. I am a lonely, desperate man, and I long to smother you in the storm of a kiss!"

How strange that it was Mr. Lewis of all people who was the real one, who struck me deepest. For he did. In class, behind my book, I pressed my mouth to the back of my hand, ignoring the taste of green lavatory soap, and imagined that it was the wide, firm lips of Mr. Lewis that I was kissing so hard. Whenever I saw Peggy walking down the hall with some pimpled, thin-necked boy, I pitied her that she thought there was anything there worth having. Could she really want to hear his puny thoughts, feel his weak flutter of a kiss? If that was all she aspired to, I pitied her very much. I felt out of place with these dull and simple students. I felt dark, wild, as if I belonged in a forest. What tepid interludes Coach Thaxter and Mr. Villendo had been; how unbelievable my long encounter with Mr. Kerr.

I could look Mr. Kerr full in the face now, speak normally, smile. I even came to like him, and I felt a great sympathy for him that he was sitting here in the Mendoza Junior High School instead of standing to an ovation at Carnegie Hall. They said he had been working on his *Europana* symphony for seven years now. Probably he would never finish it, he was too old. It was just a habit he couldn't stop, like wearing his velvet jacket and foreign shoes. In the evenings he sat bent over an old piano, slowly writing and crossing out notes with his fountain pen, while his wife and her purple eyelids brought him strong cups of tea to stimulate his tired mind. When it was late, they turned off the light and went to bed. No moonlight shone on their door. It was a small ordinary house, with small ordinary night sounds outside. A dog barking, a freight train wailing. It would never be any different for him.

It was different for Mr. Lewis. He blazed with glory. He made me desperately happy and sometimes so desperately sad that I thought of killing myself. I didn't think of a bottle of pills and a coffin. I thought of unholy music and long-flamed candles and of turning an antique dagger in my fingers, and these thoughts poured into my love for Mr. Lewis, bringing it a dimension so fateful and sublime that I could hardly breathe for the pounding of my heart as I stalked him through the halls.

After school he climbed into a green coupe and drove away. I could not follow him and knew nothing about him. His name wasn't even in the phone book. He was too remote; he filled me with frustration. I longed to be in his class, to hear his voice, to watch him move, to turn homework in so that our naked hands would meet in electrifying contact. Then, although it was almost May, I saw that there was time yet in which to hoist my math grades up so that I could enter his class in the fall.

The idea took hold with a powerful grip. But where did you start when your grade average in math was a D minus? Desperation breeds humility. I went to my math teacher and told her I wanted to understand what she was talking about. This desire was so unheard of in our class that Miss Moose—it was her real name—appeared as shocked and thrilled as if I had handed her a hundred-dollar bill. If I were truly earnest, she told me with shining eyes, and if my parents were willing to pay a tutor, she would recommend a very able student to help me.

So it came that a few days later, at four o'clock in the afternoon while the sun shone temptingly outside, I sat at the living-room table under the cool gray gaze of little Valerie Stappnagel. Little Valerie had been around as long as I could remember, a remote and colorless figure skipping grades and mingling with no one. She was now only eleven years old and in the ninth grade. She had a small, piping voice and was shorter than I and had to sit on a pillow. I supposed she was some kind of genius, but she was not like Helen Maria; she was more like a gray filing cabinet.

"We'll go back to first-grade arithmetic," she piped. "You're probably weak in your fundamentals."

I set my lips, humiliated, and watched as she took two pencils from her satchel.

"It's very important," she informed me, "to always have a sharp pencil," and she began carefully sharpening them with a pocket sharpener. Her eyes were small and slate gray behind round glasses. Her face was square and doughy, with pale brown hair growing high on the forehead and hanging thin and straight past her ears. She looked like Benjamin Franklin, but she seemed to have no idea of this resemblance. She seemed a person completely untroubled.

"Now. Addition first. Then we'll go on to subtraction, multiplication and division." She settled, businesslike, into her pillow.

At the end of the two hours she told me my big weakness was the multiplication table. "You don't know it at all. You'll have to drill yourself. Do it all the time, like when you're brushing your teeth or walking to school. At the end of the week I'll test you." She put her things back in her satchel, zipped it up, and kept sitting. "My mother has to pick me up. We live out in the valley."

"On a ranch?"

"It's called Rancho Manzanita, but it's not a real ranch. We just have a few animals."

"Like what."

"Rabbits and ducks."

"Are the ducks in a pond?"

"Yes."

"Is it deep? Can you swim in it?"

"I suppose you could, but it's scummy. There's the bell. It's probably my mother."

While our mothers talked at the door, Valerie reminded me once more to practice the multiplication table. "That's the whole thing about numbers, you have to know the combinations by rote or else you waste too much time. All the answers are right there, they never change. So study hard."

All the answers are right there; they never change. I kept thinking about this as I said good-bye. They never change.

"How was it, Suse?" my mother asked when they were gone.

"I think I'm really learning something," I said with enthusiasm.

Mama looked almost as surprised and delighted as Miss Moose.

By our third lesson Valerie had brought me up to the sixth grade. There she was met by a vacuum. Her small gray eyes took on an iron glint.

"All right. Now let's get to work."

"Not bad," she said at the next session.

I had flawlessly rattled off the multiplication table. It might be five years late, but it had been achieved in a few short days of concentrated discipline. I was proud of myself, and though Valerie was not given to wild praise, I knew she was satisfied with me on all counts so far. I felt warm toward my little tutor.

"I want to get into College Prep algebra next year," I confided.

"You have a D minus average now?"

"That's right."

"Even if you got an A this semester, it wouldn't bring you up far enough."

I sat looking at her. There was something so irritating in the tiny, piping voice that you wanted to kill her.

"It's no use getting mad. You can't change the rules. But you might be able to repeat the course in a summer school arrangement."

"Are you kidding?"

"Well, you have to decide what's important."

I knew what was important. Sun, freedom, swimming lessons. Anyway, if I got an A this term, it would be such an extraordinary leap that the whole math faculty would be flabbergasted. They would make an exception of someone so amazing, and in September I would take my place in the rich and dazzling presence of Mr. Lewis.

I didn't voice this projected chain of events to Valerie. But it was as sound and predictable as the equation she was writing down with her well-sharpened pencil.

Chapter 31

Shortly after Helen Maria moved to Berkeley I had received a few lines in her elegant, spiky hand. She was very busy, but as soon as she could have me down, she would let me know. The weeks had passed without another word, but in late May, when I had given up all hope, she wrote again: "Terribly short notice, but what about this coming Saturday? Jack and Estelle have to drive to San Francisco in the morning, and they could drop you off on the way and pick you up when they go back around six. . . ."

What had happened to our plans for a whole weekend? With dinner at a restaurant and everything? But I would not quibble; a less than perfect visit was better than none at all.

Saturday morning at ten o'clock I stood waiting on the front porch in my good Scotch plaid dress. I watched as the sun rose higher and higher in the sky. It stood directly overhead by the time the Hattons arrived, two hours late. Then Dr. Hatton had to get out in her slow, meditative way and dally in conversation with Dad and Mama at the door, and it was a quarter past twelve before we were under way.

I sat tense on the edge of my seat, my eyes boring into the back of Mr. Hatton's head. He drove with maddening leisure, now and then tapping an ash from his cigarette, as if still deep in his newspaper at the breakfast table. "Go faster, dammit," I said under my breath.

"Isn't it a lovely day for a drive?" asked Dr. Hatton, turning around with her pleasant, smoke-wreathed smile. "With the gas rationing, it's been ages since we've gotten out for a really nice long drive."

I smiled back, clutching my knees.

And then, absentminded as usual, they forgot me. Once she leaned against him, her head resting on his shoulder. Another time I saw him reach slowly across to her neck and squeeze it. And as he drove, she would light his cigarettes for him, sticking one right in her own mouth and lighting it and then leaning over and putting it between his lips. It made me uneasy; I turned abruptly to the window and kept my eyes there. The sky was bright blue, and though past its peak, the sun spread a brilliant sheen across the hills, which were already baked dry by early summer and dabbed vivid bronze and black by grazing cows. I looked at the Burma Shave signs along the roadside.

> Slap . . .
> The Jap . . .
> With . . .

Iron . . .
Scrap . . .
Burma Shave. . . .

At our rate of speed, I could read each sign about eight times.

On the front lawn of a large brown-shingled house shaded by evergreens several girls were sprawled. One of them, wearing a casual print dress and no shoes, jumped up and came over. It was Helen Maria, smiling and slouched. I sprang out, slammed the door, and stood beside her as her mother rolled down the window for a chat. The air was fragrant with the cool smell of cut grass. It was still spring down here, fresh and green. I smoothed my hair and straightened the skirt of my dress. At last the car moved off.

"Well!" said the genius, "marvelous to see you! Come say hello to everyone!"

And taking my arm, she conducted me swiftly across the lawn. "A little friend of my sister," she told the others in passing. "Wants to see the campus." Glimpsed faces as my hostess swept me on, up the step, into the house. A little friend of her sister? We hurried down a hall, the bare feet padding ahead, then up more stairs, and down another hall and up more stairs. "*Violà!*" She swung open a door.

It was a true Parisian garret, slant-roofed and fascinating. But it was barer than her salon, and messier, and there was no smell of incense, and how could she say a little friend of her sister?

"Do you want to wash up? It's just down the hall."

"No." Why should I wash up? I was very clean, cleaner than she with her black-soled feet, which she was sticking into a pair of scuffed loafers. Slinging on a shoulder bag, she led me back out the door. "You missed lunch, but we'll grab a bite on campus."

It struck me like a blow; her English accent was almost gone. And I hated the way she walked, with none of her old hauteur, but loose and slouched. I clumped sullenly behind her down the stairs, my Scotch plaid dress suddenly cutting me under the arms. Outside, she once again led me briskly past the faces on the lawn. My mouth settled in a hard line.

But down the street she said, "It's really good to see you, Suse!" And her smile was so spontaneous, so bright and unquestionable, that the little friend of her sister vanished from my troubled soul like a puff of smoke. "And I want you to catch me up on everything," she went on, taking my arm as we walked.

I looked over at her sideways, with excitement. "Well, the big thing is that I'm being tutored in math by a very excellent tutor, and she says I'm bound to get an A this term."

This was not strictly true, but Helen Maria's face lit up. "That's wonderful!" she exclaimed. "I'd given up all hope for you, but that's miraculous. Although I'm surprised your interest lies in math, I shouldn't think you had a very mathematical mind."

"I do, though. I really like numbers, the way they always come out one certain way because they can't come out any other way. You know what I mean?"

"Yes, quite. They're reliable. Which, for me, excludes the possibility of excitement. But that's no doubt my own shortcoming. If you have a mathematical mind, I'm delighted to hear it."

The air was fresh and bright around us, and there were no soldiers anywhere, no sandbags or barrage balloons or black oil tanks. Students on bikes pedaled lazily by, tennis rackets in their wire baskets, and from open windows floated soft strains of radio music, and bells were chiming melodiously in the distance.

We passed through Sather Gate into a campus of sweeping green lawns and stately buildings. As we walked, Helen Maria began describing the history and function of each building. It was not very interesting; I looked at the students instead. There weren't many to be seen on a Saturday, and because of the draft, they were mostly girls, sunning themselves on benches or strolling around as we were. It was a sunny, peaceful scene, and I felt content just to walk along, thinking a little about Mr. Lewis and a lot about lunch.

In front of a building being described by Helen Maria as the Main Library, erected 1911, I beheld a beard: small, white, pointed, attached to a book-laden old man with bicycle clips around his trouser legs.

"A beard. Look."

170

"Professor Ford, our Shakespeare expert. Please don't stare; it's rude."

But the next moment she was staring herself; then a radiant smile broke across her face. Coming out of the library was a young man in dark slacks and a white shirt, his jacket thrown over one shoulder, reminding me with a pang of Peter. But though his eyes were as blue as Peter's—even bluer, light and startling—his hair was jet black, combed straight back without a part, and he was much older than Peter, maybe twenty-five or -six, with lines around his mouth. I knew who he was, that fellow she had mentioned a long time ago, the blue-eyed, black-haired 4-F.

With a grin making deep grooves of the lines, he came striding over and stood before us with his hands planted on his hips. The two of them kept grinning and staring at each other.

"So you are here today," he said at last, speaking in a thick, guttural accent that made my ears prick suspiciously.

"I'm showing Suse the campus," Helen Maria answered, still grinning like an idiot. "I think I mentioned yesterday she was coming?"

Yesterday? That amazed me; I thought from their expressions that they hadn't seen each other for weeks.

"Suse," she was saying, "this is Egon Krawitz. And this is Suse Hansen."

At least she didn't call me a little friend of her sister. She must have gotten that out of the way yesterday. Egon Krawitz extended a large, virile hand with which he shook mine warmly, sending a good-sized thrill up my spine. He was a person who looked directly at you, with great friendliness. His eyes shone.

"Delighted. And you are having a nice visit? You have seen the Campanile?"

"No," I said politely, bringing back my tingling palm. "What's the Campanile?"

"Ah, then we shall take you there," he smiled as the three of us walked on. Egon Krawitz was solid and tanned, not like a 4-F at all. His features were large, well formed, and his light blue eyes and jet black hair made a striking contrast, and there was something magnificent about him, something polished and exceptional, foreign. Krawitz, I mused as we walked; it was not German, of

171

that I felt sure. It could be anything, Polish, Czech, Russian. And as we strolled, Helen Maria between us, I curled my fingers in and touched my palm, suddenly feeling—not only toward Helen Maria, but toward Mr. Lewis as well—a pang of treachery, a darkly immoral, yet not unpleasant feeling, and cast lowered, sidelong glances to my left, trying to see around the barrier of my hostess.

We never reached the Campanile, whatever it was. As my precious afternoon dwindled away, we strolled up sunny walks and down dusty paths, through stone archways and over broad lawns, and they walked with their arms around each other and talked so that I couldn't hear. I was hungry. I loathed their private tones. My dress was too short, too small, hideous.

Then suddenly Helen Maria recalled my existence.

"Tell Egon how good you are in math, Suse."

I gave a sullen shrug.

"It is your field, mathematics?" asked Egon.

I nodded, feeling less sullen.

"Not only that, but she reads Flaubert. Tell Egon how many times you've read *Madame Bovary*."

"Five," I murmured, blushing with pleasure at his rich, foreign exclamation of approval. And at that heady moment I realized that our endless wandering had had a destination and that we had arrived.

Chapter 32

It was the outdoor terrace of a campus restaurant, filled with sunny café tables and the pleasant sound of voices and clinking china. Everything was improving, and with a thrill of familiarity I even recognized one of the diners: Professor Ford of the beard and bicycle clips, forking up a carrot salad. I smiled at him, and as we sat down at a nearby table, I looked with confidence at Egon. Professor Ford's field was Shakespeare; mine was mathematics.

"And what's your field, Egon, if I may ask?"

"Political science."

"I think that sounds very interesting."

He nodded agreeably, picking up his menu. "Useless probably, but interesting. But tell me," he said, and the blue eyes looked warmly across the table at me, "how is it that this little town of yours produces such unusual young scholars as Helen Maria and yourself?"

I glanced horror-stricken at Helen Maria, but she only smiled, lighting a cigarette.

"I really don't know," I murmured with embarrassment, taking up my menu. A hamburger and root beer float would have been to my liking, but it was not what an unusual young scholar would order, especially with Professor Ford looking over at me now and then, stroking his beard. We had salad, tuna sandwiches, and coffee, and while we ate, everything went wrong again.

They talked in German. I had heard enough movie Nazis to know. A harsh, nasty language, as if they had sore throats. Shamefully my eyes went around the terrace, but no one was listening. Returning to my food, I chewed ignored and unhappy, listening to the horrible language, my eyes on the pair. Their eyes were on each other; when one chewed, the other talked, and sometimes they both talked at once, and laughed. I clattered my fork, I set my cup down resoundingly, there was no reaction; I might have been air, and it was *my* day, *my* visit. With a mental slash I disowned the tingle, a dirty Axis thrill—she could have him, they deserved each other. And she was shameless; you could see she had her hand on his knee under the table. When I was finished, I sat back and folded my arms in a large gesture.

This had an effect. Egon looked over at me.

"Ah, see how rude we have been. Here Suse has finished already. You have enjoyed it? Good!" And settling back in his chair, he gave me his attention. "Do you know, I wish you would tell me something about *Madame Bovary*, for I read it so long ago I have forgotten it."

Blankness and terror. Those blue shining eyes. Helen Maria sipping her coffee. I had only one wish, that they would ignore me again.

"Well?" said Helen Maria.

Under the table, my feet came nervously together. "Well, Flaubert was an unvarnished realist . . . he

173

wasn't romantic, romantics are sloppy thinkers, he didn't like them . . . he didn't even like Madame Bovary too much because she was a sloppy thinker . . . but what he really hated was the priests and notaries, and so did she, because they stifled her. And so she took poison . . ." Vainly I racked my brain for more details. "It's beautifully written."

"I am relieved to hear it," said Egon, and smiled. "Well, I must reread it now, upon your recommendation."

My heart flew to him. And Helen Maria, sipping her coffee, seemed pleased with what I had said. My eyes darted to Professor Ford, who was raising a spoon of red Jell-O, and raising his eyes too, which met mine with depths of silent congratulation. It would have been a perfect moment if only Egon weren't a German. But my mind was spiraling with accomplishment, and now I realized that he probably spoke several languages, as Helen Maria herself did, and that two such linguists might speak anything at random. German, French, ancient Greek. It didn't mean a person was German just because he spoke German. After all, no German would be attending an American, an enemy university. He was from Poland, Czechoslovakia, or Russia. I put my money on Russia.

"Where are you from, Egon, if I may ask?"

"Berlin."

I dropped my eyes. Berlin. The black heart of the Reich. He went on, not even lowering his voice as the waitress came over and poured more coffee. "That is to say, Dahlem, it is a suburb of Berlin, and a very pleasant one. It is very much like Berkeley, with all its trees . . ."

The waitress moved off. I could hear Professor Ford's spoon clinking in his dish as he listened.

". . . not that Berlin is old, in the sense of Nürnberg or Cologne, but it is a very beautiful city, nevertheless. . . ."

"It isn't anymore," I said coldly, looking up. "It's been bombed a hundred and twenty-seven times."

"Too true," he said sadly.

"Egon," Helen Maria said, "please don't let her get started on the war. She'll never stop."

"A young lady of so many interests," he remarked,

174

brightening again. "That is unusual, to know the exact number of raids on Berlin."

"I read the papers. And there's going to be an invasion. Then your whole Germany will be wiped out. Totally."

"Will you please get off your hobbyhorse!" Helen Maria snapped, and turned to him. "All Japanese are spies, and all Germans are Nazis. You haven't had to listen to it for years. It becomes boring in the extreme."

I felt a rush of resentment, looking at her annoyed, superior face. She had no understanding of war. She had never been blown up in her cellar, she didn't know the Polish family in the potato field, she didn't have a brother waiting to go in with the invasion. She knew nothing except that place, Verdun, where they had played soccer because war is a game. She wouldn't care if Egon were Hitler. She had no inkling of anything. How dare she sit there insulting me because I did know something and was honest?

But Egon himself seemed amused. "No, Suse," he said, "I'm afraid you're a bit off the mark. For I happen to be a Jew."

Jew. Though he said it casually, it seemed to be a word that settled everything, and Helen Maria looked from his face to mine with a righteous air. "And now," she said, "I for one would like to talk about something else."

"I never said anything about Nazis. How do you know what I think, Helen Maria? You're always doing that. It's unfair."

"We're dropping the subject." She spoke quietly, even pleasantly. You could tell she wanted everything to be smooth and nice. A woman was coming up the steps waving at us.

"It's true," I told Egon, "I never thought you were a Nazi."

He nodded, as if he believed me.

But what was a Jew? From Sunday school they were mixed up with bulrushes and date palms, and that's where they were, in the Bible. I didn't know they still existed. But here was Egon. How did he fit in with Germany up in the north? How could he be from Berlin and the bulrushes both?

The woman had pulled up a chair and flopped down,

vigorously shaking hands with Egon and Helen Maria. Her face was plump and smooth, with sharp brown eyes, her thick brown hair swept carelessly into a bun, her heavy figure clad in a brown cotton skirt and black turtleneck sweater. I knew who she was, one of those Rosa Luxury women, for the name had stuck in my mind along with Helen Maria's description: buns and burning eyes. They were refugees who had gotten out before the war. Even though it was not logical to have refugees without a war, I was looking with my naked eyes at a refugee.

"My cousin Ruth," Egon introduced us, and I realized that if they were cousins, then she must be a Jew, too, and that Jews must be refugees, and Egon must also be a refugee. Things seemed to be fitting together.

Her handshake was more violent than her cousin's, and her accent harsher. "So, you are visiting the campus. You have been to the Campanile?"

"Not yet."

"You must. A splendid view. *Atemberaubend!*" She reached over and pulled a cigarette from Helen Maria's pack of Fleetwoods. "*Dreck*," she murmured, lighting up with a grimace, and began conversing in German.

The sunlight was still warm on my tight plaid shoulders, but as my eyes wandered around the terrace, I saw that the tables cast long blue shadows and that Professor Ford had gone, leaving behind only a crumpled napkin, which cast its own long blue shadow. The day was slipping away. I sank my chin into my hand, but no one noticed. I wondered if Egon knew that Helen Maria's feet were dirty inside her shoes. I wondered if anyone was ever going to order dessert. I wondered how long they were going to sit there using up my visit without a glance in my direction. I wasn't just anyone to be treated so shabbily. I was a mathematics scholar, I read Flaubert, and not only did I know the exact bombing score on Berlin, but on Hamburg and Bremen as well. I heard a pause in Ruth's loud voice and took my hand confidently from my chin.

"Are you a Jew, Ruth, if I may ask?"

She looked me sharply up and down. "What does she say?"

"Who knows?" said Helen Maria lightly, but her eyes

176

slitted dangerously across the table at me. Once more my feet came nervously together.

"Why do you wish to know?" Ruth asked, and her sharp brown eyes were unpleasant.

I managed to say, with a shrug, "Just curious," but to my alarm, the unpleasant look deepened.

"We have here a young lady of many interests," came Egon's voice, calm and even genial. "What is it exactly you wish to know?"

Helen Maria's eyes closed.

But Egon's tone gave me courage. I would ask something that could not possibly make Ruth's eyes more unpleasant and that would also show that I already knew a thing or two.

"Well, I would like to know what year you got out before the war."

"What year?" said Egon. "Late in thirty-eight. You have heard of Crystal Night?"

It brought to my mind ice, snow, crystal stars. German Christmas Eve. I nodded.

"So you know then. Jews were beaten and arrested; shops and synagogues were destroyed."

And on Christmas Eve, that was horrible. Did it happen every Christmas Eve, a monstrous German custom? And had Egon himself been beaten and arrested? And Ruth? Ruth I didn't care about, let them beat her. But Egon . . . I felt a surge of anger.

"I'd like to beat *them*, didn't anybody beat *them*?"

"A little difficult, under the circumstances," he said dryly, and even smiled, but it seemed that as he spoke, a memory of the purest loathing flicked across his face and was gone.

"I think it's horrible that they do it on Christmas Eve."

"Christmas Eve?"

"Crystal Night. . . ." But even as I spoke, I realized with a cringe of my toes that I had misunderstood and had now released a profound stupidity.

Egon did not seem at all surprised by this. "No, that is not quite it," he explained. "There is no connection between Christmas Eve and Crystal Night, though I see that it might sound that way."

Helen Maria was calmly finishing her salad; she seemed relieved. As for Ruth, she had sat silent all this time, puffing on her cigarette. She no longer looked unpleasant; she didn't even look interested. She blew out a stream of smoke and looked at Egon.

"Do you always air the matter to schoolchildren?"

"Not always."

"It is in poor taste."

"I have poor taste."

But to me she seemed the one with poor taste, with her straggling bun and loud voice and the way she took cigarettes without asking. But she seemed in a better frame of mind now, so I asked, "Are you from Berlin too?" And to point out my knowledge of the city, I added, "From Dahlem?"

"Berlin, yes," she snapped, grinding out her cigarette and glancing at her watch. "Dahlem, I am afraid not. I am not quite so grand. Do you always ask so many questions? I pity your teachers." She stood up and shook hands with the others, then turned and shook hands with me too, and surprised me with a brief pleasantry. "I hope you will enjoy fully the Campanile."

I watched her go down the steps with her straggling bun. I did not really dislike her, and I hoped she had not been beaten.

"I must go too," said Egon.

My heart sank at this, but Helen Maria said we would walk with him partway, and then he and I were left alone while she went to the ladies' room—a place I needed badly to visit myself, but for which I was not willing to give up this private moment.

It was he who spoke first. He asked if I was looking forward to summer vacation. I said yes, and confided that summer was my favorite season. He said it was his too, and this, I felt, was something special between us, a bond. I asked if he liked America, and he said yes, although it was, well, very different of course. I asked if his family was here too. He said his mother was in New York, but his two older brothers were still in Germany. His father had died a few years after the war.

"Was that the First World War?"

He nodded.

"Helen Maria insists they played soccer together at Verdun, the enemies together." I watched for a scowl of denial.

No scowl appeared. "Verdun? No. But things like that

178

happened at other places. Senlis, for instance." And to this crushing reply, he added, "My father spoke of it. Or so they tell me; I was too young when he died to have heard about his experiences."

I hesitated. "You mean he was there? He fought in the war?"

He nodded. "He won the Iron Cross, First Class." And just as a flicker of loathing had crossed his face earlier, a flicker of pride crossed it now. I looked down. He was the enemy after all, with his passion for Berlin where the Führer raved from a balcony, and with his father slaughtering Yanks in the mud and getting the Iron Cross for it; but why would his father, who was a Jew, fight for the Germans, who beat up Jews? And why did they beat them up? And how were they from the Bible and Germany both? My brain creaked with confusion, and I had an eleven-year-old tutor, and all I had said about *Madame Bovary* was what Helen Maria had once said, and Professor Ford didn't know I existed, not even when he raised his spoon of red Jell-O and looked at me.

"I don't know anything," I confessed, looking up tiredly. "I don't even know what a Jew is."

Again, Egon did not look surprised. "Well, it is no disgrace. I think you consider it a disgrace not to know everything. You know quite a lot of things. I would have no worries; it will all come, by and by."

Helen Maria was returning across the terrace.

"And the Jews—?" I asked.

"—Have a long and complicated history."

"I knew it must be complicated."

"More complicated"—and as he stood up in the slanting sunlight, I was again struck by the contrast between the jet black hair and light blue eyes—"than you can ever imagine."

We walked back along the deserted campus. The sidewalks and benches shone with an aching gold, filling me with melancholy, with a sense of sun-sinking journeys. I thought of Peter in England, waiting for the invasion. I thought of Aunt Dorothy dead, and Eudene gone, and Peggy at the bottom of the sea, and of the long ride back through the evening hills.

On the street Egon shook my hand. "It has been a pleasure, Suse."

"Me too," I said, standing bereft as he took his hand away.

"See you at seven." He waved at Helen Maria and started down the street.

My eyes flashed from his back to her face. "I have to go to the bathroom!"

"You should have come with me at the restaurant," she said, heading for a gas station.

"Well I didn't!"

"Are you angry about something? Is it because I was sharp with you at the table?"

See you at seven! While I was snailing through the evening hills, they would be going out together, talking and laughing!

"I'm sorry, but you bring it on yourself. I never know what you'll say in front of people, you're such a mass of peculiar ideas."

Running off together as soon as they got rid of me, and it was my day, my visit!

"But it all turned out fine. And Egon liked you, he liked you very much, I could tell."

She spoke with real pleasure, with no jealousy at all, swelling my wrath to a peak. "I'll wait for you over there," she said, pointing at a bookstore. I slammed the rest room door behind me. Just like her, couldn't even wait, had to run off to a bunch of books.

But when I joined her there, it was to be presented with a gift, a scholarly volume called *Principia Mathematica*, by someone called Whitehead Russell. As she placed it in my hands, there was on her face that same spontaneous smile, that same warmth and interest that had made me so happy earlier. "You won't understand it now," she said. "But at some point, if you go on to higher levels, the numbers will stop being reliable, and that's when you'll want to read it."

I thanked her from the heart, for I knew her look was real, as real as Egon's blue and shining gaze. But in neither of them did it last, and that was real too. There was some gap between me and them, some distance so wide and deep and impassable that I felt tired in all my bones, and was almost glad to be going home.

Chapter 33

The invasion had become another rumor. Seven long months I had been waiting, torn between impatience and dread. By now I knew it was not going to happen, and I felt a large general disappointment, inside which burned a small particular joy.

One morning during first period a girl from the office came in with a note, an ordinary note, it seemed, since Mrs. Miller read it without expression. But when she had finished, she stood up behind her desk with a certain formality. My heart stood still. I knew what she was going to announce.

"Class, we have just learned that the invasion of Europe has begun. The Allies have landed in France." A cheer went up, a long, rousing cheer, and when it was over, Mrs. Miller said, "I think we should have a moment of silence. Let us pray for the safety of our men and for an end to this terrible war."

There was something austere, solemn, in the way she said it, maybe it was because of her grandson. She was silent, looking down at her desk. The class was silent too. I lowered my eyes and prayed for Peter.

At noon I ran home. Mama had gone downtown and bought a paper from the stand.

Invasion Extra!!

Supreme Headquarters, Allied Expeditionary Forces, Tues., June 6—Masses of troops which landed in France with little opposition were fighting their way inland early today along a 100-mile stretch of the Normandy coast between Cherbourg and Le Havre....

My eyes flicked up. Little opposition. The goose-stepping troops were reeling, defeated, their cities bombed, their spirit broken. Peter, helmeted, was running crouched through French lanes, firing his machine gun in every direction. Let him trample them down straight to Berlin; I wanted to be with him, I wanted to smell the smoking ruins, see the hordes of trembling prisoners, hear the burst of fire as Hitler was riddled to a jelly against a blackened wall.

"I kept worrying about Peter before," I told Mama. "But I have a feeling now, now that it's finally started, that he's going to be safe."

"Peter will be all right," she agreed firmly.

I ran back to school, hot with joy. There was a lot of invasion talk on the lawn, but not hot, bursting talk. The only excited person was Dumb Donny, who ran around with an imaginary machine gun blazing, and whose legs the others swacked irritably as he plowed through them. I would have liked to join him but didn't want to be swacked like an idiot.

That afternoon when math period was over, Miss Moose called me to her desk and with a glowing face took both my hands in hers. My final semester grade was an A. In view of this unusual achievement, I would be allowed to try College Prep algebra in September.

I shouted the news at Valerie, collaring her in the hall.

"Well, that's good," she piped. "That's very nice. Congratulations."

You couldn't get her excited about anything. But I was grateful for her stern methods, and I had even grown to like her.

"Maybe we'll see each other this summer," I said. "Maybe you could come out and visit."

"When?"

"Well, I don't know."

"I can come anytime. Just tell me." And I hurried down the hall for a triumphant glimpse of the beloved.

That night, when Dad came home from work, he was as delighted with my accomplishment as Mama had been. It was an even better moment than when I had feasted my eyes on Mr. Lewis today. Standing there in my parents' pleasure after so many years of miserable grades—puny, bug-low grades that they had worried about, but over which they had never made me feel dumb or belittled—I understood the depths of their long faith, not necessarily faith that I could do better, but faith that even if I couldn't, I was valuable and worthwhile. I felt this with a sense of rushing gratitude, and then they were taking me around the block to a neighbor with a telephone, to let me call Karla in San Francisco. I had never spoken on the telephone before, and I shouted my news into the mouthpiece. I heard Karla's disembodied voice rise high with congratulations; then I shouted a few more things, and Dad said I didn't have to shout, so I spoke with strained moderation, my hand damp around the strange instrument. We talked only briefly, since it was long distance, and I hung up shakily but honored and pleased with all this excitement. At home we turned on the news on the radio, "Men and women of the United States, this is a momentous hour in world history. This is the invasion of Hitler's Europe, the zero hour—" and I realized that my parents had set aside the invasion itself for my moment of glory, and I felt again that deep rush of gratitude.

Losses were light, the next few days' papers and broadcasts informed us. What did that mean? It meant few deaths, but for the one who got killed it was no light loss. I tried not to think of it. I tried to think of the end of school coming up. I tried to write Helen Maria about my math triumph, but my spelling was too bad and I didn't feel like looking up all the words. So I tried to look forward to my visit to Valerie's ranch. At school I kept badgering her to set a date.

The first morning of vacation I was fetched by Valerie and her mother and driven to Rancho Manzanita. It was no ranch at all, just a white modern-looking house with rounded corners and some of its windows like portholes, which sat on a dry field surrounded by manzanita bushes and big oaks.

"Where's your pond?"

Valerie led me through the trees, and there it was, not very big and already beginning to sink in the summer heat, but dark glassy green and only a little ringed around the edge with yellow scum. White ducks paddled on its surface.

"I won't disturb them," I said, unbuttoning my shirt.

"What are you doing?"

"Just going for a swim."

"You can't. It's dirty."

"It's not dirty." In my undershirt and underpants I waded out, soft mud squishing between my toes, and dove under. The chilled, enveloping smoothness, the deepening green murk, then cleaving up into a sunburst, into the cool smell of mud and wet ferns, the soft busy barrage of quacks, and diving again.

It was afternoon when I crawled out.

Valerie was in her room, listening to *Concert Matinee* on her radio. "Did you come to visit me or to swim?" she asked.

"Both."

"You could have brought your suit. You didn't have to be sneaky."

"Sorry." But I was prepared to be even sneakier. If Valerie kicked me out, I would come back whenever I wanted—it was only a six-or seven-mile walk—and swim secretly in her pond.

Valerie did not kick me out. With lips only slightly pursed, she suggested a game of two-handed bridge.

I was fetched again by Valerie and Mrs. Stappnagel, in what was to become a weekly visit. I didn't like or do well at two-handed bridge, but Valerie allowed me my swim each time, so I had to allow her her game. In a yellow sunsuit, a well-sharpened score pencil at her side, Valerie played with none of the hilarity that had punctuated Peggy's and my blackjack games, but she did smile at moments—a pensive lip curl accompanied by a slow, strategic upward glance from her cards, as if we were engaged in our own great war. A noble winner and stoic loser, she would have made a fine general, of the old school, with a plumed helmet.

I liked Valerie, but ours was a friendship without much conversation because of her quality of contentment. She seemed to like her life exactly as it was and to require nothing from the outside. Although she was very intelligent, it was a little like being with Mario.

At home, Mama and I began to share something, though it was never mentioned. It was a fear about the doorbell, that whenever it rang unexpectedly, it might be the Western Union messenger boy. The sudden jangle sent a faint stiffness into Mama's face. She would cross the room, and in the time before she opened the door an

184

unreality descended, a sense of slow motion and sound-lessness, though your heart was racing and your eyes felt so sharp they felt they were cutting through the wood of the door. It always turned out to be the paper boy collecting or a neighbor wanting to borrow the mower, their ordinary faces dazzling and beloved through the screen, like those of great biblical saints.

When the Red Cross swimming lessons started, I had four days a week of swimming—three in the rowdy splashing of the pool and one in the dark mystery of Valerie's pond—and I should have been very happy, but I wasn't. The main reason was that I worried over Peter. But another reason was that I no longer loved Mr. Lewis. Instead of absence making the heart grow fonder, it was making him uninteresting. He seldom opened the moonlit door, and when he did, his face was so badly recollected that my thoughts passed on to other things. He was like Mr. Kerr. One day sudden and overwhelming, and one day nothing. Gone.

Parti avec le vent. And where did it *parti* to, where was it now? Somewhere behind me. I felt there was a place behind me now that had not been there when I was younger, a place filled with faces and scenes and moments. Peter shining his loafer. Eudéne running away from us in the rain. Professor Ford raising his spoon of red Jell-O. It was time that had accumulated behind me; it was the feeling of a past.

On my third visit to Rancho Manzanita, I stayed overnight. With permission I dragged a sleeping bag out onto the garage roof, which opened from a door in the living room and which was used as a terrace and outfitted with garden furniture and potted lemon trees. Valerie had no desire to join me, but her mother said she should, since it was healthy for a person to sleep outdoors in the fresh air. And so from then on, zipped up in her sleeping bag, her bathrobe and spectacles folded neatly beside her, Valerie too became acquainted with the black, star-clustered sky and with the first coral streaks of dawn. But she never became an enthusiast.

It was the day after my third visit that we had a letter from Peter. It said Somewhere in France, June 12, 1944. Well, he said, it's really something, this invasion. Too bad he couldn't write a long letter, he had enough for a book, but he would just get this note off to let us know he was okay. He was writing in the dugout, there were three of them in it, Zafich, onetime butcher from Detroit, who was always talking about his snazzy wife back home, and Dolan, onetime interior decorator and habitué of the theater, and himself, Hansen, onetime shoe salesman, who never missed Buster Brown's till now. It wasn't bad though, the worst part was waiting seasick in the landing barge, he'd rather be shot at than seasick. It was a funny thing shooting and being shot at, hard to get used to, but he was getting used to it. He was lucky too, once a machine gun opened up in front of him, but out of about eight bullets he only got one, just barely grazed his arm. He had a souvenir scar now, which Zafich said was good for a free drink in any barroom in the states. As for France, it was a pretty place, old farms and cows. He was looking forward to Paris. He was beginning to feel like a world traveler, London, Paris, a special cutrate tour for fifty thousand. . . .

He had a new dashing style, he was getting sophisticated, and he had a bullet scar on his arm. Let him never be hit in the head. Please let him stay lucky.

The month passed with banner headlines.

JUNE 19:   **Nazis Mowed Down
                    In Cherbourg Trap!**

JUNE 20:   **Cherbourg Nazis in Wild Panic!
            Confused Germans Reel Back
            In Great Tank Fight for Caen!**

JUNE 29:   **Bayonets Slash Path to Nazi Base!**

JUNE 30:   **Nazis Smashed
                    In Caen Attack!**

Yet by the time Caen was actually captured, by the British, on July 9, I realized that the invasion had progressed exactly thirty miles in over a month. We weren't cutting through the Germans like a hot knife through butter. It was going to be Italy all over again, inch by bloody inch, with staggering losses.

186

Chapter 34

Nighty-night," Mrs. Stappnagel called across the roof.

"Nighty-night," Valerie called back.

Of methodical habits, Valerie's parents went to bed precisely at ten-fifteen, leaving the night bigger and better. Not that I didn't like them, they were very nice, but the darkness took on greater depth and mystery when the house was silent.

The night air was warm, motionless, heavy with the smell of the potted lemon trees. There was no moon, not even a thin crescent. The sky was so black that you could scarcely make out the big oaks or the nearby mass of hills behind which Mendoza lay.

"No bomber's moon tonight," I observed.

"Of course not. It's a new moon. That's when it's hit so obliquely by the sun that you can't see it." Little Valerie lay straight and narrow in her sleeping bag, like a mummy. "Astronomy is interesting."

"Do you believe in fate?"

"No. That's astrology."

I lay propped on an elbow, listening to the crickets, to the frogs croaking from the pond, breathing the lemon smell.

"Why do you say nighty-night? Why don't you say good night?"

"I have no idea." She gave an irritated squirm in her bag. "This roof is so darn hard."

"It's not hard."

"It's as hard as—"

A mammoth blush instantaneously filled the sky behind the hills. A towering, fan-shaped glow of dull red, veined all over with long descending silver streamers. Large dim shapes bloomed high in the rosy light, turning over and over with immense languor. I watched as if mesmerized, frozen on my elbow, feeling somewhere inside me a remote groping toward astonishment. Then a

187

gigantic blast struck the house broadside, slamming my head back with shattering impact.

I was running inside a nightmare, on a treadmill where blows kept knocking me back, until I realized I was in a dark room and the blows were the hard edges of furniture I was colliding with, reeling back from, tangling up with Valerie, whose face suddenly lit up harsh white. I was pulled into someone's arms, a blinding flashlight in my eyes.

"Everybody be still," whispered Mr. Stappnagel, beaming the flashlight before him and making his way carefully through the room. My eyes followed him from his wife's arm, which was so tight that it bunched up the skin on one side of my face. My bangs fluttered with the drilling breaths from her nostrils. Her husband pushed wide the half open door to the roof.

"My God," he whispered.

The huge glow was still there, paler now. I felt the glow reach my eyes, but it went no deeper, as if my skull, instead of having been shattered, had been cemented solid.

Mr. Stappnagel closed the door and stood leaning against it. He seemed not to know what to do. He beamed the flashlight on his wristwatch. "Ten-twenty-two."

"Is it an air raid?" his wife whispered.

"I don't think so. I don't hear the warning." He listened.

She listened too. She kept plucking and smoothing Valerie's hair, strands of which were caught in my mouth.

Suddenly Mr. Stappnagel went over to the light switch on the wall. Brilliance filled the room, showing his face chalk white. The floor was littered with glass, the windows framed by a few remaining pieces. Pictures had fallen from the walls and lay among overturned lamps and broken vases. There was an unearthly sense of stillness, except for a small sound of creaking from above. It was the chandelier, swaying gently to and fro. Mr. Stappnagel reached up and stopped it, slowly lowering his arms. Again he seemed not to know what to do. Then he stepped hurriedly to the radio. But with his hand on the knob he paused, turned around.

"Maybe you should put them to bed," he said, his eyes flicking down from his wife's face to mine and back. A

188

tiny movement, sending a hairline crack through the cement of my head. It was as if he wanted me out of the room. As if the radio would say something I shouldn't hear. As with the blow of an ax, the cement split.

"Shell!"

"Now wait—"

My legs were already running, my hands clawing the arm that held me back. I tried to bite it, then tried to bite the fingers that Mr. Stappnagel was clamping around my wrist. His voice rang in my ear. "It could be miles from Mendoza! There's no telling from here!" I kept biting and kicking, rocked inside by shock waves of grief until they turned into a surging nausea and I came to a standstill.

"I think you should go with Mother now," Mr. Stappnagel said quietly. "As soon as I hear anything I'll tell you. I promise. Go with Mother now."

I allowed myself to be led away with Valerie. After a few steps I leaned over and vomited on the floor, Mrs. Stappnagel holding my head. I didn't want her to do that. I didn't want to be touched. She led us on, holding me to her side, and at the end of the hall she opened Valerie's door. She reached inside to the light switch.

"I want to go home," I said.

"It's all right," she whispered, taking us inside. There was no broken glass here; she led us quickly to the bed.

"I want to go home."

"It's all right now. It's all right, it's all right." She kept whispering this, smiling at me as she drew the bed covers back. "Up you go. Both of you."

I climbed in with my terrifying grief, and she patted the covers around us. "It's a miracle you didn't cut your feet in there," she said, straightening up, and she stood for a moment with her hand pressed hard against her temple. In the distance, very faintly, came the wail of a siren. She smoothed her hair back. "Try not to worry now. Father and I will tell you if we hear anything. It'll be all right, just try not to worry." She went over and pulled the blackout shades down, then unplugged the radio and put it under her arm. She smiled as she turned off the light and went out, quietly closing the door behind her.

"I hope it's not Shell," Valerie whispered in the darkness.

I lay with my hands pressed against my face. I lay that way for a long time, as more sirens in the distance filled the air. Then I pulled the blankets away and crawled over Valerie.

"Where are you going? Mother said we should—"

After feeling my way to the door, I let myself out and closed it behind me. I walked down the unlit hallway to its end where it gave onto the living room. They had turned off the overhead light, a dim lamp glow bathed the entranceway. I leaned against the wall a few feet back. I couldn't see them or the radio, but I could hear the dial turning through static and music and stopping.

"—an unconfirmed report that the city of Mendoza has been leveled by an explosion—there is no communication with the city at this time—the tremendous blast was felt fifty miles away, switchboards throughout the area are in a state of chaos—you are asked not to use your telephones except for reasons of extreme emergency—you are asked to stay off all roads—we repeat—"

A sharp, bitter-tasting drool poured into my mouth. I was aware only of that, of how it slipped through my lips and slid down, hanging from my chin in a long, fine string that glistened in the lamp glow, trembling and swaying and catching on my pajama front. Then with a numbness, supporting myself along the wall, I moved slowly back to Valerie's room. I fumbled the door shut behind me and felt my way back to the bed, lying down across the end. The sirens were shooting along the road leading past the house to Mendoza, the piercing screams filling the room. A massive soundlessness was tearing through my throat. I wanted to go home and be dead with them in their arms.

The door opened, and Mrs. Stappnagel spoke into the darkness. "It's all right, they're fire trucks, don't be frightened. They'll be gone soon . . . try to sleep. Suse, we haven't heard anything yet . . . we'll tell you as soon as we do."

The door closed. I pulled myself to a sitting position, then suddenly jumped up and barged through the dark to the table where I fumbled wildly with the lamp, finally getting it turned on. My shorts were on the floor. With shaking hands I changed into them while looking frantically around for my shirt, not seeing it, leaving my pajama top on and seizing my tennis shoes. I staggered around, pulling them on. I felt I had no balance, no center of gravity. I fell against the bed.

Valerie had sat bolt upright. "What are you doing?"

"Going home."

"But you can't! You mean alone?"

"Don't tell them!"

"But they said you shouldn't—" She began pushing the covers back.

"I'll kill you!" I clasped my hands around her neck, squeezing the thumbs in. "I'll kill you."

She sat perfectly still, her small eyes wide. I took my hands away and went to the window.

In a chain of flashing red lights, fire engines and ambulances and police cars screamed by my side, their headlights illuminating the dirt and weeds I raced along, and illuminating my back, too, so that I feared a police car would swerve over and arrest me, or the Stappnagel car would come after me—Valerie had told them, or they had seen me run down the driveway, and they would say everything's all right and drag me back, and I would never reach Dad and Mama dead in the rubble, the three of us dead together, all that I wanted now, and as I ran, I was crying in loud, open sobs, deafened by the sirens; but for all that, I ran with wild speed, on the toes, hands knifelike to cut the air.

A wheel swerved off the tar, spitting gravel and dirt against my legs. Someone shouted from the back of a fire truck. I moved farther in, pounding flat on my feet now, a stabbing pain in my side. At last the stabs grew so sharp that I plodded to a standstill in the rushing lights and bent over, gasping. When my breathing came even again, I ran on with a fresh burst of speed.

After a while I began to feel a cycle. A terrific speed, then a heavy, plodding run, then the hunched-over standstill. As the cycle repeated itself I began to feel the distance bitten into, solid miles eaten up.

The traffic went in cycles too. The chain of lights would suddenly vanish down the road, leaving the night black, filled with the peaceful sound of crickets and the steady thud of my feet, the road stretching before me like a gray ribbon. Then a single vehicle would shoot by, and another, and then again came the long screaming chain of lights.

Sometimes I started crying again while I ran. Sometimes I noticed the stale vomit taste in my mouth. But at some point I only knew that noise and lights alternated with silence and darkness and that my pounding legs had no feeling.

The sirens sank in low, separate whines. Lifting my head from my jogging, I recognized the stretch of road I was on as lying just outside town. From within the slowing vehicles, the drivers' faces were turning and squinting at me as I ran by. I swung into the pear orchard at my side, stumbling over dirt clods, hearing shouts from down the road like barked commands. When I came alongside the shouts, I stopped and held onto a tree trunk, catching my breath and leaning around, looking.

Two convoy trucks were parked on the side of the road. Helmeted soldiers stood with rifles; others were swinging flashlights, waving ahead ambulances and fire trucks while ordering back private cars. A woman was arguing in a hysterical voice from her rolled-down window. A soldier kept waving her back, shouting, "Emergency vehicles only! Get off the road!" She kept arguing in her high, crazy voice. Another soldier stepped forward and raised his rifle. She pulled over to the side, opposite the trucks, where two or three other private cars had been forced, their drivers talking huddled together outside them.

They should go by foot, it was the only way. Maybe others were, and the orchard was filled with people like me running through the darkness, for I had struck off again, diagonally, to come out on the Alhambra Avenue side. I could hear vehicles passing the checkpoint, their sirens starting up again, screaming down the road and swerving onto Alhambra Avenue; all I could see through the last rows of trees was the swift glare of headlights and flashing red. As I stumbled across the clods to the orchard's edge, I held my hand pressed above my eyes, ready to block out what lay ahead. At the edge my courage failed me, and I stopped dead. Then I forced myself to step out.

The headlights illumined house after house, tree after tree, exactly the same as when I had left that morning.

My hand trembled down my face; then a rocket of ecstasy burst inside me, and I shot through the traffic, barely clearing an onrushing ambulance, and raced down Alhambra Avenue, loving everything unbearably, my hair whipping back from my ears, this pile of dog crap I leaped over, all the sirens screaming past, and this warm black night and all nights to come, and all days, and everything that would ever happen. Each fresh block revealed itself intact, perfect. People stood on their front steps, some on corners, but not many, and they seemed already used to the wild noise, more interested in my flight. It must be late, past midnight, maybe one o'clock, a dreamlike hour to be running down the street.

Coming toward me was a stream of ambulances and private cars, all turning onto the street that led to the Community Hospital. Turning my head as I ran past, I glimpsed the hospital nestled against the hill where Helen Maria had invoked the gods so long ago, glimpsed a mass of activity before the entrance, people rushing around in a blazing network of headlights. Then I turned off on Arreba Street and covered the last three blocks with a final burst of speed, throwing myself against the pepper tree in the front yard, breathing deep and ragged into its bark. I drank in the house. Dark, peaceful, a miracle of all that was beautiful and familiar. Dad and Mama lay safely asleep, or they were sitting safe in the living room, behind the blackout shades, discussing the night. And now I would climb the stairs and feel my arms around them.

But when I had regained my breath and started toward the stairs, the enormity of my misbehavior had already begun sinking in. I had disobeyed army orders, radio orders, Stappnagel orders, and had gone running through the dangerous night, in my pajama top. Even in the joy of seeing me, Dad and Mama would be upset; they would worry from this minute on that I was demented, that I would spend the rest of my life committing hazardous, lawbreaking acts and bring unhappiness down on myself. They were not dead. It was enough. I gave the house a last happy look and started back.

My vitality was sapped. I was aware of fiery blisters on my feet, a grinding soreness in my legs. But I was still happy, and I knew I would be happy forever, and after walking a couple of blocks, I forced myself into a jog-trot.

Progressing back down the clamor of Alhambra Avenue, I began wondering now where the explosion had been, what had happened. Then I wondered no more, feeling a detachment from everything but this body which might or might not get me back to my starting point. I was stumbling back over the clods of the orchard when I realized that the Stappnagels would be waiting up angrily and that they would tell my parents, and I would not have gained anything by denying myself the bliss of ringing my doorbell. But my body would not turn around. It was going back, completing a design, and that was that.

The miles passed. I felt none of the urgency I had on the way out, only a kind of dull stubbornness, and my great joy, which never decreased. The dark spaces between the oncoming vehicles were longer now, and profoundly silent, for the crickets were asleep. The absolute blackness of the sky was gone, as if a layer had dropped away, revealing a curved dome of the darkest, inkiest blue. The air was very cold. The ground felt harder than before, as if it had contracted, pebbles and twigs pressing through my shoes soles with the sharpness of metal.

Now and then I thought of the Stappnagels. How they had clamped me between them. How she had put the radio under her arm. How they had lied about coming to tell me. How they were smiling and calm, understanding nothing. They were stupid and smug and cruel; they were contemptible. But even the thought of the Stappnagels could not dim the happiness inside me.

Somewhere around the halfway mark I stopped to rest, sitting down against a fence post. I closed my eyes, and though I didn't sleep, I must have stayed there a long time. When I got up, I saw that the sky, though still dark, was of the deepest, purest blue, like the blue in Helen Maria's peacock feather. The hills and fields were blue too, with the trees and huddled cows black masses against them. I heard a birdcall, exotic in the blue darkness, and then, by degrees, as I walked along, the sky faded to a thin gray, and so did the fields and cows, and the farms I passed—everything gray and still and cold. After a while glimmers of light marbled the sky, and everything around me began slowly to flush with color. It made me feel exposed, and I walked faster. Then there was a plank of red across the horizon, and the sound of roosters crowing. I began to run, my eyes watering in the first harsh glare of the sun.

Chapter 35

It was broad daylight when I crunched down the Stappnagel driveway. They would be eating breakfast, waiting for me; there was no point in sneaking in. I went to the front door, but it was locked. Going around to the back, I found the door there unlatched and let myself in.

The house was dark. I walked stiffly to Valerie's room and quietly opened the door. The shade was up, the room bright. The clock said ten minutes past six. Valerie sat on the bed in her bathrobe, pasty and red-eyed, as if she too had been awake all night. I fell like iron beside her.

"It wasn't blown up."

"That's good," she said tiredly.

I closed my eyes.

"I didn't tell them. I shut the window and turned off the lamp." Her voice was frazzled, the piping gone. "Mother came in again, but she didn't turn the light on. I said you were asleep."

I gave a deep sigh. "I want to thank you, Valerie. And I'm sorry I choked you."

"That's all right," she said, sighing too.

My bones on the soft bed were expanding and pulsing, as if they had been squeezed inside a tight box and suddenly been pulled out.

"They ran over a dog. My father went outside and shot it." She began to cry. "He buried it outside. . . ."

I turned sorely on my back and opened my eyes.

"It kept screaming, that's why he had to shoot it. . . ." She was biting in her breaths, trying to speak, and I understood now that she had been crying a long time, that's why her eyes were red. "Oh Suse, if you could have

195

heard how it kept screaming. . . ." She wiped her eyes with the sleeve of her bathrobe.

I lay looking at the bright ceiling. The joy ebbed, sank, vanished.

A door opened down the hall, and we heard footsteps going by. A few moments later we heard the radio turned on loudly, then lowered. Presently the footsteps returned. The doorknob turned gently.

"Oh you're up already," said Mrs. Stappnagel, and in a yellow flowered housecoat, she stepped quickly inside. "Suse, no one was hurt in Mendoza. Not a person."

"Good."

She looked at me oddly.

I removed my leg from the touch of her housecoat as she sat down next to us, and I saw a line of puzzlement come between her eyes, but it faded; she gave me a smile. "I don't wonder you're cranky, you don't look as if you had a wink of sleep all night. Or you either," she said to Valerie, gently smoothing back her Benjamin Franklin hair. Her own hair was a mess, and there were bags under her eyes, and now her face turned grave, yet even so, the smile lingered, as a kind of faint and tender line; a lyingly soft look, at odds with the words she spoke.

"We've found out what happened now. It was in Port Chicago. Two ammunition ships exploded. Everything's in a confused state, Suse, so we won't be able to take you home yet. They're asking that people don't come in. We want to do everything we can to cooperate. But just as soon as. . . ."And she talked on.

So they were ships, or parts of ships, that had turned over and over in the rosy glow, with people inside them, or parts of people. And people inside the ambulances rushing to the hospital entrance, people with names and faces, blood-soaked and dying as I raced by, the happiest moment of my life. . . .

"I think you could both fall asleep on the spot. Try now, I'll roll down the shades."

The room darkened, and she went out softly. I heard the dog, the huge catastrophic night crammed into that one agonized scream.

My legs kept twitching, as with electric currents. Once more I climbed over Valerie, who had fallen asleep, and
196

creaked from the room. Passing the kitchen, I could hear Mrs. Stappnagel busy making breakfast. In the living room my vomit had been cleaned up, the broken glass swept from the floor, things set to rights. The radio was on. Next to it, unshaven, Mr. Stappnagel sat dozing.

"—and the other, a sixty-five-hundred ton Liberty ship, exploded simultaneously as they were being loaded at the magazine dock. Deaths are now put at roughly three hundred, with casualties at a thousand—"

I went out on the garage roof, away from Mr. Stappnagel, and stood listening by a jagged window.

"—reports of sabotage are as yet unfounded; cause of the explosion remains unknown at this time. The tremendous shock occurred at ten-nineteen P.M. and was felt for a radius of fifty miles, causing many people to think it was a Jap bombing attack. The blast left an aftermath of indescribable horror, 'like a scene out of hell,' according to one witness. In Mococo, more than three miles from the scene of the blast, shells and twisted metal were driven into the ground. Throughout the night, from every part of the country, fire trucks, ambulances, and volunteer doctors and nurses rushed to the disaster scene under highway patrol escort. In the tiny township of Port Chicago, property damage is devastating; in Mendoza few plate glass windows are left. Both towns have been placed under martial law, with all incoming traffic restricted to official vehicles. Private individuals are requested not to drive to these—"

The report was clicked off. I heard Mr. Stappnagel stretch and groan and a moment later, his face appeared at the window; he scratched his head and stood looking out. Then he saw me, and he smiled. "Well, Mother told you?"

I had never really noticed his face. It was an ugly face, not because it was whiskered and bleary, but because it was stupid, cruel, self-satisfied. The sort of face you would expect on someone who would go out and shoot a dog through the head. I knew it was illogical to hate him for having done that, yet I hated him for that as much as for anything else he had done last night.

"Mother told you?" he said again. "No one was hurt in Mendoza?"

Calling each other Mother, Father—it was cutesy, revolting, like nighty-night.

"Mother?" I said, enunciating the word with all the scorn I could muster.

He studied my face for a moment. "You're being very rude. May I ask why?"

I didn't reply but continued looking at him with a contempt that burned from my eyes like acid, receiving the most passionate satisfaction from such defiance toward this fool, these two fools, for his wife had come up beside him saying breakfast was ready. The loathing poured from my eyes, my satisfaction so bitterly intense that I felt this moment almost avenged the whole night, all the hours I had run in the dark, all the deafening sirens, and the torn-apart bodies, and the poor screaming dog on the road, all horror and death that had ever happened and ever would, because these two blind, smug fools were at the bottom of it.

"Have we done something to—" he started.

"Let me—" she whispered, and she left the window and opened the door to the roof, stepping out with a softly troubled look. I walked to the far end, past the two sleeping bags lying wrenched and twisted, and stood with my back to her. She didn't follow. After a moment she said, "It's all right, Suse. You just come in when you feel like it. It's all right."

It's all right. If you were dying in their arms with your throat cut, they would smile at each other and tell you it was all right. But nothing would ever be all right again, though the hills lay sunny and peaceful and the air was filled with the chirping of birds, because it had happened, after all this time, after my always knowing it would and hoping it wouldn't. It had happened.

I spent the rest of the day in bed, trying to sleep. Late in the afternoon Valerie, who had dressed earlier and tiptoed out, came in and rolled up the shades.

"We can take you home," she piped. "They're letting people in."

She seemed composed now, her usual confident, mathematical self, standing there at the window in her yellow sunsuit, except that she remained there, gazing out at the pile of raw dirt where the dog was buried. I dragged myself from bed, stood on the two fiery stubs that were my feet, and began to search for my shirt. I found it under a chair and bent down stiffly.

"Did you ever think anything like this could happen?" Valerie asked from the window.

"The dog?"

"Yes. And everything."

"I never expected anything else."

"I didn't."

"You were living in a fool's paradise." I pulled off my pajama top, enveloped for a moment in an overpowering smell of stale sweat. "You should always expect the worst, because it always happens."

"Maybe," she said reflectively. "Did it make it better because you expected it?"

"I don't know, but you can't ignore the truth."

"What truth?"

"*This.* What *happened.*" I dragged my shirt on and buttoned it with thick fingers. "You ought to think about that dog. You think it's the only dog that ever got run over? It's happened a thousand times before, and it'll happen a thousand times again. You just happened to hear this one. You ought to face it."

I stood looking at her in her yellow sunsuit; then I limped painfully to her side and turned her around by her arm, keeping my fingers there tightly. "You'd better face a lot of things. You just happened to hear that explosion, but it's happening somewhere else all the time. And I'll tell you something else. This war isn't ever going to end."

She thought for a moment, her fingers nervously working at my clamped hand. "But wars always end. And now with the invasion—"

"You think that's going to end anything? That's nothing but rumors!" I looked almost with pity into the little, childish eyes, yet at the same time tightened my fingers around her arm so that she winced. "You know what you saw in that red light last night? Three hundred people being blown to bits. That's war. That's *truth.*" I gave her a rough shake, making her eyes flutter behind their spectacles. "So accept it! Get your face out of those stupid equations!" She looked as if she were going to cry. Turning from her, I began to gather and pack my things.

The Stappnagels left Valerie home to get more sleep because she seemed suddenly tired out. We covered the seven long slogging miles in a few minutes, and they ac-

companied me pleasantly inside as if my rudeness and
silence and flinging from the car had been only general
upsetness: they understood, they forgave, it was all right,
everything was all right.

Mama opened the screen door, and her arms went
around me because, as she said later, she knew what had
been said on the radio and what I must have been
through. Dad came up too, and it was the moment of
bliss I had wanted last night, feeling them warm and
alive in my arms—but the Stappnagels had to tarnish
this reunion with their presence, standing there looking
on with their empty, smiling faces, again giving me that
crazy but absolutely real feeling that they had caused
the disaster, the whole war, all death and wrongness everywhere. When they left, I hoped their car would run
off the road, killing them both.

I told Dad and Mama about my flight home after all.
They looked shocked and also full of anxiety, as if I were
still running along the road, but they didn't think I was
demented. Not at all. They understood completely, and I
knew now that even if I had disobeyed President Roosevelt himself last night, they would have understood.

They took me through the house, which was not what
it had seemed the night before. Though the front windows were intact, those along the sides had been blown
in, and there were two deep black cracks down the
kitchen wall. Many things had toppled, and in my room
I discovered my jar of moldy oranges gone, smashed on
the floor and thrown in the garbage can, where I gave it
a last look and left it.

I went downtown the next morning. The impact had
gone in strange waves, hitting one window but not another, leaving some parts of town with windows un-
touched, and others paneless for blocks. The courthouse
was badly damaged, lights torn from fastenings, its Corinthian pillars and front sidewalk dislodged, and on
Main Street soldiers stood by gaping store windows,
guarding exposed and tumbled merchandise, while the
street itself was clogged bumper to bumper with sight-
seers. Over in Port Chicago so many cars had poured in
that the barriers had been replaced; all over the countryside people were parking and scurrying around to find
bits of metal to take home with them.

It was rumored that bodies without heads or limbs had already washed into the marshes, and down by the tracks I watched soldiers and police searching through the reeds with long poles, Sheriff O'Toole shouting at intervals through a megaphone. But it was only on the fourth day that nine bodies were washed up, near Avon, too mutilated to identify. Two days later the papers said twenty-five more were found scattered along the shoreline. On the same page stood the official list of deaths, 268 names—the sailors you saw hanging around the Ferry Street bars, sauntering down the steps of the USO, snoring on the yellow varnished benches of the train depot.

That night I dreamed of a sailor in summer whites arguing with someone. He was presenting his case badly, even crying with vexation and confusion, and finally, to show him he might as well shut up, he was shoved a list of handwritten names that reached the floor and his own name pointed out, and at that moment the blast struck, blowing every name to bits, and the young arguing sailor's name, like all the others, swirled around in a cyclone of shattered letters, finally sinking down through the sky to the water, washing up in black sticky bits of flesh among the reeds.

Already after the first day other headlines had crowded in above the disaster.

JULY 21:   New Allied Gains in France!

JULY 22:   Marines Land on Guam!

JULY 23:   Crisis Rocks Reich
            After Hitler Assn. Attempt!

New gains in France. Like the new gains they used to report in Italy. And Guam, one more of those hundreds of islands—still having to take them one by one. And this attempt on Hitler's life, what kinds of fools did the newspapers take us for, saying it had been done by his own generals? It was to make us feel good, the way the Germans would feel good if they heard MacArthur and Eisenhower had tried to kill Roosevelt. Everything was to make us feel good so we would keep working at the shipyards and collecting tinfoil and buying war bonds and putting new glass in our windows every time a couple of ships blew up. They wanted us to feel good, the newspaper and magazine writers sitting safe on their behinds in their offices; the square-jawed movie stars who died bloodily in film battles and then went off on USO tours, cracking jokes with some Carmen Miranda type with flashing teeth and a bowl of fruit on her head; the high-ups who sat at the Lisbon conference table shuffling papers and discussing death politely. Deceivers. Smilers. Everything's all right.

I never went back to the Stappnagel house, even though I didn't like giving up Valerie. She was an unexciting person, but likeable, and I had liked her very much. Now, thinking back to our last conversation, I felt bad because I knew I had smashed her cloudless spirit forever. She sat alone in her room, with the dog's grave outside her window, and she had nothing to turn to but her equations, and their answers would never satisfy her now because she knew, as I did, that math was only marks on paper. If the X of an equation stood for one absolute number, what good did it do? What did it tell you about anything else? My feverish involvement with numbers seemed a pointless dream I had emerged from. The thought of my math text filled me with impatience. The thought of Mr. Lewis in September left me unmoved.

August, and the stagnant marsh smell hung briny and pungent in the air. Brassy music rolled in waves from the USO. The buckled sidewalk of the courthouse had been repaved, the great fluted columns set back straight. Sea gulls drifted in the hot sky. The huge catastrophic night was gone.

Chapter 36

It was on Sundays that I noticed I was shooting up like a weed, because on that day I had to wear a dress and its hem seemed an inch higher every week. Possibly that was why Valerie had seemed to get smaller all summer.

Possibly it was why grown people seemed less towering. Now when I thought back to that awful day in Berkeley, brooding over my tuna sandwich in my tight plaid dress, I saw myself as an altogether different person then, a short, unworldly bore, an imbecile perhaps rightly ignored.

I went to the library and wrote Helen Maria a letter. I went to the library because they had a book there called *Roget's Thesaurus,* which was a book of synonyms for every word that existed. I also consulted the dictionary, looking up the spelling of every word I used, even ordinary ones I wasn't sure of, like *goeing* and *chainge;* and was attentive to my grammar, although I was surprisingly good at grammar, maybe because I had listened so long to Helen Maria's crystal intonations that they had only to be transferred to paper.

Dear Helen Maria,

I forgot to write and thank you for having me down. Thank you. I saw Peggy on the street the other day but I didn't stop. As you know, she is an erstwhile friend who I ceased communicating with a long time ago. I believe people change. In Peggy's case she changed into a sugar plum, that is your own term, and I find her unbearably boring, which of course you do too. In my own case I have also changed but for the better. Many things have happened since I saw you. I received an A in math and got a special promotion into College Prep algebra, but I am not interested anymore. It is my belief that mathematics are dust and ashes as far as real truth is concerned.

Of course you are well aware of the Port Chicago explosion which caused so many deaths and casualties. It was a disaster that was horrible to go through, and it makes you think deeply about things. However, I know you don't like how I am always interested in the horrible things caused by war so I will not dwell on this subject any longer. But trusting you will not be offended, it is my belief that your attitude toward war is cavalier and always has been.

However, you are right about many other things, and I give you exceptional credit for that.

I hope your friend Egon is well and that he is enjoying the summer, which is his favorite season. You may tell him that I am going to study the history of the Jews, which we discussed in your absence. I may also read up on Rosa Luxury who seems to have impressed you very much, although your Rosa Luxury friend Ruth did not impress me very much. I trust you are in good health and doing well as usual in your studies, meanwhile I will sign off with hearty regards,

Suse

It took almost three hours to find the exact words I wanted, to check all the spelling, and to write a neat copy. I liked it. It was a clear and honest letter, and I had said what I planned to say—except for the Jews and Rosa Luxury, who had appeared on the page unexpectedly and whom I would now have to look up in the *Encyclopaedia Britannica*. But I would put that off for the time being. After taking the letter down the street to the post office, I put it in the mail slot with a feeling of accomplishment.

The spine thrills had left me. I checked on them now and then, bumping casually against soldiers, grazing the grocery clerk's hand as he took the ration book, slipping into the warm chair just vacated by our insurance agent. Maybe it was the explosion that had blasted the tingles from me. I felt it had blasted much from me; some last unsteady footing had been demolished, leaving no footing at all, only a sharp, bitter airiness, as if I hung in space. Yet there was this sharpness, something that was new and in a way untrammeling: think of that letter, so certain, so pointed. As for the tingles, I was glad to be rid of them. They had taken up too much time and emotion. Now I was uncluttered, free, with a bitter sharpness.

The cause of the blast was never settled. It could have been carelessness; it could have been sabotage. Many favored sabotage, especially Sheriff O'Toole in his *Clarion* column, and there was no doubt in my own mind. One of your harmless Nisei released from camp to come back and do his dirty work, to turn the white-uniformed sailor and his 267 companions into shreds of black flesh. In the privacy of my room I did my gory artwork, and at night the holocaust of the Jap house crackled behind my closed lids. But more often than not it was whiskered Mr. Stappnagel and his wife in her flowered housecoat whose necks were severed, and it was their house surrounded by manzanitas that went up in flames. And sometimes it was the bigwig emissaries whose heads went rolling, and their Lisbon conference room that was gutted, and sometimes the movie star heroes and their flimsy studios, or the newspapermen and their type-clacking offices.

Dear Suse,

What a pleasant surprise your letter was. People do indeed change. You have no idea how astringent it was to hear you contradicting me outright on my attitude toward the war. Your belief happens to be incorrect, but I give you credit (perhaps even exceptional credit) for stating your opinion so honestly. I must also congratulate you on your success in and disavowal of mathematics, which, though in its highest form incorporates the highest truths, would seem a métier unsuited to your nature. My own studies, thank you, are going well.

You imply that I was unaffected by the Port Chicago disaster. That is not quite the case; it was the most horrifying night of my life. Radio reports led me to believe that Mendoza was devastated and my family dead, and when I learned the truth, my relief was submerged by the realization of what had happened to so many others. Do not think that you have a monopoly on human feeling. You have an obsession with war. There is a difference.

So you are spending your summer immersed in worthy projects, unlike our former consort, who is beleaguering Jack and Estelle to redo the Dungeon on behalf of cheerier jitterbug parties. Thank God I am no longer living there. But who, may I ask, is Rosa Luxury? Do you mean Rosa Luxemberg? I don't remember mentioning her, but you will find her an interesting person to study. I've promised my parents to come home for a visit during semester break, so I'll look forward to seeing you then.

Helen Maria

P.S. Egon is very well, and sends his regards.

It was a wonderful letter, even if my face burned over Rosa Luxury and even if my concern with the sufferings of war was questioned as to its sincerity; she was wrong there, but she had a right to her opinion, as I had a right to mine. It was the letter of someone writing an equal, and it was a letter of friendship, and not least of its delights was its reference to Egon, whose name I touched with my finger, feeling the warmth of his eyes and smile radiate through the ink.

I sat defeated over the encyclopedia. Rosa Luxemburg was a German revolutionist born a Jew in Russian Poland. This was of unnatural complexity, as was the whole essay, of which I understood nothing except the last sentence where she was beaten to death and thrown in a canal.

I sat fidgeting for a while. It was a hot morning; the library was warm and stuffy. If I investigated this tight-packed column of baffling terms, I would be here all day. Still, I had to know what I was talking about when Helen Maria came home. Getting the dictionary and borrowing a pencil and some paper from the librarian, I began rereading the essay and listing the words I didn't understand—*revolutionist, theoretician, agitator, Communism, faction,* and many others—winding up with over twenty.

Then I began looking them up and writing out their definitions. This was painfully slow work, since the definitions also contained words I didn't know and I had to look them up too; and those definitions contained more unknown words that had to be looked up; and so on in a spreading plague until I had scribbled down so much I had to borrow more paper. At noon I went home for lunch, wishing I had never heard of Rosa Luxemburg. But I remembered Peggy's rapture over her encyclopedia adventure, how one thing had led to another and they all wound up fitting together like rose petals and opening in a blaze of wonderful sense. When I had finished my sandwich, I walked back through the blistering heat to finish my work.

At four o'clock I finished. My hand was stiff with writer's cramp; sheets and sheets of scribbled paper covered the table. Now, with every last word tracked down,

I would reread what I had written and then reread the essay.

I did so, and when I was done, I sank back in my chair. Either Peggy was smarter than I was or she was a bag of wind. There was no wonderful sense here, just the same confusion that had greeted me on my first reading. The whole day had been wasted.

But dimly, as I sat glaring at the littered table, I sensed something happening. I saw something in my mind that seemed to be large and convulsive, like a giant pot of mush seething. I watched as it bubbled and boiled and heaved. It was the masses, the proletariat. And over there was a bowl of smooth custard; that was the wealthy people, the capitalists. Mush pot and custard bowl. And now, as if in a vision, they began to move around, and other words began taking shape. Exploitation was the custard bowl making the mush pot do all the work. Class struggle was the pot trying to explode off the stove and the bowl trying to keep it there. Revolution was when the pot finally did explode.

My eyes dazzled. So much for Peggy and her piddling triumph; it couldn't match this. And eagerly, confidently, I read through the essay once more. There were many subtleties that I would ponder at my leisure, but for the moment I relished the essentials:

Rosa Luxemburg gave revolutionary speeches which were highly agitating, agitation meaning to excite and disturb. She was head of the Spartacus party, Spartacus being an ancient Roman slave who led a slaves' rebellion, which was why the party was named so. But it was not the only revolutionary party, because of factionalism. Factionalism was many little mush pots seething and arguing because their theories differed. Rosa Luxemburg argued the best because she had brilliant theories and was a brilliant orator, and she led the proletariat to revolt and riot. Unfortunately she was beaten up by reactionary troops—reactionary was being against progress—and when she was dead, they threw her in a canal. And that was Rosa Luxemburg.

It was a tragic story, yet I felt tiredly happy. With hard labor I had wrested free the flower of knowledge, and now I sat spent and illumined in its golden light.

Chapter 37

I planned to tackle the Jews the next morning, but it was so hot that I went down to the creek instead, to cool my feet in one of its stagnant sumps, a poor substitute for my Red Cross swims, which had just ended, but at least water.

The heat was always more intense in the creek, more dusty and dry and piercing than anywhere else. Crackling and powdery, it stung the nostrils and eyes, prickled in little hives all over the body. Beds of gravel glared; dragonflies glittered in tall, chalky weeds; cicadas droned, broke off, droned again. Sweat rolled down my ribs as I walked, patching my shirt and gathering damply in the band of my shorts. When I saw a swarm of gnats, I plodded over to it and with the toe of my tennis shoe splashed aside the scum of a sunken pool. Then, after pulling off my shoes, I stepped in and stood immersed to the ankles. The water was sun-filled, warm, the clear golden brown of cider. I scratched my prickling body, rubbed my stinging eyes until little stars revolved, then slowly took off my shorts and shirt, and then my undershirt, and stretched out full length in the shallow water, rolling with lazy greed until I was wet all over. After getting up again, I stood looking down my glistening body for a while, then, picking up my clothes and shoes, walked on in my underpants. I felt sun-dazed, reckless, like an African animal, sleepy, yet somehow intent and ready for anything, a hot, loose-limbed beast prowling.

My stomach swept down smooth and flat into my low-slung underpants; I liked that, and I liked the golden tan of my skin and the slim roundness of my forearms, which I lifted, first one, then the other, and gazed at as I walked, my heart beginning to pound. Someone stood hidden in the bushes, watching, and now he would step out in front of me. . . . A crackle spun me around. Two blue jays flew noisily from a bush. On weakened legs I turned and went on. What if schoolmates were down here exploring and saw me like this, half naked, primitive, shameless? Their eyes would pop from their heads; they would tell everyone that Suse Hansen sneaked around in her underpants, looking for men.

Let them, I was too hot to care; the sun poured, pounded, quivered; it was drugging, intoxicating, so that this dry creekbed, gravelly and weed-choked, seemed a garden of paradise, seemed radiant, shimmering, eternal. And there was the footbridge hanging overhead, its weathered wood shining like silver, and he would walk across it and climb down the bank and come up to me, his blue eyes filled with the sun, his black hair shining.

I put my clothes down and stood waiting, my hands loose on my hips, my long smooth stomach curving slightly to one side in a sleepy, brazen stance. My bangs were glued itchily to my forehead, my bare feet burned in the gravel, but I didn't move. In a drugged rapture of exposed flesh, my ears ringing with the steady, drilling hum of the cicadas, I waited.

All at once the bridge overhead wobbled. Whirling, I plunged into the bushes and stared out wildly to see if it was some schoolmate who might have recognized me by my green hair. But it was just a woman carrying a bag of groceries, and she wasn't even looking.

Shaking, as if awakened on the brink of disaster, I waited until she was gone and rushed out to retrieve my clothes. I pulled them on hurriedly and climbed up the bank to hide myself under a eucalyptus tree. After a while, when the fright had died away, I lay back in the foxtails and gazed up at the leaves, where the sunlight burst through in great blinding punctures. I was hot and sleepy again, and I was thinking of Egon. For it was he who had been down there with me in that strange paradise of shimmering light and nakedness, that hot and sweetly aching moment of time everlasting. We were linked forever. It was Egon and I.

And it was odd that my thoughts about flesh were suddenly different, no longer dark and unsettling and vaguely repulsive in a Eudene-like way, but vast, golden thoughts, filling me with light and love and the feel of Egon's arms around me as I sprawled warm and brown in the foxtails.

*   *   *

The next morning I went to Reed's stationery and bought a new Big Chief notebook for fifteen cents. Then, going to the library and getting out the ITA to KYS encyclopedia volume, I tackled the Jews.

They filled forty-four pages; I noted that before I began. Then I decided not to begin. But I had told Helen Maria I was studying the Jews, and also, I wanted very much to know all about Egon. At least everything was neatly broken down into historical sections, which would make it easier to follow. And I could skip the first section, which was the boresome Bible all over again, and start with the "Hellenic Influence." Nor would I track down every word to its bitter end, as I had done with Rosa Luxemburg. I must settle for rough impressions or be here the rest of the summer.

How appropriate Helen Maria's first name was; Hellenic meant Greek! How fascinated she would be by the Greek influence on the Jews; but a quick glance was sufficient for me, and I leaped on to "Diaspora in The West," diaspora, I discovered in the dictionary, meaning spread out, and West not meaning California but west of Asia, specifically Europe. Scribbling these things down, I sped on to the Roman Empire, to *pagan, schism, papacy,* and a few other recurring terms, which I looked up and wrote down, then flew on to the Dark Ages, to *feudalism, Crusades, infidel, rapine,* and then to the Renaissance, to *pogrom* and *mercantile* and *ghetto,* and then to the Reformation, the French Revolution, the Industrial Revolution, and here I was right up to the modern period, sweeping through recognizable surroundings, greeting old friends such as Marx and Rosa herself, then coming abreast of Hitler and a new spate of unfamiliar terms— *anti-Semitism, conspiracy, racism, disenfranchisement*— whose definitions I hurriedly found and dashed off, whipping on to the last paragraph, where I was bidden farewell by the violent German riots of November, 1938.

"Crystal Night!" I scrawled in triumphant conclusion, and shut the volume with a thud. From the Bible to Egon in two hours. Flexing my cramped fingers, I glanced with pride at the librarian, but she was absorbed behind the *Ladies' Home Journal.* The only other occupant was a small girl turning the pages of a storybook. How little and dim the library seemed, how poky these two other occupants, with their simpleminded interests. I had the whole history of the Jews between my notebook covers, 2,000 tumultuous years—*tumultuous* being one of the words I had looked up.

Now I sat back and waited confidently for everything to fall into place. And soon I sensed something taking shape in my mind, something big and dim and convulsive. This time it was not a mush pot seething; it was a great tide of some sort, that swept out in all directions. It was the Jews. And now I began to see them running, chased and massacred like infidels, and this was because they had killed Christ centuries before and people were still against it.

But here I hit a snag. It was not believable that people had remained upset over Jesus' death for so long. It was like being upset over the price of shoelaces. Jesus was boring. Religion was boring. How could they get upset in the first place, much less stay that way for several centuries?

I would have to put that aside. It was better to concentrate on the later centuries when religion had been forgotten and it was economics and politics that everyone was upset over. That was the mush pot and custard bowl and made sense. That was when the tide was poured into dingy ghettos where it had no rights and where it became mush pots.

But here was another snag. Some of the largest custard bowls were Jews, like the Rothschilds, who had popped up regularly for a whole page. Who was on which side? If Jewish Rosa Luxemberg was against the Jewish Rothschilds, and vice versa, why did everyone lump them together? And they did. That was what racism meant, lumping people together because they looked alike. But they did not look alike, or Egon and Ruth would look alike and they were completely different. The only thing they had in common was that their ancestors had killed Christ, and no one had been upset over that for many centuries. So why were they all lumped together, rich and poor Jews, Communist and capitalist Jews, short and tall Jews, brown-eyed and blue-eyed Jews, and beaten up on Crystal Night?

It was too complicated. Egon himself had said, "It is more complicated than you will ever understand." So maybe I should leave it at that and go out of this stifling cave into the sunshine. But I was challenged now. I would reread these forty-four pages painstakingly, tracking every last reference to its source. I would sit upright and full of labor, and I would triumph in a burst of light.

It took five days. When I was done, I put my filled notebook under my arm and my blunted pencil in the pocket of my shorts and went slowly out the door into the abrupt heat. I had more than the Jews between my covers; I had the world's history, and I looked in a new way at the people on the street, almost staring. They were terrible and frightening. They were the same as their ancestors, and their descendants would be the same as they. It was the terrible thing I had learned. Each century was the same; history was the same record played over and over. War was war, and peace was preparation for war; it was as if man were crazy, had always been, would always be, and the people on the street were man in his daily and abiding craziness. And the Jews summed it up with their complicatedness. Their complicatedness was like a maze of chambers they had been forced into down the centuries, and why they were pushed into the first chamber no one even knew or cared about anymore. But if you came from that long maze, you were beaten up, even if you were as unlike as Ruth and Egon. It was the pure form of senselessness that was history. And I realized now that even Rosa Luxemburg made no sense, sinking to the bottom of the canal while time was already rushing on without her, already piling up more riots and governments and elections and famines and wars, and now she was only a name in a book, and that was the flower of knowledge.

Chapter 38

AUG. 26:   Paris Liberated!

My blood was roused by victory, and I thought of Peter marching through the old streets, hugged and kissed by the wildly cheering crowds whose necks had been crushed so long by the Nazi boot. It was a glorious scene
212

to envision, but with my library experience behind me, I wondered if twenty years from this dazzling moment another war might be brewing or might already be under way with running blood and arms sticking up like iron from the snow. I wished bitterly that I had never opened the encyclopedia; I should have followed my deepest instinct, which was never to ask anything.

It was time for Mama to clip my hair, but I told her I thought I would let it keep growing. The idea had come to me during Karla's last visit, which was really her last visit because she was definitely moving from San Francisco to Los Angeles to work at the Walt Disney studios. If Peggy had been around, she would have been thrilled—Karla in Hollywood! I was thrilled myself, but I would have been happier if it weren't so far away. All through her visit I was filled with the realization of how pretty Karla was; not that I wanted to look like her, I wanted to look like me. Karla's nose was straight, her eyes blue, her hair gold; my nose was snub, my eyes gray, my hair, when not green, the pale color of wheat, that's how I was and that's how I liked it; but one aspect of her beauty I did covet, and that was the loose, shiny length of her hair. It seemed to me that I could never be gathered into Egon's arms as long as my hair was cut as if along the lines of a T square. Mama said she thought it looked nice as it was; but she could understand if I didn't want a Dutch boy bob at thirteen, and she added that we had better go through my school clothes because everything would have to be let down.

Passing a restaurant window, I thought I glimpsed Eudene inside, and I went back and pressed my face against the dusty glass. It was a run-down truckers' café off Ferry Street, and it was definitely Eudene in a tight green waitress's uniform, her greasy sauerkraut hair stuck in a net. I flung open the door.

"Eudene!"

She was banging around the scarred counter, laughing her bellowing laugh with the customers, swinging her broad hips and chewing her gum with gusto. "Hi, kid!" she yelled. "Take the load off your feet, be with ya in a sec!" She seemed in wonderful spirits, and her belly was not at all enormous. Either I had imagined she was pregnant, or she had had it. I sat down on a stool and began

213

counting the months since February, coming up with seven just as she sauntered over, holding out her hand with the fingers spread. On the fourth finger was a narrow gold band. It had a quiet, dignified appearance.

"You got married?"

She dug into the pocket of her uniform and brought out a wallet, from which she extracted a snapshot, the kind you take of yourself in a bus station. It was of a soldier with a shiny, beefy face. His cap was pulled down at a goofy angle almost to his eyes, and he was smiling with dark, snaggly teeth, but he had a cheerful look, and he had written across the bottom "To my sweetheart Eudene from Acie."

"Acie?"

"He don't have a first name, just initials. A. C. Acie. They do that in Tennessee. Whaddya think of him?" The fry cook was yelling for her, but she paid no attention.

"He's good-looking."

"You bet." She took another picture from her wallet. "Here."

I looked at a white blob in diapers lying in Eudene's lap.

"Whaddya think? You wanna come over some time and see him."

Why would I want to see a baby? What was there to see? I told her the cook was yelling.

"Keep your shirt on!" she bellowed, stuffing the wallet and pictures back in her pocket and tramping off.

I wondered how long she would last as a waitress. I wondered how she could have had a baby in seven months, but apparently she had. I wondered if she was really married or if the ring was a fake. But none of it mattered. She was *partie avec le vent*, gone with the wind, a mother. During her next lull she would come back and bore me with details about her blob's appetite and disposition.

But she didn't. She told me instead about her wedding; not that it was much, just three minutes before a judge, but as if it were something she had to underline. "So it's Mrs. Acie Barnes now!" she concluded, snapping her gum, and only then did she launch into the baby's description, which was mercifully interrupted by a trucker's call from the cash register.

She had a lot of trouble, punching the wrong keys and worriedly screwing up her face, and when the drawer finally zipped out, it smashed her in the stomach, and then she counted the change wrong and had to start over again, dropping coins and yelling, "Hang on a sec!" until at last the trucker had his thirty-two cents safe in his palm and Eudene smashed the drawer back triumphantly.

I had a feeling that being married made everything triumphant for her. Even if she lost her job tomorrow, and I was sure she would, she wouldn't be dented. Never again would she snivel and groan over the righteous wrath of God. Even if a thousand men had slithered their hands over her flesh in cheap hotel rooms, she would never have to think about it and get confused and make up stories. And even if she'd never met this Acie till she was big as a balloon, the wedding ring was on her finger, and with her kind of mind and her kind of math it could have been put there a year ago. She was in a way blessed.

"How long have you worked here?" I asked when she had mopped up a cup of coffee she had capsized and sauntered back to my side.

"Two days. Acie's overseas—"

"Where?"

"Iceland."

"You don't have anything to worry about."

"And he's saving his pay, and I'm working, so when we get enough we're buying a house—"

That was a dreary thing to do with money, instead of buying a horse or a yacht. But she seemed to think it was exciting. Her smoky gray eyes were filled with plans and pleasure and with new worldliness. "So what's new with you, kid? Not much, I guess."

"I wouldn't exactly say that, Eudene." For one thing I was almost as tall as she, and fifty pounds slimmer, but I wouldn't bring that up. "I've been down to the University of California, visiting my friends, who are postgraduate students. And I'm going into College Prep algebra in the fall. And we did have the Port Chicago explosion, in case you didn't hear."

"Ya, Acie's sister told me about it. I'm living with her, she's got a trailer. She works night shift at the cannery, so she takes care of Bobby while I'm here. He don't

215

mind, but he likes me better. You wanna come around and see him."

I would rather look at a hole in the ground. I would rather look at a Ferry Street wino. I told her the cook was yelling again.

"Stuff it, buster, I'm coming!" She went off swinging her hips, pausing to refill a coffee cup with such haphazard aim that the liquid splashed high before the trucker's face. Grizzled men in sweat-stained shirts, cigarettes stuck behind sunburned ears, they looked on with patience and even enjoyment, no doubt feeling secure in the knowledge that she'd be gone by the next day.

But help was hard to come by, with everyone at shipyards and airplane factories, and Eudene remained. She never did become very efficient; but at least she learned how to count change, and she stopped splashing coffee in the customers' faces, and after a while there grew a family feeling in the place, she called the men by their first names, and they asked about Bobby, whose picture she had thumbtacked next to the flyspecked "Drink Coca-Cola" sign.

The Sunday after I found Eudene again I thought I might as well get it over with and took myself to see Bobby. The trailer was across the tracks near the cannery, nicely situated by the marsh. It was a cramped, stifling little trailer, so small that the sister-in-law had to get out for me to get in. She said something like "Thaz awlraght, ah dowen mahnd," and sat down with a movie magazine on the step, beefy and snaggletoothed, like Acie with a pompadour. I hadn't seen Eudene out of her waitress's uniform, and she looked pretty good, in her old gym shorts and an army shirt with the sleeves cut off. She looked like someone who might go exploring in the marsh, but of course she lifted up Bobby instead, who was exactly as I had foreseen, a boring, bald-headed mass of screams.

"Whaddya think!" she yelled over the noise, arranging him in her arms so I would have a good view.

"He's very nice," I said, concealing my pity.

"You oughta seen him at first!" she yelled. "He was way aheada time, he was so skinny you couldn't hardly see him! But he's all filled out now!"

"Yes, he's very nice-looking."

I stayed a polite length of time, making a few more

hypocritical remarks, and then with explosive relief I was walking back along the bank of the marsh. Here was something that could stir you, this hard, burning path covered with spidery-cracked dry silt. These caked brown reeds on one side, standing in pools of gold foil, and these brambles growing on the other, lacy and complex, powdered with fine dust, and this hot, still air droning with insects, pungent with tule reek and the cannery fumes of peaches. Did Eudene find something stirring in those midget fists that caught and grabbed in her hair? Was it stirring to save paychecks to move into some housing project with Acie and his bad teeth? You could only feel pity for someone in Eudene's position. Still, after the wrath of God and being kicked out her own door, it must be a happy ending for her.

But suddenly it occurred to me that there were no endings in life. How odd that until this moment I never thought of that. In a movie, Eudene's ending could have been when she reached for the basin to vomit in, a grainy close-up sealing her forever into misery and despair. Or it could be now, this minute, as she bounced the baby in the trailer, her grinning pleasure preserved for eternity. But neither scene was final. She just kept going on.

I came to the tracks and began walking along the oil-blackened ties. If a train ran me down now, that would be an ending. But if I stepped over the rail instead, which I did, and crunched along the weedy gravel, that would just be another scene, which would merge into a scene of me coming out on the road, which would merge into a scene of me walking home, and so on forever until I died.

Nothing ever came to a conclusion. Probably I had known it since that day at the library.

Chapter 39

SEPT. 4:   Brussels Liberated!

We had crossed a border at last, even if it wasn't the German border. We were getting somewhere. It made up for much, even for the fact that if Helen Maria had come home for a visit, she hadn't gotten in touch.

But the next morning at about eleven o'clock, as I was watering the bushes in the front yard, I looked up with a start. Peggy stood before me.

"Hi," she said politely. "Helen Maria said to tell you she's home and she wants you to come over."

I was so startled to see Peggy in the flesh that I dropped my eyes and stared at the stream of water. "Tell her okay."

"Well, you should come now. They're leaving this afternoon."

"Who's they?"

"She brought her boyfriend."

I dropped the hose and twisted the faucet shut. "I'd better change. I'll be back in a sec."

"You don't have to dress up!" she called after me—she, of course, decked out in a nice summer dress and white sandals. I ran inside and told Mama I'd been invited to the Hattons, then barged into my room. When I emerged a few minutes later, Mama and Peggy were conversing out front. Mama had always liked Peggy, and she was sorry when we stopped being friends. She looked happy to see her now, and she looked happy to see me coming down the steps in one of my new school dresses, with my hair carefully brushed. Waving good-bye, as if we were regular friends, Peggy and I went down the walk together.

I was about two inches taller than she; that was startling and made me feel good. It was also a good feeling to have my dress fit, and it was a nice dress, pale blue with white piping. I looked very good, even if my hair was not grown out and was still green.

But it was an uncomfortable feeling to hear only the sound of our footsteps. I could not speak because I did not wish to be the one to make an overture.

At last Peggy spoke. "I guess you're still taking swimming lessons."

"Obviously."

"I guess you're pretty good by now."

"Very."

"That's great."

But I knew very well what she thought of people who

218

splashed around to the blasts of a whistle, especially when their crowning glories were defiled in the process. "There are a lot of other things in my life besides swimming. And don't worry too much about the green, it always fades."

"I'm not worrying."

"I certainly hope not. Also, I'm letting it grow out."

"Really?"

"Yes. It will be shoulder-length."

"That's great."

"I don't consider it very great. I don't think hairstyles are important."

And so there were more blocks of silence. And I was growing nervous now, thinking of the moment when I would actually see Egon. I almost wished I hadn't come. I would stammer or blush or trip in the doorway, or all three. I took a deep breath to quiet the flutterings in my stomach. The unbroken sound of our footsteps was beginning to feel ominous, like the Bataan death march.

"What do you think of Egon?" I asked abruptly, blotting my palms on my dress.

"So-so."

I glanced at her with amazement, then gave an inner smile of scorn. She really was a fool.

"Better than Mr. Tatanian anyway," she added. "Her taste's improving."

The fluttering in my stomach was joined by a charge of affront. "I happen to know Egon, and—"

"You do?" she asked, her eyes swinging to mine with interest.

"Certainly. I know him very well. Did you think I didn't know him? I know him from Berkeley."

"Oh that's right," she nodded, unimpressed. "I heard you went down there. Estelle said you didn't look like you had a very good time."

"Estelle's nuts."

"Don't call my mother nuts."

"I apologize," I said, looking down the street. I had to have smoothness and serenity these last few blocks. No arguments, no confusion. But the closer we got to the house, the weaker my legs felt, the more my stomach fluttered; and my mind was blank, I couldn't think of what words to use in my greeting. Our marching footsteps echoed in my ears. And now we were turning up the pink walk; now I was following Peggy up the stairs. The march stopped. She swung open the massive door.

They were in the Dungeon. Rudy dashed barking through the gloom, flinging himself at my weak legs. Trying to remain footed, to breathe and smile and get my voice in order, I made my way through the room. Beneath the scowling matador they sat, on the chesterfield where I had sunk indecently into Mr. Hatton's cushion. A furnace blast of memory enveloped my face, and as Peggy hushed Rudy and an abrupt silence fell, I suffered an even worse clap of heat, remembering how I had stood before Egon sun-dazed and shameless in my low-slung underpants. Helen Maria got up and came forward.

"My God. You've grown."

Flaming, rigid, unable to smile, I put out my hand. "Greetings," I managed to say, sounding idiotic, and turned stiffly to Egon, coming over now, white-shirted and smiling, my Egon in the flesh. "Greetings," again, sounding weaker, demoralized, and my hand was clammy and trembling visibly; if he spoke, I didn't hear; I was even insensible to his clasp. All I wanted to do was get away and kill myself.

I sat down instead. It was a deep leather chair, and I felt less exposed. But this odd behavior—the others were still standing—sent a new blast of heat into my face, and I stared furiously before me.

"Well," said Helen Maria after a moment, "well, I'm glad you were home."

"Yes, we just came yesterday," Egon said as they reseated themselves. "And we must leave already this afternoon."

"I know." It came out loud and sour. It helped me bear my hideous entrance.

"We took a walk yesterday," he went on pleasantly. "It is a nice little town you have here."

"Oh yes," Helen Maria smiled over at me, "Egon thinks it's smashing."

"Oh, *Egon!*" Peggy, who had graced herself on the arm of the chesterfield, laughed, and threw her head back so that her throat looked like a white column.

"It is amusing?" he asked.

"She's easily amused," Helen Maria commented, curling her feet under her, wearing the same print dress she
220

had worn in Berkeley and the same old loafers without socks. Unlike Peggy, she used no lipstick; even so, she was pretty—beautiful really, like Gene Tierney, as Peter had once said—and I was bitterly aware of having chosen my seat unwisely, for it stood by a lamp that poured its cruel glow all over the green of my T square hair. It was like a war movie, being tortured by the Gestapo under blinding lights.

"So, have you had a nice summer holiday?" Egon asked me.

I knew how I looked; I hated his kindly attention. I answered with a sullen shrug, staring past him at the wall.

Then everyone ignored me.

They talked among themselves. They talked mostly about the heat. Rudy yawned. A fly buzzed. No wonder they were leaving, they were bored to death. They should leave now, I wouldn't miss them.

"We could go out in back," Peggy suggested.

"We'd roast," said Helen Maria. "Well, we could eat, I suppose. It's lunchtime."

A horror gripped me that I would be excluded. But Helen Maria motioned me along, and I responded with a put-upon sigh, walking behind them at a reproachful distance.

Coming from the gloom into the sunlit kitchen, with the prospect of food before me, I felt a little better. But no one noticed this, and I was asked politely by Helen Maria if I would kindly move because I was standing in front of the refrigerator, and then, again politely, by Peggy, if I would please let her get into the cupboard. I should probably have smiled and offered to help; but I could not bring myself to do this, and I sat down on a stool and folded my arms.

Egon wasn't doing anything either, but he didn't talk with me. He stood leaning against the sink, black-haired, blue-eyed, tan-faced, his sinewy hands resting on either side of him on the white tile, my beloved and longed-for Egon, to whom I had been so rude that his eyes, though not avoiding me and even pleasant, were bereft of their kindled attention and moved on, elsewhere, like a stranger's.

My nervousness had drained away, and my anger too; I just felt bitter. That hot-faced, bug-eyed entrance—he

221

would remember it always, and so would the others, and so would I. That stain would always be there, and now a great melancholy filled me, a hopelessness, which spread through me so heavily that it brought the whole world with it, the endless wars, the senselessness of history, the never-getting-there, the no-happy-endings, life so dark and futile that I felt my chin trembling.

How cloudless and cheerful they all were, while I sat here with my trembling chin. And now Egon had gone over to help, and the three of them, talking pleasantly together, were filled with smooth, practical purpose, as if they had no inkling that life was a black tunnel. Egon at least should know, but he was twisting off the lid of a mayonnaise jar without a care in the world, a man who had been through Crystal Night. And then I had an uncomfortable feeling, whose nature I could not place, a kind of shamed twinge that made me set my jaw hard against the tremor.

He put the jar on the table. Helen Maria checked the water boiling for coffee. Peggy was getting napkins from a drawer. The toe of my shoe made slow designs on the sunlit floor. Even if life was a black tunnel with no happy endings, there were bright moments here and there. And you had to take them. You had to take them or you would have nothing at all at the end. I got up, and with set lips and averted eyes, yanked the napkins from Peggy's hand.

Chapter 40

". . . *And she would* have gone on till dawn," Helen Maria was saying, setting the coffeepot down.

"I don't doubt it," Egon laughed as we all seated ourselves around the cramped table.

Helen Maria addressed me pleasantly, as if nothing had happened. "Grandmother and Aunt Margaret were here last night. Aunt Margaret was in powerful voice; she started at nine and was still going strong at mid-
222

night—Jack had to wrestle the accordion out of her hands."

"A remarkable woman," said Egon.

"Egon thinks it's a very odd family."

"Not odd, colorful," he corrected her amiably. "Anyway, your aunt has a fine voice."

"Like Enrico Caruso," said Peggy. She was right on her toes being witty, but I felt too sobered to be witty; relieved to be welcomed back, but pensive and formal.

"How was your grandmother?" I asked Helen Maria politely.

"In peak form. Regaling Egon with tales of old Berlin."

"Believe it or not," he said, "she was there in the summer of 1869."

"My gosh," I marveled, "that was even before the Franco-Prussian War."

"I see," said Peggy, making a thin sandwich with no mayonnaise, "that you're still preoccupied with things military."

I ignored her; that wasn't even her own wit, it was Helen Maria's. "Did she see Bismarck?" I asked Egon.

"She did not mention it."

"I don't like him anyway. He was against socialism."

"Oh yes," Helen Maria told him, "Suse has been studying Rosa Luxemburg."

"And by the way," I said to her quickly, "Rosa Luxury was an ironic pun. Because the socialists didn't go in for luxury, they were just the opposite. It was the bourgeois they were fighting who had luxury. That's what the whole struggle was about."

"I seem to have heard something along those lines," she nodded.

Egon's eyes were warm and interested again. "So, you are a socialist," he said.

This startled me. I had not considered if I was one or not. But I thought for a moment. "Yes, I am. It seems fairer to poor people."

"What if you were rich?" asked Peggy. "It's just because you don't have any money, so you may as well be a socialist."

"You don't even know what socialism is. Define it."

She shrugged. "Being fair to the poor."

"You're just repeating what I said. You don't even know anything about it."

223

"Maybe I do and maybe I don't, but you didn't answer my question. If you were rich."

"If I was rich I'd share with the poor."

"I bet."

"Suse probably would," said Helen Maria, passing the potato salad around. "She has the nature of a fanatic. She would go about like St. Francis of Assisi."

"I'm not a fanatic," I said, stung. It was one of the words I had looked up. It meant irrational zeal, and irrational was the other thing I wasn't. I wanted things to make sense, it was like a hunger. How could she say I was fanatical, like this St. Francis of Assisi? And I wasn't religious either, I hated religion.

Peggy was telling Egon that we were starting back to school next week. "Ninth grade," she said. "That's the first year of high school, except it's in the junior high building. But it's really high school."

As if that would impress him. "It's no big achievement," I told him. "They pass everybody."

"Lucky for you," Peggy murmured.

"Well, not everybody," I backtracked, flushing. "Like our friend Eudene, who wasn't very smart. They wouldn't have passed her."

"Oh, Eudene," smiled Helen Maria. "How is *La Grande Horizontale*?"

"Oh, she's married and has a baby. She's completely delirious."

"She always was," Peggy said. "She's cracked. She's the sort of person," she told Egon, widening her eyes as of old, "who *smashes* you in the ribs with her elbow and *screams* when she laughs. To me that's insane."

"Well maybe it's good to be insane," I said, "if it makes you happy."

"Our Suse championing happiness?" Helen Maria asked, giving me a smile. "*Brava!*"

I wasn't sure what she meant, but her enthusiasm lifted me. For the first time since my arrival I began to feel confident, and pouring myself more coffee, I looked across at Egon. "I've been studying the Jews. From the destruction of Jerusalem to Crystal Night."

"Have you?" he said, and waited for me to go on.

"I think the Jews are a pure form of the senselessness that is history."

He nodded reflectively, lifting his coffee cup. "It

sounds interesting, I must say. But I don't know what you mean."

"Neither does she," said Peggy, peeling an orange.

"Be quiet," said Helen Maria. "Go out and play."

Peggy's lips tightened. I held the floor. I took another sip of my coffee. "Everybody keeps persecuting the Jews because they started doing it a long time ago and now they can't stop. They've got a lot of fancy religious and political reasons, but the reasons don't mean anything, they just like to do it. It's like a habit. That's what I mean that it's the purest form of history's senselessness. Because history's the same old record played over and over, nobody thinks about anything or learns anything, it's like they're all stuck in a crazy machine."

"Well," said Egon, finishing his coffee and setting the cup down, "I suppose it's as valid an interpretation of history as any."

"It's utterly black," countered Helen Maria. "The old saw, man the absurd. It makes me impatient. It's all very good and fine to see life as a random joke, which it is, but to remain at that level of perception is perfectly useless."

"No doubt."

"You don't advise that kind of perception, certainly."

"No, I do not advise it."

"And you don't practice it, either."

He didn't answer. His eyes held something like humor, but it was not his usual warm, direct gleam; there was something distant about it, yet indulgent, something both removed and paternal. It made Helen Maria seem suddenly small next to him, the way she had seemed suddenly small when Aunt Dorothy had come staggering into her room.

"Well, you don't," she insisted. "You needn't look so mysterious."

"I just think we are perhaps getting off the track."

"Because you won't confront the issue."

"And what is the issue?"

"That you uphold this weltschmerzian view of life simply to give Suse her due, which isn't helping her at all. Given the slightest encouragement, she'll remain on that level forever."

"Aren't you being an alarmist?" He smiled.

"Not at all. She's been wallowing in the slough of despond for years."

"So? You have been wallowing about for years, Suse?"

"Well, it's not really funny. And here you are, Suse, taking up the study of history, and what do you do? You use it to confirm your temperament."

"I don't know what you mean."

"I don't *want* to see it that way, I *hate* it. But it's how "You read into it what you want to see."

it is. You said so yourself. You said it was a random joke."

"It's a great deal more than that."

"How can it be more than that if that's what it is?"

"It's what you put *into* it, don't you see?"

I tried to see. I wanted to see. I even closed my eyes to concentrate.

"Well, think about it," she said. "But not here. It's not exactly stimulating to watch."

My eyes opened. "You mean bright spots? Like going swimming—or if you're good at something, like you being a scholar? Or having a good lunch? Things like that?"

"You've got the drift, in a primitive sort of way."

Was that all it came down to? Those bright spots that were better than nothing at all?

"It's not enough," I said.

She gave a sigh. "Let's drop the subject."

I sat back in my chair. I had undone all the good of my bold, dazzling letter—my astringent letter, as she had so admiringly put it. Which word I had looked up: harsh, severe.

"You're confirming *your* temperament," I said suddenly, leaning forward. "Why do you study the Greeks? Because they saw everything balanced and whole, and that's what you like. The rest of history's a mess, but the Greeks are a big bright spot. That's what you want, so that's what you see. Well, that's not truth, that's just *your* truth. But you want everybody to think like you and the Greeks. And why should I? They collapsed like everybody else. The Romans ground them under, and then the barbarians ground the Romans under, and that's what *I* see. And it's as good as what you see!"

Helen Maria looked excited. "Good thinking, Suse! Good thinking! Maybe not right thinking, but good
226

thinking! No sloshing about, right to the point! *Brava!*"
And she looked with enthusiasm at Peggy and Egon.
"Well," she went on, "someday we'll have to go on from
here, but just now I think we've bored everyone sick."

Peggy nodded in agreement. Egon didn't look bored,
exactly, but as if he had gone off into his own thoughts,
and not especially sunny ones, for I saw that the lines
around his mouth were etched deep. It was odd how
sometimes you noticed them and sometimes you didn't.
It was because his face, I realized, had many different
things flickering and shading and changing in it all the
time, very quietly. It was because he was complicated,
like the rest of the Jews.

And what had happened to our conversation about the
Jews and about Rosa Luxemburg? Now that I was doing
so brilliantly we should return to them. But chairs were
scraping back, and the lines around Egon's mouth were
folding in pleasant creases as he thanked his hostesses
for lunch.

In the gloom of the Dungeon we sat as before, talking
of this and that. I felt very good, and even though Helen
Maria had her hand in Egon's, and I could see one finger
stroking his wrist underneath, I was filled to the brim
with my love for him.

"Did you have a nice summer, Egon?" I asked.

"Very nice," he said, and I felt his gaze tender and
deep on my face.

"Did you swim?"

"A few times,"̀ he said, and in filmy silence we dove,
we drifted with touching hands.

"So did I."

"That's why her hair's green," said Peggy.

I looked down, flushing. "Chlorine," I said.

"I see." He nodded. That was all. He was not repelled.
Nothing about me could repel him. I gave Peggy a calm
glance. Her hair tended to frizz in hot weather. I felt
very sure of myself, very comfortable, and was about to
settle more deeply into my chair when the visit ended.

"If the train leaves at two, I suppose we'd better get
ready," said Helen Maria, looking at her watch. We all
stood up, but I couldn't bear to leave Egon yet. I said I'd
walk to the depot with them; if they didn't mind, of
course.

"Fine, come along," Helen Maria said. "We'll be a few minutes."

I waited with Peggy.

"I like your dress," she said after a while.

"Thank you. Yours is nice too."

"Yours is really nice, though."

She wanted to be agreeable, in spite of her remarks at the table and the way she had pointed out my green hair. That was for Egon's sake. But now that he was out of the room, she was friendly. There had always been something good-natured about Peggy, bighearted, and now, suddenly, I thought again of the day I had been so cruel to her about Aunt Dorothy's death and felt a pang of old guilt. I wanted to tell her I was sorry.

I said instead, "It's nice. Talking again."

She gave a nod. "I know."

There wasn't enough room on the sidewalk to go four abreast, so Peggy and I walked behind. Carrying their overnight bags, Egon and Helen Maria walked leisurely, not pressed for time; the trains were always late anyway. The sky was white and blazing; there was a wonderful smell of melting street tar in the air, and hot pavement and dry grass. I feasted my eyes on Egon's tan neck and on the back of his white shirt. He had a strong back and a wonderful way of walking, relaxed, yet slightly military. Though not especially tall, he would look good in a uniform, better than most.

"Did he say why he's not in the Army?" I whispered to Peggy.

"Helen Maria said he had rheumatic fever," she whispered back. "It's nothing too bad, but you can't get in the Army. She's glad."

So was I. Peter should have been so lucky. And the soldiers on Main Street, waiting to be shipped to the Pacific.

I made my whisper smaller yet. "Did she say if they were in love?"

"She'd never tell us anything like that."

"I don't think they are."

"Estelle says Helen Maria's too immature for him," Peggy whispered. "She says you can see it on his face. I heard her tell Jack that. He thought so too. And so do I."

My eyes returned to the couple before us. I had a
228

feeling of lightness and hope, followed by a black thought. If Helen Maria was too immature for him, where did that put me?

"I think you're wrong," I whispered.

"She's smart, but it's all book learning. He's lived. That's what Jack said."

I nodded thoughtfully. "I think you're right."

It wasn't the years that counted; it was the living. I had been blown up in my cellar, I had run fourteen miles through the darkness, and I knew what the Jews and history were all about, and so did he, and Helen Maria didn't. His love for her had died, just as my love for Mr. Lewis had died. We had long since begun clearing the path to each other.

"It's there!" cried Helen Maria as we turned the corner of Ferry Street. Three blocks away, for once on schedule, the train was already moving. She and Egon broke into a run, their overnight cases held out from their sides; Peggy and I ran too. It was exhilarating to race madly down the street, with the soldiers cheering from the moving windows of the train, and steam hissing and bells clanging. We sped past the depot alongside the big turning wheels, and with a final exuberant cheer from the soldiers, Egon leaped into the moving door, pulling Helen Maria up after him. I caught a last glimpse of his face as he leaned out with a wave. He was laughing, and his eyes shone down into mine with love and promise.

Chapter 41

Soon after, I opened the paper to find that our ragged, hopeless enemy had begun smashing London with a powerful secret weapon, the V-2 rocket.

When I returned to school a few days later, I was three inches taller and many years older. At assembly I observed the usual cast of characters. There was Mother Basketball plonking down the aisle, and over there, Miss Moose, whom I had brought such happiness, and nearby was kindly, wrinkled Mrs. Miller. And there was Coach

Thaxter, and Mr. Villendo, and poor Mr. Kerr with his big nostrils, and concluding this band of dreary ex-lovers, Mr. Lewis in his eternal gray suit.

And there was Dumb Donny, green-haired and pulling someone's shirttail as always, but so shockingly tall that I stared. And now Peggy entered with her retinue, all in pink socks, pink skirts, and white blouses; it must be the newest thing, dressing alike first day. She smiled in passing, and I smiled back, but with a touch of pity for all that pink. And then the welcome-back speeches began, the voices droning on as you sank into other things, such as Egon waving from the train. . . .

Now it was all over, except for "On the Road to Mandalay." Mr. Kerr came onstage, seated himself at the grand piano, and banged out the rousing overture, while majestic Mr. Grandison raised high his arms and flung back his silver head.

The school year had begun.

Our homeroom teacher was new, a puny white-faced young woman called Miss Petain. I disliked her at once because of the name and because she was so awed by us, with big fisheyes that looked paralyzed. A wave of contempt swept through the class, followed by racketing disorder and a swiftly passed note: "Knock your books off 10:10!!!"

I felt excitement building up inside me, a wonderful sense of shared purpose, absolute accord. We all were quiet now, nudging our books to the edges of our desks. It was ten-nine, and Miss Petain was calling roll in a voice as thin and pale as her body. A click of the clock hand, and a tremendous thunderclap as seventeen books struck the floor at once. Miss Petain leaped straight into the air from her chair, a triumph beyond our greatest expectations. Then she collapsed over her desk and burst into hysterical sobs.

We looked worriedly at each other as the sobs grew wilder and more tearing. It was possible that we had destroyed her, and she would be dragged off to a mental institution. We became very frightened and looked for someone to do something. It was Dumb Donny who stood up in all his shocking new tallness. He spoke in a deep, cracking voice.

"Miss Petain, I'm ashamed of this class."

Eagerly we all agreed, sending up a chorus of dissapproval, as if each one of us were an innocent and appalled party. It made no sense, but miraculously, if slowly, it brought Miss Petain's head from her arms. She fumbled her purse from the desk drawer and dragged out a handkerchief, with which, not meeting our eyes, she sadly wiped her tears and blew her very thin nose.

"And I want to tell you," Dumb Donny went on, "that they'll never do anything like this again. You don't have to worry, Miss Petain."

We were all pretty sure Dumb Donny himself had started the note, but you couldn't hold his righteousness against him. He had stopped the sobs, and Miss Petain, red-eyed but willing to forgive, took up the roll sheet once more.

Next period I entered the room I had so often dreamed of while turning into a math whiz. Mr. Lewis called roll. His voice was impersonal, his mouth humorless, his gray eyes hard as pebbles. And didn't the man own another suit? I was oppressed by our moonlit past, not only because it was embarrassing, but because much of life was apparently a waste of time and you never knew it until afterward.

But at least he paused at my name and gave me a brief, interested look for all the Towks to see. That was worth something. And though math was no longer my field, I vowed to maintain my wizardry. With a cool inward smile, I leaned back and crossed my arms.

We met our responsibility toward Miss Petain like a group of doctors given charge of an invalid. Two girls presented her with a pretty lace handkerchief since she was probably in need of many. She never dropped a piece of chalk but the nearest pupils leaped to spare her the effort of bending. We never got out of hand; even when she left the room, we remained orderly, so as not to shock her into a fit when she reentered. Gradually she became less nervous, more social, and now and then she shared some personal tidbit, such as the fact that she came from Baton Rouge, Louisiana, where Petain was a fairly common name. I was glad to hear this, and I was glad to see Miss Petain looking very attractive one morning. Her white face glowed with a blush, her big fisheyes were bright, and her thin mouth held a smile. It was exactly at this time that rumors placed her in Mr. Lewis' green coupe, riding down Alhambra Avenue at his side.

Well, I thought, observing him in algebra class, I'm glad if someone sees something in him. If she could find moonlight in those hard pebble eyes, if she wanted that sour mouth stuck to hers, more power to her. Still, it was hard to imagine them together, the big Gestapo agent and the trembling leaf. If she was having a real affair with him, in bed—rumored to be an earthquakian activity—I should think she would be in the hospital now, squashed and broken. But maybe they were only holding hands. I wished them good luck, whatever they were doing.

We started a battle in Holland, at a place called Arnhem. After a few fierce days, Churchill came out and predicted a long battle. He was wrong; it was not very long. And the Germans won. Dad shook his head over the newspaper and said it was our worst blow to date, a bad setback. If we crossed the Rhine this year, he would be surprised.

We had a letter from Peter, written at the beginning of September. He was somewhere in Belgium. He told about Paris, how it was to rumble through the streets with the whole city running alongside the trucks, crying out and reaching up to hug you, to kiss you and press flowers into your hands, even bottles of wine. It was like something out of a wild dream, he would never in his life forget it. Paris was beautiful, and he told about the green Seine and the chestnut trees, the broad avenues and small, crooked streets, and the buildings—everywhere you looked there was this magnificent architecture, it made your mouth water. Then he said that Dolan, the ex-interior decorator, was back in England with both legs off, and that his other buddy, Zafich, the ex-Detroit butcher, was being sued for divorce by his snazzy wife back home, and what a lousy thing war was, even with the flowers and wine. . . .

I missed stern little Valerie, who was now in high school. Peggy was pleasant, but it was clear that she was not going to be seen with me as long as I was still in dumbbell class and my hair was still green and ungrown-out. As for Eudene, I dropped into the café now and then, but she only wanted to talk about Bobby and the kind of house she and Acie would buy.

My best moments came in Mr. Lewis's class. My satisfaction was great when in his gruff way, with a raised eyebrow or slight nod, he made it known to all that he held my acuteness in esteem. Still, I felt none of the melting ecstasy I had dreamed of last spring, and I thought it probable that all life was arranged so that the right things came at the wrong time.

Chapter 42

For instance, there was a conference that had just ended in Washington, D.C., called Dumbarton Oaks. I read about it in *Time*. If I had read about it a year ago it would have lifted me high, because it was described as having set up an agency called the United Nations, "to free future generations from the desolation of war." But now that I knew about history, I could put no faith in it.

I wrote the line down anyway, in my Big Chief notebook, because it was beautiful, like a line of poetry. "To free future generations from the desolation of war."

We discussed Dumbarton Oaks in Social Studies. It was one of the few interesting subjects ever to be brought up there. The teacher told us about the United Nations, then mentioned the League of Nations and asked if any of us had ever heard of it. I had read about it in the *Time* article. My hand shot up.

"It failed," I said.

The teacher was so startled to receive a response to a question that she didn't speak for a moment. Then she said, "Very good. But the United Nations will have powers much greater than those of the League of Nations."

"I don't think that will make any difference. The United Nations will fail too, because there's never been a time in history when peace wasn't a preparation for war. War always comes. It's human nature to go on doing the same thing over and over."

The teacher looked interested now. More than interested. "Do we all agree?" she asked like a cheerleader. "Do we have opinions? Is peace impossible?"

"Naw," said one boy. "Because when we beat 'em, we'll keep 'em beat. For good."

"They won't twitch, the buggers," said another, sending a pained expression across the teacher's face, but not daunting her.

"All right, fine! But what about human nature?"

"What is it?" a girl asked.

"It's how people are, basically," said the teacher.

"Oh. Well, people are basically nice," the girl informed her.

But another girl disagreed. "People are basically crumbs."

"That makes you a crumb too," challenged the first girl.

The second girl didn't answer. She was stuck.

"Nobody wants war," someone else said. "My parents don't want it anymore. They're fed up."

"My cousin got his leg shot off in Tarawa, and he says—"

"—or my uncle Alfred in France, my aunt May's fooling around because he's been overseas so long she don't even remember what he looks like—"

"Let's keep to the subject," interrupted the teacher.

"Well I am, I'm saying it's lasted too long."

"It oughta end—"

"Everybody wants peace—"

"But they never get it," I said. "It never lasts."

"That's what this thing's for, this United Nations."

"Baloney."

"Baloney's right," said Dumb Donny in his cracking new voice. "You've always got overpopulation, so you've always got to have wars to keep it down, and nobody can change that. That's Malthus's theory."

I looked at him, astonished. There were actually thoughts in that goofy head, which in fact didn't look as goofy as it used to. His face had a lean, graven quality, there was something wolfish about it, perilous, and he had a mind like mine that held lean, perilous thoughts, except that they didn't seem to bother him, since already he was cagily attaching a long chain of paper clips to the curls of the girl before him.

"All right," the teacher was asking with enthusiasm,

"what do we think of Donald's argument? Do we believe that war is caused by overpopulation?"

"No," I said, "but it's bad anyway. There're too many poor people in the world. Socialism is the only answer. I believe in Rosa Luxemburg."

Neither Egon nor Helen Maria had looked startled when I said I was a socialist, but the teacher looked as if I had leaped on my desk and done a dance in the nude. Then she became more enthusiastic than ever. "Have we any opinions on socialism? On a system where the government controls everything? Would you enjoy living in a country without the spirit of free enterprise, in a country where you could never get ahead in life no matter how hard you worked?"

There was a barrage of nos.

"Tell them about capitalism," I urged.

"Capitalism is the system of free enterprise—"

"Where the rich control everything—" I interrupted.

"—where it is possible for anyone to better himself if he has the desire and the will because he lives in a democracy. I'm not saying anything against our wonderful allies the Russians. They have their system, which they feel is right for them, but do we want a communist government for ourselves?"

Another barrage of nos.

"Yes!" I said, surprising myself.

"She's against America," a boy pointed out.

"Of course Suse's not against America," the teacher said. "I think she's just been reading things she hasn't quite understood. She needs to think them out a little more clearly."

But the boy was right. I was against America. I hadn't been a few minutes before. Strangely enough, I had never brooded over Doris Duke, sailing around in *Life* magazine on her block-long yacht drinking champagne, while on the next page sat a Pennsylvania mining town of grimed shacks and black slag heaps. America had never been included in my thoughts of mush pots and custard bowls. America was America, exceptional, blessed, and it had been that way from the start, with George Washington and the Bill of Rights and all that dreary but unquestionably fine business. Only when I heard myself say "Yes!" did I realize my opinion had changed. I didn't know how it happened. It seemed the teacher had done it for me.

"Of course I recommend outside reading," she was telling us. "Nothing is more important than to search for answers. But what must you always keep in mind?"

No one knew.

"To think your ideas through," she said, lifting a forefinger.

At this point the bell rang, and everyone departed in lively spirits, which were increased by the chain of paper clips borne innocently away like a Chinaman's queue. But I felt removed, staring in my mind at Doris Duke and the coal miners.

We never had another discussion so spirited. We returned to the legislative system, the subject we had digressed from that day, and though the teacher still tried for enthusiasm, she bored us and we bored her.

I thought dismally of my next four years, the same old blankness at test time, the same old swamp of Ds and D minuses. It had been nice that day of the discussion, having facts and opinions at my fingertips. It was nicer than being bored, which I knew from algebra class. Maybe if I studied all my subjects as I had studied algebra, they would start making sense, too. True, there would be no ultimate sense. There was no golden rose of truth. There were just a lot of parts that would never fit together the way you wanted. But I was feeling something new, a curiosity at least to know what the parts were.

Chapter 43

I rose early and studied an hour before school. I took books with me into the bathroom and would have taken them to the dinner table if it had been allowed. Dad and Mama said I should slow down, I was an extremist. But I was not. An extremist would not take time off two evenings in a row, and last evening I had written Peter, and this evening I was writing Helen Maria.

I have been very busy studying [I told her]. I don't think education is a solution to anything, but it is worth looking into. There isn't much to tell, except that I've been studying. Of course there is the election coming up, and I hope President Roosevelt will be reelected even if his enemies say he looks sick and will not last long. He certainly does not look sick to me, just elderly, and many elderly people last a long time, look at your grandmother. I see his enemies also call him a Communist because he helps poor people. He must abhor rich capitalists like Doris Duke and be working against them, that is entirely to his credit and I feel the same way. For a while I thought I was against America and it was a weird feeling, but now I see I am just against everything that's wrong with it, but it's still a weird feeling. However, you must face facts, such as the Negro sharecroppers in the South whom I have been reading about in *Time* magazine, and even the conditions that prevail here in Mendoza where everything is different down by the cannery where my friend Eudene, the erstwhile La Grande Horizontale, lives. But I will not bore you with the obvious.

Do you cherish any hope for the United Nations? I think that it is a premature organization, to say the least, but well intentioned. We discussed the subject in Social Studies. Our social studies teacher recommends outside reading in government and politics, which reminds me may I ask a favor: since Egon's field is political science he could advise me on what books to read, so could you send me his address so I could dash him off a note? I am anxious to get a good grade in Social Studies. In fact I must get back to it now, so I will sign off prematurely with hearty regards.

                                                        Suse

The mornings were like cut glass. The big dry hills, burned off in patches during the summer, stood gold and black against a sky of purest blue. The sidewalks were cool under your shoe soles, and here and there the fruit from a fig tree had fallen and splattered during the summer, slowly congealing in a hard crust that now gave off a cold winy smell as you passed. There was a wind moving high in the air, and the fronds of the tall palm trees rustled with a sound like sand sifting. It was going on three years since Pearl Harbor now. Two weeks ago General MacArthur landed in the Philippines. He had said, "I will return," and he had. It was one of the few things that anyone ever said that came true. Yet even with this triumph, the papers concentrated on the European front. It was because the Pacific war was so spread out that it would take a long time yet to reach Japan; but in Europe distances were smaller, and headlines could sound more encouraging. Even if the enemy still had us stuck in Belgium and Holland.

Helen Maria took her time answering, then scribbled a few lines on a postcard. She was up to her ears in work but would write more fully later. She was glad Roosevelt had won and glad that I was studying hard, and she was sure Egon would be happy to help me, and there, printed clearly at the bottom, was his address, sending a burst of warmth through me.

It sounded as if she hadn't seen him lately, or else she would have asked him. It sounded as if they had finally broken up. I hoped she wasn't taking it too hard, but the note sounded cheerful enough. There were plenty of other fish in the sea, after all.

I sat down immediately and wrote "Dearest Egon," but it was too intimate. Then I tried "My dear Egon", but it was too formal, and "Dear Egon" was too dull. Putting the salutation aside, I asked about the books, but after that everything got knotted up and an hour later I threw my pencil down in disgust.

Every evening I returned to the letter, but the more I worked the more knotted it became. Finally I was forced to put it away because of tests.

The cut-glass mornings disappeared. I walked to school in tule fog, listening to the foghorns muffled and ghostly, like the dead sailors' voices rising from the bay. Gradually you became aware of dim figures walking along, and then suddenly you were in a glare of electric light, lockers banged, feet hurried, and you stood still for a moment, as if coming out of a dream.

I liked these fogged silent days; they made it easier to concentrate on your work, pushed out everything else. Dumb Donny had taken to snapping his ruler on my rear

238

end whenever I bent over the water fountain, but this attention passed into the fogged silence; so did the interesting sight of Mr. Lewis and Miss Petain chatting openly together in the hall; and so did Peggy, who stopped to tell me my hair was beginning to look better. There were only the tests I was studying for, and Egon's letter waiting to be finished, and the fog.

On November 18 General Patton's Third Army crossed the German frontier. And my tests were returned with marks ranging from B to B minus. I felt suddenly happy and relieved about everything, except for Egon's letter.

I couldn't get the tone I wanted, a mixture of passion not too forward and brilliance not too bombastic. It always came out like the worst kind of showoff essay mixed with mushiness. Through the following week I struggled off and on with the thick heap of scratched-out, question-marked, thumb-smudged pages; then it was my birthday, and I said I didn't want a party because I had too much studying, which was true. Mama told me again that I went to extremes, and Dad agreed; first I never studied at all, and then I did nothing but study. Wasn't there a golden mean? I meant to get into the golden mean very soon, I said, but right now I was pulling myself up by the bootstraps because I was sunk down so far. And then it occurred to me that maybe they were right, after all, that I was an extremist because only an extremist would have gotten sunk down so unbelievably far. What a lot they had to contend with, I thought, as the three of us sat at the dining-room table with birthday cake and hot chocolate; an extremist was probably not easy to live with; an extremist plunged down to rock bottom or shot high in the air, it was always all or nothing at all, and it was true of me because I felt it inside, that sudden whipping high or smashing low, and it was no fun for me to live with, so why should it be for them? And as we sat there, eating and sipping our chocolate and talking, I was struck by something, by the absoluteness, the trueness of my parents' faces, of those eyes and lips whose every nuance was carved so deeply, so dependably into my life; I felt at that moment an almost painfully deep sense of love for them, and it seemed that this birthday party, the smallest and quietest of them all, would be the one that I would always remember.

I was fourteen. Walking through the fog the next

morning, I carried a purse, my birthday gift. I had long fought against having a purse, purses seemed cumbersome, but then I had changed my mind. A purse would be a good thing, a shoulder bag you could just sling on. In it you could carry your pencil, pencil sharpener, handkerchief, jackknife, candy bars, even a pack of cigarettes as Eudene did, and especially Egon's letter. It would be a long letter, his handwriting would be clear and firm, and he would probably use blue ink.

But how could he answer a letter he had never received? When I got home that afternoon, I tore up all the pages I had written and started over again, determined to send the result no matter how it sounded.

Dear Egon,

Helen Maria sent me your address because I wrote and asked for it. My social studies teacher recommended outside reading in politics and government, and since that's your field maybe you could recommend some good books for me to read.

It's very foggy here, is it in Berkeley? I like the fog, but summer is still my favorite season. I'm studying a lot right now because I will confess that I was not a good student but now I want to catch up. What you said about the Jews in Berkeley started it, I got interested in history and now I realize there is a lot to be figured out about mankind, even though I don't believe it can be figured out. But I believe you should try anyway.

Isn't it terrific that the Allies have smashed into Germany and maybe the war will not be so long in ending now? But maybe I shouldn't mention smashing into Germany because you are a German as well as being a Jew. I know it is complicated, as you mentioned. It was also complicated what I said in Berkeley about Berlin being bombed. I only meant because it is the capital and Hitler is there. I hope the bombing will soon stop everywhere and that your house will be all right and your two brothers also. What do you think about the United Nations? We discussed it in Social Studies, and everyone believed it would end war for good. I would sure like to think so too, but I'm afraid it is more like poetry.

I am looking forward to winter when it rains and

thunders, it is inspiring, but summer is still my favorite season. I hope that you are in good health
and enjoying your studies, and I will thank you very
much if you will please send me a list of those
books.

Sincerely yours,
Suse

It read plain, plain. No brilliance, and no passion either, and I had wanted so badly to send him my soul.
But if I started rewriting, it would never reach the mailbox.

Chapter 44

DEC. 1:   Funeral Notices

Pelegrino, Mario—in San Ramon, November 29;
adored son of Anna Pelegrino and the late Franco
Pelegrino; loving brother of Ezio Pelegrino; devoted
nephew of Sergio Borsanti; a native of Mendoza,
aged 17 years.

Rosary Sunday evening at 8 o'clock Harmon &
Co., 1124 Sanchez St., Concord. A Mass of Christian
Burial will be offered Monday at 9 A.M. at St. Moni-
ca's Church, followed by interment at Holy Cross
Cemetery.

Monday morning, while Mass was being said for Mario,
Miss Petain announced that she was no longer to be
addressed as Miss Petain but Mrs. Lewis. We stared at
her face, which was extremely red and embarrassed but
happy; it took a few moments for the words to sink in;
then a chorus of congratulations filled the room.

In algebra class, while Mario was being buried, Mr.
Lewis took us through our lessons without a word
concerning the great change in his life. I began to wonder if Miss Petain had made up the story—how terrible
for her, how humiliating. And as the hour drew to a close

and Mr. Lewis remained as hard and sour as ever, I became certain that Miss Petain had lost her marbles. Then, just before the bell rang, a girl gave a nervous cough and stood up from her desk.

"Mr. Lewis, on behalf of the class I would like to congratulate you on your marriage to Miss Petain in Room Fourteen that we just heard about, and we all wish you much happiness and prosperity."

I waited apprehensively, but a touch of pink appeared in the hard, blocky cheeks; the mouth unclamped; it widened a little. It was a smile.

"Thank you, class. Thank you very much, from both of us."

I sat back with relief. I hoped they would be happy. I hoped that they would get a nice apartment with big sunny windows and that they would not be lonely anymore. A new life, together and in love, and now the bell rang, and Mario's burial would be over, the people would be walking away from his grave, leaving it to silence. Poor little Mario, not to have enjoyed this day: the church with its tolling bells, the priests praying in their fancy robes, the long line of cars driving through town, the bright flowers massed around the grave, and so many people standing there together, just for him, taking him seriously, the way he liked. How he would have been crazy with excitement, how his little squint eyes would have blazed with pleasure. But his eyes were closed, deep in the earth, and I walked down the hall to my next class, thinking both of Mario's closed eyes and of the sun streaming through the newlyweds' windows.

At noon Dumb Donny came over as I was getting my lunch from my locker. He banged the locker door against the wall.

"Want to come to the noon dance with me?"

"What for?" I asked, taken by surprise.

"Do you or don't you?"

"No."

He shrugged, popped his bubble gum, and sauntered off. He had a new gangling way of walking. He also had pimples on his chin and a pronounced Adam's apple, but you couldn't deny that he was good-looking with his lean new face and his hair combed back from his forehead in thick overlapping layers like gold leaf, the green tint gone. The green had faded from my hair too, and it hung a graceful inch or more below my ears. I wouldn't really have minded showing up at the dance except that I didn't feel like it, because of Mario.

I ate in the auditorium, watching poor Mr. Kerr conducting "Anchors Aweigh." Afterward I put on my coat and walked around outside in the fog. Dumb Donny came up to me again.

"You want to go to the show Saturday night?"

Again I was taken by surprise. "What for?" I said again.

"What for?" He looked frustrated. "To see the show!" He snapped his gum again, glaring at me. But it was a great moment anyway, now that it had sunk in. If I had kept a diary, I would have put down in capitals: "ASKED FOR FIRST DATE TODAY."

"What's playing?" I said, walking on.

"I don't know yet."

"Well I don't want to see something I might not want to see."

He gave his knuckles a nasty crack. It was a habit left over from his short, goofy days.

"You're not exactly Miss Charm of 1944."

"I don't care." And I didn't care about going to the show either. I just liked being asked. "I'm too busy for movies anyway. I'm studying a lot."

"I know. You're turning into a real drip."

"Thank you."

We walked along in unfriendly silence.

"May I ask why you would want to invite a drip to the movies?"

"I don't know, it's my big heart—treat a drip to the movies."

"You give me a pain."

"You look like a pain."

"I'm depressed, if it's any of your business."

"Tell me. I've got this big heart."

I shook my head.

We walked in among the pepper trees where, dimly, in the fog, you could see the lurking figures of noon smokers. Dumb Donny fished up a bent, old-looking cigarette and a kitchen match from his shirt pocket. With a smart crack of his thumbnail, he ignited the match. Taking a puff, he handed the cigarette to me. From the gym you could hear the song they were dancing to, "When the Lights Go On Again All Over the World."

"What do you think of Miss Petain?" Dumb Donny asked.

"I think it's nice." I took a puff; I still didn't do it right. "But I don't want to get married myself."

"I don't either. Marriage breeds overpopulation."

I handed the cigarette back. "Tell me about that theory you mentioned in class, Malthus's theory."

"It's simple. We're all war meat, every twenty-five years."

War meat. It was an ugly term.

"At least we've got twenty-five years," I said with a bitter smile, listening to the song from the gym.

He was silent, taking a deep drag and exhaling slowly. "People are stupid. There's a quotation about it: with stupidity, the gods themselves battle in vain. That's the tragedy of life."

It was something Helen Maria herself might have said. Dumb Donny Woodall, of all people, a thinker. Suddenly his eyes narrowed. Flicking the cigarette to the ground, he stepped on it and grabbed my hand. "Come on, peaches, let's scram!"

It was Mr. Lewis coming through the trees, patrolling.

"You can let go of my hand now," I said when we had hurried away to safety.

"You know what your hand feels like?"

"No, and I don't want to know." He was feeling my calluses. I pulled my fingers free. "When do you think we'll cross the Rhine?"

He snapped to attention. "Pretty quick now, sir."

"I'm being serious."

"Serious? I'd say another week."

"Really? I'd say about another month."

"We'll be in Berlin in a month."

"There could be another Arnhem."

"Not a chance. That was their last stand. Plus it's winter now, they haven't got what it takes for winter fighting."

"What does it take? Just some snowshoes."

"Snowshoes!" He laughed.

"What's so funny?"

"You need more than showshoes, for God's sake. Look what happened at Stalingrad. Cold is *murder*."

"I know all about it." The vast plain of white, arms sticking up like iron. "They were cut off at Stalingrad. They're not cut off here. They can get supplies; all they need extra is snowshoes."

"They haven't *got* supplies."

"How do we know? We don't know anything. We didn't know about the V-2 rockets, did we? They could have all sorts of things up their sleeves."

"Listen, peaches, by now they don't even have sleeves."

"Don't call me peaches. Anyway, you just go by what you read in the newspapers."

"I don't either. I come to my own conclusions."

"Based on what? The papers."

"What about you? I guess you've got a direct line to von Rundstedt? Is he the one who told you about snowshoes?"

"I'm just skeptical, that's all."

"I'll bet a dime. We cross the Rhine in a week. The war's over in a month."

"That would be bloody money if I won. I wouldn't do it."

"What's bloody money?"

"I don't know. But I wouldn't do it."

We came around the corner of the main building, and Dumb Donny hurried to the door and opened it wide, bowing with a great flourish. "Welcome to the halls of poison ivy!" And he grabbed my hand again. "You know what your hand feels like? A dumpling."

"Really?"

I left it in his for a moment before grabbing it back.

Chapter 45

The days went by. I mourned Mario's death. Egon's letter didn't come. We didn't cross the Rhine. Peter wrote from a forest in Luxembourg which he said was very cold and very quiet and which he called the ghost front. It made me nervous.

December 7 was a school day, but exactly the same as that Sunday in 1941: bright, wrong, out of kilter. Sounds held in by the fog were suddenly released: dogs barking, a train rumbling over the railroad bridge, shouts and truck motors from the garrison, and "Invasion!," a rifle shot, a pounding torrent of water. All this glaring light, a God-made day for bombers. It would happen yet, God's little saved-up surprise, God's little reminder, like Port Chicago.

I remembered in Sunday school long ago a girl described God with a white beard and golden halo, and He had a wise, kind face, and little children were gathered around Him. But in the encyclopedia I saw how everyone slaughtered each other over Him, and it seemed He was just a bad joke, and if you had to give Him a face, it would be a laughing, sharp-toothed one. I'd like to see that girl in London or Berlin crawling through her bombed cellar, with her little sisters and brothers a pile of entrails, and I would like to know if she saw Him standing there in the blood with his kind, wise face; and if she did, that would be the biggest joke of all, He would laugh so hard it would sound like the bombs coming down again—

—a shock out of the blue; I was being attacked, ripped into.

"What're you doing!" I cried. It was Dumb Donny, tearing my books from my arms.

"Just being chivalrous—"

"Give 'em back!" I was furious. "You came at me like a dive bomber!"

He dumped the books back in my arms and told me to dry up.

"And what about the Rhine?" I said, my heart still racing. "You're such a military genius. We haven't crossed it yet!"

"So what, just a few more days."

"Huh!" I wanted to hit him, and I wanted to hit the weather, too, all this bright, glaring light. But he was talking on, about ordinary things.

"You want me to quiz you on the Four Freedoms for the test today?"

"Quiz yourself," I said shortly.

"Okay, I'll recite them in all their glory." And he held up four fingers. "Freedom of speech. Freedom of religion.

246

Freedom from want. Freedom from fear. Which one's the most important? She'll ask that."

"Freedom from Dumb Donny."

He was silent for a moment; then he walked off.

All day he ignored me. In Social Studies I glanced a few times at the frigid face, but I was more involved with the weather, how a certain blue sky and certain slant of light could bring back something so violently, an old moment of horror thrashing up before your face, like a whale breaking from the ocean.

The teacher was passing out our test. "List the Four Freedoms. Which do you consider the most important? Explain in full." I listed them and then wrote, "Freedom from fear is the most important." But I could not think of an explanation. I still hadn't thought of one when the bell rang, and I put down, unsatisfactorily, "Fear is terrible."

It was there, a white envelope lying on the lace cloth of the dining-room table. His name and address were in the upper-left-hand corner. His handwriting was foreign; intricate and graceful. And his ink was blue.

"Suse, who is this person, Egon Krawitz?" Mama asked.

My eyes lifted happily. "That friend of Helen Maria's, remember I told you about? That's studying social science? I asked him to send me the names of some books."

"Oh," said Mama pleasantly.

I took the letter to my room. Thudding down on my bed, I tore it open.

My Dear Suse,

I wish I could help you, but I'm not sure what kind of reading your teacher has in mind. I can only recommend *History of Political Thought*, by Gettell, but I'm afraid it is very involved (and very long). Maybe your teacher himself could recommend something better.

Thank you, I remain healthy, and I suppose I am enjoying my studies. And you, studying so hard! I hope you will not try to figure out mankind all at once.

Yes, the Dumbarton Oaks conference was interesting, and it is to be hoped their goals will be realized. You say you would like to think so but it is more like poetry. That is true, perhaps, but poetry is more than beautiful words. Someday you must think just what poetry is.

Please never worry over your remark about Berlin. Of course, I understood how you meant it. Nor should you feel you can't write about the Allies pushing into Germany. I too hope the end will come soon. It has not been foggy here, just cold and overcast. Sometimes I forget where I am and think it will snow. Now I send you best wishes for a happy Christmas, Suse, and thank you for writing me such a good and interesting letter.

Sincerely,
Egon

I read it haltingly, slowed by the alien handwriting. Then I went back and read it again, and the words flowed into my heart. He cared what I thought about Dumbarton Oaks, he soothed me not to worry about my war remarks, he understood everything, and he thanked me for such a good and interesting letter. We were two hearts that beat as one, he walking beneath the overcast sky and I walking here in the fog—two souls against the world! And as I read it a third time, the dazzling day in the creek flooded through me; if only we were there now, and his arms were around me, his lips pressed hard to mine. . . .

Dear Egon,
I'm writing right away to thank you for the name of the book. I'll try to get it right away at the library. I enjoyed your letter very much and am glad to know you're fine. I wish you would get snow in Berkeley, though I don't think it ever happened, but I know it is your natural condition in winter and I know how much you must miss it. I am going to think about what poetry really is, and then I will write you what I think, if you wouldn't mind. And so I will sign off now with all my best regards and with many warm wishes that you will enjoy a very merry Christmas.

Sincerely,
Suse

It was strange how it would not come out right in a letter. It was so polite and without a scrap about our dazzling embrace in the creek. But maybe our feelings could not be expressed in letters—for though his was beautiful, it was polite too. Our feelings could only be expressed in person. I must get to Berkeley.

With Egon's letter deep in my shoulder bag, I walked to school the next day in a cold, blowing drizzle. The halls smelled of damp wool and damp hair; everyone's cheeks were stung red; my own felt poreless and tingling, my eyes brightly washed. Buoyantly I banged my locker door open.

"You really burned me up yesterday," came Dumb Donny's voice at my side.

I turned around. I had forgotten all about him.

"Don't you ever call me that," he said.

"Call you what?"

"Dumb Donny."

"What d'you mean? It's your name."

"You think I ever liked it?"

"I never thought about it."

"A lot of people don't call me it anymore."

"I didn't notice."

"Well, notice."

He was snotty, but I felt too great-hearted to care. And there were good things about Dumb Donny. He could discuss the war; even if his conclusions were wrong, he was more interesting on the subject than Peggy or Valerie or Eudene had ever been. He had even spoken of a map on which he moved around different colored pins representing armies. I would like to see that.

"So what do I call you?"

"Don."

"Okay."

I slammed the locker door shut, and with Dumb Donny—Don—at my side, started off for Miss Petain's—Mrs. Lewis's class. But Egon was Egon forever, and deep inside my shoulder bag, pressed close to my side, his letter shone like buried light.

Chapter 46

In the middle of December we were routed by a massive attack in a forest called the Ardennes. It was the forest Peter was in, the ghost front, and it was to become one of the bloodiest battle sites of the war, a swollen Nazi protrusion through the Allied lines into Luxembourg and Belgium, pointing us backward, away from Berlin. That was how it was as Christmas approached: our troops, with Peter among them, retreating, scattered to the winds in the Battle of the Bulge.

I wondered if after all this time, after coming so far, we might actually be going to lose.

"Not a chance," said Don, ushering me over to the table where his map lay. We were in a glassed-in sun porch streaming with rain, like a glass submarine in a gray ocean. In a new raincoat, my old slicker outgrown, I looked down past the pointing finger.

"It's just a matter of time," he said.

It always was.

"The black ones are them. These blue ones are us. The greens are British. The reds over there are Russians. The way I look at it—"

But now that I was here I couldn't get interested in these pins, these neat little dots of color. I gazed around the porch. Wicker chairs, potted violets, issues of the *National Geographic*. Behind us in the living room Don's younger brother and sister were stretched out on the floor reading comic books. They were about eight and ten, and I had a sudden urge to leave Don and squeeze in between them. I belonged with them. All I had ever wanted was to lie content on the rug with my comic books. The rain would beat down, then spring would come, and summer, and autumn, and winter again, and nothing would ever change. . . .

"I thought you wanted to see this!"

I swung around, my face flushing red. It was mortifying to want his ten-year-old sister's body and her comic book, unbearable to feel his eyes bore into this infantile relapse. I had to give a casual toss of my hair to get back to fourteen.

"I was looking."

"You weren't either!"

His face was tense. When people got tall, they seemed to break into raw, touchy spots like a measles rash; they became unpredictable, like overbred horses. You had to humor them.

"I was concentrating. You've got to look away to concentrate. You've got to see things in your mind's eye."

"All your fancy talk," he muttered, flinging down a red pin that bounced from the map to the floor.

You didn't have to humor your friends when you were small; you never hung on each other's words and glances and threw things down. I picked up the pin and flung it back on the map. "I was concentrating on the Russians. I was visualizing where they'd meet the Western armies."

"That's what I was trying to *explain*."

"Well I'm *listening*."

He walked me home afterward, his good spirits restored, his big, bony fist punching out through the rain at hedges and bushes. The Bulge would collapse in two weeks; we'd cross the Rhine in three and capture Berlin in four. It would be the Yanks who dragged Hitler screaming from his Chancellery. It would be the Stars and Stripes that flew over the ruined city.

I couldn't see why. The Russians were closer.

"I know," he said. "But that's my calculations. Wait and see."

For all his pins, he just went by what he wanted. Well, I wanted it too. I would like to be there with them when they threw Hitler against a wall and machine-gunned him to a pulp, but I didn't care who did it, the Yanks or the Russians or anybody else. I just wanted it done. But there was no glory in it. Hitler would slide down the wall, the firing squad would crunch off through the rubble, and the rest was smoke and silence, whichever flag flew over it.

"You want to make a bet this time?" Don asked.

"No. But I'll tell you one thing. Those hills will be green by the time anybody reaches Berlin." The hills

251

stood high in the driving rain, abrupt and massive, a sodden grayish brown. "They'll be green with spring, like tremendous emeralds."

"That's poetic. That's very beautiful."

I looked at him to see if he was making fun, but he was serious.

"Thank you," I said.

"But I think you're wrong."

"I hope I am."

We were passing the garrison in its field of mud, where lakes were already forming, pocked white by the downpour. Soldiers slogged around the mired buildings like big bats in their flapping rain capes.

"I'd never put a garrison where it floods," Don said. "They should've put it on a hill. I could've told them that. I could tell them a few things right now, like about the Ardennes."

Just give him an army and he'd lead it to instant victory. But I didn't even know what victory was any longer, though once it had been simple: everybody against us dead. Not the Italians, necessarily, I'd never gotten them straightened out in my mind. But the Germans, and absolutely the Japs, every last rotten one in the world, dismembered and burned to a crisp. A pile of burning corpses five miles long, and our armies massed alongside with flying flags and booming cannons. But it no longer did anything for me. Something in me that had been black as pitch and hard as a diamond, something strong and unbreakable, had broken, and in its place was a strange spread-outness, like a thin, flickering sea, pointlessly awash.

Don was talking about the blue pins and the black pins in the snowy Ardennes, but if you looked at their boots, I thought, you wouldn't know what color they were, you would just know it was a boot with a frostbitten foot inside; and that was the thin, flickering sea, that loss of boundaries, that absence of discrimination, all feet the same, all frostbite the same, and Helen Maria was probably right that they had played soccer and exchanged snapshots and there had never been a hard black diamond inside them, just inside me, and now it was gone, and there was nothing.

* * *

252

Hills like tremendous emeralds. I wrote it down in my Big Chief notebook. I wrote down everything that was connected with poetry and had several pages of notes now, including Webster's definition of a poem: "A composition designed to convey a vivid and imaginative sense of experience." I saw no connection between that and the aims of the United Nations, and I was stuck. Egon must be looking in his mailbox every day, wondering why he hadn't heard. If only I had something really brilliant and amazing to say.

The reason I couldn't concentrate on my poetry notes was Peter. When we listened to the radio, I would look at Mama and Dad. They listened with a special thoughtfulness, and sometimes Dad's cigar would move back and forth in his mouth, as if he were not sitting here in the living room, but were deep in the bitter snow of the Ardennes. More than ever before, the house hung heavy with the threat of a sudden doorbell ring. In that heaviness, Christmas Eve came small and thin, like Pearl Harbor Christmas, as if nothing had changed since then, had gotten only worse.

Then the tide turned. The Bulge began to collapse. By New Year's Day of 1945 it was clear that we had won the battle, though it wasn't yet finished. Battles never stopped all at once; they died away, and many soldiers died with the dying away.

"Hey," Don said the first day of school, "what'd I say about the Bulge?"

"It's not over yet."

"You're pretty hard to please."

"No I'm not. It's just facts."

"Where're you going? You're going the wrong way."

"New homeroom, I told you. I'm in College Prep now."

"Oh, that's right. Hot stuff, up with the big brains."

"They're not big brains, they just get decent grades."

"You can have it."

"You could have it too. You're not dumb. I always thought you were, but you surprised me."

"You surprised me too. You always struck me as a complete moron."

"Thank you," I said, walking away. What was wrong with him, always so insulting? I was glad to get away from him into a new class. But I felt out of place as I sat

253

down among the Towks, lonely for my careless, bogged-down companions of the last two years. There was something prim about these College Prep types, too neat, too much like each other. In dumbbell class you had variety. You had bold, sleazy girls, with penciled eyebrows and greasy lipstick, and boys in pachuco haircuts and leather jackets, who slouched around narrow-eyed like Humphrey Bogart, and you had certain Okie kids who never got rid of their Okieness but still looked unwashed and farm-bred and talked in a gray-sounding drawl, and you had a girl who was more like a boy, with her hair short and slicked back and a leather jacket over her dress, and a boy with a harelip, and then there were some goofy, talkative types like Dumb Donny had been, and some slow dreamy types, and then there was me, and for all our differences we got along, we were joined together in not caring about schoolwork, all bogged down together, cozy. We didn't care about the rest of the school; there was something ridiculous about the way they ran for puny school offices and took it as seriously as if they were Roosevelt and Dewey, and the way they aped college students, screaming themselves hoarse at our dinky basketball games, and how they walked home after school in couples, some of them holding hands, like something they'd seen on a *Saturday Evening Post* cover, whereas our sleazy girls and pachucos punched each other and exchanged racy jokes, which was more lively and real. These others were a herd of sheep, and here I was among them.

At least I was only here on probation, my grades having improved greatly but not extraordinarily, because of the Battle of the Bulge. I could always fall back again.

The middle of January we had a letter from Peter. He said they were stunned by the Germans striking back, nobody thought they had it in them to put up such a tremendous offensive. But it was their last hope, and now their stuffings were knocked out for good. He said our stuffings had been pretty well knocked out for a while too. Everything was loused up by fog, and then the snow came, and maybe he'd have enjoyed it under other circumstances, since he'd never seen snow before, but it wasn't exactly *Holiday on Ice* when you were in massive retreat. It was the roughest countryside he'd ever been in, it reminded him of a high school field trip he'd taken up around Mendocino, rugged hills thick with trees and brush. And everything snowy and icy. Had we ever seen a bona fide icicle? He was looking at one a foot long from his dugout as he sat writing. Amazing, a real icicle, he'd thought they only existed in Andersen's fairy tales. What an education, join the Army and see the real icicles. He said if he sounded slaphappy, his buddy had found a bottle of wine in what was left of the village of censored, and they were feeling no pain. He was in good shape, not a scratch, and no frostbite either since he'd learned to take off wet boots and socks at night, but it was strange how slow everyone was about learning things, like getting tanks whitewashed and putting sheets over their fatigues. If he never saw the color white again, he'd be happy, but *c'est la vie;* at least the shoe was on the other foot now, and it was the Germans who were in retreat. He said his unit had been reduced to censored; a lot had been taken prisoner the first day. He didn't envy them, but at least they wouldn't be prisoners for long, it was the last leg. . . .

JAN. 24:   St. Vith, Last Bulge
                  Holdout, Falls!

We could breathe again. I hoped Peter had another bottle of wine for the long tramp to Berlin, and I hoped I was wrong about its being spring when he got there, but at least he was on his way, unscratched, with the Bulge behind him, and I felt so good that I got my Big Chief notebook out and attacked my poetry letter to Egon.

Dear Egon,
    You are probably wondering why I haven't sent you my thoughts about poetry before now, but there were some extreme reasons why I couldn't get down to it, even though I was very eager to. I am happy to say that the reasons are gone now, and I am enthusiastically studying all the notes I have been making, in order to consider just what poetry is.
    First of all, poetry is beautiful, which life is not always, so I think poetry is not like life. I think life is sometimes beautiful, but only certain moments, and it seems that poetry only concerns these mo-

ments and not all the other moments in between when you are having arguments or worrying and have a dark feeling or a knotted-up feeling. I think poetry must be written to make you remember the beautiful moments and have faith in them. Therefore, what I meant about the United Nations was that it believes in something beautiful, which is the idea of peace, and it wants to give us hope in peace. But history shows us that peace is only a very brief part of life, and so it seems to me that the United Nations is having faith in one small part and not taking the biggest part of life into consideration.

Webster's definition of a poem is: A composition designed to convey a vivid and imaginative experience. I have to admit that this does not make any sense to me. It doesn't say anything about a poem being beautiful, just that it should be vivid and imaginative. With that definition you could write about an explosion or even a dog scratching itself. That doesn't seem like poetry to me, it seems more like those moments in between, the terrible ones and the plain ordinary ones.

Maybe I haven't read enough poetry yet, but I've read The Windhover, by Gerard Manley Hopkins, and Alfred Lord Tennyson's The Eagle, and William Wordsworth's My Heart Leaps Up When I Behold, which are all magnificent, and John Keats's Ode to a Nightingale, which is my favorite—Thou wast not born for death, immortal Bird! I think it is so full of greatness, it makes my blood race! Anyway, those are the poems I have been reading, but I will read more in order to see if I have missed something about what poetry is. I am profoundly interested to know what you meant in your letter, because I'm sure if I understand what you meant that it will clear up everything. Unfortunately, the library did not have the book you recommended, but I am sure it would have been excellent outside reading. I will close this letter on poetry now, hoping I haven't gone on too long. I am sending my very best wishes to you.

Sincerely,
Suse

Again it was too polite. I had wanted to use as an example of life's beautiful moments our talk on the sunny terrace and when he leaned from the train waving, but I left them out. Somehow, you couldn't do it in letters; something held you back. You had to wait till you saw each other.

Chapter 47

"*Oh, by the way,*" Mama said to Dad one night, "I heard downtown today that Mr. Nagai's back."

"Is that right? Well, good, I'd say it's about time—except I wonder what the man's going to live on."

I saw him on the street soon after, not on Main Street, where his florist shop was now Modern Miss Apparel, but coming out of a corner store with a bag of groceries. He looked the same, too old to have gotten older: quiet-faced, a dainty man in a neat dark suit and little fedora. I was relieved to know he was no longer withering away behind the barbed wire of a detention camp, and I said hello. He replied in the same rather low, soft voice, with a polite smile, and when I walked on, he was not only out of the camp but out of my storeroom as well, two troubling Mr. Nagais merged into one home-again Mr. Nagai, and I was happy.

I was not so happy about the rest of the Japs returning. Still, I was not thrilled to know what was happening to some. One had been assaulted on a street in Seattle. In San Jose a couple had their house burned down. In Fresno night riders had shot through the window of a recently returned family, just missing two children asleep in their beds. I wanted to feel excited and fulfilled, but I couldn't get the feeling started. It was the thin, flickering sea; it couldn't be whipped into a storm, it was too big, too broad. I knew I would never like Japs, but I also knew, with an acute sense of loss, that I would never hate them again either, with my black pointed passion, because there was no black pointed passion left in me for anything.

* * *

"Why don't you come over to my place after school tomorrow?" Peggy asked me in the hall one day. "We get together and play records and talk."

I had been expecting it. I was out of dumbbell class. My hair was no longer short. It was no longer green.

"All right," I said.

Karla had left some sloppy Joe sweaters, and the next morning I put one on. It was salmon and came far down over my skirt, so you saw only a strip of the skirt. That was how you were supposed to look. It was supposed to look good. My hair was getting on toward the shoulders, and the bangs were long enough to comb back. I had a forehead, a good high one without being Benjamin Franklin high like Valerie's, and my eyelashes were dark, which I had not noticed before, with the gray of the eyes set off pale like pewter. And Aunt Dorothy had been correct. My bone structure was first-rate, very clean and smooth with high, mysterious cheekbones, a face with no spongy padding, but full of sheer sweeps and fascinating angles, a kind of hungry face, a perilous face. Perilously I smoothed the sloppy Joe sweater, got into my raincoat, and picked up my books.

After school I went over to Peggy's. She answered the door and took me through the Dungeon, dark and gloomy as ever, with the chesterfield still standing at its pulled-out angle, and Rudy came barking and leaping as always, and then we were in Peggy's room; but that had changed. It was extremely neat now, and there was a blue and gold University of California pennant on the wall. Her phonograph was on the dusky pink rug, and someone was singing "Long Ago and Far Away." Bottles of Coke also stood on the rug, and piles of records, and there were three girls lying around: the eternal Bev, and two Jeans from my homeroom, all in sloppy Joes and all saying hi pleasantly as I sat down in their midst. The charmed circle.

One of the Jeans was looking into the mirror of a compact and carefully powdering her face. The other Jean, sitting next to me, was sorting records and copying their titles into a notebook, using green ink and dotting her Is with circles. Bev was sipping a Coke and leafing through a *Calling All Girls* magazine on her lap. From a little

258

manicure set on the rug before her, Peggy picked up an orange stick and began pushing her cuticles back.

"I love your sweater," Bev smiled at me. "That salmon color is beautiful."

"Thank you."

"Gorgeous," said powdering Jean.

"Thank you."

"I wouldn't dare wear salmon," said the other Jean, looking up from her notebook, "not with this awful coloring of mine, but it looks terrific on you."

I couldn't say thank you again, it would sound repetitious. Besides, her color wasn't awful; it was perfectly normal. I was reminded of the time Peggy and I had bombarded poor stupid Eudene with compliments like that. I was offended.

"Maybe it's a nice color, but I'm afraid that my opinion of sloppy Joes is that they're abnormal."

"Abnormal?" Bev asked politely.

"Yes. They're so huge that they're the only kind of sweater you wear out in the back, from sitting on it. I consider that abnormal."

"That's interesting," she said.

"Here, have a Coke," Peggy interrupted briskly, handing me one.

"There!" Notebook Jean announced, making a final entry in her green ink and passing the notebook to Peggy. "I'm taking three Ginny Simms."

"And you brought one Dick Haymes and two Mills Brothers," said Peggy, running her finger down the list. "Here, give me your pen, you got a title wrong."

They were trading records, apparently an exacting procedure. I reached out and patted Rudy, who was waddling by. He was getting old, there were white hairs on his muzzle. Peggy was getting old too, she would be fifteen in four months. She had a bust now, small but there. So did Bev, who was getting up to change the record. And so did Notebook Jean. In fact, almost everyone in ninth grade had a bust. I was a slow starter. So was Powder Jean, who had closed her compact and sat up straight, her chest flat. She was looking around at the others, waiting.

"Oh no, it's absolutely no good," said Bev, sitting down again. "It looks cheap."

"You used too much," said Peggy.

Notebook Jean took a sip of her Coke and shook her head. "I think we should vote against it."

"No, wash it all off," Bev said. "Then put it on light. I don't think we should vote until we see how it is light. Don't you, Peggy?"

Peggy nodded, queenlike, preoccupied, back with her orange stick.

"What are you voting on?" I asked as Powder Jean went out.

"If we should use powder," said Bev, "but I think she got the wrong color. It should be kind of pinky, and this is more like white."

"It looks like that white powder Mother Basketball puts on her feet," I told Peggy, "She's always taking off her gym shoes and shaking this white stuff on her feet. They're huge."

"I haven't noticed," said Peggy.

"I think this is Helena Rubinstein," Bev told me with a pleasant smile. She was certainly the friendliest of the four, and I felt a little pang that I had ever blown her to bits in a Zero.

"Fine," she said as Powder Jean returned with her washed face. "Now try it on light. Right, Peggy?"

Peggy nodded. She was definitely the important one, the leader. Bev was her second-in-command. Then came Notebook Jean, who could make suggestions but wasn't listened to. And finally, there was Powder Jean, who did whatever was asked of her. It was interesting, just like a stepladder. The stepladder was in the boys they went around with, too. The two Jeans went around with a couple of ordinary Towks, whereas I had seen Bev eating lunch with the student body president's best friend, and I had seen Peggy holding hands with the student body president himself. And the stepladder was in their looks, too. Peggy was very pretty, I had to admit, with her fiery hair and luminous green eyes. Bev was pretty too, but not strikingly, soft-eyed and sweet-faced. Notebook Jean was attractive, but her nose was a good deal too long. And Powder Jean just made it over the line with a lot of curly bronze hair, but her eyes were terribly close together.

I wondered if the stepladder was in everything: in their wardrobes, and the size of their houses, and how many people in their families had gone to college. Best

Everything, right across the board; then second best, and so on down the line. It didn't seem possible; it would be too well ordered. But they *were* well ordered. The meticulous list in green ink. The way they voted, like a committee.

Powder Jean opened the compact again and dabbed her face with little darts. When she was finished, she lowered the puff.

"Well? What do you think?" asked Bev, looking around.

"You can't even see it," said Notebook Jean.

"But if she puts more on, there'll be too much. What do you think, Peggy? Should she put more on?"

Peggy gave a shake of the head, working on her nails.

"I agree," said Bev. "Now the question is, do we want to vote yes for it the way it is, if you can't *see* it?"

"There doesn't seem much point," said Notebook Jean.

"I agree," said Bev. "You want to see some results if you're going to spend money."

"It would be a waste of money," said Notebook Jean.

I wondered if the emissaries at the Lisbon conference had gone on like this. They probably had, for days on end, pleasant and polite and pointless, sipping their glasses of water, or maybe they too had Coca-Cola, or more likely champagne.

"What's your verdict, Peggy?" Bev asked.

Peggy gave a brief thumbs-down gesture.

Then they all voted no. I hoped they were finished. I hadn't been so bored since Sunday school. Peggy looked bored, too, and it seemed more than just her queenlike manner. This wasn't much of a pinnacle to arrive at.

Now suddenly there were little squeals as they put on another record and Sinatra's voice oozed forth with "You'll Never Know." Notebook Jean clutched her sides and shut her eyes tightly. Powder Jean did the same. Even calm Bev threw her head back with rapture. But Peggy was above all this and just kept pushing her cuticles back. I sat listening to the crooning voice and to the jangle of charm bracelets as hands rose to weave softly in the air. Sometimes there were sighs, once even a moan.

I thought of pictures I'd seen in *Life* of Sinatra in auditoriums packed with thousands of girls who squealed and moaned like this and even tried to tear his clothes off and fainted, so that attendants had to carry them away. There was something very wrong with this, because he had a voice with no oomph; it was a tired voice, and I would think you would be more likely to fall asleep than get excited.

It would be different if you were hearing someone magnificent from olden times, some great pianist crashing the keys in a Parisian concert hall; that would be thrilling, but the audience wouldn't scream and try to tear his clothes off. Frank Sinatra brought out tired taste and bad manners, he was a sign of the times; people were getting lower and more like a herd of sheep, and it wasn't like the olden times, when there was passion and grandeur and glittering manners.

There was another spate of squeals as the hollow, syrupy voice came to an end. Bev got up to turn the phonograph off and smiled over at me. But then she must have noticed my unappreciative face. "Don't you like him?" she asked.

"No. And neither does Peggy."

"You must be insane," Peggy said in her quiet, queenlike way. "I've always loved Frankie. I was one of his first fans."

"How can you not like him?" Powder Jean asked me with wonder.

"He's too tired."

"He's just the *opposite*," she said with a kind of breathlessness. "He's just so full of . . . life and love and everything. He's just Frankie . . . there's nobody else like him."

"Nobody as boring," I agreed. "But just because I think he smells, that doesn't mean anything. To each his own."

I was trying to be nice, but I could see that the word *smell* offended them, and now another displeasing thing was happening because I was remembering something Helen Maria had once said about Franz Liszt, the great composer and pianist who had given dazzling concerts throughout the best drawing rooms of Europe. She said the women in the audience, those women with their lorgnettes and tiaras and lovely gowns, would run up to him like football players and grab him and pull his hair, which was very long, and tear the buttons from his beautiful frock coat and scream and beat their temples and faint in piles around him.

I should have been used to it by now: never arriving at a fine solid theory but that it was immediately wiped out by a nasty contradiction. But at least, I thought stubbornly, at least it was the magnificent Franz Liszt they had lost their marbles over and not puny little Frank Sinatra.

The others had begun talking about a Valentine's dance Notebook Jean was giving. She was going to send out invitations saying "Hop on over to the Valentine Hop." She wanted opinions. Powder Jean thought it was cute. Bev said it sounded a little like rabbits. Peggy was consulted. She said it sounded like rabbits, but it was sort of cute anyway. Notebook Jean said she wouldn't send it if it sounded funny. They decided to put it to the vote.

I pulled my shoulder bag against my thigh, so that I could feel the buried light of Egon's letter. It made everything more tolerable—the boredom, the offense I had caused, even the women screaming and pulling Franz Liszt's hair. It was comforting, like a touch of magic. I felt restored, and when they had all voted in favor of the invitation as it stood, I turned to Peggy.

"Have you heard from Helen Maria lately?"

"Not lately, she's very busy," Peggy replied with coolness; she was not pleased with my behavior.

"Is she still going with that what's-his-name?"

"I don't know." And she looked around at the others. "He's this very, very handsome guy. Very terrific. A grad student."

"Why isn't he in the Army?" Powder Jean asked, and then blinked. Peggy was leveling her a disdainful look, as if everyone should realize that no sister of hers would be dating a 4-F; obviously he was doing essential scientific research, or maybe he was a returned hero with the Purple Heart. It was an eloquent look, and in it I could see Helen Maria as she had been presented to this group: popular, busy, dating only the biggest men on campus, dashing around to football games and dances, her room filled with pennants and pressed corsages. The genius had become one of Peggy's great assets. I sat wondering if I should pop this bubble. I decided to—only the truth was moral and just. But Peggy was giving me a friendly look, as if she were going to pay me a compliment. Pay me to keep my mouth shut, maybe.

"You know, Donald Woodall is really good-looking now. Are you going around with him?"

"Sort of." Though we were in different classes, he still ate lunch with me, and we had attended a noon dance, and I had gone home with him again to look at his pins. He was still insulting at times; but I insulted him back, and we got along all right.

"He's the one that's very tall with the blond hair?" asked Bev.

"He used to be sort of funny?" asked Powder Jean, and blinked again at Peggy's look.

"I don't think he was funny," Peggy told her coolly. "I don't think there was anything funny about him."

"He was funny," I said. "He's still funny."

Peggy was in a corner. She looked irritated to have to defend him. But she did. "Well, *I* don't happen to think so."

"Let's give it the vote," I said. It was meant to be humorous, but it didn't come off. Peggy said they should put on "Begin the Beguine" and practice some dance steps. As a fifth wheel, it was my dismissal. I got up, and Peggy walked me to the door of the room.

"Thank you very much," I said.

"Don't mention it."

She was clearly delighted to see me leave, yet she didn't seem delighted with what she was returning to. There was still that touch of boredom on her face, that quality of presiding over something that didn't grip her talents.

I walked back through the Dungeon, thinking with a dry smile of the time I had waited on the chesterfield for Mr. Hatton, feeling so depraved and depressed, envying the lives of this little group behind the closed door.

Chapter 48

The Valentine Hop was a great success, from what I overheard one morning in homeroom a couple of weeks later, as Notebook Jean's friends enthused around her desk. But it was lost on me; I was sliding down in my seat, reaching into my shoulder bag.

Mr dear Suse,

First of all, I don't know why a poem could not be written about a dog scratching itself, as long as it showed a true dog scratching itself in a true way, so one felt what it actually is to be a dog. You are right to say that poetry is always beautiful, but beautiful can mean many things. It can even mean pain and sorrow, and I believe there are more poems written about death than about love. Those moments in between, as you call them, the terrible moments and the ordinary moments, are really more the material of poetry than the moments of bliss.

Not being a poet, it is hard for me to explain, but I think we go to poetry not to find faith in the blissful moments, but because we know other people have felt as we. They have known all our own emotions; they have known the same questions, and have stood awed by nature, and have lived with all the small familiar things that we have lived with (including scratching dogs), and this is somehow, though I do not know why, a necessary thing to feel inside oneself. If you will forgive me for sounding pompous, I think it has to do with being part of the enduring spirit of man.

And so with the United Nations. It is true that to plan a lasting peace sounds like a high-flown poem painted in the air, for I can only agree with you that peace has not played a large part in the history of our world. But it is the spirit that has prompted this organization; it is mankind's old tough hope and its

265

willingness to try, which, if we are to call the United Nations a poem, makes it a beautiful one. Whether it succeeds or not is another matter entirely.

I see that I have borne out the fact that I am not a poet, for I have wound up on a very clinical note indeed. Let me allay that note by saying strange things happen, even miracles, and who knows? Maybe we will really come through this time.

Now, Suse, I must end this, for I haven't much free time—translating German texts for the present, having quit my studies. Thank you for giving my brain such a good workout, and with best wishes that you are busy and happy—

Egon

I closed my eyes, savoring the words. Trying to savor them.

"They were completely unique—"

"They were absolutely darling, Jean—"

"Oh thanks, I just used this heart-shaped cookie cutter—"

"Did you notice Dick Johnson, the way he dances?"

"You mean like a spastic?"

"What does Lois see in him?"

"She could do much better—"

"I adored the punch—"

"My poor mother, she's *livid*—I used up all our sugar stamps for the next twenty *years*—"

"Did you see what Barbara was wearing?"

"She should never wear pleats—"

"You'd think she'd *realize*—"

Poor Barbara, not to realize about her pleats! I was about to put my fingers in my ears when it occurred to me that I was hearing poetry. This was one of those small ordinary moments we all shared, a moment beautiful in its own way, part of the enduring spirit of mankind.

"At least if she turned the hem up—"

"It's hard with pleats—"

"And that sick green, why bother?"

No, this could not be what Egon meant. If this was what endured, God help us. I would have to ask him. But I couldn't do it right away because he was busy with his new job; I would have to respect that, hard as it was.

Meanwhile, it was interesting that he had broken from his former life and was no longer a student. It seemed a final statement of his distance from Helen Maria. He had never mentioned her once in his letters, never said Helen Maria is fine or Helen Maria sends her regards. They were finished, and Helen Maria was stepping out with someone else; but Egon was not.

The bell rang; order descended. I returned the letter to my shoulder bag, tenderly placing it next to the first one, two lights shining deep in the dark. And the light of his blue eyes, and the light flowing through my veins, and the light of mankind's miracles, for we might really have peace forever.

Dear Helen Maria,

I'm dashing this off in study hall. You'll be happy to know I'm in College Prep now, but you won't be happy to know I've only got a B minus average. I realize that I'm not a scholar, because I don't stick to things. My mother says I run hot and cold, and that's true. Right now I'm hot for poetry, I think there may be more truth in it than in book learning. For *me*. I would never be so presumptuous as to tell others where they should look for truth. To each his own, as I mentioned in Peggy's room the other day. Yes, she invited me over, I was quite flabbergasted. Her friends are extremely dull, in fact everyone in my class is dull. The class I came from was dull in their studies, but they were more original to be around, I can't explain it. But I guess I will stick here now that I am here, because as Thomas Wolfe says, you can't go home again. I have a friend named Donald who is reading Thomas Wolfe. Personally, I think the tragedy of life is that you can't go home again, but recalling your attitude about the melancholy aspects of life, I will not belabor this point. Anyway, I'm not melancholy at all. I'm cherishing some hopes for mankind. As for Peggy, who I brought up a minute ago, she is practically queen of the school but she looks bored. All her friends talk about is powder puffs and Frank Sinatra and I think it's getting to her. Maybe she will turn serious and become a scholar like yourself, or at least start acting more interesting and original. That's about all

the news, I thought you'd like to catch up on everything. I wish we could get together again. We never
finished that history conversation in your kitchen
when it got so exciting and you said brava!

> Your friend,
> Suse

For a long time I had felt guilty about writing Helen
Maria, in case she was still hanging onto Egon, eating
her heart out. But now I was certain of their break, and I
knew she had recovered, because to brood was not in her
philosophy. I felt with a rush how much I had missed
her; I wanted to see her again and talk about history and
life. And there was no reason why the three of us
couldn't be friends, without any hard feelings. Maybe we
could even go out on a double date, my hair was long
enough.

I picked up my pen again.

> P.S. My hair is almost shoulder length. If I came
> to Berkeley you wouldn't even know me.

Chapter 49

One day, in early March, Peggy stopped me in the hall.
"Why don't you come over this afternoon? Nobody'll be
there."

I was surprised. But I nodded. "All right," I said.

It was a stormy, dark day, but with moments of dazzle
when the rain came flashing down like gold needles. The
leaves on the trees were new and green and wet, and the
wind shook them hard on their branches. We didn't talk
because the wind was too strong. It blew at our backs,
pushing us along almost at a run, as if to get us home to
her room in a hurry.

"You want a Coke? Or how about a cup of hot tea?"
Her face looked eager, and I felt that mine did, too. She
went off to make the tea, and I stood at the French windows, looking out at the trees shaking dark and light in

the garden. Rudy came over and sat at my side. He liftd a short back leg, cocked his head, and scratched behind one of his long hanging ears. With his black, blunt claws he scratched long and passionately, making a harsh noise painful to hear. His muscles worked fast and rippling under his smooth brown coat. His eyes were slits, with deep grooves of concentration between them. At times he looked as if he'd fall off-balance, but he never did. Then suddenly he stopped, gave his head a shake, so that the ears made a snapping sound, and settled back on his haunches. With a sigh of satisfaction, he gazed out again at the garden.

Yes, why couldn't you write a poem about that? I saw now what Egon meant. It had to do with Rudy's soul.

Peggy came in with a tray of tea things and set it quickly on the rug. We arranged ourselves on either side, and she poured for me, offered me milk and sugar, asked if I was comfortable. We lifted our cups and sipped.

"That day you came over," she said, "you didn't like my friends."

"It's just that I don't have anything in common with them."

"But look at Helen Maria. She never had anything in common with anybody, and look how she never had any friends."

"She had us."

Peggy gave a little sigh.

"I liked those days," I said. "I thought we had fun."

"I don't know, it was kind of pathetic. She was a screwball. I was fat. You had green hair."

"It was fun anyway. Remember when we went up on the hill that night and she invoked the gods? I'll bet none of your friends would do that."

Peggy laughed, almost with her old gusto. "God, if they'd seen us! I can imagine their faces!"

"Well, what do you want them for then?"

"Oh, you always see things black and white," she said, setting her teacup down. "Nobody's perfect."

"They don't have to be perfect. Just not zombies."

"Zombies. That's disgusting. Are you calling Bev a zombie?"

"Not her so much, but those two Jeans. If you think about the enduring spirit of man, you can't fit them in at all. There's nothing in them you'd want to endure. I can imagine Keats writing a poem about Rudy scratching himself, but can you imagine an ode to a pleated skirt?"

Peggy was silent for a moment. "I have to tell you something, Suse. You bore people. You bore them because you don't make sense. You bored my friends as much as they bored you, but at least they were polite."

"Pin a rose on them!"

"Oh, honestly." She sighed.

It was falling apart, all our eagerness and intimacy. "Let's start over again," I said.

"All right," she agreed, drawing Rudy to her as he waddled by. He lay down with his head in her lap. A few moments of silence passed. "Well, how's your family?" she asked. "How's Peter?"

"He's in Germany. They're getting close to the Rhine now." I held up two fingers and pulled them back as I spoke. "Normandy. The Battle of the Bulge. He's been through them both, and he's been lucky all the way."

"I'm glad. I really am."

"But it's odd," I said uneasily. "He's been lucky so long it makes you worry. You keep holding your breath."

"You've got to have faith, Suse. That's the only thing you can do. Have faith."

"I know."

"How's Karla?"

"Fine. She's in Hollywood."

"*Holly*wood?"

"That's right. She's an illustrator at the Walt Disney studios."

"Is she working there waiting for a break? She could get a screen test easy with her looks."

I put my hand inside my blouse and rubbed my chest. The skin there felt tender these days, itchy, and there was a slight swelling on either side. "Karla's an artist, that's her career. She doesn't want her face plastered all over the screen."

"I'll bet. I'll bet she'd be thrilled. Anybody'd be."

"I wouldn't."

"You would be too. You'd love to have millions of people come and ooh and ah over your face."

"Do you think they would?"

She cast me a brief look. "They might."

Ten feet high on the Technicolor screen I saw my wheat-gold hair streaming in a wild wind, my silver eyes flashing, my skin smooth and gleaming over the perilous cheekbones. A face in a thousand. I stretched out on the rug, smoothing back the long, wild hair.

"Well, maybe I belong in the movies, but I still wouldn't want a bunch of strangers gawking at me."

"Who said you belonged in the movies?" She looked irritated. "If you really want to know, you're still way too thin. And your hair's too straight. They'd have to fix you up plenty before you'd be ready for the cameras."

"What are you mad about?" I asked with pleasure.

"I'm not mad. It's just embarrassing when somebody takes themself so serious. You can't have a decent conversation that way."

"Well, let's start over again then."

"All right." And she was silent, stroking one of Rudy's long ears.

"Listen," I said after a while, "since we're being really honest today, I want to ask you something. How come you've always been so interested in good looks?"

She thought about it. "Because they're like a sword."

"A sword?"

"They can get you places like nothing else can. People stand back like you had a sword. But you've got to know how to use it. Helen Maria, for instance, she doesn't know how to use it. She just wants to be a classical scholar. It's a waste. She might as well look like Eudene."

"Well, Eudene's happy. A lot of homely girls are happy. Remember little Valerie Stappnagel? She was happy."

"Maybe they're happy, but they don't have any power."

Power. Having a sword in your hand. But where were you advancing as the crowd parted before you? You weren't storming a citadel or throwing out a government; there were no flags or leaping flames at the end of the crowd, just the student body president, or a movie producer, or a rich husband, or many rich husbands, like those of Aunt Dorothy, and all Aunt Dorothy left behind was a little yellowed sketch of a boy and a pool of tears on Helen Maria's floor.

"That's not power," I said. "That's just going after men."

Peggy gave me an indulgent smile. "Grow up," she said, still stroking Rudy's ear.

"I have, for your information. I'll tell you something, Peggy. Nobody else knows it. I'm in love."

"With who?" She was interested. She put down Rudy's ear.

I paused; I didn't want her to suspect Egon. "You don't know him."

"He's not in junior high?"

"God, no. He's out of college. He's a friend of a friend."

"What does he think of you?"

"He's in love with me."

"That's ridiculous," she said flatly. "You're fourteen years old."

It was like a bucket of cold water. I sat up angrily. "Age is in the *soul*, it's what you've been through *inside!* I've been through a lot inside, and he knows it, and that's why he doesn't care if I'm fourteen!"

"Don't get mad, or we'll have to start all over again."

"I'm not mad," I said, picking up my teaspoon and putting it down again. "I'm just surprised that you have such a small mind."

"I don't have a small mind, I'm just realistic. Look, they've got all sorts of girls their own age, what do they want with some kid in junior high? Besides, they could be arrested."

"Just for holding hands? Or kissing?"

"I'm not sure. Probably."

Frowning, I moved the teaspoon back and forth on the tray. "Well, it doesn't matter. You would do it where nobody saw you."

"They wouldn't take a chance. Why should they ruin their lives to kiss somebody in the ninth grade? I mean I don't like it either, I'd rather go around with some older guy instead of Jerry, but you've got to face facts. I've gotten very realistic."

"You've gotten full of hot air," I muttered, giving the spoon an angry twirl so that it clattered against the china.

"All right." She sighed. "Let's start over."

"I told you. I'm not mad."

"Then I'll give you my honest advice. Forget this guy, and concentrate on Donald Woodall. He'll do you a lot

272

more good. I hear he's got a lot on the ball, and if you could get him to crack his books and get out of dumbbell class and sort of influence him not to be so rude—"

"Why should I spend my time changing Donald Woodall? I've got better things to do."

"Like what? You're not in activities. You don't go to parties or dances. And you're not a grind either. It seems to me that you just sort of . . . float around."

"Well, that's freedom."

I thought she would argue, but she nodded slowly in agreement. "That's what I miss. Freedom. I'm being honest. You saw how it was, you think the same and talk the same and dress the same. You have to agree on everything."

I was surprised to hear this confession, surprised and pleased. It made my words gentle. "But you're the top one, you could change it any way you wanted."

"That's just it, you can't. Oh, I can say I like Dick Haymes better than Perry Como, and they will, too. Or I can say pearl necklaces are out and lockets are in, and they'll put on lockets. But if ever I said I liked Enrico Caruso or put on antique jewelry—well, I'd just lose my position. I wouldn't have any influence at all. It's something bigger than all of you, and you have to stay inside it. Not that I like Caruso or antique jewelry—but if I *did*. Or if I went up on top of a hill at midnight, believe me it wouldn't make them do the same thing; it would make them drop me. You can't go outside this thing, even if you're the top one."

"What is this thing?"

"I don't know. Customs, I guess, the way things are. And the question is: do I stay, or do I go out?"

"Oh, go out, definitely."

"Oh, it's easy for you to say, you're already out. I've got a lot to lose. Like Jerry."

"You don't sound very crazy about him."

"Maybe not, but he's student body president." She put her hand out at me like a stop signal. "I know, I know, that doesn't mean a damn thing to you. But I want to tell you, when I think back to what I was in the seventh grade, I shudder. I wouldn't have dreamed of even *looking* at the student body president. We were from different *planets*. It makes me sick when I think how low I was—"

"You were never low!"

"Don't be polite. I was low. I was a dumb fat slob. And if you think I went on that damn diet and knocked my brains out studying and figured out exactly how to dress and act for the *fun* of it, you're crazy! If you think I'm going to throw all that out the window just to climb some stupid hill in the middle of the night, you've got another thought coming!"

"I didn't say anything."

"No, but you're sitting there thinking it! You really irritate me!"

"All right, we can't talk then. We'll have to start over."

"That's fine with me!" She poured herself more tea, not offering me any. The gray room lightened a little, went dark again, and was suddenly irradiated. The French windows trembled with wet, sparkling light, the trees in the garden blew back in a wild glare, and just above their tops, but far in the distance, probably miles beyond Shell Hill, the fluid darkness lit with the steep, lofty end of a rainbow. I could feel a sudden happiness soar through me; I reached out perhaps to squeeze Peggy's hand, but squeezed Rudy's paw instead.

"I'm going to be a poet."

"Fine," said Peggy politely.

"I'm going to write about storms and things, and I'll write about Rudy, and a lot of other things. How's Helen Maria, by the way?"

"Well, like I said the other day, she doesn't write much."

"You say you don't know who she's going with now?"

"She never tells us personal things, it's all guesswork with Helen Maria. But she was really blue at Christmas."

"She was home for Christmas? Why didn't she come and see me?"

"Because she didn't do anything. Just sat around and moped."

I was sorry to hear this. But it was in the past now, and she was over it. "So you think she broke up with what's-his-name?"

"Egon. I think so."

"That's too bad," I said, rubbing my chest again. "But those things happen."

"You shouldn't rub there. It doesn't look good. It looks like you're feeling yourself."

I took my hand away. "That's disgusting, Peggy."

"That's why you shouldn't do it."

"There's nothing there anyway. Hardly anything."

"There will be. That's how it starts, by feeling tender."

I knew it. I knew what was happening. And it was strange, because I always thought I would be fearful and angry when my body began to change, but I had been feeling a pleasant anticipation. I realized I wanted something there, small, shapely, unobtrusive. Because if you were going to be held in someone's arms, you didn't want to be a complete ironing board.

"And after that," Peggy went on, "you'll get your period."

There was nothing romantic about menstruation; it was just disgusting. "Who wants it?"

"You don't ask, kiddo, you just get it."

"Well, I'm going to ignore it."

"Just try to," she sneered, "when you're moaning and groaning with the cramps."

"I won't be getting the cramps. I don't believe in all that Mother Basketball junk. Anyway, I'd like to change the subject. I'd like to talk about something inspiring."

"Like what," she said shortly. She would rather have talked about menstruation. Maybe it was something she couldn't discuss with her other friends. If so, I was with them.

"The United Nations," I said. "You know where they're having their first meeting? Next month? San Francisco. The public's invited and everything. President Roosevelt will be there in person."

"He doesn't cut any ice with me. I'm a Republican."

"I never knew that."

"I'm a Republican because everybody in my family's a Democrat. I believe in freedom. And I believe in freedom of speech. So I'll tell you something. I know who you're in love with. Egon."

It was like those days after Pearl Harbor when I never showed anything on my face. Bombs exploding everywhere, death all around, I never gave a twitch. "Really? I'd like to know where you got that silly idea."

"Because you know his name as well as I do, but you keep pretending you can't remember it. And you keep asking who Helen Maria's going with. It's plain as day—"

"It's none of your business—what're you sticking your big nose in for!"

"I'm not." She looked offended. "I thought we were letting our hair down. I thought we were sharing our deepest thoughts."

"Baloney!" I said, getting to my feet. "We've had to start over three times—we don't even know each other anymore. And if you tell Helen Maria about him and me, I'll kill you. Or if you dare write *him*, I'll strangle you with my bare hands!"

"Don't you talk like that to *me*, you assy moron!" she snapped, jumping up.

"I mean it! If he thought I was going around blabbing to everybody—it's unfair! I didn't blab anything, you just stuck your big nose in! Well, it's between him and me! It's private!"

"Do you think I care about your stupid crushes?"

"It's not a crush!"

"Don't you yell at *me*, you assy moron!"

"You call me that again, and I'll smash you!"

"I'll call you anything I want! We're not friends!"

"You've made that clear enough!"

"*You've* made it clear!"

We stood breathing in each other's faces while Rudy gazed up from the floor, his tail thumping worriedly. Peggy wiped her mouth angrily with the back of her hand.

"You must think I've gotten pretty low if you think I'd go talking behind your back to Helen Maria or Egon. That was insulting. Because I'll tell you this, whatever else I am, I'm no informer. That was a low thing to say!"

I looked away from the injured face. "All right, I'm sorry. I apologize."

"All right. I accept your apology." She crossed her arms. "Do you want to start over again? I don't think it's worth it."

"It's up to you."

"I don't give a damn one way or another."

"I don't either."

We stood in silence, each waiting for the other to decide. Then warily, both at the same time, we finally lowered ourselves to the rug again.

276

Chapter 50

—EUROPANA—
by Raymond Kerr
Performed by the Mendoza
Jr. High School Symphony.
Orchestra, under the
direction of Raymond Kerr.
March 16, 1945—8 P.M.
Jr. High School Auditorium
Admission Free—

Dad never got home early enough from the shipyard to go anywhere, so on Friday evening Mama and I walked over together, putting up our umbrella under a heavy downpour; this boded ill because no one would want to come out in such weather. But a block or two before the school, I saw that it was going to be a full house; the sidewalk was alive with people hurrying along under their umbrellas like those crowds you saw in the movies rushing to the opening night of Carnegie Hall. Ahead of us, in the rain, the building was bright with lit windows, stately and gala, and as you crowded up the wet steps to the open doors, you could hear the busy, heart-thrilling toots and pipings of the orchestra warming up.

We got good seats on the aisle, and pulling off my galoshes and coat, I looked around to see who was here. I didn't see any of my dumbbell friends; but every Towk in school had shown up, some in groups, some with parents, and every single teacher was present, sitting with husbands or wives never laid eyes on before. Mrs. Miller, for instance, had a flesh and blood mate with a stiff gray mustache and bald head, and Mr. Villendo of the double-sized eyes sat right next to me holding hands with an enormously pregnant wife in a flowered smock.

There were outsiders, too, mostly society women whose pictures you saw in the Local Events section of the

Clarion, and there were a lot of soldiers, sitting quiet and self-conscious with their caps in their laps. And there—I pointed her out to Mama—was the famous Mrs. Kerr, whom I recognized by her purple eyelids and because she was the center of attraction. She was sitting in an aisle seat, wearing a long wine-colored gown with a white corsage pinned to her shoulder, and people kept stopping and shaking hands with her and laughing and talking and then patting her hand in congratulation as they made way for the next well-wisher. She had blue-black hair worn in a very unusual style, pulled straight up on top of her head in a shiny tight bun. Her purple lids were big and droopy, with black spiky eyelashes, and she was gaunt and haggard-looking, with long teeth under her red lipstick. She wasn't pretty, but she was striking—so ruined and yet passionate-looking, for under the purple lids the eyes flashed, and the great toothy smile was dazzling in its pleasure and excitement, and yet there was something tragic about that smile, something that cut my heart—

Some people had stopped at our side. It was the Stappnagels, bland and smiling as always, talking pleasantly with Mama and greeting my lifted eyes with friendly hellos. My ferocious hatred of them was gone, but like the Japs, they were people I would never be able to give a spontaneous smile; something of them was embedded in my flesh like old pieces of shrapnel, no longer painful, but not to be forgotten. I ignored them as they talked. I didn't notice Valerie at first. She was at their side, but being so small, she was half lost from sight in the streaming crowd. I had feared that my last conversation had left her disillusioned and empty, and I was relieved to see her looking the same as ever, very serious and mathematical and content. We exchanged a brief hello, and then the three of them passed back into the crowd to find their seats.

Then it was Peggy leaning down to chat, while Jerry, the highest of all Towks, stood next to her, patient and courteous, with her raincoat over his arm, smiling brightly as he was introduced to Mama and smiling at me, too.

"What a nice boy," Mama said when they had gone on.

"He's student body president. She likes to impress people with him."

"Now don't be like that. I'm sure she likes him for himself. He seems very nice."

It was true. He did. But I knew Peggy better than Mama did; she only got Peggy's sweet side, I got the dozen other sides. We had had another afternoon session since the first one, but for all our shared confidences there was still a circling-around quality that I felt might go on forever, like a basically false equation that could never be worked out.

Up on the stage the orchestra players were dressed in neat white blouses and dark trousers or skirts. They looked serious and professional as they warmed up trilling and blaring and turning the music sheets on their stands seemingly unaware of the audience, and there was a special and festive smell throughout the room, a mixture of perfume and brilliantine and wet umbrellas, which added to the feeling of drama and gaiety.

I took up the program I had been handed at the door. "EUROPANA," it said, "A SYMPHONIC POEM." There was a good deal underneath about a wanderer coming under the spell of many different countries, and how he begins to hear the tremors of war and then its terrible clash, and then at last how through the smoke he glimpses the dove of peace descending. It was a wonderful theme, my kind of theme. How right I was to have sensed something great and remarkable in Mr. Kerr. And now everyone began to clap, and I looked up.

Mr. Kerr was crossing the stage, his face sterner than I had ever seen it, the nostrils positively gigantic. He was not in his velvet jacket and old woven sandals, but wore a dark suit and black shoes. His long gray-streaked hair was combed smoothly back along the sides. Turning his back to us, he stood waiting as the claps died down. You could hear a few coughs and the sound of seats being settled into more comfortably. There was silence. Then Mr. Kerr raised his baton.

A thin flute note blossomed through the auditorium, so weak and wobbly that it was a relief when the string instruments joined in, not exactly on time, but quickly getting straightened out as Mr. Kerr leaned forward pointing his baton at various players and with his left hand making deep, scooping movements. It was a nice melody and you could feel youself wandering over hill and dale, and then the whole orchestra came rushing in

279

and you weren't sure where you were—maybe being carried down a turbulent river, over a huge waterfall— and Mr. Kerr stood on his toes and threw his arms out quiveringly, so that it was thrilling and inspiring, and I glanced with excitement at Mama.

But then I lost track of where we were. There seemed to be a lot of modern zigzags and repeatings, like the records of Alban Berg that Helen Maria sometimes played; it got more and more complicated and mathematical until all at once it tangled up in a knot, and all the eyes of the players hung worriedly on Mr. Kerr's face. Somehow, with skids and lapses, they were dragged out of the tangle onto a dark mountaintop, and you were filled with the music's sadness, a sadness that became slower and softer until it was as desperately forlorn as Mahler; in fact, it sounded exactly like Mahler. These soft passages seemed hard to do, because you could hear flat notes twanging through like hiccups, making Mr. Kerr's neck stiffen each time; but after a while Mahler disappeared and we were back with the zigzags.

My mind drifted. I thought of the headlines a week ago—"Yanks Cross Rhine at Remagen"—and wondered again if Peter had been among them. I thought of the Russians advancing from the other direction. I thought of Hitler trembling in his Chancellery and of the hills around Berlin growing more emerald green every day, as our own hills in Mendoza were growing.

I was brought back to the music by the wobbly flute again. It was going on in a long solo, which made you feel sorry for the player, an eighth-grade girl with black bangs who looked cross-eyed with nervousness. The passage was torture to listen to, but at last the violins came sweeping in again, this time in unison, ominous, reminding you of gray skies and swirling wind. Bassoons and tubas sounded through, deep and fateful, and a girl in the back row holding a triangle now gave it a great bop, and it sounded like the peal of a bell, echoing bodefully, and very slowly the violins faded away to a whisper, and then suddenly there was a crash of cymbals.

The war had begun. It was the longest part of the symphony, and the best—brilliant with trumpets and trombones, the kettle drums booming—and Mr. Kerr was directing with his whole soul, crouching, leaping, arms shooting in every direction, his long hair flying.

He had a wonderful lead trumpet, just a short old seventh grader but he knew what he was doing and his solos flashed and shimmered, sweeping the other trumpets into magnificent fanfares like something from the medieval age, with banners and plumes and glinting armor—war as it should be, thrilling the soul—and now the cymbals clashed again and the kettle drums boomed, and unfortunately a clarinet player knocked over his music stand in his haste to turn a page; but even this could not mar the tremendous crescendo that was building up, and now it came, an earsplitting blast that sent chills down your spine, and Mr. Kerr was on his toes, his elbows tight against his sides, his whole body quivering.

Then a slash of the baton. Abrupt silence. The flute player lifted her instrument to her lips again. The long, wobbly note again, but this time growing steady, gradually gaining resonance. She lifted your eyes upward, for you could see the dove of peace flying overhead; it swooped and careened in a sweet, clear melody, and slowly, very slowly, it descended, its wings fluttering, folding, settling, and with infinite grace, the sweet, clear melody shaded to silence.

Mr. Kerr brought the baton down. He stood as he was for a moment, then turned around as the auditorium exploded with applause. His face shone with sweat, and it was still stern, the nostrils huge. He bowed. He bowed again. He gestured to the flute girl and trumpet boy, and they bowed, embarrassed, but covered with smiles. Mr. Kerr bowed again, deeply.

It didn't seem that the deafening applause could grow greater, but it did. My palms hurt with the glory of their beating, my heart was pounding, and I exchanged delighted looks with Mama, who was clapping almost as hard as I but in a more ladylike way. Across the aisle, people were urging Mrs. Kerr to stand up, and now she did. She must have been an actress once because now she was thrilling—she threw her arm out at the audience and then at Mr. Kerr, and then she bowed graciously, her smile radiant with pride for her husband, a pride that shone with the most naked, unabashed love, and even if all this glory was taking place in the Mendoza Junior High School auditorium instead of Carnegie Hall, I saw no tragedy in that smile now. As my palms throbbed and stung, I looked around me. There was Notebook Jean giving her all, and Powder Jean, too, and Bev and Peggy and Jerry and every last Towk in the place. For all their pleats talk and stupidities, I would forever respect them for coming here and giving Mr. Kerr his moment, for honoring and appreciating those eight long years of labor.

Still stern, passing his hand through his wild hair, Mr. Kerr bowed again and turned to accept from the principal's wife, who came swishing across the stage in a blue evening gown and a tremendous smile, a bouquet of red roses, which he held stiffly, bowing to her, and then to us again, and then to the orchestra. Then he strode offstage, and with a final surge the applause died, replaced by new excitement and commotion as people began getting up, most of us leaving but others hurrying backstage—Mrs. Kerr, of course, and teachers, and the parents of the players, and the society ladies, and even a photographer from the *Clarion*, holding his flash camera high above him in the crush.

Leaving Mr. Kerr to his triumph, we filed back up the aisle, down the hall, and into the wet night. The rain pounded off the umbrella, but I was lit up in my blood.

"Wasn't it beautiful!"

"It was. It was absolutely beautiful," said Mama, linking her arm in mine as we walked. "Your school is lucky to have such a talented person teaching."

"I know."

I loved Mr. Kerr, and I even loved my school—every bright window gleaming through the rain, and every teacher and student I had ever cursed.

Chapter 51

Dear Egon,

I have had a wonderful experience, our music teacher composed a symphony called *Europana*, and it was performed at night. It was so powerful and beautiful that every one was totally demolished. It was about Europe and the war, and then the dove of peace descended. I believe he's a genius, and I believe you are too. You said you weren't a poet, but your letter was a supreme poem that I will keep forever. You have given me so much to think about and hope for, you have really changed my life and made me a deeper, happier person. I would love to see you in person again, because there's so much that's impossible to say in letters. I could come down by train for a visit, and I could go home on the train too. Transportation is no problem.

I want to tell you I understand about the dog scratching, it came to me in a flash of illumination as a dog I know scratched himself. I saw his soul. I think I understand about souls now, thanks to you. I never liked my College Prep classmates because they're trite, but I think each one of them has got a small something in their soul worth enduring. I saw this in a flash of illumination at the symphony when they came through the rain to cheer Mr. Kerr, our music teacher, in his moment of well-earned triumph. I will always respect them for that. I know I would not have had this illumination if it hadn't been for your letter, which has made me a deeper person.

There is so much to answer in your letter that I can't even begin to do it in this reply. If you had a free Saturday I could just jump on the train and be down there in forty-five minutes. I must end this now because I don't want to take too much time away from your translation work. That is why I didn't write all this time, but believe me, that's the only reason! I will sign off now with deepest regards, hoping to hear from you soon about coming down.

Suse

I didn't allow myself to reread this letter. With a racing heart I took it to the corner mailbox and thrust it in. Then a horrible nervousness overcame me, a sense of having done something rash and irrevocable. What would he think of my asking so brazenly to come and visit him? It was true that our two hearts beat as one; but there was such a thing as good manners, and I had thrown them to the winds. It was *Europana*, it had lifted me too high. What if I had undone all his love, if he would see me now as just another pushy, babbling bobby-soxer, hardly worth getting entangled with?

But he could never misread me that badly, not when we were as close as we were.

A few days later I came home from school to find an envelope waiting for me on the dining-room table. It was addressed in Helen Maria's elegant, spiky hand. They were engaged. They had read my letter. She was furious. So was he. I opened it with a sick feeling.

Dear Suse,

Thanks for your nice note, sorry I haven't had time to answer till now. Yes, it was a stimulating discussion we had that day in the kitchen; I was impressed by your thinking; it struck me as having evolved enormously. I would enjoy picking up that discussion, and we must do it as soon as I see a free day ahead or next time I come home. Speaking of which, I'm sorry not to have gotten in touch when I was home for Christmas, but I was feeling somewhat under the weather.

So you're seeing Peggy again; most interesting. See if you can knock some sense into her head, though I think she's too far gone. She wants pennants (and *pompoms*; I desisted) and squeezes me (implausibly) for all the fine points of campus social activities. This is what college means to her. She's become more consistently trivial than I had ever feared in my worst moments. I allow for fads and tender years, but there's something self-willed in Peggy which transcends ephemera. I agree that she shows a certain ennui, but whether this is one of her many poses or a sign of true boredom I'm not sure. If the latter, bring to bear on it all your resources.

It's raining fiercely here today, pouring off the eaves like a waterfall. Your great friend Ruth (who lives on the second floor) just left a minute ago. I know you don't like her—she has an abrasive quality—but she's a good person, and was very kind to me a while back when I was somewhat under the weather for various reasons.

But now I want to tell you exciting news. If the

war ends in the next few months, I'll be sailing for England in the autumn. I've been waiting so many years that it should come as an anticlimax, but I'm quite beside myself. One of the reasons this letter is so long is that I can't concentrate on my work—but I'd better get down to it! In closing, let me say I'm glad you're beginning to cherish some hopes for mankind. And if you've decided you're not a scholar, so be it. The important thing is to seek, and you are doing that.

Helen Maria

What a relief on all counts. Our friendship was intact. Her split from Egon was absolute. And she was beside herself with joy to be sailing for England at long last. A world of white swans after winter, released across the blue of open seas.

"Helen Maria's going to England!" I told Mama, waving the letter. I told Dad, too, when he came home from work that night. "At least she will be if the war in Europe's over in the next few months. And it will be, don't you think?"

"I don't know, but it could look like it," he said. "Maybe even by next month."

"Then everybody'll be free and going everywhere—"

I stopped one morning before a notice on the bulletin board.

IUNITED NATIONS CHARTER MEETING!
Anyone interested in attending this
historic event, please sign up at
the office. Transportation to San
Francisco by school bus. Leaves
from here 9 A.M., Thurs., April 26.

I went directly to the office and signed up. At noon, eating lunch with Don, I learned that he had signed up too.

"It's history in the making," he said, cracking a hard-boiled egg against his forehead. "We owe it to ourselves to see it. Not that they'll make a dent in Malthus."

"I don't want to sit next to you on the bus if you're going to talk that way. You know what you don't have? A soul."

285

"I've got as much of a soul as you do," he returned, peeling the egg with his long, clumsy fingers. "Only it's got its feet on the ground."

"Baloney. Mine are more on the ground than yours— mine got frostbite in the Bulge and all you ever did was shove those little pins around that don't have a toe to get cold."

He bit the egg in two, giving a slow shake of his head. "I never know what you're talking about."

"Just don't sit next to me on the bus."

"Who wants to? I don't want to sit by you. You bore me."

"Good."

"Or we'll talk about the weather. You can bore me about the weather."

"Just don't talk about Malthus. I'd like it to be a nice day."

"It'll probably rain."

But it was more than a month away; spring would be in full flower. And the war might even be over by then.

I talked to Peggy in the hall. "Everybody'll want to go because they'll get the whole day off. You'd better sign up now."

"Who says I want to? You'll probably have to stand in line over there for hours."

"It's worth it, isn't it? It's history in the making. Even if you don't like Roosevelt."

"Maybe I'll sign up, but I don't know if I'll go. School excursions bore me out of my mind."

"Pretty soon you won't have a mind to be bored out of," I said, remembering Helen Maria's instructions.

"You give me a pain."

"It's a crucial decision, Peggy. To go or not to go. At least put your name down. Then you'll have a whole month to think it over."

"Maybe," she said, walking off to link arms with Jerry.

The end of March we had a letter from Peter. He had crossed at Remagen with the first breakthrough, over the Ludendorff Bridge. He said the Rhine wasn't much, at least where they crossed, brown and still and surprisingly narrow. He said in Remagen, civilians came running to show them where German soldiers were hiding in

286

cellars; the soldiers were so demoralized that they had actually sent the civilians to bring the Americans in. But the bridge itself wasn't such an easy nut to crack, and when they finally set foot on the east bank, they didn't even have time to think about it because they had to take a hill. You'd think climbing a hill would be simple enough, but it was steep and covered with loose rocks, and it was here he met his downfall, wrenched his ankle and knocked two teeth out . . .

Thank God for such a merciful downfall, thank God his luck had broken in that small way, like the Normandy nick in his arm. It would keep the fates satisfied.

. . . so he was off his feet for a few days, taking it easy. It was good weather, the countryside was nice, and he was studying German from an old phrasebook he'd picked up in London. Now he could say such useful things as "Will you please direct me to the opera house?" and "Kindly take my trousers to be pressed." . . .

Chapter 52

I never knew when the barrage balloons were taken down. Maybe months ago, but the weather was so thick and dark you didn't notice. I only noticed in early April. There hung the sky a deep pure blue, with nothing in it but a couple of sea gulls.

It was a Saturday, and I had gone to the Market Basket to buy some potatoes for Mama, wandering on through empty lots with the sun roasting my shoulders. The tall, springy grass, bright with dandelions and poppies, made me stop every few minutes with my nostrils wide. There was a sharp grassy sweetness mixed with the rich dirt smell, as if the sun had all at once unlocked these smells and released them in a steady, overpowering uprush, while overhead white butterflies tumbled high and low in the breeze, which blew over your face as clear and cool as the sun shone hot. Out on the sidewalk the pavement felt warm through your shoe soles, and the store windows looked newly washed and polished, and everything inside them stood in fresh, bright display.

It was too much to expect the sandbags to be gone just because the barrage balloons were. They still stood shored against Sheriff O'Toole's office: hard, shriveled, streaked and blotched with long years of sun and rain. But the sky was blue, and the air sweet, and beneath my shirt my chest had put forth two very small mounds, so that I too felt a sense of beginnings.

There was the usual bustle around the train depot and USO, but as soon as you crossed the tracks and started down the long road to the wharf, you walked in midmorning silence. Birds chirped in the trees that lined the road. They were olive trees, small and gnarled, with pale grayish leaves flickering. Behind them stretched the tule marsh with its sharp smell of mud and salt. The water lapped brown among the reeds, but farther out it graded into a smooth sheet of green with a long, broad strip across it like a shining mirror. I looked up at the sky again, holding nothing in its blueness but the sun and a few gulls gliding.

On the wharf radio music and boisterous voices rolled out from the baitshop-saloon, a long weathered shack built on pilings. A group of society ladies carrying boxes was clattering up the gangway to the Bass Club, which was an old ferryboat where social events were held on Saturday nights. Down in the water, laid out in rows along swaying wooden walkways, fishing boats were bobbing, while men in black knitted caps or dirty white yachting caps with gold braid worked on the motors or puttered around with a bottle of beer in their hands. The boats began rocking wildly; it was the ferry coming in, the *City of Mendoza*, sending out a storm of waves. I hurried over and watched it churning into the slip, heaving from one side to the other against the pilings, setting them creaking and groaning, and finally hitting the dock with a tremendous thud as the water below fumed white and gnashing. The steel apron banged down, men leaped off pulling ropes to fasten to the pier, and the cars rolled out with a thump, one by one, while bells clanged and gulls swooped above in wild circles.

After a tour of the people fishing, sitting along the dockside as always, waiting patiently for the bass too oily to eat, I remembered the potatoes I was carrying and started back. The air was clear as glass, and looking

288

across the water at the hills, I felt them close enough to touch with my hand. I would write a poem about their emerald greenness, and the white swans streaming across blue seas, and the United Nations, and the dazzling sun in the creek and Egon's arms crushing me to him. Walking between the olive trees and the marsh, prowling like a sun-warmed animal along the soft dirt path, I wanted suddenly to feel the ground with my naked feet. Stopping, I pulled off my tennis shoes and stood working my toes into the dirt.

"Here, boy," someone said.

I looked around. Behind some bushes there was a washed-up beam of timber where you could sit and look out across the water. I could see bits of a khaki uniform through the leaves and the white, moving blur of a dog. There was something about the nakedness of my feet, their sudden freedom and freshness, and the feeling of the sun pouring warm all over me that impelled me to prowl around the bush to where the soldier sat, and stand nearby with my shoes and bag of potatoes, as if taking in the view.

The soldier looked over. He was throwing twigs for the dog, whom I recognized as the depot mutt.

"His name is Whitey," I said with a sideways look.

"Here, Whitey," the soldier said.

"He belongs to Mr. Moroni," I added, turning around a little, casually. "That's the stationmaster. He's part Alaskan husky."

"The stationmaster?"

"No, not the stationmaster. Whitey."

He smiled at this. I didn't think it was much of a joke. But his sleeves were rolled up, and his arms were muscular and hairy. I moved a little closer, small thrills of danger darting through me. "He swims in the slough," I said, feeling that I must keep talking. "Whitey. He's a good swimmer. He'll swim for anything you throw." There was a loud toot from the bay. The ferry was starting back. "That's the *City of Mendoza*."

"I thought that was the city of Mendoza," the soldier said, nodding toward the town.

"It is." He wasn't a very sharp soldier. "They've both got the same name. One's a town and the other's a ferryboat. The boat's named after the town."

He smiled again, at what there was no knowing; a dim

sense of humor. But under his cap his hair was black, like Egon's, and as he leaned forward to pat Whitey, his khaki shirt stretched tight across his shoulders. I moved closer yet, still talking.

"Whitey got into a train once and rode all the way to Sacramento. It was on the front page of the *Clarion*. That's our newspaper, the Mendoza *Clarion*."

"What's your name?" he asked suddenly, looking up.

"Suse," I said hesitantly. He shouldn't ask that; it was forward.

"Suse, you're a mine of information."

I shifted the load in my arms. "It's because I live here."

"Oh," he said with a look of illumination, nodding.

He was slow-witted, and it was a pity, because he was so nice-looking, with dark liquid eyes and those nice solid arms. I hoped he had a kind-hearted girlfriend who didn't make fun of his dimness.

"Are you from a long distance off?" I inquired.

"All the way from Camp Stoneman."

"I mean originally."

"Originally? From a place called Rye, New York."

"Oh," I murmured, concentrating on what I was doing. I was sitting down next to him, in a casual way I hoped, yet with a feeling of stiffness. My eyes were fixed on the ground. I had never in my life gotten into a conversation with a soldier. It was the one thing I had been warned over and over not to do, so that it was second nature not to by now. Yet here I was sitting next to one in the bushes, with my feet naked and the sun hot all over us. But he stood up, and that made me feel easier. He went over and picked up a stick and threw it for Whitey.

"I suppose you're shipping out to the Pacific?"

"That's right," he said, crouching as Whitey raced off.

"I don't think the Pacific theater will last long after Berlin capitulates. Our troops will outnumber the Japs two to one."

He glanced over at me. "You seem to have quite an interest in the war."

I nodded. "I want it to end."

"That," he said, opening his arms for Whitey racing back, "is a sound sentiment."

He didn't sound so dim anymore. And his thighs under the stretched khaki were hard and muscular, too, like

290

his arms. I wished he would pay less attention to Whitey.

"I'm also interested in the United Nations. I'm attending their charter meeting on the twenty-sixth."

He stood up and threw the stick again. "That should be quite an occasion. Are you going with a school group?"

He needn't have asked that. Instead of answering, I threw a twig for Whitey, confusing him. He didn't know if he should go for the stick or the twig. Then he lost interest in both and began sniffing around the reeds. The soldier seemed to be losing interest, too, brushing the dog hairs off his pants as if getting ready to leave.

"It's a terrific view, isn't it?" I said, putting down my shoes and potatoes and going over to him. "This is the Suisun Bay, well actually it's where the Suisun Bay and Carquinez Straits meet, and those are our big hills over there, that's Port Costa you can see down the way, can you see it down there?"

He nodded, looking. He was taller than Egon, but not as good-looking. If you noticed, his lips were a little too thin, and his nose had a bulge at the end, but a nice bulge, and his bare arm was only a couple of inches from my bare arm; I felt an overwhelming urge to move closer so they would touch, just to see how it would feel.

But he was saying, "I guess I'll be getting on," and smiling down at me. "Suse, it was nice talking to you."

"It was nice talking to you, too," I said, looking up into his face. His dark eyes, in the light of the sun, had flecks of gold in them, like a tiger's, and his lids were heavy, knowing, full of dark nights and passionate embraces. My own eyes felt wide, so wide the sun hurt in them, they felt widely waiting, rigid, and it seemed as he smiled down, adjusting his cap, that he wanted to crush his lips to mine, to grind the hot flesh of his face into mine, to press me down in the bushes and lay his big hands all over my body—my thighs, my stomach, my two new mounds, he lusted for them, horrible, disgusting! I was only fourteen, how dare he come crashing through that barrier with his snorting lust and big hairy arms, was he blind, was he insane? I stepped back, swung around, and ran.

He didn't come after me, thank God, and by the time I had put a good distance between us and thrown myself behind an olive tree he was walking on toward the wharf, Whitey trotting beside him.

As I watched, my heartbeats subsided. The water in the reeds slapped softly, a sparrow pecked peacefully at my feet. After creeping back for my shoes and potatoes, I started home along the path. Once more I drank in the morning silence and salty tang, and the unsettling experience sank away as I thought again of my great poem—the emerald hills, and the white swans streaming, and the United Nations opening, and the creek's dazzling sunburst, with Egon's strong arms crushing me to him.

Chapter 53

I liked art class because there were dumbbells mixed in with the Towks. And I liked the art teacher, Mrs. Pinelli. We used to have a clean, simpering teacher who was more interested in having you weave baskets and make pretty bookmarks than in drawing and painting, and I hated her. But Mrs. Pinelli's hands were dirty with charcoal and paint. She didn't frown and pinch her lips when you sketched Hitler being riddled by bullets against the Chancellery wall. Mrs. Pinelli said, "Make his torso shorter if he's falling forward." Mrs. Pinelli didn't say, "Good heavens, what is that?" when I began a big watercolor illustration of the great poem I was going to write. The picture was mixed up because everything had to be there together, but Mrs. Pinelli said, "Interesting composition! Good tension!"

I wasn't sure how I would go about showing Egon and me. Our twined arms and pressing lips were too private for the eyes of Mrs. Pinelli and fourteen classmates, yet that was the most important part of the picture. I finally decided to place the sun right in front of us, so all you saw was a blaze of light. I had done that, very cleverly, and now I was reworking the emerald hills, slapping and splashing down new layers of brightest green, while Don, across the room, was reverting to his short, goofy self by screeching a Conté crayon across the tabletop, until now at last someone threw an eraser at his head.

It was just at this moment that a girl from the office came in with a note, and with a face so profoundly serious, so sorrowful and bowed and filled with hushed importance that the voices and bustle of the class abruptly died away. Mrs. Pinelli, standing by one of the tables, glanced at the girl's face and took the note. When she had read it, her hand dropped down at her side; she looked as if she were going to cry. We were all very still, looking at her. Green paint dripped from my brush. Don was holding the eraser that had bounced from his head. But Mrs. Pinelli didn't speak. She walked slowly back to her desk. There, after a long moment, she said, "Class, I've just received word from the office . . . the president is dead."

It was not possible. There had never been another president. He was eternal, like God, but God as He should be—great, yet ordinary, too, caring about coal miners and sharecroppers, our FDR with his flashing smile and jaunty cigarette holder, and the way he said, like someone you knew, "My friends," yet so great that you didn't count him among the bigwigs, he was so far above them, so grand in his black cape, so serious, and he had worked so hard for the United Nations, and now he wouldn't see the flags flying and hear the cheering crowds, he would be in the darkness of his grave like Aunt Dorothy and Mario. . . .

These thoughts seemed eternal, too, as if they had been going around in my head for centuries, yet the sad important girl was just stepping back out the door, and Mrs. Pinelli was just pulling out her chair and sitting down at her desk, where she took up a drawing someone had turned in, but you could tell she wasn't looking at it. I laid down my paint brush. The room was still quiet. Then, though we had not been given permission, we began putting our things away. Mrs. Pinelli said yes, we could leave.

In the hall we saw that the whole school was leaving. There wasn't the usual shouting and laughing, except for some seventh graders. I saw Peggy walking along with some of her Towk girlfriends, and I wondered if she was pleased with the news. Roosevelt cut no ice with her, she was a Republican; maybe she was even rejoicing. I went

293

over to her, to become angry, to relieve the soreness in my chest. But Peggy looked as cast-down as everyone else. I walked along with her and her friends. I had never walked with a bunch of Towks before, but today was different; it seemed to join everyone together. Even the teachers seemed joined to us, standing at their doors as always, but not eagle-eyed for misbehavior; it was as if a barrier between us had been removed, and we looked at them openly with the great strangeness of what had happened, and they looked back the same way, even hard Mr. Lewis, and especially Mrs. Lewis, who stood with her lace hankie in her hand.

At my locker I nodded good-bye to the Towks, and they nodded back. Everything was formal; everything was strange. Don was formal, too, waiting silently for me at the door. Silently we walked out into the spring afternoon.

Then he spoke majestically, almost like Roosevelt himself. "Today is the end of an era."

I gave a sad nod.

"He was a great man. We'll never see another like him."

"I know."

"This is a date the world will remember."

"April twelfth."

When we walked by the garrison, we stopped and looked through the storm fence. The busy atmosphere was gone; everything was quiet, as if a string had snapped. Soldiers stood by the open door of a barracks building, listening to a radio news broadcast.

"Do you realize," Don said as we leaned against the fence, "that he was voted in thirteen years ago? That's one hell of a long time."

"I know."

"It's a crime he couldn't have made it to the end of the war."

"That's what I wish too."

"It's the irony of life," said Don, and we walked on.

A young woman walking along the street had apparently not heard the news yet, for she was walking briskly, with a cheerful face. Don felt she should be told. He went up to her.

"Pardon me, lady. Did you know President Roosevelt died?"

She gave him an angry look. "If you're making some kind of joke, you should be ashamed."

"It's no joke. You can just look around."

She did look. She looked at a group of students walking along without the usual loud banter. She looked through the storm fence at the silent soldiers. Faintly, from the open door of the barracks building, you could hear the sound of the radio broadcast.

"My God," she whispered, "it can't be true." And there before us, clapping her hand to her face, she broke into tears.

"It was hard to do," said Don as we walked on, "but I felt I had to do it."

We passed the park.

"Do you think they know?" asked Don, indicating the old men on the benches. It was hard to tell. They were quiet, but they were always quiet. Still, they didn't look stunned and grief-stricken. Don crossed the lawn and spoke to one.

"They knew," he said, coming back.

Maybe when you got that old, nothing stunned you. Maybe you used up all your grief on the way.

"Well," sighed Don as we approached my house, "I guess we'll have to get used to what's-his-name now."

"Who?"

"What's-his-name, the VP."

"I don't care about him."

"Truman." He tasted the name on his tongue. "President Truman. It doesn't sound right."

"It sounds awful."

At my front steps we parted soberly.

Mama's eyes were red when she opened the door, and as I stepped inside, I saw them fill and overflow. It loosened the soreness in my chest, and my own eyes wetted. She had been sitting at the kitchen-table with a cup of coffee, and we went back there and sat down, and we had a cry together.

It was odd how the kitchen table was always there in the things you remembered after. Mama sitting there the day the Germans invaded Denmark. The night we came up from the cellar alive and had hot Ovaltine. The last breakfast we had together with Peter. And now again the same faded green oilcloth, the same salt and pepper shakers, the same old metal toaster, and the big round clock on the wall, ticking.

We listened to the radio the rest of the afternoon and ate alone together. When Dad came home, at about eight o'clock, he put his lunch pail on the kitchen table, and his and Mama's eyes met in a long look, as if someone in the family had died, and then he shook his head with a sigh, and Mama bent down and took his dinner from the oven where she kept it warm. I didn't say anything either. It seemed that there was nothing at all to say.

We listened to the radio again afterward, late into the night.

". . . I walked across town, toward Broadway, and exchanged glances with hundreds of people who looked stonily back. . . . A group of businessmen halted by the foot of an elevator shaft. They had exchanged jokes for years about little boys who thought there had never been another president and never would be, who thought that Roosevelt was immortal. In a way, the businessmen had thought so themselves. Now, they knew he was. . . ."

What did he mean? The whole terrible point was that Roosevelt was not immortal; he had died.

Some of the voices were from churchmen. I didn't like churchmen, but I liked them tonight, they said truthful things. ". . . Thou hast taken from us Thy servant, who has led us faithfully and truly through twelve fateful years, and we are stricken and bereft. . . ."

Some of the voices were full of purpose and spirit. ". . . I can't help but believe that the force of his personality will continue . . . I can see that wonderful face saying to every one of us, 'Go ahead, keep going!' "

One of the speeches was very long, by a war correspondent. "For myself, who spent most of the war years abroad, when Mr. Roosevelt was in the White House, I would like to say this: When President Roosevelt died today, the Fascist dictators lost their greatest enemy. . . . And just as the Nazis feared him, the people, whom the Nazis conquered and enslaved, loved and revered him above all foreign statesmen. . . . In France and in Belgium, when they were liberated last summer, the people there felt somehow grateful to the President personally, but that was not all. Somehow, too, he represented to them the great hope of achieving lasting peace on this sorry planet. . . ."

Very late at night, there was a hymn sung, "Now the day is over, night is drawing nigh. . . ." Then there was a moment of silence.

"April 12, 1945, has closed."

Chapter 54

APRIL 17:   **Nuremberg Falls!**
Luftwaffe Shattered!
1,345 Planes in 2 days!

APRIL 18:   **Yanks Smash into Leipzig!**
Russ. Gain on Berlin!
Open Up All-Out Assault!

APRIL 20:   **316,940 Nazis**
Taken in Ruhr!
U.S. Troops Break
Okinawa Stalemate!

APRIL 21:   **Red Army 7 Miles From Berlin!**
Moscow Announces Final
Drive Across Oder!
Fierce Fighting on Okinawa!

You no longer saw one headline or two across the page; there were always three or four, sometimes more. So much was going on that you could hardly keep up. Berlin almost reached. Prison camps revealed, full of emaciated slave laborers. Hitler rumored to have fled south, the coward. Montgomery's troops pushing north to Denmark. Pétain facing trial in France. Okinawa falling fast. Baguio taken, the last Philippine holdout.

APRIL 22:   **Russ. Reach Berlin!**
16 Armies Drive
Into Burning City!
Reich Ripped to Shreds!

The emerald hills loom high in the sky,
as the last day of war grows near,
and soon the swans so white on the sea
will cross its blue without fear.

APRIL 23:   **Welcome United Nations!**
Russ. Smash Deep
Into Heart of Berlin!

The United Nations will meet on high
to make our vict'ry eternal,
so that we will not have to die
in smoke and flames infernal.

APRIL 24:   **Red Armies Linked Inside**
Berlin! Great Tank Battle On!
Molotov, Stettinius, Soong Here

The sun will shine in the creek like gold,
our two hearts will beat together,
while world peace comes like glory untold,
a moment to last forever!

I couldn't stop writing. I wrote a long letter to Peter, whose ankle had healed and who was tramping across the rubble of Germany, heading east toward the Russian advance. I sent him my poem, leaving out the last stanza. I wrote Karla, too, and sent her the poem. And I wrote Helen Maria, but I didn't send her the poem because I feared her literary opinion. I thanked her for her letter and said I hoped I could come down and see her soon. . . .

I am really happy to know you will get to Oxford at last, it is a wonderful reward that you have awaited many long years. And now that the Russians have smashed into Berlin, the end of the war can't be far off. I am sorry President Roosevelt could not be alive to see it. I realize now that he was in failing health, but at the time I thought it was political propaganda, and also, I did think that it was *impossible* that he could die, that is an honest statement.

He would be happy to know that the United Nations is opening tomorrow, as he planned. Will you be going? I will be going on the 26th, I'm going with the school. Which brings me to Peggy. I will give you a report on her progress, I mean her lack of it. You're right, she's too far gone. Concerning the United Nations, I told her she should sign up to go, and the other day she told me she had; but she's still not sure she will go because school excursions bore her. I will tell you about the long talks we had in her room. She always seemed to be wavering on the edge of giving up her stupid life and getting free, but she would get mad at the last minute, as if you were trying to take something away from her, as if she were frightened, too, like someone being pushed into deep water. So I have stopped harping.

You may think I'm being melodramatic, but I have a strange feeling about Peggy these days, that she is choosing her life's direction for good and will not change later on. It's a feeling in my bones. This is why she must come to the United Nations; to me it is a crucial decision on her part. If she will attend this historic event which she has heretofore called dull and uninteresting, it means she has seen the light. But I can't tell what is going on underneath and if she has seen the light. We will just have to wait till the 26th to see if she will make the correct crucial decision. . . .

I wrote a lot more, and when I was finished, I was still in a writing mood, but there was no one left to correspond with. The one person I wished most to write and send my poem to I could not. Egon had never answered my last letter, and it was five weeks now. I was often struck with a shuddering certainty of having offended him and ended everything. Yet I did not really believe that he could feel that way; I felt sure there must be another reason for his silence. More and more it seemed he must be away on vacation, someplace where there was the snow that he longed for, up at Tahoe, where it still lay thick on the mountains; and I could see him skiing down the slopes in the keen mountain wind, crouching as he soared high in the air, his blue eyes narrowed.

APRIL 25:   **Berlin Overrun!**
                S.F. Welcomes
                World Leaders!

I looked at the photographs of crowds massed around
limousines from which famous figures stepped out, and
then I matched up the figures with the names below.
There was Governor Warren and tall, snowy-haired
Secretary of State Stettinius. There were the Russians—
Commissar Molotov, short and gray-haired, and a handsome aide called Gromyko. There were Anthony Eden
and Clement Attlee and Lord Halifax, all very English-
looking—I hoped Helen Maria would be there. And
there was Trygve Lie from Norway, and Field Marshal
Smuts from South Africa, with his pointed white beard
like Professor Ford's, and slender Soong from China, and
Arabs in dark robes and flowing white head-dresses, and
Carlos Romulo from the battling Philippines, and
Masaryk, the Czech foreign minister, and there were Negroes, too, Endekatau from Ethiopia and Clarence Simp-
son from Liberia. Every nationality was represented—
eighty percent of the world's population, the article said.
Eighty percent in agreement, the other twenty being the
crushed Nazis and Japs, who would have no say-so. How
could we go wrong?

Chapter 55

I arrived at school early the morning of the twenty-
sixth, wearing my good Sunday dress, which was blue
and white flowered, with puffed sleeves. Our bus stood
waiting. It was yellow, with prominent black lettering
along its sides: "Mendoza Unified School District." The
delegates from Mendoza.

I sat down by a window, putting my coat and shoulder
bag and lunch bag in the seat next to me, saving it for
Peggy. The three teachers who were accompanying us
sat up front, nice little wrinkled Mrs. Miller, and Mrs.
Pinelli from art class with her hands washed, and Mr.

300

Villendo, all dressed up today in coats and hats, the two women in small white spring hats something like Aunt Dorothy's and Mr. Villendo in a smart gray fedora.

It was a warm morning, with a soft golden haze hanging over everything. I sat looking out, and gradually as it grew nearer nine o'clock, the bus began filling up, and the walks and lawns filled with students going to class, and still Peggy hadn't come. Neither had Don. Don I didn't care about, but what if Peggy had made the wrong crucial decision? And everyone seemed to be aboard now because the motor was starting up. I rolled the window open and craned my neck out. There was Don, racing along the street like a maniac, waving his lunch bag, zooming past my head, and crashing up the bus steps, where Mr. Villendo told him not to be so god-awful noisy. Then I saw Peggy, but she wasn't running; she was walking with Bev and some other Towk girls, and she had her books in her arms.

I leaned down as she passed, cupping my hands around my mouth. "Peggy! Come on! You signed up!"

She turned and looked up.

"You've got to!"

From the front of the bus Mrs. Miller told me not to shout.

"You'll never have another chance!" I took my hands away.

Peggy looked embarrassed to be shouted at, annoyed. Giving me a small shrug, she went on, the fiery hair battened down, the bobby socks rolled to just the proper length, and around one sock the latest fad, an ankle bracelet with a little locket, giving a final tiny glint as the bus pulled away from the curb.

Don flung my things in my lap and sat down, breathing hard from his run. Like the other boys today, he was dressed in slacks and a sport jacket, the collar of his white shirt spread out over the lapels. "We're off!" he exclaimed as we started down the street.

"And it's perfect weather!" I wasn't going to let Peggy's decision ruin the day. Nothing was going to ruin it.

After a stop at the high school, where we fell in behind their bus, we zipped down Alhambra Avenue into the countryside with its orchards lush and green in the warm haze. The bus crowd was noisy and cheerful, and Don didn't talk about Malthus. We discussed how we would sneak off and find closer seats if we couldn't see well, because the opera house was said to be huge. We discussed the Burma shave signs. We discussed the invasion of Berlin and where Hitler had fled. We had a good conversation all the way.

San Francisco Bay was bigger than Suisun Bay, and not green but dark blue. We sailed high over it on the windy bridge, seven miles long, Mr. Villendo informed us, raising his voice over the noise, and completed in 1937 after five years' labor. Peering out the window with his big double-sized eyes, he pointed out Coit Tower and the Ferry Building as we came down the ramp, and then we wanted to know what street we were on, because it looked like Ferry Street, even sleazier and more interesting, and Mr. Villendo said Third Street as a drunk wavered into the traffic, laughing and talking to himself. Cheer abounded; flags flew from buildings, on Market Street streetcars clanged and crowds of shoppers bustled along, and then we were driving into an area of green squares and fountains and large white buildings, and now we drew up before the War Memorial Opera House. A big crowd had gathered already, though it was only ten o'clock by Don's wrist watch, and the session wasn't to open till three-thirty.

We were to spend the morning at the Veterans' Building next door, where there was an international art exhibit, then eat our lunches at the civic center square, and then line up and wait for the opera house doors to open. It was to be a very full day, and here we were stepping out one by one under the smart green-striped awning of the opera house, to join this crowd of ladies in three-quarter-length fur coats and men in overcoats and fedoras.

The air was sunny and brisk, and the opera house soared into the sky brilliantly white with great columns and arched windows and flying flags. Military police stood guard by the doors in white helmets and white belts, but you could hardly see them for the crowd, which was very noisy considering that they were mostly adults. They were clamoring about lining up, where and how, and the military police were shouting advice and pointing at the immense glass doors, through which, in the lobby, you could make out a five-abreast line already formed.

"What if we can't get tickets!" I exclaimed to Don; but he was lost from sight, and I stood crushed into the deep fur of a stout lady's coat.

"Hello, Suse," a voice piped at my side.

It was little Valerie. I was glad to see her, so calm and content, though she could hardly breathe among the tall pressing bodies and had to stand on her toes.

"Did you come with the high school group?" I asked.

"Yes. I think it will be an interesting day, don't you?"

"If we ever get tickets!"

"I certainly hope we will," said Valerie.

"They can't turn us back!"

But one of the teachers, Mrs. Pinelli, was now pushing toward the doors, looking worried and nervous. Everything was falling apart; we would never see the inside of the opera house.

"If we can't get tickets, we'll sneak in!"

"Oh, I wouldn't want to do that," said Valerie.

Just then Mrs. Pinelli grinned and waved to someone in the lobby. A minute later Don elbowed his way back. "Mrs. Pinelli's got a cousin getting our tickets. He came down at eight o'clock." *Brava* for Mrs. Pinelli, a far-sighted woman who arranged things well. And now at last we were being herded away from the crowd to the Veterans' Building, which was almost as large and elaborate as the opera house. I introduced my two friends as we walked, and they nodded politely, two serious people bound by a historic event, and we went up the steps into the building. It was crowded here too, and the teachers decided it was useless to form us into a line to look at the pictures, and said we could look on our own, as long as we all met outside at eleven-thirty on the dot.

There were a lot of rooms, and they were interesting at first: art from Mexico, art from Alaska, art from China. But after a while they all began to look the same and we wandered back into the lobby. Official-looking people wearing blue United Nations buttons strode through the crowd to the elevators, and a guard told us that all the offices involved with the meeting were upstairs on the second floor. I looked quickly around, in case Commissar Molotov or Anthony Eden was striding by.

But I didn't see them. I saw Egon. Just a glimpse;

then he was swallowed up in the crowd. I plunged after him, feeling a huge, wild grin stretching across my face. "Egon!" I yelled, pushing through to his side. "Hello Egon!"

He turned around and looked at me, surprised. "Suse. What in the world are you doing here?"

"I'm with my school!"

"So." And he smiled, holding out his hand. "That's nice, that you could come."

"We just got here!" I said as we shook hands and the electric shock jolted through me. "We came by bus!" I knew that I was talking too loud and not saying anything sensible and that the wild smile was still pasted across my face, but I didn't care. He was here in the flesh, smiling, his blue eyes warm and filled with love.

He was with some friends, whom he introduced me to. They looked like grad students, a couple of fellows and a girl who was attractive but thankfully not with Egon; she had her arm linked with one of the others.

"Are you coming to the meeting?" I asked Egon.

"We had better, after getting in line for tickets at half past six."

"That's early!"

"It is," he agreed, and his friends agreed too, but I sensed they didn't want to stand there being knocked against by the crowd, they wanted to move on.

"That's really early!" I elaborated, not knowing what else to say. How could we converse with no privacy? What if his friends dragged him off and this was all we had said? And now, pushed and squeezed by the crowd, he too looked as if he wanted to move on and held his hand out to say good-bye.

"Egon, I've got to talk to you. Privately." I glanced at his friends, who were looking at me with an expression I didn't like, one of amusement and indulgence, which made me flush. But at least, as they were looking that way, they were moving off, saying they'd meet him later by the door.

"What is it?" he asked, but now all my headlong courage disappeared. I didn't know what to say; my brain whirled. Then I caught hold of something. "I've decided to become a translator. I wanted to ask you about it."

"Yes, all right," he said, and we walked on.

"I'm taking French in school. I could take either Spanish or French, but I decided on French. Flaubert was French."

"Ah, yes, *Madame Bovary*."

We went over to a corner of the lobby where there was a bench with some people sitting on it. They made room for us. "Did you go skiing?" I asked as we sat down.

"Skiing? No, why? I do not ski."

"Oh, I thought you did. Have you been busy with your translation work?"

"Yes," he nodded. "It keeps me busy."

"I was surprised you quit the university."

"I may go back," he said. "I haven't decided what I should like to do." He seemed preoccupied, gazing out at the crowd, at the important officials striding past with their blue buttons. There was a sadness in his eyes, a deepness, something bitter.

"Aren't you happy about the United Nations?"

He looked surprised, and I realized he had not even been noticing what he looked at. "Yes, of course I am," he said.

"I am too. And that the war's almost finished in Europe. It could even end today."

"I suppose it could."

"But I'm really sorry about Berlin. I wish they could take it all at once instead of smashing what's left of it."

He gave a nod.

"Egon," I said suddenly, "I hope your brothers are all right. I hope they're not in the middle of all the fighting."

"Thank you, Suse. But I think they are not in Berlin."

"You think they got out?"

He gave not a shrug and not a nod, but a kind of mixture, and said again, "I think they are not in Berlin." And there was again that preoccupation in his eyes, that look of sadness and bitterness; but now he seemed to push the expression away and concentrate more on me. He asked about my French and what I could say.

"*Avez-vous trouvé votre parapluie vert et votre grand cheval blanc?*"

"No," he smiled, "I have not found my green umbrella and great white horse."

"*Quel dommage!*"

"Yes, a great pity. I need them."

"Egon, I've written a poem."

"Have you?"

I recited it for him; only the first two stanzas, I couldn't bring myself to say the third with people around.

"That is a good poem," he said when I was done. "I like the swans on the sea, that's especially nice."

"Of course," I said, reddening with pleasure, "I don't think swans *go* on the sea—"

"It doesn't matter. It is very nice."

"I've gotten so interested in poetry, Egon. It's because—well, of the things you wrote. I've read your letters over and over."

He was silent for a moment. "Yes, I'm glad that we're good friends, and can write about the things that interest us. And someday—when you're grown-up and a famous poet—I'll tell people I knew you when you wrote your first poem." He was standing up as he said these things, folding his coat over his arm. "And now, Suse, I think my friends are waiting for me. It was good to have seen you again."

"Maybe we'll see each other at the opera house," I said as we shook hands once more.

"Yes, perhaps," he said, and smiling good-bye, he turned to make his way through the crowd.

I wandered around, replaying our conversation in my mind. It had been so short. If only his stupid friends hadn't been hanging around the door. And we couldn't talk freely, because people were listening. If we had been alone, he would have talked of love, not friendship; he would have explained why he hadn't written. But I was pretty sure now it was because he was bogged down by his work. You could see that he was worried and preoccupied. Translating was difficult work.

"Where did you go?" Valerie piped at my side.

"I saw someone I knew."

"Don's looking for you."

"Oh, why doesn't he leave me alone? I want freedom. I want to breathe."

"You seem to be breathing," Valerie said.

Chapter 56

At twelve-thirty, having eaten our lunches, we lined up with the other ticket holders in front of the opera house. Now we would stand for three hours. Peggy was right, but her decision was wrong; sore feet were a small price to pay for a convention of peace, and even Don felt this way, and he was wearing new shoes that had given him blisters. He had been curt when he found me, as if he owned me—which I told him—but now he was back in a good mood, and another good thing was that he liked Valerie; he seemed to appreciate the way she looked at you without blinking or smiling, then came out with something pipingly to the point. I hoped he would transfer his infatuation to Valerie.

We all stood talking and laughing, listening with half an ear to Mr. Villendo explaining that the opera house had been built in 1932 after three years' labor and could seat 3,200 people. We shifted our feet and stretched and waited, and the hours crept by, and the line grew four blocks long. Mrs. Miller looked tired, but there was no place to sit except on the pavement, and when some of us tried to sit there we were told to get up.

But now photographers and men with newsreel cameras were arriving, and a mob of onlookers was filling up the broad sidewalk so that you could hardly see the street, and Don kindly offered his foot for Valerie to stand on; she said thank you, no—I knew she would consider it undignified to stand on someone's foot—and remained solemnly content, viewing the back before her. As we stood craning our necks, an electric excitement was building up in the crowd, and now the first cars began drawing up, official olive drab cars and long dark limousines which you could only catch scraps of through the mob. Dignitaries must be stepping out under the striped green awning because everyone cheered and applauded and the cameras popped and flashed, and then the military police were clearing a path through the crowd, and you could see better.

There were the Arabs in their dark brown robes and flowing white headdresses like sheets, and other dignitaries in suits, tall dignitaries and short dignitaries, hurrying up the steps talking solemnly together; and then at a roar of applause I turned to see Molotov, short and stocky, hurrying along with his retinue, smiling and raising his arm in a wave at the cheering crowd. Another roar, and it was Smuts of the pointed white beard, and then Stettinius, after which the roar never let up, and now it was Anthony Eden in the flesh, tall and elegant, striding along with a dashing smile, and the newsreel cameras were grinding, pigeons swooped, flags whipped—a crowd-roaring moment in history. I grabbed Valerie and pulled her up by the arm.

After the photographers and movie men had followed the last dignitaries inside, there was another wait. Then the glass doors swung open, and the line moved. It was a palace inside. Marble floors, columns, gold filigree everywhere, lit chandeliers, wall-length mirrors reflecting the gold and glitter and the crowd as it hurried along in a din of clattering footsteps. Mr. Villendo led us forward with an arm held high. We surged up a stairway like a tunnel that amplified the headlong clatter to a mad pitch; then the pitch dropped as we rushed into a lofty hall, swinging sharply to our left and up another clattering stairway; then out into another hall and swinging up another stairway, until it was like rushing up the spirals of a corkscrew, and you dizzily kept your eyes on your feet. But suddenly, as if commanded by fate, I glanced up as we swung into a hall, and there in the crowd was Egon, glimpsing me as I swept by and throwing me his warm, loving smile.

A few stairways later, Mr. Villendo, his arm going up again like a general's, led us into a balcony where the noise left off. All you heard was a vast, hushed murmur of voices. Everything was soft, the velvet drapes you brushed by as you entered, the carpeted stairs of the steep aisle, the plush red seats you sank into. Before us hung an immensity of space, with the stage very far down at its bottom. I had no time to be disappointed, because Valerie was producing a pair of opera glasses in a neat leather case.

"Are they yours?" I asked, hesitating as she offered them to me.

"Of course."

"I thought maybe they were your parents'."

"No, they're my own. I've been to several operas."

"Here?"

"Yes."

How modest of Valerie not to have mentioned that she had been here, how admirable. Taking the glasses from their case and putting them to my eyes, I saw nothing. Then Valerie showed me how to adjust the lenses, and the stage was right before my nose. Against a royal blue backdrop was lined a palisade of flags from every nation, set off at intervals by square gold columns. On the stage itself sat an aquamarine rostrum with a bas-relief of green garlands, and before that was a smaller rostrum, below which was a section filled with busy people—court reporters and translators, Mr. Villendo was informing us. The photographers were there, too, running around getting ready for the great moment. Mr. Villendo was informing us that the ground-floor audience was composed of delegates, and I trained the glasses on the backs of their heads; then I swung the glasses to one of the balconies where the newsreel cameras had been set up, and then to the curved and glamorous box seats where I was met, as if only a few feet away, by other opera glasses staring back at me.

"They're powerful," I said, passing them to Don, who was loosening his shoes from his blistered feet, and I looked around. I noticed with a jolt that Mrs. Miller wasn't with us, and I had a sudden vision of her falling with a heart attack on the way, stampeded—but here she came now, small and wrinkled, carefully making her way down the steep aisle. She had taken the elevator, she told us, sitting down nearby, and she had arrived not a moment too soon, for a man was walking out onstage.

But he only leaned down and talked with the court reporters, and it was another long half hour before the great moment actually arrived. Six men filed across the stage, five seated themselves at the large rostrum, and one stood behind the smaller one. There was a respectful applause, then silence.

The man at the smaller rostrum began speaking, his voice clear and penetrating even without a microphone. I was anxious to know who he was, but I had to wait because Valerie had the opera glasses. The man was welcoming us to this historic occasion, going on in a manner both flowery and official, so that you didn't care too much if you heard or not, but by the time I got the glasses from Valerie he was saying real things. Adjusting the lenses, I saw that he was Carlos Romulo of the Philippines. He was pausing now for a moment; then he looked up.

"We are here to determine whether the human race is going to exist or is going to be wiped out by another holocaust."

He didn't mince words. He gave me a chill. I trained the glasses on the men behind him, of whom I recognized only Molotov, whom I studied. He had rimless spectacles, a broad, thoughtful forehead under thinning dark gray hair, and a gray mustache under a small nose. He didn't look like a Russian—Slavic, wild-eyed, exotic—but he looked very nice anyway, and then I had to give the glasses to Don, who was bopping me in the side.

We learned later that the session had lasted three hours. It seemed thirty because every speech, no matter how long, was given again in French, Spanish, and Russian, and during these translations the only interesting thing was the flash of the cameras as the photographers bobbed around, falling on one knee or stretching high with their shoulders hunched, but after a while even that got boring.

It was a different matter when the speeches were in English. Having taken out my Big Chief notebook from my shoulder bag, I scribbled down highlights in the dark.

"Lofty phrases and great promises were forgotten after the last war, but this time they must have full realization!"

and

"Believe me, if you had lived under blitzes and rocket bombardment, you would find it a powerful stimulant to turn your thoughts to world security. That is something to remember, the range and power of modern weapons. . . ."

and

"For centuries to come, men will point to the United Nations as history's most convincing proof of what miracles can be accomplished by nations joined together in a righteous cause. . . ."

and

"We do not expect to change human nature. All we need to do is draw out the very best that is in it."

When Molotov spoke, it was in Russian, and as I sat listening to the foreign words, I saw fur-capped soldiers on galloping horses, riding to meet the Western armies, and I saw Red tanks crashing through the ruin of Hitler's Chancellery and the snowy steppes of Stalingrad with arms sticking up like iron, and it seemed odd, like a clap of light, that when the English translation was given, there was no war in it, only the future: "We are confident that the United Nations' aim will be achieved by joint effort of all peace-loving nations. . . ."

There was one other speech, at the end, that I scribbled down: "Let us with all the creativeness of which we are capable, by constructive thought, by willingness to cooperate, in order to keep faith with those who have made the supreme sacrifice, offer ourselves and our sacred honor to the building of a new united world."

Then came the applause, with everyone getting to their feet. It was like the end of Mr. Kerr's symphony, a thunder of triumph everlasting. Mr. Villendo was completely beside himself, turning this way and that as he clapped, as if he had supervised the entire proceedings, and Mrs. Pinelli lifted her hands above her head in applause, and even little Mrs. Miller beat her old weak palms together with vigor, while Valerie clapped steadily, with sober satisfaction, and Don, standing half out of his new shoes, applauded as hard as anyone, harder—Malthus apparently *parti avec le vent*.

The great crowd poured back out into the lofty hall, down the endless corkscrew stairs and into the street. It was dark now, and across the street the City Hall's green copper dome was brilliantly lit. Lights glittered everywhere, traffic flowed by with big-city honks, yellow cabs were lined up along the curb. The speeches still rang in my ears, and the overwhelming applause, and though I couldn't see Egon in the crowd, I knew he was there, looking back at me with love and longing as he was swept along.

Chapter 57

After school the next day I went to the library to read about yesterday in the San Francisco papers and to look at the pictures. But the picture on the front page was of a mass of white tangled worms, extremely large, with a couple of people standing in them knee deep, each pulling a worm out. Then I saw it wasn't worms they were pulling, but a pair of long arms. In shabby overcoats, leaning over, the two men were trying to extricate a corpse.

They were standing on a pile of them, and the worms were the corpses' long arms and legs tangled up. They were so scrawny and crazily meshed that it didn't seem they could be bodies, but they must be because they had heads, unmistakably they were heads, for they had mouths, slack holes, black against the whiteness.

I looked abruptly away. I knew the Army had found work camps filled with starved prisoners, many of them dead, but these weren't prisoners; they seemed more to be things; flung down like things, tangled up like things, stood on like things. I felt an urgent need to turn the page and never look back, but I forced my eyes again to the picture, then to the caption below: "Townspeople of Belsen are ordered to bury concentration camp dead." There was an article underneath, which I read quickly, skipping, for it gave me the same feeling as the picture had.

> Political prisoners, slave laborers, civilians of various nationalities ... 30,000 believed to have died at Belsen, near Bremen ... 21,000 liberated at Buchenwald ... the camps were run by a policy of calculated brutality ... in Buchenwald, prisoners were mostly Polish Jews brought there to work ... almost all Jews in prison camps have been destroyed ... after them the most cruelly treated were Russians and Poles ... bodies stacked like cord-

wood . . . hanging from hooks . . . shoved into furnaces . . .

Jews. Then, that was why Egon had looked as he did yesterday. That was what he meant when he said he didn't think his brothers were in Berlin.

The next day there was a picture of the Yanks and Russians meeting on the Elbe. *Historic Junction at Torgau!* the caption said.

"Did you see the picture?" Don asked me at school. "All hugging and shaking hands? It was historic!"

"I know." And they had worn fur hats, the Russians, and were on horses . . . but I couldn't get the other picture out of my mind. "Did you see the other one, the day before? Those bodies at that Belsen camp?"

"I saw it. It made me sick."

"It made me sick too," I said, thinking of the gaping mouths, the wormlike arms and legs; things that had been people once. "It makes you realize one thing—the UN's got to work out."

"Agh, the UN—they're already arguing. I thought you read the papers."

"It doesn't mean anything—they're just minor things!"

APRIL 29:   **Mussolini Assassinated!**
              Nazis in Italy Giving up!

"I see old Benito got it!" said Don.
"About time."
"His girlfriend too, strung 'em up by their feet."
"It's too damn good for them."

MAY 2:   **Hitler Killed**
              Nazi Radio Says!
              Fell at Chancellery!

"Well, old Schicklgruber's done for!"
"He should've been done for against a wall."
"I think he committed suicide. That's my theory."
He probably had, the coward. Afraid they'd tear him to pieces, now the concentration camps were discovered. But you couldn't put the blame on him alone; it took hundreds of Nazis to run those camps, maybe thousands.

313

And if that was so, if it was in the human nature of so many people to commit such a crime—even if they were Nazis—if it could be done by anyone at all, what hope was there?

MAY 3:
Hitler a Suicide,
Nazi Officials Say!
Berlin Garrison
Gives Up!
A City of Flames!

"What'd I tell you? Suicide."

"I hope he took arsenic. I hope he suffered."

"They don't use arsenic. Those guys all have cyanide capsules. Two seconds and kaput."

"It's wrong. They should suffer."

"I thought you were Miss United Nations—peace and goodness."

"So what? Why shouldn't they suffer anyway?"

MAY 4:
1,000,000 German Troops
Surrender: War in Europe—
The Last Act!

The last act. The bombed cities, the Polish family, Peter dodging his way through machine-gun bullets, it would be over. A last shot, and silence would fall across the Continent.

But what about human nature?

MAY 5:
Nazis Wail for Peace!
North Reich Falls!
Denmark, Holland
Freed!

"*Skaal!*" said Dad.

"*Skaal!*" said Mama.

"*Skaal!*" said I, and we clinked our glasses.

I hadn't seen my parents so happy for a long time; maybe I had never seen them so happy. They were truly from another country, I realized in a kind of dawning light; their hearts were there, they didn't belong to the soil of this town, the way I did. I had never caught that accent Peggy had mentioned, but I believed now that she had spoken the truth. It was there. It was strange to know this, that they were foreigners. Yet it didn't mean anything. It didn't change them in any way from what they were the day before, when I didn't know they were foreigners. They were who they had always been, even as they sat there listening to the liberation news with their wineglasses, and they would always be who they had always been.

But it was a curious thought that the Japs in the valley were less foreigners than my parents; they had worked the soil here for generations. The young ones had grandparents born here. I didn't. What if they had argued that truth with me while I was dragging them to the firing squad? What would I have said?

A blackness of realization: I was no better than the Nazis. For I would have said nothing. I would have kept dragging them.

MAY 8:   **Full Surrender!**
                5 Years, 8 Mos.
                Of War Ends Today!

We were in Mr. Lewis's class when we first heard. The door opened, and the same office girl who had brought the note about Roosevelt's death came in. This time the importance on her face was open and exuberant. Mr. Lewis took the note, beaming as much as that hard face could beam.

"It's over in Europe!"

We went wild, clapping and cheering, reaching around to grab arms and swing hands—Towks that I'd never before had an urge to grab—and at this glorious moment it came back to me with a burst of light, what that UN speaker had said: "You don't have to change human nature; you only have to draw out the good that's in it."

It was true, and I was the great case in point, brutal as a Nazi once, but look at me now, the good had been drawn out; I would never drag anyone to the firing squad anymore. I had thrown out my burned Jap head long ago. And if good could be drawn out of someone like me, as black and hard as I had been inside, it could be drawn out of anyone!

On the radio that night Mama and Dad and I listened to a reporter on Market Street in San Francisco. The

315

mobs were so thick that streetcars and autos couldn't move. People cheered and waved their hands with Churchill's V for victory sign; drunken soldiers and sailors waved bottles and grabbed girls they didn't know and had long, passionate kisses. A woman pulled off her clothes and jumped in a fountain. They had been there all day, yelling and laughing themselves hoarse. "For one joyous moment," the reporter said over the roar, "our nation feels entitled to forget the other war still waiting to be won. . . ."

But the Jap war would be over quickly; the victory in Europe made you feel Axis doom in an avalanche—huge, unstoppable.

MAY 10:   Japan to Get
                            More Bombs
                            Than Reich!

MAY 11:   38,857 Japs Killed
                            On Okinawa!

"Want to bet on V-J Day?" asked Don.

"I don't mind this time. I'll bet a dime. Three days."

"Three days? Are you crazy? Six weeks!"

"You're the crazy one."

"Okay, peaches, it's your dime."

"Don't call me that. And don't grab my hand!"

"I can't help it, baby, you do something to me—"

"Why don't you go out and visit Valerie Stappnagel?"

"Why should I visit her?"

"You liked her, didn't you?"

"Aha—jealous!"

MAY 15:   Yanks Split Jap Line,
                    Take Okinawa Airfield!

"You owe me a dime. It's three days."

"You'll be wrong too."

"I won't be wrong. But I won't be here to collect in six weeks."

"Good, where are you going?"

"Nevada. Work on my grandfather's ranch for the summer. You gonna write me?"

"I don't know. If I have time."

But it was Egon I wanted to write. The day I realized what had happened to his brothers, I had sat down and tried to write him a letter. But no matter what I said it sounded wrong, intrusive, and I had torn it up.

"Well, find time, baby."

"There you go again—don't keep grabbing my hand!"

"You know what you are? An ice cube."

"Well, I know somebody who's not. You want to know who I heard rave about you once? Peggy. You should hear the terrific opinion she has of you."

"I don't like redheads. I like blondes."

MAY 16:   Yanks Beating
                       Back Banzai!

Beating back. It didn't sound like an avalanche, it sounded like slow work. Italy, Normandy, the Bulge again; after all this time I hadn't learned to keep my hopes from sweeping out my brain. Suddenly Don's six-week date sounded overly optimistic; it could be months, even with reinforcements from Europe. And as I realized this, all my fears for Peter came rushing back.

MAY 17:   U.S. Okinawa Dead—3,781,
               But Jap Loss Is 47,543!

It was a gloating headline. I was glad it wasn't the other way around, but it was a gloating headline. Gloating was human nature. There was too much about human nature that set your teeth on edge. Thank God it didn't have to be completely overhauled, an impossible job. Just draw the good out of each person.

Even the Nazis. Commandant Kramer of Belsen had said, "I love my wife and children. I love children. I love God." You had to have hope; you had to believe that even in the blackness inside Commandant Kramer there was a drop of good. And every tiny drop was going to be drawn out, on a grand scale, throughout the entire world. It would be the first time in the history of our miserable world that such a thing would take place.

Peter wrote from near Leipzig, and the first thing that crackled through my brain was that he wasn't being sent to the Pacific. He talked about a point system, one point

317

for each month in the Army, one for each month over-seas, five for each battle you fought in, five for each wound, and five for each medal. If it added up to eighty-five, you'd be sent back to the States for demobilization in the first batch this summer. He fell two points short, but it wouldn't be long anyway, probably late fall, he hoped his clothes would still fit. . . .

Mama stopped reading aloud, lowering the letter. "It's the first time it's real to me," she said slowly, almost as if to herself, looking across the room, but not seeming to see it.

I thought she was going to cry, but after a few moments she took up the letter again. Germany was a shambles, refugees, black marketing, ruins everywhere, but as for himself, he had to say life was like one long rest period now, and by God it was nice just to walk around in the sun—nice wasn't the word, there was no word for it, and there was no word for what it had been, for everybody, the whole of Europe, and why and for what. . . .

I thought of this letter often, the picture he painted of the ruins, the desolation; not a country, not a person un-touched. And the deepest scars of all, the death camps. I began feeling something disgusting and cowardly about myself, how I lied inside. How could I have persuaded myself that Commandant Kramer had good inside him, except that it was too frightening not to think so? But he was a mutation, a monster, and not the only one; there were the thousands who ran the camps, and maybe thousands or millions in the world that we didn't know about, like black beetles under a log that would scurry out at any go-ahead signal. For good to be drawn out, there had to be good there. What would Commandant Kramer yield? Not even blood, but some kind of yellow juice like an insect's. And my whole idea of drawing good out seemed not only false and disgusting, but overwhelming in its stupidity. Had I imagined that the UN would go around with syringes, lining people up and drawing the good from their arms? Like a community blood bank? A community goodness bank?

The social studies teacher was right. I didn't think my ideas through. I had great hopes, wild fears, and a miser-able brain that never caught up.

Chapter 58

We had a graduation ceremony, not a real one with diplomas, but a farewell ceremony with parents invited and stout Mr. Grandison present. We were in our best clothes, and some of the girls tottered to their seats in semi-high heels and their older sisters' nylon stockings. You had to hold them up with a garter belt or girdle. I didn't want either, or a brassiere, and planned never to get one. To be strapped up from chest to thighs was an insult to good firm flesh.

I had plenty of opportunity to think about these things, and many other things, because there was never anything important to listen to on important school occasions. Don told me his thoughts also grew interesting on these dull occasions, and once, staring at the back of Miss Moose's head, he had even grasped the meaning of life, but lost it later.

I would miss him, but I wouldn't tell him because he would grab my hand, maybe even try to kiss me. I was Egon's. My hand had already been grabbed too often by Don, I felt the keen newness of hand-holding already used up before I had even twined fingers with Egon; but by God the first keenness of a kiss wasn't going to go down the drain the same way, wasted on that big fool butting in. I would suck my lips between my teeth; I would hit him in the face. But I liked the part of him that was just a friend, and that part I would miss.

I wouldn't be seeing Valerie either this summer. I didn't want to set foot in her parents' house, and I didn't want her coming to mine if her mother had to bring her. I would miss our long hot afternoons of two-handed bridge, her eyebrow slowly going up like that of a great general, pondering in a plumed helmet.

Nor would I be seeing Peggy. The day after the United Nations she had ended our tottering friendship. Cordial and pleasant in passing, she made it clear that that was to be all. And strangely I didn't care very much; I had never gotten back my old fat Peggy, and even old fat Peggy wasn't real anymore, but hazy, far-off, like Ezio and Mario.

It would be a solitary summer but I had things to do. Swimming lessons, poetry to write, trips to Berkeley; I must write Helen Maria right away and ask about coming down. And I must write Egon, even if I still couldn't find the right words . . . and now it must be the end of the ceremony because Mr. Grandison was giving his speech, was in fact ending it, and Mr. Kerr was coming onstage and sitting down at the grand piano; and now Mr. Grandison took his "Mandalay" stance, setting his feet firmly apart, loosening his arms at his sides, a deep breath expanding his chest. This was the part of assemblies I liked best, and now it came—Mr. Kerr's rousing overture that sent his long hair leaping and Mr. Grandison's powerful silver voice bursting over our heads.

I looked around at the teachers I was leaving and felt an unexpected pang. Little Mrs. Miller with her kind, tired wrinkles. Mother Basketball, misguided, but vigorous and happy with her great powdered feet. Mr. Villendo, who had burst with pride on the United Nations balcony. Miss Moose of mathematics, whom I had given the happiest day of her career. Hard Mr. Lewis in his everlasting gray suit. Mrs. Lewis, our Miss Petain, who had put on pounds and never wept into her hankie. And Mr. Kerr, our Liszt, our shining glory, flinging himself up and down the keyboard as Mr. Grandison's arms rose high, his silver head thrown back:

> and the dawn comes up like thunnnnnnnder
> out of China 'cross the bay!

Chapter 59

Dear Egon,

I have been wanting to write to you for a long time, but I haven't known how to say what I would like to say. I think it sounds intrusive, no matter how I say it. I am speaking of what happened in Germany, and maybe to people in your own family. I can only say that I am deeply sorry. It is all I can say. I wanted you to know it.

Sincerely,
Suse

I wrote Helen Maria too, asking her if she was staying on for summer session and if she would like me to come down for a visit. Don I didn't write, though I had his address. If I wrote first, he would misinterpret it. The one thing I had learned from him was that when a person was in love, they blew up out of proportion every ordinary thing the other person did and saw it as a sign of returned passion. There was a name for this kind of love: unrequited. It was the subject of many poems.

Very shortly I received such a poem from Don, along with a letter. The letter told about his train trip and the ranch and was interesting. The poem wasn't.

> With eyes so blue and hair so long
> You really make my heart go bong.
> I know you think that it is wrong,
> You'd rather go and play Ping-Pong
> Than hear my heartbeats like a gong,
> But as you walk among the throng
> At home or in far-off Hong Kong,
> Remember always my bonging song,
> Because my heart's where you belong,
> And if you wonder why this poem I prolong,
> It's because this train trip's so goddamn long.

He would have to tack on that last line, and didn't he know you never tried to rhyme every single line? Look at the result. It was a horrible poem. I wrote and told him that. I told him he should take his bongs to Valerie Stappnagel, who led an uneventful life. Or to Peggy, since she was bonging for him. As for me, he was right, I would rather play Ping-Pong, and my eyes weren't blue, they were gray.

And so we began a summer correspondence.

Helen Maria wrote back that she was staying on in Berkeley for the summer, taking a couple of courses just to keep busy before leaving for England in late August. Why didn't I plan to come down early in July? She had Mondays free. If I took the train, she would meet me at the depot.

I got permission from Mama and wrote back, setting the date for July 2.

JUNE 22: **The Battle for Okinawa Is Over!**
              90,000 Japs Killed in 82 Days!

Again, I was glad it was 90,000 Japs instead of 90,000 Americans, but again it was a number so great that you wished they had left the exuberant exclamation point off; you felt satiation, a vision of the world's crust spongy with blood by now, soaked dark and deep like swampland.

JUNE 27: **U.N. Charter Signed—And Now**
               Says Truman: Avoid Disunity!

Two months ago, when I attended their first session, it had not occurred to me that there could be disunity among them; they had sounded in such powerful accord. But since then I had read of their arguments: who should be allowed in, who kept out, how many votes for this nation, how many for that? It had become clear to me that there was nothing miraculous about these men; they were hardworking, dedicated men, but they were not magically equipped to soar over practical problems, just as they were not magically equipped with golden syringes to draw out goodness from such as the black beetle Kramer. Only one thing I knew for sure, and that was that they would never give a go-ahead signal for the black beetles to come crawling out.

Peggy would have been glad to see how realistic I was becoming; to be realistic was a great virtue, she seemed to think, and she was correct. The proof of a virtue was that it was not enjoyable. And it was not enjoyable to make do with common sense and good intentions. Such as the newspaper article about Congress hearing the report of a committee who had seen the death camps. The report said: "Through the spectacle we have witnessed, we realize that the world must come to a fuller understanding that men of all nations and tongues must resist

322

encroachments of every theory and ideology that debases mankind." It was not a spectacular or miraculous statement; it smacked of good faith, hard work, and nothing more. But it was the spirit behind those things that counted, and that was what we must put our hope in.

As the days went by and I didn't hear from Egon, I felt my new realism taking hold of him too. He was not skiing anywhere. He was not so busy with his work that he couldn't find a minute to write just a line saying he'd received my note and letting me know how he was. He didn't answer because he didn't care.

It was like walking into a meat grinder and walking through it anew each day. The pleasure of the hot summer vacation crumpled; the sun shone, but I didn't feel it. I felt a grieving, as I had felt for Mario, but even worse, like that of a widow, for it was as if Egon and I had had a marriage of some kind, that no one else would have understood, but that we understood. Mama and Dad asked why I was so droopy, but I couldn't tell them. They would probably be sympathetic, but I feared their sympathy would be set inside a realism even greater than my own, and my own was bad enough.

At night, in bed, I would drag the pillow over my head, the way Karla used to when I plagued her with questions. But these questions refused to be blotted out. Why didn't he write? Because I meant nothing to him. Nothing, nothing, and yet I wondered if real widows, grieving because their mate was dead, somehow did not grasp it; kept some small senseless gleam of hope. For in the face of all my realism, down in my ground-up insides, there remained such a tiny, flickering gleam.

The Saturday before my trip to Berkeley a letter came.

My dear Suse,
    I have just read your very kind letter—thank you, Suse, it is something I appreciate very much and will always remember. I was away on the East Coast, and if things work out I shall return there soon, from there to return to Europe. I will drop you a line from there, I'll be in Nürnberg, and you must write back and let me know how everything is with

you. Meanwhile, take very good care of yourself, Suse, and again, thank you for writing as you did.

Egon

The joy of receiving his letter was like a thunderclap, a release of light and life, and yet the contents were confusing—he was going away, when, and why Nuremberg? But of course, it was where they planned to hold a trial for the Nazi bigwigs, Göring, von Ribbentrop, Hess, all those. Was he going there to watch them hang? I understood it, I would like to watch too, but how long would it take before they swung? Weeks? Months? And was he coming back? And when was he leaving, how soon? Maybe already by Monday I would know, because if I saw Ruth, I could tactfully squeeze the information from her.

Chapter 60

The train coach was hot, and crammed with soldiers and sailors and duffel bags, the way it must have been for Aunt Dorothy and Roger on that long terrible trip that was the beginning of the end for them. But this trip was like the beginning of a beginning; it was exciting to travel alone, and I felt pleased to be meeting my best friend at the depot, and outside, as we rattled swiftly along, the sun beat down in a glitter on the green water. Except that the sailor beside me and the two soldiers opposite were all asleep with their mouths open, there was a feeling of hurtling like a rocket to some great and dazzling destination.

I was the only person to get off at the Berkeley station. Helen Maria was standing on the platform, reading. When she saw me, she smiled and stuffed the book back into her shoulder bag. She gave me a hug and stood back, holding my wrists.

"My God, you're right, I wouldn't have known you. *Mais où sont les neiges d'antan?* Come on, we must make a dash for it."

324

I ran after her to a bus around the corner of the depot, just starting up. We flung ourselves aboard, and it rumbled off, a hot breeze flowing through the open windows.

There was no trace of Helen Maria's past sorrow on her face. She looked happy and excited and very fit in a pale green dress that set off a nice sunburn.

"Have you been swimming? You're really sunburned."

"No. I'm taking a botany class, don't ask me why. We march about campus staring at trees. Not that I need the credits, but I need to keep busy. Whenever my mind's unoccupied, I start worrying that the British Isles will be snatched from under my nose."

"They won't be. That's unrealistic."

"I realize that."

I wondered if the real problem was that she remembered Egon when she wasn't busy. I hoped it wasn't true; I hoped she had a new boyfriend.

We were rumbling up a long street at the end of which I could see the green campus. How long ago it seemed that the three of us had strolled across those lawns, I in my tight plaid dress and T square hair, a Dutch boy midget smoldering with neglect. Now it was the other way around; it was Helen Maria who was on the outside.

"You *are* happy, aren't you?" I asked.

"Of course I am. Very."

"And you're having a social life too?"

"Well, I'm hardly the Miss Campus Queen type."

"But you go out, I mean with fellows?"

She was silent for a moment. "You probably want to know about Egon, don't you?"

"Egon?" With a heart thud I glanced away, but only momentarily, my long years of pretended calm standing me in good stead. "I've wondered, of course," I said politely.

"Yes, of course. Well, we came to a parting of the ways a few months back—quite a few months back, actually. It bothered me very much at first, but I'm over it now. I've begun seeing someone else."

"Oh I'm glad. Do you like him a lot?"

"He's quite decent. He's not Egon, of course."

"But you're over Egon, you said."

"Yes, yes, I'm over Egon," she muttered, pulling the cord for our stop and looking at nothing for a moment.

"I think it was Pascal who said, 'The cause of love is *Je ne sais quoi,* and the effects are dreadful.' " She threw me a smile as we got up. "See what you've got to look forward to."

"Me?" I asked, following her to the door.

"Yes," she said as we got off. "You'll fall hard when you fall. Well, be forewarned, but don't be turned aside. One must take life by the horns. Now, shall we just potter about campus, or is there something special you want to do?"

"No, nothing special, but what if you run into Egon?"

She gave a shrug and slouched off across the lawn. "So what? Anyway, Ruth says he's quit school."

"I know. He has."

She looked over at me surprised. "How do you know?"

"Remember I wrote to ask him about some books? Well, he wrote back, and I wrote him back, about poetry and the UN and different things, so we started corresponding."

"How utterly charming. How utterly like Egon."

"How do you mean?"

"Oh I don't know. I suppose I'm trying to be sarcastic. However," she sighed, "Egon really *is* charming. Most men I know wouldn't take the time to write some schoolgirl acquaintance, but he would. I can't fault him on consideration."

"I saw him in San Francisco," I said, stung. "We had a long talk."

"Did you? In San Francisco? What were you doing there?"

"It was when I went to the United Nations. He was there too."

"Oh, I see," she said, walking toward a bench in the shade of a tree. "Rather ironic, if you think of it. Here I am totally out of touch, and here you are corresponding with him, running into him—"

"But you don't mind, do you?" I asked as we sat down, looking carefully at her face as she answered.

"Of course I don't mind. I think it's very nice. But you should watch out a little, he tends to see life in rather dark shades. You don't need more of that."

"But he's not like that at all. He has an inspiring view of life."

"So I thought too, but he doesn't. It comes through.

Not that one wants a hebephrenic." She took her cigarettes from her shoulder bag and lit one.

"May I bum one?"

"Oh, sorry. Here." She passed me the pack.

I lit up and leaned back, drawing on the cigarette. I still didn't do it right; but I was improving, and as I puffed, I watched the sprinklers on the lawn swinging around and around. The cool greenness was pretty, but it seemed somehow like a stage set, unconnected with real life; you would never smell the baking marsh here or see swarms of droning gnats or Shell workers tramping home from work, sweat-stained and grimy. . . .

"I only mean," said Helen Maria, exhaling deeply, "that one doesn't relish being looked upon as insubstantial simply because one happens to lack the qualities of Hamlet. Or what it boils down to, I suppose, as if you were some kind of poor joke because you were eighteen."

"I don't think age has anything to do with anything."

"Exactly, but try getting that through his head!" She gave a sigh, then shook her head. "But I'm being unfair, I make it sound as if we did nothing but argue and insult each other. We never did. It was just something I felt more and more, and then one day he said it wasn't working out. He was very nice about it—concerned, you know, and unhappy, I could tell. Because we had been very close. I mean really close . . . like man and wife. . . ."

She lowered her eyes as she said this, maybe sensing that I would be shocked, which I was. Helen Maria was not a virgin. She had done it. She had done it with Egon.

I had never imagined them that way together. I would not dwell on it now; it was done with. She had had a sex experience, which was only natural and good; she herself had said you must grab life by the horns. And he had probably had many sex experiences, and this was just another one. His great experience was still in the future.

"Well, it's done with now," I said. "I hope you're not brooding."

"Do you see me brooding? I'm just telling you because you must have wondered why I never mentioned him in my letters. Did he ever mention me, by the way?"

"No."

"No, I suppose not. Well. Enjoy your correspondence."

"I'm glad you don't mind."

"Why should I mind? You don't have a lot of people in that godforsaken town to communicate with. Except what's-his-name . . . Donald? Tell me about Donald who reads Thomas Wolfe."

"Oh, he's nothing. We talk, but he's not on any very high level."

"And Peggy. So she didn't go to the United Nations."

I shook my head. "*Parti avec le vent.* And she dropped me like a hot potato the next day. Didn't want any more nagging, even if I wasn't nagging, but she knew I was inside. I don't think she'll ever change now."

"No, I don't think so either."

"It was as if she closed a door."

"There's a good deal of door closing in life. It's something that dawns on you." She blew out smoke, her green eyes reflective.

"I know," I said.

"Fortunately, there are also doors opening."

"Like going to England?"

"Yes, like going to England."

We had lunch at the same terrace café we had eaten at last time. There was no alien language grating on my ears, no anxiety and anger; there were no long blue shadows growing. We talked about Oxford, and the United Nations, and French grammar. We had cigarettes with our coffee, and I leaned lazily back in the sun.

"*C'est plaisant ici,*" I said, exhaling. "*Et Rosa Luxury, comment vat-elle?*"

"Rosa Luxury?"

"You know, Ruth."

"Oh, fine. You'll see her later, she's coming to dinner with us."

"I thought she didn't like me."

"Don't worry, she doesn't even remember you."

I took a short puff of my cigarette. It was irritating to inquire after someone who didn't even remember that you had met.

"Of course I don't bracket her with Luxemburg anymore; that was sloppy thinking. She has none of Luxemburg's power and brilliance."

"I'm sure I fail to understand how you can judge anything about Ruth, since you scarcely know her. I also fail to understand why you keep associating her with Rosa

Luxemburg. Ruth is a perfectly ordinary, garden variety socialist who will never accomplish anything spectacular, but she's a very good person."

"She's got a bad memory, though."

"Be glad. Incidentally, please don't bring up the concentration camps."

"What sort of idiot do you think I am?" I asked, flushing.

"I don't think you're an idiot at all. I think you've evolved remarkably. But it's a subject everyone's talking about, and it would be natural enough to—"

"Well, I wouldn't. I would assume she might have had family over there."

"Yes, she and Egon both. What's become of them they don't know yet. But one can surmise."

"There's going to be a war crimes trial. In Nuremberg. I suppose you know Egon's going?"

"Yes, I know."

"I wonder if he'll come back afterwards."

"I have no interest in where Egon will spend the rest of his days—Berkeley, Germany, or Inner Mongolia. I shall be in England. And just because I brought his name up doesn't mean I wish to discuss him."

"Well," I said, "let's discuss poetry then."

We spent the rest of the afternoon strolling around the shady parts of campus and browsing along Telegraph Avenue, talking mostly of poetry—Homer (Helen Maria's favorite), Keats, Gerard Manley Hopkins, and a name I'd never heard of, T. S. Eliot, whom I didn't like when she quoted him:

> I grow old . . . I grow old . . .
> I shall wear the bottoms of my trousers rolled.

Who cared how he wore his trousers? It was carrying the small ordinary things of life too far; next thing, poets would be writing about brushing their teeth or going to the toilet. I told this to Helen Maria, not without a blush for my coarseness.

"You have a point," she said, shading her face as we walked along the white, glaring street. "I prefer the grand image myself. But you must read Eliot in context. His rolled trousers are a lament for greatness ungrasped."

"But you don't like laments, do you?"

"There you go generalizing. I don't like lament as a *way* of life, but it's a part of life. You can't get around it." And she said it again, slowly, as if to herself, "You can't get around it. . . ."

We had to eat early because I was taking the six-forty-five train back. The street still blazed with light but inside the restaurant it was dim. It was a French restaurant, shabby and scuffed-looking, but picturesque, like the cafés of Paris. There was sawdust on the floor, and French travel posters were tacked on the walls, and on red-checked tablecloths stood candles stuck in bottles rough with wax that had run down. There weren't many people there yet, just a few students; it seemed to be a student hangout. Helen Maria knew them and smiled and said hello as we passed; how different, I thought, from the days in Mendoza when she didn't know anyone and strode swiftly along with her head in the air.

Ruth was already there, sitting at a table with a glass of wine, smoking. She had on the same black turtleneck sweater she had worn before, despite the heat. She looked different, though, because her hair was down, frizzy and loose, and it gave her a younger appearance. But her crushing grip was the same.

"So we have met before," she said. "I have not such a recollection, or perhaps vague. If you had the hair of a Dutch doll, it crosses my mind. It crosses my mind you asked numerous questions."

"Suse doesn't ask so many questions," Helen Maria said as we sat down. "She has evolved greatly."

"I am happy to hear it."

We were only there a few minutes when the waiter came over. "Look at your menu," said Helen Maria. "You must speak French with him."

I was able to say, "*Qu'est-ce que cela?*" as I pointed to this item and that, and then, "*Merci, monsieur,*" when he translated.

"Very good," said Helen Maria, when he had gone off with our orders.

"I may become a translator," I announced pointedly, for Ruth's sake, to stir her thoughts around Egon.

But she only said, "You will have some way to go."

"Of course, you have to have a knack for translation," I went on, "I know certain people have a knack for it."

330

"Was ist ein knack?" Ruth asked Helen Maria, and they slipped into German, like the first time. But I didn't mind because I had pleasant thoughts to absorb myself in: what a nice day it had been, and how well Helen Maria had taken my involvement with Egon; and now, obligingly, she got up and said she would be back in a moment, going over to the students she had said hello to.

"I hear Egon's going to Nuremberg," I said at once, to make the most of her absence.

Ruth nodded. "Yes. Or at least he hopes to. They must inform him if he has been accepted."

"Just to watch them hang? You have to be accepted?"

The brown eyes took on a slightly narrowed, criticizing look, as if I had spoken frivolously.

"I don't mean to sound frivolous," I said quickly. "I'm not belittling it. It would be great to watch, I'd like to watch myself. I'd like to see them starved and tortured first. They should be beaten with rubber hoses."

She looked at me for a silent moment. Then she said, "You have an ugly way of speaking."

My face reddened, as if she had slapped it. "Well," I ventured in defense, "war is ugly. . . ."

"Yes, and you would do well not to babble about it."

I, a babbler? I who had existed with war night and day for years, who had felt every minute of its terrors and sufferings and lived only for the moment when it would be over? I was no babbler; only to this woman who was always so strange and unpleasant, who must have a demented streak. There was no way of holding a conversation, I realized that; I could only hope to calm the atmosphere before Helen Maria returned.

I had lowered my eyes to the checked tablecloth; I raised them now, to the unpleasant face. "I don't know what I said wrong, Ruth. But I didn't mean to offend you. I apologize."

She took a sip of her wine, slowly, still looking at me. Then she gave a nod. "It is not necessary. It is perhaps I who am not used to the way Americans speak. We will talk of something else." And she set her glass down and tried to think of something else to talk about. "So you will become a translator, like Egon?"

"Yes," I nodded. "I think I should talk to him about it. Do you know when he's leaving?"

"Perhaps now, perhaps later. It is uncertain. He must be accepted. He has applied as interpreter."

"Oh," I said. "And I suppose he's coming back?"

"I would think so. He would not want to stay there."

"Do you think it will be a long trial?" I asked.

"Yes," she said. "I think it will be long."

"I hope the food comes soon." Helen Maria was pulling her chair out. "I'm starved from all that walking."

"Eat well now," said Ruth. "In England they serve *Dreck.*"

They both saw me off at the station. I gave Helen Maria a hug and held out my hand to Ruth, who crushed it in her stern grip. But she smiled. *"Au revoir,"* she said, *"reviens à la maison sain et sauf."*

And Helen Maria said, "Come down again. On a Saturday, and stay over."

I seemed to have passed a test; I had been invited back. "I will!" I said as I climbed aboard. "It was a wonderful day, thanks a million!"

Chapter 61

Dear Egon,

I was in Berkeley yesterday, and I saw your cousin Ruth, who said you weren't sure when you were leaving. If you should be leaving any minute, I could come down right away and wish you bon voyage. It's an easy trip by train. I know you're busy getting ready and I wouldn't want to interfere, so I could meet you on a street corner and say bon voyage, if you were going on an errand anyway, so that I wouldn't take time from your preparations. It's just a thought. Ruth says she thinks it will be a long trial.

Votre bonne camarade,
Suse

When the swimming program started, I did something I thought I would never do: I wore a bathing cap. My

332

skull felt tight and deafened, and I looked like a pinhead; but I didn't want to say good-bye to Egon with green hair.

I was in lifesaving class this year and was special aide to Peggy's bête noire with her clenched teeth and blasting whistle. An instructor in my own right, I enjoyed my position of greatness, yet I missed my old freedom when I was unimportant and could slip away unnoticed for long underwater voyages. With power came clamps; it was the opposite of what you would have expected.

But when everyone else had climbed out and was heading for the dressing rooms, I stayed behind, pulled off my cap for just one plunge, and soared, unimportant and irresponsible, over the side, feeling the great green whoosh in my ears, the green rush slitting my eyes, the depth and perfect silence of this perfect world whose sunlight, dappling down in pale turning coins, I slid through like a fish.

JULY 14:   **1,000 Yank Carrier Planes
                Hit North Japan Targets!**

JULY 18:   **Mighty Allied Fleet
                Fires War Factories!**

JULY 19:   **Carrier Planes Blast
                Remains of Jap Navy!**

It had been hard to wait for victory while Germany crumbled, but not as hard as it was now, waiting the second time around. Sometimes, for no particular reason, you felt you could smell the last day of battle in the summer air, and your heart jolted with realization of the whole thing over; then you sank back waiting again, maybe for years, and the contrast was too much. You grew weary of the black headlines, the big numbers, the exclamation points. When you heard about signs going up in the valley, "Japs, go back where you came from!" or read about a Jap couple returning to Los Angeles, escorted from the train by armed guards for their own safety, you almost wanted to say, for God's sake, leave them alone, enough.

Well, it's way past your six weeks' victory date [I wrote Don], so you won't collect your dime. I don't want to bet again, I'm sick of war. I always have been, but now I've begun to imagine the crust of the earth soaked through with blood like wet sand. I suppose that's morbid, so I'll refrain from saying more and ruining your carefree life up there galloping on the range.

I told you about my trip to Berkeley, well, I'm going back in early August for another visit. My girlfriend's boardinghouse is giving her a going-away barbecue party, and she's invited me. I'll miss a day of swimming because I'm going on a Sunday and staying through Monday, but it will be worth it. I'll write you about it. Thank you for your last letter. I'm glad you're not sending any more poems, they're really painful.

Suse

He would answer by return mail, but it wasn't a letter from Don I wanted.

In the late afternoon, when the shade of the house crept over the old card table in the backyard, Mama and I would bring out our pitcher of lemonade and sit down. We talked about its being a year since the Port Chicago explosion. The crickets chirped in the cooling dry grass, and I thought of how they had fallen silent on my walk back, and how beautiful the deep blue night sky had been, and how I was going to be happy forever. I was less of a fool now. Like someone on a wild airplane flight, I had dropped from height to height until I now saw everything clear, steady, unvarnished. No one was happy forever. That was in the realm of magic, the same realm as world peace unfolding without effort. What you had to have faith in was what they had said at the UN: constructive thought, creativeness, and cooperation, and that was what I saw, flying low, steady and clear-eyed.

But the war had to end first. Nothing could begin until the war ended. Until then I would still lie in bed at night with my ears half listening for the air raid siren. Until then the Polish family would be lying out in the open. Because when I spread my hand on the warm tabletop, I still saw them that way. I had somehow thought that when the war in Europe was over, I would see them at peace under a headstone, with grass and flowers growing over them; but that hadn't happened, and I knew they wouldn't be laid to rest until the end.

JULY 24:   **1,000 Carrier Planes Hit**
                  Largest Jap Naval Base!!

Two exclamation points. Someday the whole headline would be nothing but exclamation points. No words, no sense, just exclamation points going on forever.

There had been a letter from Don, but no letter from Egon. I was waiting for one, and I kept waiting for one; but now a change of direction slowly took place in this waiting. I was no longer waiting for a letter from Berkeley because it was a fact I must face with my new realism: he was no longer there. He had received word, packed, and gone before my note ever reached him. What I waited for now, bitterly disappointed, but patient, because there was no other course to take, was a letter from Nuremberg.

Downtown a strange sight met my eyes. The side of Sheriff O'Toole's office was bare in the pounding heat. The stucco was discolored, the exposed ground damp and dark. I stood there for a long time, staring, then walked on. At the corner I whirled around and looked back. The broad, bare, discolored wall, with the sun pounding against it.

Sheriff O'Toole would never have taken down his sandbags unless the end were in sight. And these old posters along the street, still hanging from storefronts and fences, faded almost white. "Deliver Us from Evil," "Back the Attack!", "The Walls Have Ears." So old, so unbelievably old, and now they would be taken down, too.

JULY 27:   **U.S., Britain, China Give**
                 Japan Surrender Ultimatum!
                    Quit or Be Destroyed!

Prompt and utter destruction, said President Truman, was the alternative to unconditional surrender.

"What do you think he means?" I said at the dinner table. "Prompt and utter destruction—how can we all of a sudden promptly and utterly destroy them?"

335

"You've got me, Suse," Dad said. "Maybe it's a bluff."

It must be. Yet the sandbags were down, I smelled ceasefire in the air, I felt it in my blood. The Japs were going to surrender because they didn't know if the bluff was real or not and they didn't dare take a chance. It was a great bluff, and it was going to work. It was a stroke of genius.

JULY 28:   Carrier Toll for Week—
               752 Jap Ships, 928 Planes!

Why didn't they surrender? Were they going to call our bluff?

AUG. 2:   Mightiest B-29 Fleet Strikes—
               800 Fire Four Honshu Cities!

They weren't going to surrender. They had called our bluff, and the war was going to go on forever.

AUG. 4:   Streetcar Strike Dispute
               To Go Before Grand Jury

I lowered the newspaper with the same feeling I had had when I saw Sheriff O'Toole's blank wall. A headline that was not a war headline? Since Pearl Harbor there had never once been such a thing. A streetcar dispute ... how beautiful it looked, like a poem.

And so it was true, what I had smelled in the air was real; it was surrender coming, it was peace.

Chapter 62

I wore my Sunday dress, newly washed and starched. My hair, unchlorinated, was also washed, and my shoulder bag was polished to a deep gleam with Johnson's wax. In it, lying near but not cramping Egon's letters, were my toothbrush, a tin container of Ipana tooth powder, and a clean washcloth, wrapped in wax paper. Helen
336

Maria would supply pajamas. She said to bring, primarily, a good appetite.

The big dark-shingled house was up and busy. The door swung open at my first knock, and a girl in a bathrobe, holding a carpet sweeper, said come in and proceeded to attack the hall runner. In the living room to my right there was a flurry of activity, people busily dusting and tidying up. Helen Maria, in her old sea-green robe, which was rather soiled and had a cigarette burn on front, came over waving a dustrag.

"It's our housemother. She goes insane over the mess at the most inconvenient times. Go to the kitchen and have a cup of coffee. I'll be along."

In the kitchen a radio was playing loud Benny Goodman music, and half a dozen girls, or women, I wasn't sure which, were doing dishes and carrying garbage out and bumping into each other. The one who was directing must be the housemother; she was old and wore a lot of makeup like Mrs. Kerr, but had a long braid down her back like a schoolgirl and wore some kind of peasant outfit. She boomed at me in the door. "You must be Hatton's friend, don't mind us, we're all at sixes and sevens! Come in, have some coffee! If there's a clean cup—"

She took me over to the table, a clean cup was supplied, and she poured my coffee, something the way Eudene poured coffee. "I'm Pendleton," she introduced herself, setting the pot down.

"I'm—Hansen."

"Have you ever seen such a mess? And they want to have a party? You'd think they were a bunch of freshmen!"

But she looked good-natured as she said this, and the girls didn't seem cowed. One threw a wilted lettuce leaf in her direction. They seemed an easygoing lot, and I began to feel at ease; then Ruth came in from the back porch with a bucket of water and a mop, and I felt completely at home, waving hello to someone I knew.

"*Comment allez-vous?*" I asked her as she wrung out the mop.

"*Ça va. Ça va.*"

"*Avez-vous* heard from *votre cousin?*"

"*Comment?*"

"Have you had a letter from Egon yet?"

"A letter? Why? He is not gone."

I felt a conflicting rush of emotion—still here, I could still see him! But still here, and never answered my letter.

"I thought he'd gone...."

"In one week he goes. Stand back, I must have room!" And she swung the mop around to make space among the busy feet.

Don had once mailed in a Wheaties box top for a baseball picture, which he had never received. He told me that a long time ago, and I remembered it now. The U.S. mails were not infallible. I knew I wasn't being realistic; but it seemed that I must concentrate on that undelivered baseball picture or else the party would be dust and ashes in my mouth, and it wouldn't be fair to Helen Maria if I brooded through her special day. Nor was it a wild fantasy I was grabbing at: it was a solid fact that that baseball picture had not been delivered, and the more I dwelled on this fact, the better I felt. By the time the house was back in order so was I. Helen Maria and I went up to her garret.

Her grandmother's big black trunk, with all its foreign stickers, stood open and partly filled in the middle of the room. There were suitcases on the bed, clothes draped over chairs, book-filled boxes on the floor. The walls were stripped bare; the closet stood open and half empty.

"I suppose I'm a bit early in packing," said Helen Maria, lifting up some dresses, looking for something. "But I can't seem to keep from it."

I was reminded of when she had packed to move down here, restless and eager to leave, walking around, unable to find anything. "Actually," she said, rummaging through a suitcase, "you'll find this less a barbecue party than a potato salad party. We have invested in three tons of potatoes and only half an ounce of steak, rationing being what it is. But I think it'll be fun. Ah, here," she murmured, pulling out a slip and a pair of stockings. "Well, you're looking very sprightly. Did you get some coffee? You met Pendleton?"

"Yes. She's nice. She looks like a bohemian."

"Oh, Pendleton is that. She studied art on the Left Bank years ago and never recovered. Where are my shoes? She's not bad in a quasi-Braque sort of way, but the representational's beyond her. Sit down, you'll have to clear off a chair. She has a Christ on the cross who looks like an arthritic banana. Where are my—ah, there! Read something if you like. Then we'll set up your cot. I'm off to take my shower."

The party was held on the lawn of the backyard, and the food was mostly potato salad, as Helen Maria had said, with only the smallest bit of steak for each; but it didn't matter since there were also two chocolate cakes which Ruth had baked, and an endless supply of Pepsi-Cola and orange soda, and wine if you cared for that sort of thing.

People strolled around with glasses in their hands or sat in little groups on the grass with plates in their laps, a cosmopolitan lot: refugee types, and women in Indian saris and men with black beards and turbans, and a Scotsman who could have passed for an Englishman in his dark blue blazer like Roger's, and two Chinese girls in long slitted dresses. Helen Maria looked beautiful in a simple white dress with a gardenia behind her ear, and she was very happy, sipping wine and talking with everyone and laughing. She introduced me all around, and everyone was very pleasant, and Ruth was very pleasant too, cutting me a large wedge of chocolate cake, and even a second large wedge, her hair worn loose and free, her stout form outfitted in a big polka dot dress with strings of pearls. She drank a good deal of wine and grew red-faced and mellow and eventually sank down in the arms of a bespectacled refugee type, who it later turned out was her intended.

Helen Maria's boyfriend was there too, the new one. At first glance he looked heart-wrenchingly like Egon; but on second glance his dark hair was not so dark, and his blue eyes were not so light, and he was taller, thinner, and he had no accent, being from Los Angeles, and no lines around his mouth. He was like a poor twin, but decent enough. He was very fond of Helen Maria, I could tell; she seemed to like him too, but not in a special way. She would find someone really good at Oxford.

The sun blazed down, sparkling in the tall evergreens, whose cool dark blue shade moved slowly across the lawn as the day lengthened. Glasses and bottles clinked, voices were lifted, I could hear Pendleton booming with laughter. The orange soda glittered in my glass as I drank from it, the sky soaring blue and boundless above the trees, and then suddenly everyone began to sing.

> For she's a jolly good fellow,
> For she's a jolly good fellow,
> For she's a jolly good fel-low. . . .
> Which nobody can deny!
> Which nobody can deny. . . .

And Helen Maria, pleased and smiling and embarrassed, looked around at all the faces, and at the ground, listening as we sang on to the last rousing line. Then she cried. I had never seen her cry. It was very swift. A couple of hard blinks, a swipe of the hand across the eyes, and then she was thanking us all, smiling and shaking hands with everyone who crowded up to wish her a happy voyage.

Though most of the guests left early in the evening, some stayed on, and the party moved inside with more potato salad, more wine, and dancing. I was thankful they didn't jitterbug, but of course they were too cosmopolitan for that. They did the fox-trot mostly, and I could manage that once I had some wine and got my courage up. At first no one asked me, seeming to think I preferred to sit there with the potato salad and remaining cake; but Helen Maria brought the boyfriend over, and there I was, doing the fox-trot to "Is You Is or Is You Ain't My Baby?" with his arms around me, and they were Egon's arms if I narrowed my eyes slightly so that his face was blurred; I crunched his toes a few times but he didn't mind, he was very decent, and it was an exciting dance, after which I danced with one of the turbans, who had fierce dark eyes and smiled flashingly through his black beard, and that was exciting too. After that I danced with Ruth's intended, and then I danced with everyone.

It was a party that didn't want to end, nor did I want it to. Sometimes it almost died out, with everyone collapsing on sofas or the floor, smoking and drinking wine, and guests yawning and departing; but new ones would come through the front door, and a new record was put on, and everything started up again fresh and lively. I kept awake by going down the hall to the bathroom and splashing my face with cold water, which left me ready for anything. But by four o'clock even that didn't work, and it was a joy to see the party breaking up, though it had been a joy of a party.

I staggered up the stairs behind Helen Maria to the garret, where I pulled off my dress and fell to the cot in my slip. But I couldn't seem to fall asleep. I lay looking at the window, at the dark sky thick with stars, reliving the party until the stars had gone and it was almost daylight.

Chapter 63

Sunlight lay hot on my face. I opened my eyes, stretched powerfully, yawned, groaned, and flung my arms down. Helen Maria's bed was empty; the garret was silent, heavy and still with heat.

"Good morning!" Helen Maria called from the door, kicking it shut behind her. She came over in a pair of shorts and an old shirt, carrying two mugs of steaming coffee.

"Is it morning?"

"No, actually. Going on three. Here, this will wake you up."

It was black and bitter, not to my taste, but it seemed a perfect thing to be lying in bed in your slip drinking black coffee after a wild night of partying.

"I only just got up myself." She yawned, sitting down on her unmade bed with her mug. "I'm totally fagged. What do you say we just potter about today?"

"That's fine with me. I had enough excitement yesterday."

"Good. Maybe we'll take a walk or something. And you can have dinner here before you take the six-forty-five."

Then we began talking about the party. I learned many interesting things, such as that Pendleton was carrying on with the Scotsman though he was donkey's years

341

younger, and that Ruth and her intended were moving to Palestine, and that the turban I danced with was sick—

"With what?"

"A Sikh. It's a religion; they're not allowed to cut their hair."

Under the turban his hair was all wound up, yards long, fascinating; and even the boyfriend was fascinating, an author, for he had written a novel that was going to be published, about growing up in Pasadena.

But Helen Maria hadn't read it.

"I would rather, as Alexander Woollcott once said, fall facedown in a pile of Italian garbage."

"Why? Why Italian?"

"I have no idea, rancid olive oil perhaps. Preferable, in any case, to reading about Pasadena—come in," she called at a knock on the door.

A girl poked her head through. "Did you have your radio on? I just caught the tail end of a broadcast, something about a bomb they dropped on Japan."

"A bomb? Aren't they always dropping bombs?"

"I don't know," she said, withdrawing her head, "it sounded different," and she closed the door behind her.

Helen Maria took her mug over to the radio and turned it on, but there was no news. "Well," she said, finishing her coffee, "I guess we'd better have something to eat. Here, I'll give you some shorts and a blouse. Have a shower if you want. I'll be down in the kitchen."

Under the shower I contemplated this bomb the girl in the door had spoken of. It sounded as if it were a special one. Which meant that we hadn't been bluffing after all. Which meant that the surrender would take place quickly now and that this bomb would be the last, the final bomb of the war to drop.

Awake, refreshed, I hurried back to the garret and dressed, looking out the window at the motionless evergreens, not a breeze in the heavy, glaring air. A broiling day, but I felt light and cool thumping down the stairs barefoot, my hair damp and slicked back. While we had eggs and toast, Helen Maria tried to get a news station, twisting the dial around. She left it on, at a music station, in case there was a bulletin.

"I have a feeling this means the war's finished," I told her. "They'll give up."

"It could be," she said. "Let's hope so."

"Do you think people would dance in the streets?"

"In this heat? Only mad dogs and Englishmen."

"I will. I'll dance with a mad dog."

"Such oomph. I'll watch from the shade."

I looked around the empty kitchen. It would be nice to have people here for the excitement of the surrender broadcast. "Where's everybody gone?"

"To class, mostly. It's Monday."

"You'd never know by you!" Pendleton boomed, coming through the door. "Sleeping half the day away! What degenerates!"

Helen Maria laughed and poured her some coffee as she sat down with us. She looked rather bleary-eyed, though she hadn't been present at the late party, and I wondered if she had come from a long night of passion with the Scotsman in his blue blazer. I sat thinking about this and also keeping track of the radio music with one ear, while with the other ear I took in their party gossip. Then I heard the music end and a news broadcast come over the air. I didn't like to interrupt them as they rattled on, but at last I couldn't restrain myself. "I think they're talking," I said, pointing at the radio.

". . . that the hour of final victory seems near in history's most horrible war. The United States has unleashed against Japan the terror of an atomic bomb more than two thousand times more powerful than the biggest blockbuster ever used in warfare, ushering a new epoch in science and war, the age of push-button warfare. The atomic weapon, harnessing the basic power of the universe, struck squarely in the center of the industrial city of Hiroshima with a flash and concussion that brought an exclamation of 'Oh my God' from a battle-hardened Superfortress crew ten miles away. The returning fliers' report gave reason to believe that the Jap city has ceased to exist. . . ."

Helen Maria and Pendleton sat staring at each other as they listened, but I couldn't hear more for the rush of blood in my ears. Suddenly standing up, I murmured, "I think I'll go outside."

In the backyard I sat down on the lawn and began picking blades of grass, kneading and shredding them. What did it mean, a city that had ceased to exist? The basic power of the universe? A new epoch of push-button warfare? Dropping the grass, I clasped my arms around my knees and sat rocking to and fro, trying not to hear the radio voice, a faint buzz from the kitchen. After a while the music came back on.

"I thought you wanted to hear it," said Helen Maria, coming down the back stairs.

"Not really." I unclasped my shaky knees and lay back on the grass, my arms behind my head. "I want to get some sun."

"Not exactly what I had in mind, splitting the atom," she said, sitting down beside me and shading her eyes with her hand. "But I guess we shouldn't be so surprised; they've been talking about it for decades."

"Splitting the atom . . . what does it mean?"

"Don't ask me, I have no grasp of atomic physics. But basically I suppose it's breaking the smallest unit of an element, which somehow releases a huge natural force. Want a cigarette?"

I shook my head.

"Gives you the shudders, actually," she said, taking her cigarettes from her shorts pocket and lighting one. "Still, it's just as well we had it, rather than the Axis." She blew the match out. "Curious, though . . . we should be the ones to use it."

"Curious. You could say that."

"Horrible."

I lay looking at the sky.

"I must say you're taking it well," she said. "It's rather a nasty windup."

I shrugged, not wanting her to know how I felt, tightened up and sick inside, with a light, airy, trembling feeling in my arms and legs. I wondered how she could smoke, how she could keep her hand from shaking.

"Anyway," she said, "I guess that's it. The end of the war."

The end of the war. All these years I had waited, and now it had come, like this, with the power of the universe unleashed.

"Maybe the end of everything," I said. "What if the world blows up?"

"I don't know, I doubt it will."

"The power of the universe—why didn't they leave it alone?"

"I don't know. But maybe we should think what the

alternative might have been. Probably a long invasion, thousands of lives—"

"What about the people in that city? A whole city!"

Helen Maria shook her head.

A whole city of people, ceasing to exist. And who had done it? Not the Nazis or the Japs themselves, but us, the good ones, the ones we were supposed to have faith in, who talked of constructive thought, creativeness, co-operation, drawing the good out of people. They themselves were the black beetles. I felt my throat ache; the sky blurred and sparkled. I closed my eyes so Helen Maria couldn't see them.

"I don't know how you can take this heat. It's too much."

"I like it," I managed to say.

"Well, I'm going in."

I followed her a few minutes later. It had been such a wonderful party, and it was still her day; I didn't want to ruin it lying bitter and solitary in the backyard.

I passed through the kitchen, where some of the girls had returned from class and were sitting around the table with Pendleton, listening to another broadcast. The words followed me as I went out the door.

". . . If the European war had gone on another six months, it is quite possible that this planet would have ceased to exist, because it is quite possible that someone would have learned to break the atom without controlling it. . . ."

I had to stop for a moment and lean against the banister.

In the garret, Helen Maria was lying on her unmade bed with a book. She looked sleepy.

"I think I'll have that cigarette now," I said, trying for a normal tone.

She gave me one and took one herself. I lit my own, turning away, because my fingers were trembling, and sat down on the cot, stretching and rubbing my face. "That was the best party I've ever been to."

"It was smashing, wasn't it? I'll miss them; they're a wonderful crowd."

"But think of the wonderful crowd at Oxford. And those cool mists."

She nodded, looking at me through her cigarette

345

smoke. "I'm glad you're not too upset. It *is* upsetting, it's terribly upsetting, and I know how you are about these things."

"Things military?" I said, managing a half smile. "No, I've evolved past that."

"So you seem to have. I must admit."

"Parti avec le vent." I yawned, setting my cigarette in the ashtray, because it was making me nauseated.

Helen Maria yawned too, putting her book aside. "If you're as fagged out as I am, what do you say we have a nap?"

"Sure," I said. But I couldn't bear the thought of lying still with my tight, sick feeling, just lying and thinking. "Or maybe I'll take the five o'clock train back. I'm so fagged out, I think I'll just go home and go to bed early."

"It's a shame I wore you out."

"It's no shame," I said, reaching down for my dress, which lay crumpled on the floor. "It was the best party I ever went to."

When I had dressed and combed my hair and gotten my overnight things together in my bag, Helen Maria said she would come with me to the depot and got up from bed. But there was no need; she might as well have her nap. She walked me to her door, where we said good-bye; not the ultimate good-bye, though, because she was coming home before leaving.

"Get a good rest," she called as I started down the stairs.

"You too! Thanks again for the wonderful time!"

Then I was alone with the tight, sick feeling, going down all the sunny stairs.

Chapter 64

After a block or two of walking I stopped and snapped open my shoulder bag. It was done suddenly, as if out of the blue, yet maybe it had been there in my mind all along. Pulling out one of the letters, I looked at the address on the corner of the envelope.

I asked directions of someone walking along and was told the street was on the other side of campus. It took endless time to find; first, I lost my way on campus and couldn't discover where it came out the other side and had to ask more directions; then, when I finally came out the other side, the streets there were winding and confusing, and when I asked more directions, they took me in circles, until my despair of ever finding him grew as great as my other despair.

I knew by the length of its shadow how late it was when I found his house. It was a tall white stucco building, a little run-down, and not a boardinghouse like Helen Maria's but more like an apartment house, with mailboxes by the front door and names and room numbers on them. The door was unlocked. I went inside, and on the third floor I found number nine.

He was typing. I knocked, and the clacking stopped. I could hear his chair scraping back, his footsteps crossing the room. Then the door opened, and I was looking into his blue eyes.

"Suse," he said, and the eyes were not lit up, but quizzical. "What are you doing here?"

I hesitated, not having expected questions, expecting only that he would see the need on my face at once and take me inside.

"I just . . . wanted to talk."

"But you have not come all the way from Mendoza? Alone?"

I nodded, then shook my head, unable to concentrate, wanting only to be inside with him.

"Yes? No? What do you mean?"

". . . I was at Helen Maria's," I managed to say, looking at the not unkind but not welcoming face.

"I see," he nodded. "So you are staying over there?"

Again I shook my head, and suddenly the undelivered baseball picture swirled down and took its place with the skiing trip and all the other lies I had served up to myself. And with my eyes going to the floor, I saw, as if it were an old fact I had always known, that he had not written because he didn't wish to encourage me. It was as simple as that. And strangely, it was of no importance now. I wanted to tell him that. He needn't fear being arrested; I wouldn't expect him to hug and kiss me; he didn't have to do anything at all, if only he would let me come inside and be near him for a while.

"What is it?" I heard him ask at last. "What's wrong, Suse?"

"The atomic bomb," I said, my eyes still on the floor.

"So." I could hear a small sigh through his nostrils. He opened the door for me, and I stepped into the room, a warmth of relief and comfort unloosening the tight, sick feeling. It was a small room, but that was as much as I noticed, all my awareness taken up by his presence, the touch of his hand on my elbow as he offered me a chair.

"Now, let me understand. You are visiting down here?"

"No, I was," I said, sitting down, "But I left to go to the depot . . . only I came here instead."

"But aren't your parents expecting you? They will be worried."

"No, I was taking an early train, because I was upset . . . about the bomb . . . but I'm supposed to be on the six-forty-five."

"I see. Then I shall take you at that time to the depot."

"You don't have to."

"Yes, of course I will," he said, sitting down in the chair by his desk. There was a clock ticking on the desk; it was already twenty past five. I would not have much time with him before I had to go back out into the world again. But at least I was here. It was a room drenched with the late-afternoon sun, its two windows open, and the curtains pulled aside, so the light could pour through.

"It's a nice room," I said.

"It is not so bad."

Mostly it consisted of books, books in bookcases, and leaning along the floor against the wall, stacked on the desk. The furniture wasn't much, a couch with a green spread, a spindly table with some loose change, some notebooks, and a box of Ritz crackers on it, the small plain desk, and a bureau. On top of the bureau I could see a silver-backed hairbrush and a smaller silver-backed clothes brush gleaming in the light. There was also, in a heavy old-fashioned silver frame, a large photograph of

348

three young men standing with their arms around each other. Egon was the youngest, maybe in high school then, thinner in those days, but with the same smile. The two brothers looked like him.

He was looking at the window, through which you could see the green clustered trees of the Berkeley hills, bluish now in the late-afternoon haze. They held a great sense of stillness.

"You'll be leaving soon. Ruth told me."

He nodded. "Next week."

"Will you be coming back here afterwards?"

"I don't know, Suse. Perhaps not. Perhaps I'll stay somewhere in Europe."

I looked away from him, down at the carpet.

"Suse," he said after a silence, "there's something you should realize. . . ."

"I do realize it," I said quietly, still looking at the carpet.

"Do you?"

"I understand perfectly," I said, and looked up at him. I felt a deep wrench inside, but I was glad to have everything out in the open and cleared up, so he wouldn't sit there worrying that I would throw myself at him and embarrass us both. But now that it was cleared up, I wished never to speak of it again.

"I came because of the bomb."

He leaned back in his chair, closing his eyes. It was strange to see his face without the startlingly blue eyes in it. He must look like that when he slept, with the dark lashes down, and the lines around the mouth finely etched, except that he was moving, slowly taking from the pocket of his white shirt a pack of Fleetwoods, the eyes opening now as he reached to the desk for a box of matches.

"I see it has been put in my lap."

It was true. The bomb, the world, all life.

He lit his cigarette and sat back again, blowing the smoke out. "You're quite a taskmaster, Suse."

I thought about this. I nodded.

"You deal in absolutes. Black and white. Mostly black."

"No I don't, Egon," I said, sitting forward. "At least I wasn't doing that anymore. You made me see things differently."

His face, with all its complex shadings of expressions, was hard to follow. He seemed almost dryly amused, and at the same time he seemed to be contemplating, in a tired sort of way, as if he would rather talk about the weather. My warm, comforted feeling began to diminish, like a circle closing.

But these expressions resolved themselves into a smile: small, quiet, reassuring. "Well, I'm glad. You're too young to go around with heavy thoughts all the time. It's a time of life to be free in; you should never waste it."

"But if it's all going to end anyway! If the world's going to blow up—"

"Suse, look. I don't think it will blow up."

"You don't?" The circle of warmth stopped narrowing. "You really don't? But are you sure?"

Once more I heard a small sigh through his nostrils. "I am not a physicist. And I am not a prophet either, though you seem to think I am. I can only say I don't think it will happen. There is too much at stake, too much to lose and nothing to gain."

"But that's the same reasons as not to have war, and it never stops war. And what about mistakes? If they break the atom without controlling it? What about accidents?"

He ground out his cigarette in his ashtray, mashing it unnecessarily hard, it seemed. "Do you want the world to blow up?"

"No. My God, no."

"Then maybe you should think that it won't."

"What good will that do!"

"It will do good, believe me."

"How? So I. tell myself it won't—how can that help anything? It can't keep me from being destroyed."

"It will, Suse," he said with a quiet nod. "That is just what it will do."

"I don't understand that," I murmured, sitting back in my chair. "It doesn't sound realistic."

"It is the most realistic thing I can tell you."

"To believe it won't. That's realistic."

He nodded again.

"And you believe that way."

"Well," he said, and smiled, "you don't see me climbing under a table."

It was true. He was unfrightened, as Helen Maria was
350

unfrightened, and the people I saw on the streets; not that their normality gave me comfort, but Egon's did. The circle of warmth began expanding, widening and widening, filling me with a kind of golden weariness, as if I had been running for hours and I could finally stop now and fall asleep. I felt my eyes actually closing as I sat there; but I opened them and sat forward again. There were other things that must be settled.

"There's that whole city, though. All those people killed."

He said nothing. He looked weary too, as if he would like to stop talking. But I could not leave these terrible things up in the air. "The ones who did it, I thought they were the ones we could depend on. That's what you said. To have faith in the spirit that moved them."

Still he said nothing.

"But their spirit's no good; it's rotten. There's nothing to depend on." I kept looking at him, afraid he would never contradict me. "I was right about history, it just goes on and on, and there'll be another war—"

He spoke at last, but with a rough edge of impatience. "This one is just ending, and already you start a new one."

"I don't *want* to, it's all I've waited for all these years, just for it to be finished! I thought it would be such a wonderful day—"

"It is. It's finished. And it's a wonderful day."

He got up suddenly and came over to me, taking my arm and pulling me up sharply, startling me. He took me over to one of the windows, where he stood behind me, his fingers hard around my arm.

"Are you looking out there? Do you see what's there? Hills and trees and houses, a blue sky? How much do you want?"

His voice was as hard as his fingers, making my eyes blur, so that I could hardly see what he was pointing out.

"It's a beautiful day. And the war is over. You say that you have waited all these years, well I have waited too. And now I want to be glad that it's over."

His hand loosened and came away. "Are you looking?" he asked again, more quietly.

I nodded, trying to keep the blur from spilling, trying to see through it.

"Then remember it." And he put his hand on my head

351

and gave my hair a slow, downward stroke to my cheek, where he left it, firm and gentle, and warm as the sun, sending a rush of happiness through me.

"Well, Suse," he said with a pat, "I think the time has come for us to go, if you're to catch your train. It's getting late."

The train was already there when the bus pulled up in front of the depot, and as we climbed out, we could hear bells clanging and the conductor calling, "All aboard!" Running around the building to the platform we saw that the train was moving, steaming and hissing, the wheels slowly turning as the conductor leaned from the door, waving us on.

There was time for nothing as we ran, not a word, not a look, and I suddenly realized that none of the mysteries I had brought him had been cleared up, that his words had in a way been like air, the black beetles were still with us, the bomb still hung overhead, nothing had been settled; there was just a window with some hills outside that he said to remember, and the feel of his hand on my cheek, and now as we ran, he was swinging me up onto the steel step, and I couldn't see him when I turned around because the conductor was blocking my way, steering me up the steps as if I were a child, bustling and guiding me inside. Breaking away, I rushed down the aisle of the coach behind me, turning sharply at the first open window I saw, squeezing in and sticking my head out between the elbows of two leaning soldiers.

Egon was walking now, a distance back, his white shirt bright in the low rays of the sun. He saw me leaning out and waving, and he lifted his arm, waving back, how much do you want? he had asked, and the true answer was everything, peace, glory, love, life everlasting, and all he had shown me was a window, a summer day, and what he meant I didn't know, but I would remember it, I would remember it and keep it.

"I'll remember it, Egon!" I shouted.

If he heard me or not through the noise of the train I couldn't tell, but I felt in my bones that he did, still waving his arm back and forth as he grew more and more distant on the platform, and then we passed some boxcars and he was cut off,